ALISON INGLEBY

Infiltrators

The Wall Series Book 2

Dedication

For Michael Garvey (Grv), Rachel Majumdar and José Barretta. You shone so bright and left us far too soon. You remind me to make each day count because we never know how many days we have left.

Shine until tomorrow.

A Note on Language

This story is set in a future London and is written in British English. For my readers who are more accustomed to U.S. English spellings and terms, I hope you don't find this too distracting.

1

Aleesha

I look up at the two faces displayed on the huge screens that line the square. The evening news headlines have run, and this is the final announcement before the advertisements start up again. A murmur of excitement ripples through the crowd in front of us as two words flash up underneath the faces. Wanted criminals.

Excitement. Not fear or alarm, but excitement. But then, these people are Insiders. They don't understand fear. Not real fear. The kind that has you constantly looking over your shoulder and viewing each person who smiles at you with suspicion. The fear that causes you to hide from the world, to choose to starve rather than reveal your identity and to betray your own neighbour to the government.

But admittedly, the two faces staring out at us don't really look like dangerous criminals. They look like what we are: teenagers.

Names flash up above the faces. Aleesha Ramos. Darwin Trey Goldsmith. Such an odd name, Darwin. Trey suits him better. On the screen, he looks happy and relaxed, wearing a light blue shirt that I guess was his old school uniform. Today, he's wearing a hat to cover the blond roots that are starting to show through the black hair dye. His blue eyes flick nervously to mine as though he's looking for protection from the words that track continuously across the bottom of the screen.

Wanted criminals.

I inspect my own face, wondering when they'd captured the image. Unlike Trey, I have no official record. Tight, fearful brown eyes stare down at me, framed by wisps of dark hair torn loose from my usual braid. I must have been having a bad day.

I pull my pink scarf up over my head, take Trey's hand and lead him around the edge of the crowd. We keep our heads down, trying to look like a couple out for an afternoon stroll. I catch a flash of yellow on black ahead and turn sharply, almost dragging Trey down a narrow alleyway.

"Metz patrol."

Trey doesn't reply, but his fingers tremble in mine. We turn left at the end of the alleyway and left again further up the street to bring us back to our original route. We both memorized the directions, but Trey lets me lead. For an Insider, he doesn't know much about the layout of the city Inside the Wall.

"What was your friend called again?" I ask.

"Theo."

"And you're sure this is the right thing to do?"

He nods and glances down at me nervously. The small lump in his throat bobs up and down. "Yes. I thought we'd agreed on this. People need to know the truth. If they know what the government has done and why our city has ended up like this, then perhaps they'll finally do something about it."

But what will they do?

I know Trey's right, but I can't get rid of the nagging voice inside my head that's telling me this is a really bad idea.

I'm so lost in my thoughts that I don't notice the rhythmic pounding ahead until Trey pulls me back against a wall. The chatter of voices around us dies and is replaced by a low murmur of fear. A woman steps back onto my foot and stammers an apology.

"S'okay," I murmur, too quietly for her to catch my Outsider accent.

The press of people intensifies as the crowd parts to make way for the Metz patrol. Glancing up from under my scarf, I watch them as they round the corner onto our street. They tower above the crowd, taller and broader than even the tallest Insider, and are protected from head to toe in black armour that seems to absorb all light. The only splash of colour is two parallel yellow stripes on either side of their helmets. These are our protectors. Our law enforcers. Our judges.

My fingers twitch toward the knife that's hidden in my secret pocket. It would be pointless to attack them, but I'd feel better with the blade in my hand. But I stop myself. If someone were to see it, they'd know I was an Outsider and call me out. Insiders don't carry weapons. They don't need to.

The footsteps get closer, pounding in perfect time as if made by one being. And then, as the front line of the patrol draws level with us, they stop.

I stare resolutely at the ground. A bead of sweat trickles down the back of my neck. Surely, they can't have spotted us in this crowd? My heart hammers in my ears and my fingers creep down again to tug at the handle of my throwing knife.

A heavy silence falls over the street. Everyone's waiting. I risk a glance up, but all I see is the back of the man in front of me. I'm not even tall enough to peek over his shoulder. I take a step to the side, but Trey's hand reaches out to grip mine. His palm is slick. He gives a tiny shake of his head.

Don't do anything stupid, Aleesha.

A child whimpers. The kind of whimper that's a precursor to a full-blown tantrum.

"Who is the guardian of this child?" The Metz officer's voice is toneless and gravelly. There's no way to tell if the person inside the armour is male or female. If there is a person in there at all.

I stretch up on my toes and strain to see between the heads of the Insiders in front of me but it's no use. All I can see are the helmets of the Metz officers.

The child begins to cry. The officer repeats his question but is again met with silence. I move sideways to a break in the crowd, feeling Trey's eyes bore into me. The child's cries reverberate in my skull. Adrenaline fizzles through my veins and I fight to control my breathing.

The only reason they would detain the child would be if he was illegal. Like me.

The child's cries turn to a scream as the officer reaches down and lifts him into the air. He's perhaps two years old and dressed in Insider clothes, which is odd. A thread of doubt weaves its way into my stomach. Perhaps he isn't illegal after all.

Just then, there's a cry of fear and the sound of running footsteps. A woman appears, her hair flying loose from the tight knot on the back of her head. She runs awkwardly like she's wearing high heels, and her face is a mask of terror.

She skids to a halt in front of the officer and reaches up her arms for the child. "Please, he's mine. He just ran off ..." She looks pleadingly up at the impassive black mask towering above her. For a second, they stare at each other, then, slowly, the Metz officer lowers the boy to the ground. The woman picks the child up and tries to soothe his sobs as she backs away.

"Wait."

The woman freezes, and I feel the crowd around me tense.

"Your chips."

The woman holds out her right arm and the officer runs a gloved hand down the trembling limb. He does the same with the child. There's a slight pause and then he nods.

"Keep a closer eye on your son in future, ma'am."

I let out my breath in a rush, a strange sense of disappointment flooding through me. So, he was just an Insider boy after all. I could have risked everything, put myself up in front of the Metz, to save someone who didn't need saving. A few weeks ago, the thought wouldn't have even crossed my mind. But that was before Lily.

The Metz move off and the crowd thins around me.

"What do you think you were doing?" Trey sounds pissed.

"Nothing," I mutter. "Let's go."

Trey's friend lives down by the river, or at least what was once the river. To me, it's always looked more like a sea. Or, in the summer months, a muddy swamp. You can't really smell it at all Inside. Out in Area Four, it stinks, especially when the tide is out. But I guess in here people don't use the water as a toilet or a handy dumping ground for bodies.

We weave our way through an ancient part of the city that dates from the time before the Great Flood. The stone buildings are dwarfed by the glass towers behind them. The streets are quiet, even though it's a weekend, and it doesn't take us long to reach our destination.

"This is it," Trey says as we turn down a street lined with modern apartment blocks. They're blindingly white and each has a neat balcony with pot plants or small trees. I never realized that there were so many different types of plants until I saw Inside. Outside, everything dies.

We pause in front of one of the apartment blocks. "Are you

sure you want to go in alone?"

Trey nods. "It'll be fine. Best that they don't see you, just in case." He sounds as if he's trying to convince himself as much as me. I reach out and squeeze his hand. His skin is cold and clammy.

"He's your friend, right?"

"He was my friend." Trey sighs and steps forward, scanning the list of names by the apartment door.

How his life has changed. A few weeks ago, he was an Insider boy, son of a government minister, being educated at a posh school outside London. Now, he's an illegal citizen, forced to live Outside the Wall. I wonder if he wakes up some days thinking his old life was all a dream.

Trey tugs the cap down over his eyes and presses the comm link up to his friend's apartment. A voice answers.

"Is Theo there?"

There's a pause, then another voice comes on the line, too faint for me to hear.

"Theo? It's me, Darwin." There's a muttered conversation, then the door clicks open and Trey disappears into the building.

I wander down the street, keen to get away from whatever security cameras may be around. The road is a dead end, the apartment buildings sloping down to the river wall. It's a low, brick wall. I wonder what they do when the waters rise, but as I get closer, I spot the retracted flood barriers on either side. The evening sun casts a warm glow over the rippled surface of the water. Sunset is getting later. Spring is on the way.

My mother took me to look out over the river once, on an evening like this. We'd sat on top of a low building looking out as the sun bathed the city in red. I'd asked her who lived in the towers that jutted up out of the water. She said no one did. Not

6

anymore.

I don't remember what we did after that. My memories of that time are few, and as every year passes they seem to fade a little more into the blur that was my early childhood. But I think that wasn't long before she left.

Before she was murdered.

The sound of footsteps cuts into my thoughts.

"Hey." Trey rests his elbows on the wall and drops his head into his hands. "I'm glad that's over."

"What did Theo's dad say?"

Mr Johnston owns one of the news networks in the city. An important man.

"He took copies of the documents. Said he'd think about it." Trey lifts his head to stare out across the water. "It was strange though. He didn't seem that surprised by the information. Almost like he already knew."

"He knew?"

Trey shrugs. "I don't know, maybe I'm wrong. We'll have to wait and see. Theo was pretty riled up about it." He smiles and pats the backpack on his shoulder. "And we've still got the originals."

The originals are plastic films. We found them in some ancient cabinets in the basement of the government headquarters the first time we broke in. I haven't read them – I can't read that well – but Trey's told me what they contain. They're records of what happened after the Great Flood when London was one big city. Before they put up the Wall. Before there were Insiders and Outsiders.

"Let's go. We're more likely to be noticed if we're out on the streets after dark." Trey starts back up the street. I take one final look at the dying sun, then turn and follow him.

We walk in silence until we're almost back at the Wall. It towers behind the apartment blocks and houses, a shimmering array of colour that lights up the dark sky. I yawn, feeling suddenly tired. Perhaps Abby will let me stay at her house tonight.

Trey turns down an alleyway. I follow, stumbling on a loose piece of paving. Recovering, I frown as I try to place where we are. "Isn't this a dead end?"

Ahead of me, Trey rounds the corner, then takes a step back. "You're right. Sorry, wrong road."

I'm just about to tease him about not knowing his way around when he turns toward me and the colour drains from his face. His eyes lock onto something over my shoulder. I turn around and draw a knife from my pocket. But I know at once that it won't help. There's no weakness in that black armour.

I take a step backward and the three Metz officers take a step forward.

We're trapped.

2

Trey

Aleesha backs up until she's standing in front of me. My limbs feel suddenly weak and lifeless and I take a deep breath to try to force oxygen into my muscles.

"Is there any way out?" Aleesha whispers.

I shake my head and then realize that she can't see me. "Nothing. No door or ladder. Just a high brick wall."

I glance around, looking for something to use as a weapon. A length of broken metal pipe catches my eye. It's hanging off the wall and almost rusted through. I take a step toward it.

"Don't move!"

My body freezes instinctively.

"I'll distract them. When you see an opportunity, run." Aleesha's voice is low and controlled, showing none of the panic I feel. But that's always the way. If she feels fear, she doesn't show it.

"No, I'm not leaving you." My voice betrays me, cracking on my final words.

Aleesha's eyes tighten. "Don't be stupid. You can't defend yourself."

Her words cut through me. The worst of it is, she's right. I don't know how to defend myself. They didn't teach us that at

St George's. The closest we got was rugby, but I don't think I'll have much luck trying to tackle a Metz officer.

"Darwin Trey Goldsmith. Aleesha Ramos. You are both under arrest. Place your weapons on the ground and raise your hands." The middle officer twitches its gun threateningly.

I lift my hands and look to Aleesha.

"See that passageway on the left, behind them?" Aleesha whispers. "I think it's too narrow for them to fit. If we can reach it, there may be a way out. Let's split them up."

A security light high on the wall throws long shadows in front of the three giants in front of us. Behind them, a dark gap cuts between the buildings. If it is a passageway, it barely looks wide enough to squeeze through.

Aleesha begins to take slow deliberate steps toward the far side of the alley. I move in the opposite direction.

"Don't move! Put the knife down."

But Aleesha's ploy is working. Two of the officers are turning to her. The third takes a step toward me. I stare up, transfixed by its blank, expressionless mask.

There's a flash of movement in the corner of my eye. The officer turns as a harsh, grating cry rips through the silence, and suddenly I can move again. I run to the broken pipe, yank it from the wall and am running for the gap between the officers by the time it turns back to me.

It reaches out an arm. I duck around it. A glint of metal in the corner of my eye gives me a split-second warning before a shot fires overhead.

There's a scream. *Aleesha.*

I skid to a halt but can't see past the bulk of the two black figures in front of her. I throw the battered pipe at the nearest officer, then stumble after it. The pipe bounces harmlessly off the hard, black armour, but before I can think what to do next, Aleesha explodes from between the two officers.

"Run!" She grabs my arm and pulls me around. My foot catches on something and I lurch forward. A bullet cuts through the air where my head had been a second earlier.

The narrow passageway is two paces away. Aleesha disappears into it, swallowed up by the darkness. I misjudge the width of the opening, overshoot it and grab for the edge of the wall.

Another shot. Something thuds into my shoulder and an electric shock jolts my arm, causing it to spasm and throw me off balance. My shoulder smashes into the wall and a burning pain shoots down my arm as I stumble into the narrow gap between the tall buildings.

"Trey?"

Aleesha's voice comes from up ahead. I scramble blindly in the darkness toward it, running my hands along the concrete walls.

The passageway opens up and I let my left arm fall to my side. I trail my fingers along the right wall, feeling the smoothness of Plexiglas windows.

The bright beam of a flashlight slices through the darkness of the passageway and bounces off the walls. I emerge into an old-fashioned light well between tall office buildings, barely three metres across. Ahead, the passageway turns a corner, and Aleesha stands at the bend, face flushed and eyes wide.

"Get down!"

I press my back against the wall as a knife whistles through the air in front of me. There's a clatter and the light goes out.

The darkness seems even blacker. Aleesha's hand grabs mine, pulling me forward. I follow her blindly, my arm outstretched to ward off any obstacle.

11

My foot catches on something and I lurch forward, falling to the ground, my hand slipping from Aleesha's grasp. Pain shoots from my right kneecap, and I bite my lip to stifle my whimper of pain.

"Come on! They'll start shooting soon."

As if on cue, another flashlight shines down the light well. It comes to rest on me, and I drop flat to the ground as a bullet shoots through the air above me.

I look up. I'm just a few metres from the turn in the passageway. A few metres from safety.

Aleesha's face appears around the corner of the wall and she mouths something at me. Words of encouragement perhaps. I squirm forward on my belly, feet scrabbling to push me forward.

Bullets thud into the ground around me. Aleesha reaches out and grabs my belt, yanking me behind the shelter of the wall. I lie with my face pressed to the dusty ground, gasping for breath.

"Damn."

I push myself up and follow Aleesha's gaze. The flashlight reflects off the office windows, providing enough light for us to see the concrete wall ahead of us. A dead end. I swallow, tasting the iron-tang of blood in my mouth.

"You hurt?"

"I'm okay. Just banged my knee." I heave myself into a sitting position and examine my shoulder. The fabric of my top is torn, and my finger comes away wet with blood. I look away and roll my shoulder experimentally. "They shot me ... but it felt like I was being electrocuted?"

"Stun bullets." Aleesha picks up a small cylinder and holds it up to the light. "They're designed to shock you. Like a taser but in a bullet. They're pretty nasty." She glances at my shoulder. "How did you get it off you?"

I squint at the object held neatly between her fingers. It looks like a tiny electronic device encased in clear plastic, with a set of spikes at one end. "My shoulder hit the wall. I guess it must have ripped it out?" I shudder and swallow down the nausea that rises in my throat, trying not to think about the blood trickling down my arm.

Aleesha nods approvingly. "Good. If you'd have tried to pull it out, the shock would have been worse. You'd most likely not have made it into the passageway."

I lean back against the wall and close my eyes. The throbbing in my knee is fading to a dull ache. "I guess it's too much to hope for that they'll just go away?"

I can almost feel the look she's giving me.

"They're not trying to kill us at least. Otherwise they'd have used proper bullets. They want us alive."

"Great. That makes me feel *so* much better."

Aleesha ignores my sarcasm. I feel her shift beside me. There's a soft tapping sound. "The lower windows are proper glass. Breakable. Not like Plexiglas."

There's a sound like a child's rattle followed by a small thud as something hits the ground on the other side of the skylight.

Why are they throwing things a—

There's a blinding flash of light and the air is sucked from my lungs as a deafening blast reverberates in the narrow space. I try to draw a breath, but the air is more dust than oxygen and my lungs spasm in protest. Spots of light dance in front of my eyes and there's a loud ringing in my ears.

Aleesha's hand closes over mine and tugs me forward. I crawl obediently toward her, gasping as my knees grind into the hard surface and tiny daggers bite into my hands.

I blink and the spots of light fade. A steady beam of light

13

reflects off thousands of shards of glass scattered on the ground. The bottom windows are ringed with glass teeth, the panes shattered by the explosion.

Aleesha is already inside the building, beckoning to me and mouthing silent words. I scramble through the window, not caring that the glass tears at my clothes and skin, and drop down into the room beyond. Aleesha pulls me forward and we half stagger, half run out of the room and into a long corridor. A high-pitched wailing noise intrudes on the ringing in my ears.

At the foot of a flight of stairs, Aleesha pauses. There's a sign on the wall indicating we're in the basement. "Up!" she mouths and points at the ceiling.

I pause on the ground floor but Aleesha keeps on going up, taking the stairs two at a time. Panting, I follow, struggling to keep up. She pauses for breath on the third floor.

"Where are you going?" My words sound muffled as if I'm underwater. I rest my hands on my knees and gulp in air.

"To the roof. They won't expect us to go there."

The roof? "Is there a way out there?"

Her teeth flash white in the dark. "I hope so."

"You hope so?"

But she's right. A trapdoor leads up onto the roof and we soon find a way back down a fire escape to a different street. The Metz are nowhere to be seen.

We reach the Wall, a shimmer of colour that stretches into the clouds. The patterns are constantly changing and shifting, like the swirling water in the brook that runs through the forest beside my family's home in the Welsh countryside. I push the thought to the back of my mind. Thinking of the house, of my family, is still too painful.

Aleesha runs straight through the Wall, barely pausing for

breath, but I hesitate, reaching out a hand toward it. Why am I nervous? I've been through it so many times. But we still don't know why Aleesha and I are the only people who can pass through unharmed. Everyone else dies almost instantly.

I was always taught that the Wall was there to protect us. That inside it, we were safe. That was before I discovered I was an illegal child, my birth covered up by the man I thought was my father. Before the Metz came for me that fateful day at school. Before I cut out my chip and threw away my identity. Before I went on the run.

Now I know that nowhere is really safe. Insiders and Outsiders, we're both at the mercy of the government.

I take a deep breath and step through the barrier. There's no resistance, just a slight tingling.

Then I'm through. Outside.

* * *

It doesn't take us long to weave through the streets of Area Five and reach the back alley to Abby's house. Light glows from the kitchen window, but the blind is pulled down, obscuring the scene inside. An overwhelming sense of relief makes me stumble on the cracked paving stones and I sag against the wall of the house for a moment and close my eyes.

We made it.

The back door is unlocked. As I push it open, a stench of dirt, sweat and something else hits the back of my throat and I cough violently, my eyes watering.

What on earth?

The kitchen is in chaos. A bare-chested man lies prone on the kitchen table, which is covered with plastic sheeting. His hands grip the table edge and his eyes are squeezed shut. The

15

hairs on his chest shine wet in the light and a deep wound on his stomach leaks fresh blood.

"There you are, Trey. Can you come and give me a hand?"

I tear my eyes from the man to look at Abby. She's pouring water from the kettle into a large bowl. Her long dark hair is loosely tied back, and her olive skin is creased with worry lines.

I walk over and take the bowl from her. Jars full of pastes and ointments are neatly lined up on the counter. Healing remedies from the few ancient books on herblore Abby's collected over the years, or those she's learned to trust. It's a far cry from the sterile, mechanical environment of the medic centres where bots carry out delicate surgical procedures and drugs can heal almost instantly. But, as Abby keeps reminding me, the medic facilities out here are overrun and not everyone can access them.

"Wash your hands. Then put some gloves on and start trying to clean up this gentleman's wound." She points to a pile of neatly folded white fabric and then to the man on the table. "Aleesha – please put more water on to boil. Bryn? How are you doing over there?"

It's only then I notice that there are other people in the small room. A pale-faced woman sits in the rocking chair, clutching a small child to her. The boy appears to be asleep. Next to her, Bryn's busy wrapping a white gauze bandage around the head of an elderly man whose eyes are glazed over. Another two people wait in line for treatment, slumped against the wall.

I walk over to the table, rest the bowl on the edge and pull on thin plastic gloves.

"What happened?" Aleesha asks. There's an edge to her voice and I wonder if she knows these people. If they're from Area Four.

"The Metz have been taking a heavy-handed approach again.

There was a bust-up a few streets away, plus things in Four are so bad, Amber's had to send a couple of people up here to get patched up." She brushes back her hair with the back of her hand and sighs. "It's been a busy day."

I dip a cloth in the warm water and dab cautiously at the man's chest. He lets out a moan. When I rinse the cloth in the bowl, it tinges the water pink. I swallow hard and force myself to look at the wound on his stomach. The raw gaping flesh moves as he breathes, revealing what looks like a giant worm.

Is that his intestine?

A wave of nausea washes over me and the room seems to shift sideways. I close my eyes but that doesn't get rid of the smell. It reminds me of another place. Another man. *Mikheil.*

"Trey? Are you okay? You look about to faint."

The room swims back into focus. Aleesha is staring at me, concern in her eyes.

"I-I just …" I make it to the sink just in time. My eyes burn as I retch, and the smell of vomit mingles with the stink in the room, making my stomach heave again. I close my eyes and force myself to take a couple of deep breaths.

Behind me, there's a faint splash as Aleesha takes over my washing duties. Abby walks over to her. "Once the wound's clean, smear this inside. It'll help stop infection. Then I'll stitch it up. If he starts screaming, give him a bit of this on his tongue."

"Tronk? You're giving him tronk?" Aleesha's voice sounds strangled.

"Just a bit, for the pain. And to sedate him while I stitch up the wound."

Aleesha doesn't reply. I glance back at her. She's staring at a small packet of white powder on the table. Her eyes are hungry. They dart to me and I look away, wondering if Abby would have handed her the tronk so willingly if she'd known about Aleesha's addiction.

"Here, drink this." Abby shoves a cup into my hand. I rinse my mouth and take a couple of sips before using the rest to wash out the sink.

"Sorry ..."

She pats me gently on the back. "It's okay. Why don't you and Bryn go into the front room for a bit? I can manage fine with Aleesha. Besides, you two need to talk. You've been tip-toeing around each other for too long."

Bryn growls from the other side of the room. "Abby, it's—"

Abby gives him a silencing look. I stumble from the kitchen, grateful for any excuse to get away. The air in the hallway is comparatively fresh and I gulp it in, trying to shake the nausea.

Bryn pushes past me into the small front room. He seems angry, but then he always seems angry around me. Like he wants to be rid of me. The son he never knew he had.

The room is dark and sparsely furnished. There's a blanket on the sofa where Bryn has been sleeping. He turns to face me, his hands on his hips.

"What trouble have you two been getting into now?"

"W-w-what do you mean?" I bite my lip. *Damn that stammer.*

"You come in with a limp, covered in dirt and with blood on your hands. I hardly think you got that from walking in the park."

"It's none of your business." The words come out sharper than I'd intended and Bryn's eyes narrow.

Though we're the same height, his hefty build makes it feel as if he's looming over me. For a moment, his outline is silhouetted against the lamp in the corner of the room. Then he sighs, rubs one hand over his eyes and sits down on the sofa. "I'm sorry,

Trey. It's just, I worry about you, you know? I promised your parents I'd take care of you."

I perch on a high-backed chair. *Your parents.* To him, I'm still the pathetic Insider boy who he's been lumbered with the job of looking after. If everything had gone the way he and my father had planned, I'd be up at a school in Birmingham, banished from London by the government, and he'd have been able to forget I exist. Instead, I'm still here, a lingering reminder of an old affair.

My father. I still can't think of Bryn as my father. My genes may be his, and my blond hair and blue eyes come from him, but my father is still the tall, dark-haired man who brought me up. The man who I always failed to please, but who I know loved me as if I were his own flesh and blood.

I wonder if it hurts Abby too, now she knows the truth. She never had the opportunity to have children, never found the man to love her as she deserved. If it hadn't been for my mother, perhaps her and Bryn's story would have been different.

"I couldn't just leave. Not now I know how wrong things are in this city. If I went away it would be like I was burying my head in the sand, as if I was accepting that it was okay for the government to treat Outsiders like … like they don't matter."

Bryn snorts. "Oh, to be young and idealistic." He sighs. "I was like that once."

We sit in silence for a moment. "You know, you don't have to stay in London because of me," I say. "Don't let me stop you from going back home. Where is home anyway?"

He yawns. "I've never really had one. Always been too busy moving around, working. But I had my eye on a little place up in the mountains in the south of France. It's cooler up there in the summer and quiet – not many people around. I figured it would be a peaceful kind of retirement. Anyway, I may be able to leave soon. Now Lamar's replacement's arrived."

I sit up straight. "Milicent's replacement?"

"Lamar's replacement. Milicent was never supposed to take charge."

The door bangs open and Aleesha walks in. "Abby needs a hand moving the big dude, Bryn," she says without preamble.

"Sure." Bryn gets to his feet.

"Wait, who is he?"

"Who is who?" Aleesha looks from Bryn to me.

"Lamar's replacement," I say.

"*Her* name is Katya. She's Russian," Bryn says, as if that explains everything.

"And ..." I prompt.

"And she seems competent enough. The Leader trusts her implicitly."

There's a "but" hanging in the air. Aleesha senses it too. She folds her arms, blocking the doorway. "So, what's the problem?"

"No problem." Bryn shrugs. "She's a beautiful woman. And I never trust beautiful women."

Aleesha rolls her eyes. "You never trust anyone."

"You can talk." He glares at her and Aleesha meets his gaze defiantly. "Anyway, she wants to see both of you tomorrow afternoon. Now, are you going to let me give Abby a hand or are we going to stand here chatting all night?"

Aleesha steps aside to let Bryn past, then leans against the door frame. "Who do you think the person is behind all this? The one they call the Leader?"

I shrug. "Don't know. I can't even work out how big the Chain is. From what Bryn and Murdoch have said, they've people in different cities all over the world."

20

"Bryn knows, doesn't he?"

"I think so. He seems to be the only one here who's actually met him face to face. Maybe he's a recluse."

"A what?"

I forget sometimes that Aleesha's vocabulary is limited. She's smart, but never went to school. "A recluse. Someone who hides away from the world."

She looks thoughtful. "Maybe that would explain why he doesn't just come here and sort things out himself."

"Maybe." I stand and prod my knee experimentally. It's sore, but sound.

"Trey, how do we know that what the Chain is doing is right?"

I walk over to her. "They say they want to create an equal city. Take down the divide between Insiders and Outsiders."

"Do you believe them?"

I sigh and stare into her brown eyes. They have flecks of green that I've never noticed before. "I guess we just have to trust them and believe they're doing the right thing. You've got to believe in something, after all."

"What do you believe in, Trey?"

I consider the question for a minute. "Justice. Trying to right the wrongs of the past."

"Justice." Aleesha rolls the word around in her mouth as if it's new to her. Perhaps it is. "It's a good word." Then she turns and disappears back into the kitchen.

3

Aleesha

T he grey light of dawn filters through the small bedroom window. Beside me, Trey's breathing is light and even. He insisted on me taking the bed, even though I'm used to sleeping on the floor without even a mattress for comfort. I roll over to look at him. His hair's all mussed up, framing his pale face. He looks so peaceful as he sleeps, like a child who knows he is safe. Did I feel like that once? Maybe a long time ago.

I push the blanket aside and crawl to the end of the bed, then tiptoe over to the window. I crane my neck to see past the back yards of the houses to the end of the alleyway. No sign of Metz officers. But that doesn't mean they're not there.

It was late by the time we finished treating the injured people last night and I'd been about to leave when Bryn had stopped me. "There are Metz stationed at the end of the road and the back alley," he'd said. "It may just be coincidence or the fact that we've had all these people traipsing in and out, but we can't risk them seeing you. You'll have to stay here tonight."

To tell the truth, I was glad to stay. A hot meal and a warm room to sleep in? I'll take that any day. Though it felt strange to share a room with Trey, even if I was on the bed and he was on a thin mattress on the floor. It took us both a while to fall asleep.

I dress then crawl back over the bed and leave the room. There's no noise from behind Abby's door and only a duet of snoring from the front room downstairs. The man with the stomach wound had been in too bad a condition to send away last night. I can't see him surviving unless Abby can work some miracle. I've seen wounds like that before and they usually mean a slow, painful death.

I slip out the back door and pad silently down the alleyway. But there are no Metz around and the streets of Area Five are quiet as I weave through them and cross the unmarked boundary into Four.

My hand moves automatically to the knife pocket in my trousers before I remember that I'd lost both of them last night in the fight with the Metz. Without my knives, I feel almost naked. Area Four is a dangerous place, and while I can defend myself hand to hand, my size and weight work against me. I need to find a blade, preferably more than one, soon.

But knives mean money. Chits. Which is why I duck into a narrow alley opposite a row of boarded-up shops to wait for the city to awake.

After half an hour, a light goes on in an apartment above a disused kebab shop. I know that apartment well. Lived there for most of the past two years, until a few weeks ago. My belly twists and I feel the smouldering fire within me, so quick to leap into flames. Anger. Hurt. Betrayal.

I lean back against the rough wall.

Calm down. This isn't helping.

But the more I tell myself to calm down, the stronger the fire burns.

Two silhouettes appear at the bedroom window. They move into the other room and I lose sight of them in the dim light. I hesitate, wondering if I should go now or wait until *she's* gone. I'd rather not have to see her, but if they both leave, then I'm screwed. And I really do need those chits. They'll still be there – even Jay didn't know about my secret stash under the floor.

I wait until the bedroom light goes off and my emotions are once again under control. But as I step out from the shelter of the alleyway, the sight of a figure walking up the road makes me freeze.

Him.

I pull back, my heart racing. He's a big man, as tall and muscular as the biggest Insider, but he moves smoothly, almost gliding up the street. His black clothing is standard. The dark dreadlocks that hang to his waist are anything but.

Samson.

Part of me still wonders if I'd imagined his presence in the President's room. Perhaps it was a hallucination. I'd been pretty beaten up by the guards, after all. But the smell that lingered in the room was so distinctive. And when Trey had told me that the President seemed to know that he had been in the building, despite not being caught on any of the cameras, I had been sure. Because who else could have told the President but Samson?

Which begs the question, why was the Brotherhood, the most feared of all Outsider gangs, doing business with the government?

The man pauses at the door leading into the apartment block. His body blocks the keypad entry system, but a moment later he pushes the door open and steps inside. I lean back against the wall. More waiting.

Ten minutes later, the door opens again, and Samson walks

out. He doesn't even glance in my direction but heads off down the street.

Checking up on Jay, huh?

I wait another five minutes and am about to move out when a rustling behind me makes me instinctively duck to one side. A heavy hand lands on my shoulder and spins me around.

"Aleesha. Fancy meeting you here."

The whites of his eyes are bright, locking me in his gaze. I feel like a rat in the flashlight of a hungry hobie. That smell again – sweet wood and needled trees – tickles my nostrils.

He glances around, checking we're not being watched. "Come. I need to speak with you."

His hand clamps around my arm. I stumble unwillingly after him.

If only I had a knife. Then I'd show him that just because I'm small doesn't mean I can't bite.

He drags me down the trash-filled alley until we reach a warped metal door. He kicks it in and pushes me in front of him into a dark room. It's empty apart from a water container and a pile of rags, and stinks of urine. The only light that filters in is from the door.

Samson releases my arm but remains standing between me and the door.

"Why are you working for the government?" The words spill from my lips.

Samson raises an eyebrow. "With, not for. Why do you think?"

His response throws me. I thought he was dragging me in here to beat me up, or to question me some more about the Chain.

"Because you're one of them?" I hazard a guess. "An Insider."

He chuckles. "I may have been once but not anymore." We

stand in silence for a moment, and I sense he's weighing up how much to tell me. Finally, he continues. "As you seem to have worked out, we – the Brotherhood, that is – are working with the government. For the benefit of Outsiders." He holds up a hand to forestall my protests. "Just listen to me. I know this divide in the city isn't right. The Wall, Outsiders being treated as second-class citizens, it's all wrong. But the Chain are going about it the wrong way. If they manage to take down the government then all they'll replace it with is another dictatorship. Or they'll create a war, pitting Insiders against Outsiders. Do you really want that?"

"So what do you want?"

"I want what's best for everyone. Insiders and Outsiders. And at the moment that means stopping Outsiders killing each other."

"Says the man who's killed half the gang leaders in this part of the city." I fold my arms. "For someone who's trying to save Outsiders, you're doing a pretty good job of bumping them off."

He tenses and takes a step forward, his bulk silhouetted against the pale grey light. "I thought you would understand. But if you're not even going to let me speak, then—"

I flinch and take a step backward. "No, go on."

There's a moment of silence. "The death of some of the gang leaders was unavoidable. They were so focused on fighting each other that they didn't realize who the real enemy was. Besides, the number of deaths from gang-related fights across Area Four has halved in the past month. The death of a few idiots can save many."

Is he right? I've got no way of knowing. I don't know of anyone who keeps track of deaths. Probably only the government, and I doubt they know half of what goes on

Outside. Most bodies end up in the river rather than the official crematorium.

"We need a long-term solution, Aleesha. The government is open to change, but they need to see that Outsiders can work together – that they're capable of more than just fighting each other. All their attempts to improve education and healthcare have failed. The facilities have been attacked and people are now too scared to work there. The government want a solution to this as much as you or me, and they're willing to put some resources forward *if* we show we're willing to help them."

He sounds confident. Passionate even. I shake my head. "You're wrong. If the government want to stop fighting and killing, then why are there so many more Metz patrols now? The number of gang murders may have fallen but more people are dying at *their* hands."

"Because the Chain have been inciting rebellion. They're not bringing Outsiders together, they're spreading dissent. They don't *care* how many Outsider deaths it takes to win, and believe me, if you try to take on the Metz, it will take a lot!"

"So you think we should just lie down and let them walk all over us?" My voice echoes in the empty space. I take a deep breath, trying to control my rising anger.

Samson walks forward and grips my shoulders. His closeness suffocates me, and I feel lightheaded.

"No, I don't," he says tightly. "But if you – if we – attack them, they'll only attack back. And they have the bigger army. They're always going to win. We need to make them see that Outsiders aren't the stupid, violent people they believe them to be. That they can be valuable to society rather than being a burden."

"But what if you're wrong?" I whisper. His fingers dig into the thin layer of flesh on my bones and his scent fills my nostrils, making my head spin.

White teeth flash. "If they don't take us seriously? Well, that would be their mistake. When you invite a viper into your home, you'd better treat it nicely. Because the viper watches and listens and learns. And if you don't play fair, the viper will bite." His teeth snap shut and my heart jumps.

"So why are you telling me this?" My voice trembles and I wish, I *really* wish, he'd let go of me. His strength radiates through his hands and I feel as if he could just pick me up and crush me in an instant.

"Because you care about what happens to these people. The Chain *say* they're working for Outsiders, but they don't know what it's like to be right at the bottom of the food chain." He takes a deep breath. "And, unlike many Outsiders, I don't believe you want to harm Insiders. You lied to the President to save the boy."

"That doesn't mean I like Insiders," I mutter under my breath.

"I can protect you. I can get the government off your back. If you help me take down the Chain. You may think they're doing the right thing. I'm sure their lies are pretty convincing. But their motives are twisted – right at the top. They aren't seeking justice. They're seeking revenge."

He lets go of me and I stumble backward. I can still feel the imprint of his fingers on my skin.

"What do you mean?"

"Figure it out, Aleesha. You have all the pieces of the puzzle. You just need to put them together."

"But ..."

But he is gone. Disappeared out of the door as silently as he'd snuck up on me. Leaving me wondering what the hell just happened.

* * *

I pace the rooftop. Forty paces by thirty. The corrugated iron roof of the small building in the centre rattles in the wind. Lily had thought it a monster the first night she'd spent up here. The things kids dream up.

Lily.

I scowl at the building and flex my fingers. What I would give to have my throwing knives back. At least then I'd have something to focus on. The wooden beam that runs along the side of the building is notched from years of practice. I can hit it from twenty paces, right in the centre.

Dropping to the floor, I start doing press-ups. Ten full ones. Then sit-ups. Twenty of those. Ten press-ups. Twenty sit-ups. I switch between the two methodically. Grey dust on the rooftop. Grey clouds in the sky.

My breath comes in gasps and my arms begin to weaken. *Come on, two more.* The muscles on the backs of my arms tremble. I lower down so my nose almost touches the ground then push up again. I make it half way before my arms buckle.

Panting, I roll over and stare up at the sky. Where can I get a knife? I've used up all the favours I was owed. Snakes' headquarters? There are always some spares lying around there. I sit up and lean forward, resting my chin on my knees. I *could* go to the gang headquarters. I'm sure someone would let me in, even though I don't know this week's password.

But I know I won't. I don't want to see the thoughts written so clearly on their faces.

Jay's reject.

My stomach spasms. I look down and realize I'm grinding my knuckles into the ground.

I guess they know now I'm illegal. Even Jay. Now my face is

29

on the screens, branded as a criminal, he can't have missed it. I wonder how he feels about having sheltered me for the past two years. The penalty for sheltering an illegal person is almost as harsh as the penalty for being one.

My gut twists again, and there's a bitter taste at the back of my mouth. A raindrop hits my forehead, trickling down to the end of my snub nose. It's followed by another and a gentle patter starts up.

I push myself up and walk over to the sheltered side of the building where the roof juts out. Even the strongest rains don't reach to the back, but my few possessions are wrapped in a waterproof cloth, just in case. I slump down beside them and unlace my boots, pulling them off to let my feet breathe.

You have all the pieces of the puzzle.

What had Samson meant? I frown, trying to remember what else he'd said. That the Chain weren't seeking justice, but revenge. But aren't they the same thing?

What does he expect me to be? A mind reader?

Perhaps I should have told him about what Trey and I had found in the government papers. That the government had caused all this; that they were still poisoning Outsiders. Perhaps then he wouldn't be so keen to take their side. But I'm not sure I trust him that much.

I lean my head back against the rough brick wall. There's just too much to think about. And my survival depends on figuring out who's telling the truth. If any of them are.

Is that all you want? To survive?

I swirl my finger, making patterns in the dust at my feet. A couple of weeks ago survival would have been enough. But now? Now, I'm not so sure.

You're just like your mother. So passionate.

30

That's what he'd said. I can still scarcely believe it. The President of Britannia – the most powerful man in the country – knew my mother. Went to school with her. Friends, perhaps … It must have been an expensive school, for the President to have been there.

How she had fallen. From a rich Insider to struggling with a young child in a mouldy one-room basement apartment in Area Four. All because of me. Because for some reason, she couldn't register my birth and make me a legal citizen.

Because of him.

That's what the President had said. He had blamed my father for her death. And he knew who he was. He knew!

And still, I don't. My father is a mystery to me. A codename on a file. LC100.

I untie the thin cord that's fastened around my ankle and hold it up to the light. The amulet hangs down. Green glass with an outlined pattern in a bronze coloured metal. I try to remember what Trey had called it. There was a special name for it. A tri … triquetra, that was it. Apparently, it was some kind of religious symbol. Is my father a religious man? I struggle to believe it.

I twist it over and over in my fingers. It is the only part of him I have. And the only part of her. A gift from my father to my mother before I was born. She had given it to me on the day she left the flat. The day she'd gone to meet him. The day she'd died.

Why did you leave me, Mama? Why not take me with you to see him?

Sometimes I wonder if I'll ever find out the truth about what happened that day. The truth about *him*.

I turn to the brick wall and gently ease out the loose block to retrieve the lockbox hidden inside. It rattles as I pull it out and

I quickly open it. A single chit. I sigh. One chit won't get me very far.

I run my finger around the inside of the box. It picks up a white residue. Before I can stop myself, I bring my finger to my lips and lick it off.

Ah. The trace of tronk is barely enough for a glimpse of the happiness it brings. Like a flicker of a beautiful bird at the edge of your vision, so fast that by the time you turn to look, it has gone.

I wipe at the saliva pooling at the corners of my mouth and rummage inside the hole in the wall. Perhaps I'd stashed some away somewhere for this very occasion. But all I find is brick dust and rubble.

The voice in my head starts up again. The annoying little voice I thought I'd got rid of.

It would be so nice just to have a few hours of peace. To escape the world.

I curl my knees up to my chest and bang my head back against the wall. I am stronger than this. Tronk is bad. Besides, I made a promise. And I don't have any. There's no point in wanting something I don't have.

But every fibre in me wants it. Craves it. My fingers curl into claws and the three points of the triquetra dig into my palm.

Abby. Abby has tronk. For medical use.

I could take some. She wouldn't know.

No. I made a promise. A promise to Lily.

But Lily isn't here anymore.

A sharp pain shoots up my arm and I realize I've been clawing at the brick wall. Another broken nail. A drop of blood wells up and I suck on it, my mouth twisting at the sour metallic tang.

I must be strong. I'd seen the look of disappointment that

Trey had given me last night. Like I was going to let him down again, that I would be too weak to resist the temptation.

I can be strong. For him. And for Lily.

I force myself to stand and walk over to the crumbling parapet. The rain on my face provides a little distraction. Enough to think of something else. I open my hand and look down at the amulet.

I'd always hoped he was a rich Insider, that he'd make me a legal citizen and give me a better life. A normal life.

"Who are you?"

But of course, the amulet doesn't answer.

It's a cruel thing, hope. It keeps you going, until one day it crumbles. And all you're left with is despair.

4

Trey

Aleesha turns up at Abby's just in time for lunch. She doesn't offer any explanation for where she's been or why she felt the need to sneak out of the house in the middle of the night. Lunch is a thin soup using the last of the winter greens from the garden. Four small flatbreads sit on a plate in the centre of the table beside an empty bag of flour.

Abby smiles apologetically as she sets the bowls in front of us. "Sorry, it's all I've got left."

I bite my lip as she turns away and dip my spoon into the thin liquid. It's tasty but more like a herbal drink than a filling meal. I use the bread to wipe the bowl clean and chew it slowly, trying to convince myself that I'm full. My grumbling stomach betrays me.

Aleesha gives me a sideways glance. She's already finished her portion. She eats so fast, almost inhaling her food, as if someone's about to take it from her. And she's so thin. Mum would say she needs feeding up.

My throat constricts as I think of my mother and the final piece of bread turns to cardboard in my mouth. I keep chewing and try to think of something else. You'd have thought missing them would make me want to think of them more. And I do want to think about them … But only when I'm alone. When I don't have to pretend that the tears in my eyes are from a dry piece of bread catching in my throat.

Footsteps sound on the path outside and all three of us stiffen and look up. A brief knock on the door, then it opens and Bryn steps inside. My shoulders relax, and I look back down at the table.

Who were you expecting it to be?

He walks in, places a backpack on the table and starts pulling out food. Another bag of flour. Brightly wrapped protein bars and chocco. A handful of withered carrots – real carrots from the earth, not a factory. With a final flourish, he pulls out a pack of burgers. Not real meat, obviously, but they're Steakhaus and they taste pretty much the same.

"Where …?" Abby stares at the food, her expression both awestruck and suspicious.

"I finally got some of the pay I've been owed," Bryn replies. "You really need to charge people for treatment, Abby. You can't help anyone if you're half starved."

Abby turns to fill the kettle. Her hands tremble as she pulls a bottle of water out from under the work surface. We're nearly out. I should offer to go to the pump to refill them.

"They don't have any more than we do, most of them." Her voice cracks slightly.

Bryn sighs and walks over to her. He hesitates for a moment then reaches out and touches her lightly on the shoulder. "I'm sorry, Abby, I wasn't criticizing. But people take advantage of you. Not everyone, but some people. And if you don't take payment, then you won't be able to afford to buy what you need to treat those who can't afford to pay."

"I know." Abby turns and smiles brightly up at him.

There's an awkward silence, then Aleesha clears her throat. "So, when do we get to meet this Katya then?"

"Ah, yes." Bryn glances up at the small clock on the wall. "We should be going."

Abby starts putting the food away. She holds the frozen pack of burgers in one hand. "We'll have these for dinner. They won't keep without a freezer."

Of course. I keep forgetting how limited Abby's kitchen is. All the things I took for granted at home seem to be luxuries out here.

"Where are we heading? To Six?" Aleesha asks as Bryn leads us down the back alleyway and out onto the street. He nods in reply and sets a quick pace, dodging through the smaller roads and back alleys to avoid any Metz patrols. As usual when we go out, Aleesha and I wear hooded jackets, pulled up to hide our faces.

Area Six is one of the better areas Outside the Wall. It's where Insiders live if they can't get an apartment Inside, and where Outsiders who have more money aspire to live. It's got proper shops, schools and a medic centre. It almost feels like being Inside. The Chain have a large old house here that they use as a headquarters. Two figures loiter at the bottom of the short set of steps leading up to the door.

"Murdoch." Bryn nods slightly to a stocky, dark-haired man with a scar on his jaw who straightens as we approach.

"You here to see the new boss?" The two men stare at each other. There's no love lost between them.

Aleesha steps forward and raises her arm to deliver a ringing slap to Murdoch's cheek.

"What the—"

"That's for Area Four, you lying bastard!" Aleesha spits on

the ground beside him. "You told us there was going to be a Cleaning."

Murdoch scowls and rubs the red mark on his cheek. "Well, I needed you to agree to help us," he says, unrepentant. His lilting Irish accent makes his words sound almost mocking.

Aleesha glares at him and raises her hand again but he grabs her wrist. "Oh, I do like a feisty woman." He smirks.

Aleesha jerks her arm from his grasp and takes a step back.

"Stop bickering, you two," Bryn says. "He's only trying to wind you up, Aleesha."

"I know." Aleesha folds her arms. "He's just grumpy because the only woman that'll have him is a street whore." She turns and marches up the steps toward the front door of the house.

Murdoch mutters something that I don't catch. I suspect it's nothing flattering.

A slim woman with short brown hair and a sad face greets us as we step into the house. "Aleesha, Trey, nice to see you again," she says without enthusiasm. "Katya is waiting upstairs."

"Thank you, Matthews," Bryn replies.

I hesitate at the foot of the stairs, wanting to ask how she is, but she's already disappeared into a small room that leads off the hallway. Matthews had accompanied us and Murdoch through the tunnels when we broke into the government building. Her partner, Sanders, was killed trying to get in.

At the top of the stairs is a landing with a series of doors leading off it, one of which is slightly ajar. Bryn walks over to it and pushes the door open.

The room is small. In the centre is a small square black table about waist height with a surface as smooth as glass. A holo table. There's a metal cupboard against one wall and a handful of chairs scattered around. A woman stands in front of a tall window that looks out over the street below. She turns as we enter.

"Trey and Aleesha. Thank you, Bryn, you can go."

I barely sense Bryn leave the room. My eyes are locked on the woman in front of us, tracking her as she comes to stand in front of us. My heartbeat thumps in my ears like a dull drum and the air in the room feels suddenly thick and hard to breathe.

She's every boy's fantasy of the perfect woman. Like an avatar in a VR game: too perfect to be real. Thick blonde hair that cascades down her back, a sculpted face and emerald eyes that seem too bright, too dazzling, to exist in the real world. She even wears the figure-hugging, all-in-one suit that clings to every curve of her body.

I swallow hard, feeling heat rush to my groin. A sharp dig in my ribs jolts me out of my daze. "Close your mouth," Aleesha mutters. "You look like a dead fish." She sounds angry.

Katya laughs, a tinkling laugh that bounces around inside my skull. "Don't be jealous, Aleesha. I'm afraid I cause that reaction sometimes. Don't worry, I'm not interested in boys."

My cheeks burn, and I tear my eyes away from her to stare at the floor.

A boy. Is that all she sees?

Aleesha snorts. "I'm not jealous."

"Now, I want you to tell me exactly what happened when you broke into the government headquarters." Katya's tone is suddenly business-like.

"Surely Murdoch and the others have brought you up to date."

"They have indeed," she replies, ignoring Aleesha's sullen tone. "But I'd like to hear it from you, in your own words."

Aleesha starts off, and when she pauses I take over the tale. Between us we explain everything that happened from the moment we left Murdoch and Matthews in the basement of the government headquarters to the point at which we'd escaped back into the tunnels.

Aleesha leaves out some of the details, including her conversation with the President. I know from what she told me afterward that there was more to that than she's letting on. But she doesn't leave out anything that might be important to the Chain, just her personal stuff, so I keep quiet and don't say anything.

When I come to describe Mikheil's death, my voice cracks and I have to pause to clear the thickness in my throat. As much as Mikheil's father hadn't blamed me for his death, I can't help but feel responsible. I should have done more to save him.

"And what happened to the microchip with the information that Mikheil did manage to retrieve?"

"The President took it from me when I was searched," Aleesha answers quickly.

I stare at the floor, hoping Katya takes my silence as assent.

It's destroyed anyway. You made sure of that.

The crunch of plastic and metal underfoot. Dust blowing away in the wind.

"And you chose to come back, Trey. To leave your parents and help us?"

I start at the question and look up. Those eyes captivate me, locking me in their gaze. "Y-yes."

Heat flushes through my cheeks again.

Katya frowns slightly but says nothing. She turns to Aleesha. "And you, Aleesha. You're willing to continue working with us?"

"That depends on what you've got planned." Aleesha folds her arms. "If it's as dumb as the plan Millicent came up with, then no."

"I-is she okay, Millicent?" I ask hesitantly. An image of the elderly Insider appears in my head. Aleesha was right, her plan had been wrong, but I can't help but feel a pang of sympathy for her. She had helped me find my family after all, and I sensed there was some hurt buried deep inside her.

"Millicent is taking a well-earned rest. But she is continuing to assist us with her connections and financial support."

Funds. Of course. From the size of Millicent's house, she obviously isn't short of money.

"So, what's your plan?" Aleesha asks.

Katya walks over to the window and stares out. "Breaking into the government headquarters was a mistake. And the plan to just take down a section of the Wall without any preparation work was … ill-advised. Too extreme. Taking the Wall down should be the *final* element of our plan."

Her accent is slightly odd. Like an Insider's but more clipped, and she elongates some of the syllables, drawing them out as if she takes pleasure in the words.

"And the first stage?" I ask hesitantly.

"Remove the threat." She turns back to us. "If we remove the Metz from the equation then the government has no power. They rule by force, by fear. If we can remove that fear, people will support us."

"You're going to take down the Metz?" Aleesha stares at her as if she's gone mad.

"Yes." There's a certainty in her voice, as if she's stating a simple fact to a child. Grass is green. The sky is blue. We will take down the Metz. I wonder if she always gets what she wants.

"We've developed a tool that we think we can use to take control of them."

Take control of them.

The Metz are trained law enforcers. Inside, it's an honour if your son or daughter is chosen to join the Metz. Lucrative too, for the family. But out here, there are rumours that they're bots. Machines designed for a single purpose.

"They're not people?" I blurt out.

"They're cyborgs. When the officers are recruited, a chip is implanted in their brain. The government use it to control them. To override their emotions and make them do the job they're designed to do: put fear into the heart of the population."

"Was that the tool that Bryn didn't think would work?" Aleesha says into the silence that follows Katya's words.

Surprise flickers in Katya's green eyes, but her expression doesn't change. "It's still in its test stages. We're planning to try it on a small scale. If that doesn't work, then we may need to take more active measures to find out how they're controlled."

"And that's it? Surely there must be some failsafe or something. If it was that easy to take control of the Metz someone would have done it by now. We're not *all* dumb Outsiders, you know."

Katya gives her an appraising look. "You're right. It may not be as easy as all that. We need to know more about their compound. What their setup is, how officers are controlled when they're out on the streets. Who controls them. That's my job to investigate."

"How can you investigate?" Aleesha shoots back. "You're from out of town, right? You're not even chipped."

"That's not for you to worry about." Katya smiles coldly.

A shiver runs down my spine. Being in her presence puts me on edge. Part of me – a *large* part of me – wants to be close to her. To touch that perfect porcelain skin and … I shake my head.

Get those thoughts out of your brain.

Was this what Bryn had meant when he said he didn't trust beautiful women?

"Bryn said you were from Russia."

Katya turns her gaze to me. "I have lived in many places. But yes, originally, I'm from Russia."

"Where's Russia?" Aleesha asks.

Katya gives her a patronising look. "It's the largest country in the world. Don't they teach you anything at school here?"

Aleesha's jaw clenches and her hands ball into fists at her side. *Uh oh.*

"We don't get taught much about geography outside of Britannia," I say quickly.

A half smile turns the corner of Katya's mouth. "Obviously not. Well, that's enough for today. I'll be in touch once we have a use for you."

She walks over to the door and opens it, giving us no choice but to leave. There's a slight click as the door locks behind us.

We walk back downstairs and follow the sound of voices into the small room Matthews had disappeared into. Bryn looks up as we enter. "Everything okay?"

I nod.

"Fine," Aleesha says tightly.

Bryn guides us back through Six to the boundary with Area Five. To our right, the wide road leads up to the East Gate, one of the three official routes through the Wall. There's a queue of people waiting to get in. We hurry over to the other side of the road, where Bryn pauses. "Look, are you guys okay to get back from here? Got something I need to do."

I look at Aleesha. "Sure." She shrugs. "I know my way from here."

"What do you think about what Katya said about the Metz?" I

muse as we walk slowly through the streets. "If she's right and they're not in control of their actions, well, that changes things, doesn't it?"

"How? They're still killers." I glance at Aleesha, surprised by her harsh tone, but she stares straight ahead, an expression of grim determination on her face. "Killers. They need destroying."

I look away. The Metz killed her mother and her friend Lily. I guess that's not something you can just forgive.

"I'm sorry." Aleesha's hand grasps mine, pulling me to a halt. She gives me a brief smile. "I just want justice. Justice for Lily and my mother." She lets my hand drop and looks away down the street. "You don't know what it's like to lose people you love."

I reach out and take her hand back, giving it a squeeze. "I know. But destroying them won't give you justice, Aleesha."

"It would avenge their deaths."

I try to catch her eye, but she refuses to look in my direction. "Revenge isn't justice," I say quietly.

"Maybe in your world it isn't, Trey." Her voice is hard again. "But Outside is a different place."

5

Aleesha

I don't sleep much. It's a cold night up on the roof and the thin thermal blanket Jonas gave me barely keeps off the chill. Perhaps I should have taken him up on his offer to stay at his place. But he shares a two-room apartment with a couple of other members of the Snakes and what he'd really meant was for me to share his bed. And I'm done with that. I don't want to rely on anyone else for help anymore.

My stomach gurgles. Food is going to be a problem. I can't keep taking Abby's rations. Though that dinner last night was the best food I've ever tasted. I close my eyes and try to bring back the smell of the hot burgers.

Saliva pools in my mouth and I shake myself and stand up, stamping my feet to get my blood moving. Thinking of food is just another form of torture. Today I'll go back to Jay's apartment. Get my chits back. At least then I can replenish my stash of food and maybe get something to pay Abby back for all the meals she's fed me. We'll be even. I won't owe anybody anything.

I drop down from the roof and start the laborious climb down to the street. It's awkward getting up and down from the roof, but I don't mind. So far, the convoluted route has stopped anyone else coming up here.

The noise filtering up from the street gets louder as I get closer to the ground. Usually, I find the background hum of the city kind of comforting. But today something's different. Every so often the streets are filled with fearful murmurings about a Cleaning or a Metz raid, but this is something I haven't heard before. Anger.

I join the river of people on the main street, keeping my head down so I don't get recognized. There are shouts up ahead and some people start chanting. I can't make out the words. The crush intensifies as more people push onto the street. I try to turn around and get out of the crowd, but a shot of panic jolts through me as I realize I can't. My pulse quickens as the memory of another crush, another crowd, forces its way into my head.

A panicked crowd. The Metz. Lily.

I shake my head to try to get rid of the thought and draw in a deep, ragged breath. I just need to stay calm.

"What's going on?" I whisper to the woman next to me. A scarf is wrapped around her head and neck for warmth, and her drab clothing is held together by rough needlework.

"Some big announcement on the screens. Somethin' about a gov'ment cover-up. We're goin' to Rose Square to see what's what."

My heart leaps in my chest. Suddenly the crowd is moving too slowly.

Come on, people.

I try to push through them, but just get an elbow in my chest and a sour look. I wait impatiently as the broiling mass of people inches closer to our destination, carrying me with it. Then finally, we arrive.

Rose Square is one of the largest open spaces in Four and one of the few places where large screens still cover the buildings. There used to be screens everywhere. You can see the outlines of them in the weathering of stone walls and the odd wire or screw that peeks out between the cracks of the buildings. But most of them have been long since torn away and dismantled, their parts put to better uses. The government hasn't bothered to replace them. I guess they know they wouldn't last long. Besides, what would be the point? Even the ones in Rose Square are largely ignored by the citizens of Area Four. People here don't want to know how perfect life Inside is. Not when every day out here is a struggle for survival.

The crush of the crowd eases slightly as people spill out into the square. Out of the corner of one eye, I see the market traders hurriedly packing up their goods. I take that as a warning sign. If the traders are getting out, that means trouble's ahead.

More people spill into the square from every side, most of them heading for the largest screen at the far end of the square. The screen that overlooks the spot where my mother was murdered. I let myself be carried along with the tide until I'm close enough to hear the newsreader's voice and read the tagline that runs along the bottom of the screen.

The words scroll past a few times before I finish reading them. I have to turn the words over in my head a couple of times before they make sense. *Leak of secret government files reveals plot to drug population.*

I strain my ears to catch the newsreader's voice over the hubbub around me.

"In a moment, we will speak to the President about this news. But, if you've just tuned in, here are the headlines again. Secret government files reveal that the government deliberately introduced the drug co-tronkpretine, commonly known as tronk, to government rations more than sixty years ago. An anonymous source within the government laboratories has stated that co-tronkpretine has been found to have a long-term impact on brain function and that prolonged ingestion of the drug over generations could negatively impact on intelligence levels and a person's ability to carry out complex tasks."

The newsreader pauses for a minute and glances off-screen. "And now we welcome the President to comment on these allegations. Can you confirm this shocking news?"

The President appears on the screen. His face is smooth and composed but a slight twitch at the corner of his eye reveals his anger. When I'd been brought before him in the government headquarters, he'd looked tired and worried. Now, his grey hair has been dyed dark again and it's slicked back from his forehead. A few of the worry lines are gone – or maybe that's just the cameras being kind – and his face wears a look of grim determination.

"Firstly, I must apologize for this breach in our internal security. The documents you're referring to pre-date my term in office and that of my predecessor by many years but they were never supposed to be made public. I have instigated a full investigation and will find out who is responsible for this traitorous behaviour. They *will* be punished."

His eyes bore into me from the other side of the screen.

"But is the information correct? Did the government use a drug that hadn't been properly tested and is co-tronkpretine still part of the government rations that many citizens rely on today?" the newsreader presses.

The President smiles. A hard, cold smile that doesn't reach his eyes. "One question at a time, please. After the Great Flood and the dark time that followed, our country was left in a desperate situation. I am confident that the government of the time did everything in their power to keep their citizens alive. You have to understand that our country was very different then to now. People were fighting for survival!"

And we're not now?

"I have spoken to my chief scientist and she has assured me that they will be carrying out tests on this substance immediately to determine if there are any negative side effects from its use decades ago—"

"But surely those tests would have already been carried out and recorded?" the newsreader interrupts. "Our source says—"

"I'm sure they were, back at the time of these papers. But unfortunately, the large fire we had at the government laboratory archives some years ago destroyed many of the records from that time. It was an oversight that the electronic records and films were held in the same place, but ..." The President shrugs. "And it was so long ago that anyone working on that project would no longer be with the department. I'm afraid your 'source' is probably just someone eager for their five minutes of fame." His smile is that of a parent humouring a child. "Of course, the government rations today are safe. We wouldn't be giving them to people if they weren't. We're not about to poison our citizens!"

Poison our citizens.

"But tronk is a real issue in this city, one we have covered before. Its addictive nature and ability to take away hunger pangs—"

The newsreader's voice is overwhelmed by the voice of the crowd. Shouts ring out around me.

"Poison?"

"They poisoned us!"

"It's their fault we can't get jobs."

"My mother died from tronk …"

"It's *their* fault!"

Gradually their cries come together in a single chant.

"Poison! Poison!"

The sound builds, swelling like the storm surges that rip up the river.

"Poison! Poison!"

Around me, people are pumping their fists in the air. Tears run down the face of the woman next to me as she screams the word. *Poison.*

The newsreader talks on, ignored and unheard. The anger in the crowd pulses, barely contained. My skin tingles with electricity.

This is it! This is why we did it. So that people would know the truth.

The government can't ignore this.

"Poison! Poison!"

I'm dimly aware that I'm shouting along with the rest of the crowd. My fist punches the air, buoyed by the energy and passion around me. People's anger at this injustice.

The thumping fills my head, a regular pounding that beats in time with my heart. And then, suddenly, I realize it's not just the cries of the crowd that pound in my head. There's another noise, equally rhythmic. The drum to accompany the chanting.

"Poison …"

The word falls from my lips and I'm left rooted to the spot. I can't be the only one who's heard it? But no, murmurings of fear spring up from every side. I cast my eyes around, seeking some way out of this crowd, but I'm right in the middle of it and we're packed so close together that there's no easy escape.

I lick my lips, unable to quell my rising panic. The pounding echoes in my skull but I'm not sure if it's my heartbeat getting louder and louder or just *them*.

The Metz.

The crowd begins to move around me. Whispers reach me from people tall enough to see. But rather than the usual screams of fear and terror, the chanting around me just intensifies and gets stronger. And people aren't moving away from the thumping beat but toward it.

"Poison! Poison!"

I'm dragged along, stumbling over my own feet as I attempt to stay upright.

Need to get out of here.

I claw my way through the throng of people, twisting my body to squeeze through the gaps that open up as people move. An arm pushes me into a tall man who curses and lashes out. I duck but the blow catches me on the side of my head and sends me reeling with a ringing in my ear that momentarily drowns out the pounding feet of the Metz officers. I stumble forward until I trip and fall, sprawled on the steps that lead up to the monument, a stone spire put up to commemorate an ancient war.

Finally, space to breathe.

I gulp in air, my fingers digging into the gritty stone steps. Then I push myself up, scramble to the smooth stone column and gaze out across the crowd.

An army of Metz officers are marching in from the two main streets that feed into the north part of the square. Facing them is the crowd of ragged Outsiders. Some people wave pieces of wood and metal and there's the odd knife, but most just beat the air with their fists.

Then, as if someone has flipped a switch, the regular chanting and monotonous pounding cease. What comes next is chaos.

The first wave of people hit the line of Metz officers. They bounce back as if they've run into a brick wall, but the press of the crowd is so strong that more people are forced to take their place. Slowly, they begin to penetrate the ranks of the Metz. The officers lash out. The hiss of tasers and the thumping of batons punctuate the screams of the crowd. Screams of pain and anger and fear.

Why don't people run away? Don't they see it's useless? How can we defend ourselves against them?

But from my vantage point, I see the black figures spill like wasps into the square from all directions and I realize why people haven't turned to run.

There is nowhere for them to go.

Nausea washes over me and I grip the stone column so tight that it feels as if I could crush it. I'm on a tiny island, surrounded by a raging sea. But I can't stay here for long. It's only a matter of time before the Metz spot me. Up here, I'm exposed.

People fall, their bodies crushed under the stampede. The Metz have the upper hand, but even some of them are brought down by the sheer weight and volume of people around them. A young man jumps onto a Metz officer's back, wrapping his arms around its neck and pulling at its helmet. The officer tries to beat him off, but the man clings on and someone else raises half a brick and strikes at the black and yellow helmet, again and again. The officer is disarmed, and its own gun is pointed back at it.

Blood stains the ground and the smell of dirt and sweat mingles with vomit and blood, creating a heady cocktail that threatens to choke me. I slump against the monument, my legs feeling suddenly weak.

What would Trey think if he saw this?

We wondered what people would do if they found out about the truth. And here's the answer I suspected and feared. They fight.

There's a dull thump at my feet and I stare down into a pair of sightless eyes. Blood from the man's cracked head trickles down the steps toward the feet of his assailant. But the attacker has already turned and is fighting his way back through the crowd. All around me Outsiders are fighting the Metz. And each other.

I take a deep breath and dive into the chaos. A Metz officer makes a grab for me, but I duck under its outstretched arm. I catch a glimpse of a baton looming over me just in time to run my shoulder into the man's stomach. Winded, he pushes me away and I stumble forward, only to trip over a motionless figure and hit the ground.

My breath comes in gasps. I lift my hand and find it smeared with blood. The bright red blood of a fresh wound. I turn to the person I tripped over, but the woman is already beyond help. It's her blood on my hand. In front of me is another man, no, barely a boy. I vaguely recognize him. He's not one of the Snakes, but I think I've seen him around. A member of one of the other gangs perhaps. He, too, is dead.

I shakily get to my feet, but a glint of metal in the boy's hand catches my eye. His fingers are still warm as I prize them apart to get at the knife. Quickly, I run my hands down his legs and find another blade concealed in a pocket. One in each hand, I get to my feet.

I lose one of the knives distracting a Metz officer who blocks my path, but eventually I make it to the edge of the square. I head down a narrow street, desperate to get away from the massacre behind me, and then dive into an alleyway on the right to avoid the black figures running up the street. Turning a corner, I skid to a halt.

Three pairs of terrified eyes look up at me. A girl of about eight shrinks back, pushing two younger boys behind her. They're twins and can't be more than four years old. On the ground beside them, a woman lies unconscious and bleeding. By the rise and fall of her chest, she's alive, though from the amount of blood pooling around her, not for long. The alleyway stinks of trash and piss. Most dead-end alleyways do.

I lower my knife and kneel beside the woman, trying to work out where the blood is coming from. There's so much of it.

Heavy footsteps sound in the alleyway behind me.

No.

I get to my feet and stand in front of the children, holding my knife up as if somehow this small, measly blade can defend us all.

It may not be ...

But it is. The dark figure turns the corner and looms over us. I take a step backward. *It's so big!* Behind me, the girl whimpers and one of the boys begins to cry.

I stare down the barrel of the officer's gun and wonder if it's shooting bullets or just the paralyzing taser.

"Aleesha Ramos." It's a statement, not a question. I stare up at the blank mask of the officer, wondering if there's a person inside that suit or just a robot.

The officer twitches the gun. "Come with me."

I glance back at the children behind me and realization finally hits. *Three children. One mother.*

I lower my knife and take a step forward. "Fine, let's go." I'm impressed at how calm my voice sounds.

"Wait."

The officer turns its head toward the children. "Helen Gollin." The girl utters a squeak, her eyes wide.

"I do not have any data on you two." It motions to the two boys who cower behind their sister. "You will come with me."

"No!" I lift the knife in what I hope is a threatening stance, but my hand shakes, and I can't keep the tremor from my voice. "They're only children. Just leave them. I'm the one you want."

The officer pulls a pair of cuffs from its belt. "All illegal persons must be apprehended," it intones in that dry, gravelly voice.

I step back and feel the girl's breath on the back of my arms. "If I can distract him, you have to make a run for it," I whisper. "Get your brothers out of here."

I scan the Metz uniform. Plates of impenetrable material, interlocked to give no point of weakness. Apart from one. Yesterday, when Trey and I had been trapped in the alleyway, I'd stabbed my knife desperately in the crease of the officer's elbow and felt the material give under the point of my blade.

The officer opens its arm and I take my chance. Lunging forward, I aim my knife at the tiny gap between the plates at the elbow joint. Instead of bouncing off the hard uniform, the tip of my blade penetrates something soft.

There's a cry, an almost human cry, of pain. Then a blur of movement and I'm flying across the alley. My body slams into the wall and I slump down, the breath knocked from my lungs.

Run! I want to shout at the girl, but I can barely breathe, let alone speak. The kids stand frozen in place. Then as if waking up, the girl seems to remember what she's supposed to be doing and tugs her brothers forward. But it's too late. The officer blocks their path.

I crawl forward, barely able to move. Pain racks my body, but I'm pretty sure that nothing is actually broken. I look around for my knife, but it's nowhere to be seen. I must have dropped it when I hit the wall. Above me, the Metz officer blocks out the little light that filters down between the tall buildings.

All three children are now crying. The girl pushes back her mop of dark curly hair. The curls remind me of Lily, but Lily's hair had been blonde. Like a baby angel.

And I let her die. Like these children will die.

I clench my fists and push myself slowly to my feet. I sway slightly, trying to get my balance on legs that feel weak and wobbly.

"Please." My voice is thin and cracked. I cough and wince as the movement washes a new wave of pain through my chest. Maybe I've cracked a rib. "Please. They're innocent children. They've done nothing wrong."

My legs give out and I fall to my knees. More pain. I open my hands. "Take me but leave them. Please?"

I stare up at the officer. Was it my imagination or did it hesitate slightly? For the first time, I notice a tiny label on the top left of its chest. There's something written on it. A number.

"ML486." I read out. "Is that your name?" I look up into the blank mask. "Or do you have a real name? Is there a person in there or are you just a machine?"

The officer lifts its arm and blood drips from its elbow to the floor. Blood.

Machines don't bleed.

"You are under arrest—"

Without thinking, I stumble to my feet and rest my hand on

its chest. *His chest.* He's so big, even for the Metz, that I think he's male, though I could be wrong. I crane my neck to search his face, but all I see is my own face reflected in the visor.

"Innocent," I say quietly.

"You are ..." The voice trails off and the arm holding the gun falls to the officer's side. I hold my breath, wondering what to do next. But before I can decide, the other arm, the one whose elbow bleeds, comes up to my head. I flinch but the blow I'm expecting doesn't come.

A gloved finger reaches out and gently touches my hair. "Innocent?"

"Yes." I swallow to moisten my mouth. Every muscle in me is tense.

"Go."

The word bounces around inside my skull. It takes me a moment to register what he's said.

The officer takes a step back and turns away. "Go," he says again, more quietly this time.

I don't wait to be told again. Grabbing the twins' chubby hands, I drag them down the alleyway. The girl follows, sobbing loudly. Back on the street, we turn away from Rose Square and join the other people stumbling away from the carnage. There are no more shouts of anger coming from there now. Just screams of pain.

But as we get to the end of the road and turn a corner, I can't help but look back. And when I do, I see the outline of a black Metz officer silhouetted against the light. For a moment I feel as if our eyes meet. Then he turns and walks up the street away from us.

6

Trey

The moment Aleesha barrels into the kitchen pulling three small children behind her, I know something is wrong. She's limping slightly, and blood is smeared across her cheek and hands. But it's the haunted look in her eyes that makes the breath catch in my throat.

My fingers fall from the strings of the guitar and the final notes of the simple melody I'd been playing linger for a moment in the silence between us.

"Aleesha, what's happened?" Abby looks up from the dough she's been kneading and takes a step toward the children who stand awkwardly in the doorway. She beckons at them. "Come in and close the door behind you."

Aleesha sways then takes two steps over to the table. She grips the edge of the wooden surface, her knuckles white, but she can't stop the trembling that runs up her arms. "I-I'm sorry, Abby. I wasn't sure what else to do ... Their father's at work."

Her voice trails off and she looks at Abby beseechingly. A glance passes between them and Abby nods, obviously understanding some unspoken words that I can't grasp. She walks over to the sink and washes the flour from her hands, then turns to the eldest of the children, a dark-haired girl.

"Where do you live …?"

"Helen," the girl supplies in a small voice. "Helen Gollin. We live on Underwood Road. Me da works at the food factory in Area Three."

"Davie Gollin? Is that your da?"

The small girl nods, surprised. Abby smiles warmly at her. "Well, if he's on shift now, he won't be finished until this evening. I'll take you back home myself once he's done."

The girl hesitates. "But me ma …" Her voice trails off and tears start to roll down her cheeks. One of the boys flops down onto the floor and starts wailing. The other quickly follows suit.

"Ah, come here, the three of you." Abby bends down and envelops the weeping children in her arms, making soft soothing noises.

I place the guitar carefully back on the wall and walk over to Aleesha. I hesitate for a second, then reach out and gently rub her shoulder. She flinches at my touch and I whip my hand away.

"Sorry," she says. "I'm a bit sore."

"What happened?"

She glances over at the children then jerks her head toward the door. "Not here."

We go into the front room and Aleesha lowers herself gingerly onto the sofa.

"He did it, Trey. Theo's dad. He released the information in the government papers, about tronk. It's all over the news."

I close my eyes as relief washes over me. *Thank goodness.* I'd made out to Aleesha that I'd been confident about Theo's dad releasing the information, but the truth was I hadn't been at all sure. He'd sounded so dismissive of it, but also slightly nervous.

I smile and open my eyes. "That's great!"

Aleesha stares at me and the smile drops from my face. "No, Trey. Not great." She sighs and drops her head into her hands, digging her fingers into her dark, braided hair. "I've never seen anything like it. People gathered to see the news on the screens in Rose Square. They got angry. Really angry. There were so many people there, the whole square was full. Then the Metz came, appearing in every direction, and rather than run from them, people fought back."

My stomach gives a lurch as if I've just been dropped ten feet.

She looks up at me, her eyes full of anguish. "They didn't have a chance, Trey. What use are homemade weapons and fists against Metz armour and guns? People were cut down, massacred ..." Her voice trails off and she wipes her eyes with the back of her hand, smearing dirt and blood across her forehead.

"What have we done?" I whisper.

"Started a war."

I stare at the faded paint on the walls. *A war. We started a war.* "The children ... Their mother?"

"Dead," Aleesha says shortly. She blows out a breath. "At least, I think she's dead. She was losing so much blood ... I couldn't stop to check. W-we were trapped by a Metz officer. Just one, on his own. He knew who I was, and he didn't have any record of the twins ..."

"Three children. They had the girl and then two boys?"

Aleesha nods. "I guess under the two-child rule, you're supposed to give one of them up at birth, but how would you choose? She must not have registered either of them. But, the strange thing is ... he let us go."

"What, the Metz officer?" I stare at her.

"Yes. I pleaded with him to take me and let the kids go, and at first he was just like they normally are. Just doing the job, like a machine. But then something changed. I don't know what, but it was almost as if he *felt* something. It was like he knew what he should be doing but couldn't bring himself to do it." She stares at me. "And he bled. Like a person."

My mind whirrs. *What can this mean? That whatever it is that controls the Metz can be overridden? Or that they make their own decisions?*

"We should tell Katya," I say slowly. "What you saw, well, it proves what she said – that they're at least partly human. And that there's some way of connecting with them, of making them see that what they're doing is wrong."

Aleesha looks doubtful. "You sure? She sounded like she had her own plan very much under control."

"Look, I don't know what you've got against her, but—"

"Just because I wasn't hanging on her every word and drooling over her, doesn't mean I've got anything against her!"

"Huh?" *Where did that come from?*

Aleesha pushes herself awkwardly to her feet, wincing as she straightens her back. I put out a hand to help her, but she shoves me away with a scowl.

"Let's go tell Katya," she says in a false, high-pitched voice.

I stare at her, confused. "Wh—"

"Don't be stupid, Trey. Remember what Bryn said about not trusting beautiful women? That sexy look she's got going on? It's designed to make men want her. That's how she works. They'll agree to anything to get just a little bit closer to her. Tell her all their secrets, promise her the world. And you fell for it."

Her words sting. "I—"

An image of Katya jumps into my head and I feel my cheeks

begin to burn as heat flushes through me. "She can't help being beautiful. And she seemed nice ..." I realize how lame the words sound as soon as they're out of my mouth.

Aleesha snorts and begins to hobble toward the door. "Nice? She wouldn't have been put in charge if she were nice. She's a pro. Charming, manipulative, dec—"

She stops short. A fleeting expression crosses her face as she turns away from me.

"What do you mean?" Now I'm really confused.

She pauses in the doorway. "It doesn't matter. You're probably right. We should tell her."

I follow her into the kitchen, still puzzled.

Abby is trying to get the kids to help her make bread. The two younger boys seem happy enough punching dough, but the older girl just stares at it, occasionally pulling off a tiny piece and rolling it between her fingers.

"We're just heading to the house in Six," I say as we squeeze past the table. "Won't be long."

"Wait a sec." Abby reaches into a battered old tin and pulls out a protein bar. She hands it to Aleesha. "I bet this is the first food you've had all day."

"Umm, thanks," Aleesha says awkwardly, shoving the bar in her pocket.

She turns toward the back door, but the dark-haired girl starts, as if only just noticing us, and runs to block her path. She looks up at Aleesha with wide, round eyes.

"Th-thank you, Aleesha," she says in a tiny, high-pitched voice. Her hands are twisted in front of her as if she's not sure what to do with them. Then she seems to make up her mind and throws her arms around Aleesha's waist, pressing her cheek to her chest. Aleesha freezes and stiffens, and the girl releases her grip and steps back awkwardly.

"It's fine," Aleesha says, her eyes shifting to the back door. "I … really, it's fine." She chokes slightly on the final word and turns it into a cough. The girl steps aside and Aleesha rushes out the door.

"You okay?" I ask, catching her up at the bottom of Abby's small back yard.

"Sure. Let's go."

But as she pulls open the back gate I catch sight of a solitary tear trickling down her cheek.

I don't recognize the two men who lounge against the stone pillars at the bottom of the steps leading up to the Chain's headquarters, but they seem to know who we are. One of them raises an eyebrow when I say that we want to see Katya, but he disappears inside and, a few minutes later, beckons to us from the doorway.

"Now remember, no drooling," Aleesha mutters as we walk up the stairs.

"Don't be an idiot."

We're shown to the small room on the ground floor and told to wait. After a few minutes, the door opens and Katya walks in. She's dressed in a tight sleeveless suit, similar to the one she was wearing yesterday but with a few additions: more pockets and a gun holster on the belt. The added bulk doesn't take anything away from her figure.

I gulp in a breath and tear my eyes away from her to stare out the window, trying not to think about what she'd look like if she wasn't wearing that suit. Of course, that means it's hard to think of anything else.

"What's up? Trey, are you okay?"

"Y-yes, fine." I force myself to look at her. *Concentrate.*

"Aleesha has something to tell you, about the Metz. It might help."

Katya runs her fingers through her long, loose hair and I notice that her right forearm is bandaged. "Okay, well what is it?"

Reluctantly at first, Aleesha describes her run-in with the Metz officer. When she gets to the point where she stabbed him in the elbow, Katya is suddenly alert.

"There was definitely blood? Your knife went through the suit?"

Aleesha nods. "It's only a tiny gap and you can only get at it if their arm is held out, like this." She demonstrates, holding her arm out straight at ninety degrees to her body.

"Interesting," Katya says, narrowing her eyes. "Go on."

Aleesha continues the story. Katya's eyes widen in surprise when she describes how the officer let them go. It's the first time I've seen a real emotion play over her face.

When she finishes, Katya looks at her appraisingly. "So you think it realized that what it was doing was wrong?"

Aleesha shrugs. "Why else would he have let us go?"

Katya doesn't answer. She walks over to the window and stares out, drumming her fingers lightly on the windowsill. "If this officer was feeling guilty, perhaps there was some malfunction in its system. Something that disrupted the connection between its chip and the main control system. I can't believe they give them autonomy over decisions like that."

She turns back to us. "Have either of you seen anything like this before? Where an officer seems to change its mind?"

I shake my head.

"No," Aleesha confirms. "Even when they're taking people, during raids or Cleanings, when people beg them to let them go, I've never seen them back down." I sense her stiffen and, glancing down, see that her hands are balled into fists.

"And you say you got the officer's number?"

Aleesha nods. "ML486."

Katya seems to reach a decision. She walks over and stands in front of us. A whiff of her exotic scent reaches my nostrils, making it very difficult to focus on her next words. "You need to find this officer again. We've got no way of knowing whether it was something to do with you specifically that triggered this. We need to know if it was a one-off, or if it can really think for itself. If it feels guilt then maybe we'll have a way in."

"Into what?" I blurt out.

"Into the Metz compound, of course." She catches the look of disbelief on my face and waves a hand dismissively. "Don't worry, I'm not going to send you two in on some suicide mission. But if there's any way of getting this officer on our side, then we'll have a person on the inside should we need it."

"And how do you expect me to find him?" Aleesha asks. "They all look identical."

"You've got his number."

Aleesha nods. "But you have to be really up close to see it, and I'm not going around poking my nose at every Metz officer's chest in the hope it might be him. I'd be arrested before I got fifty paces." She glares at Katya.

"I'll spread the word around for people to keep a look out for it. Did you say you thought it was male?"

"I don't know for sure. Their voices all sound the same. He was big though, one of the biggest I've seen, and I just felt ... I dunno, I just had a feeling he was a guy."

Katya nods. "Fine. Also, if he remembers what happens, he may go back to the same place. Worth a try anyway." She reaches into a small pouch on her belt and pulls out a bag that clinks. Opening it, she reaches inside and pulls out a handful of small rectangular scraps of metal. She drops some into each of our hands.

"Thanks for coming to me with this. Aleesha, I want you to keep an eye out for this officer. If you spot him again, try to engage him in conversation." She turns to me. "Trey, see if you can get any information out of your father on who in the government is really in charge of the Metz, and anything he knows about the compound. We need more intel."

I stare down at the four warped scraps of metal in my hand. They're stamped with a double circle. Chits. The currency Outsiders use. Those who don't have a regular bank account. It's not legal tender, but the government must turn a blind eye as there's little they can do to control it. It's the first money I've had since I dug my chip out and lost the connection to my bank account.

Aleesha's already pocketed her chits. We walk toward the door, but it opens in front of us.

"What do you want doing w—" The man stops short when he sees us and begins to back away, closing the door. But not before I catch a glimpse of what's behind him. A woman's body, strapped to a hover float, her long blonde hair tickling the floor. She's dressed in the familiar blue uniform of a junior government official. Her left arm hangs limply off the float; a glint on one finger indicating a thin wedding band.

I stare at the cracked plastic door, the image of the woman burned on my retina. A ringing laugh makes me start. "It's okay, Trey. She's not dead. I just needed to take her chip for a while." Katya smiles at me. "You look as if you've seen a ghost."

"You took her chip?" Aleesha says slowly. She sounds more

thoughtful than shocked.

Katya ushers us out the room. The hallway is empty. I flinch as she moves toward me, but she just steps past me to open the door.

"Remember, anything you find out, come to me first." We're gently, but firmly, pushed out onto the steps. The front door slams shut behind us.

I stumble down the steps, still trying to process what I've just seen. Aleesha catches my arm as I trip. "Hey, steady there."

At the bottom of the steps, I pause and look back up at the door.

She was young. And married. Will her husband report her missing? Is he even alive?

"Trey!"

There's a tug on my arm, and when I look down I realize I've taken three steps back up toward the door. I finger the chits in my pocket. The thought of the woman's face tugs me forward, but Aleesha shakes her head. I let her guide me back down onto the street. She's probably right. What could I do? But when the guards nod a friendly farewell to us, I look away, unable to meet their eyes.

We walk in silence for a minute until, finally, I can take it no more. "She took that woman's chip!"

"Looks like it. I don't know why I didn't think of it before. I guess I just assumed that it wasn't that easy. If it's just a case of cutting the chip out of one person's arm and putting it in someone else's …"

I stop and stare at her. "Aleesha, this isn't okay! She's *taken* that woman's identity. Stolen her money, her apartment, her job … Everything!"

"A new life …" Aleesha seems lost in thought.

How can she be so cold? So practical about it? And Katya ...
It's sickening.

Aleesha places her hand on my arm. "I told you she wasn't nice, Trey." Her voice is soft, not the sarcasm I was expecting. "You should know by now what kind of people these are. If Millicent was willing to let hundreds of Outsiders die as part of her plan, what's one woman?"

I pull my arm away. "But that woman was innocent!"

"And Outsiders are all criminals who deserve to die?" Anger flares in her eyes.

"That's not what I meant." I glare at her. "Stop twisting my words. It just ... well, it's just *wrong*."

"Because she's an Insider? Is that it? *Her* identity and rights are more important than other people's?" Her voice is tight and controlled. "Dozens of Outsiders died today, Trey. Hundreds, perhaps, and more will die in the coming week as they can't get the medical help to treat their wounds. I'm not saying it's right to take someone's identity, but just remember that there are people who die in this city every day because they've never been given an identity in the first place."

"That doesn't make it right." But I'm talking to Aleesha's retreating back. I think about running after her. But she's the one in the wrong. I don't see why I should apologize.

I sigh and look around, wondering how long it's going to take me to find my way home.

7

Aleesha

I run through the streets of Area Five, not caring who might see me. It feels good to stretch my muscles and work my lungs. Channel my frustration into something productive. As I reach the boundary with Area Four, the atmosphere changes. Wounded people wander the streets in a daze. There are more Metz on the street, but though a hobie may spit in their wake, there's no real challenge to their oppression.

There are two figures at the window in Jay's apartment, so I slouch against the wall of the alley out of sight. Half an hour later, Beth walks out the front door and down the street without a backward glance. I wait five minutes then stroll over to the door between the old kebab shop and a boarded-up tattoo parlour. The outer door code hasn't changed, and I run up the stairs inside and stop in front of a familiar faded green door. My fingers beat a rat-a-tat-tat.

The door opens six inches. "I thought I told you not to come here." Jay scowls at me and I stick my foot out just in time to stop the door slamming shut.

"I've come to get the rest of my stuff."

A look of puzzlement crosses his face and I use the momentary distraction to push the door open and step into the room. It looks just the same. Bare apart from a table and chairs and a thin counter in one corner with a hotplate.

Jay limps across to the table and takes a swig from a bottle of Chaz, the sickly sweet drink that's cheaper than bottled water. There's a fresh cut on his arm and another slash across his broad chest that's still leaking blood.

I'll bet he hasn't treated that.

Even after he won the Snakes' leadership contest it was me who had to make sure his wounds were clean, who made him take the anti-infection pill. That was part of my job.

The role of a girlfriend. To look after her man.

I realize I'm frowning and force my face to relax.

"You were involved in the fight?" I ask. "Did anyone get hurt? In the gang, I mean?" I glance around. "Why aren't you at the headquarters?"

Jay makes an exasperated noise. "Will you stop with yer questions? I came back to check that Beth was okay."

"You should be with the gang, not here with her."

That earns me another scowl. But I'm right. He's the leader of the Snakes. They should be his first priority.

"Anyway, you've got no right comin' here and having a go at me. Not after you've spent years lying to me. I saw your face on the screen." He jabs his finger at the window. "Illegal citizen? No wonder you were always beggin' me for food."

I sigh. "I'm sorry." He gives me another scowl. "Really, Jay, I'm sorry I couldn't tell you. I didn't know if you'd turn me in."

He turns away and mutters something under his breath.

Fine. I walk over to the corner of the room. "Can I borrow your knife?"

"What have you done with yours?" But he tosses a short-bladed knife in my direction. I catch it by the handle, more by luck than skill. "Nice to see you haven't lost your touch." He smirks.

"Lost mine in the fight in Rose Square," I say, using the blade to ease up the loose floorboard in the corner of the room.

"You were at Rose Square?"

I nod. "I went to see what was on the screens, and then couldn't get out when the Metz came."

Jay walks over and crouches down beside me, his eyebrows bunched together in a frown. I swallow, trying to ignore his closeness. His musky scent cuts through the smell of sweat and dirt and I shuffle further away from him.

"You've been hidin' stuff here all this time?"

I nod.

His eyes narrow. "I always wondered where you kept your stash of tronk."

"I've quit," I say through gritted teeth, swallowing down a pang of longing.

Dammit, Jay.

I can almost taste it on my tongue.

My hand shakes as I reach into the void under the floorboards and pull out a metal lockbox. Inside, there's a handful of chits, a few protein bars that are well past their use-by date and a couple of half-used packets of pills. I reach back down and run my hand around the void. Nothing.

Damn. I thought I'd left a knife here.

"Any chance you've got a spare knife I could have?" Jay looks at me suspiciously and I roll my eyes. "I'm not going to stab you. But I need to be able to defend myself. You know that."

He sighs and goes into the bedroom, returning a moment later with a battered plastic box containing an assortment of knives and makeshift weapons. I raise an eyebrow. "That's quite a horde you've got there."

He shrugs. "There's plenty more at headquarters, but I like to keep some stuff here. Help yourself."

I route through the box, selecting two knives that are well-balanced enough to throw and a stiletto blade that should fit in the hidden pocket in my trousers. "Thanks."

"No worries." Jay leans on the back of the chair. "Are … are you okay, Aleesha?"

The question and the concern in his voice surprise me. I stand and tuck the lockbox under my arm. "Yeah. I'm fine." I hesitate, and then hold out the pack of blue pills. "Take two of these. They're anti-infection pills." I eye the trickle of blood on his chest. "And make sure you keep those wounds clean."

Jay shrugs. "They're just scratches."

Irritation flares inside me. "And you know how many people have died from infected scratches out here." *God, sometimes it feels like talking to a kid.*

A flash of anger crosses Jay's face. "Weren't you leavin'?"

He walks over to the door and yanks it open.

I follow him, but then remember what else I needed to talk to him about. I take a deep breath. "I saw Samson leaving here the other night."

Jay's face darkens. "And?"

"He's working for the government, Jay. I saw him inside the government headquarters, talking to the President."

Jay's eyes widen. "What were you doing in t—"

"That doesn't matter. He was there."

He shakes his head. "You're wrong. Samson doesn't work with the government. It must have been someone else."

"Did you take those people off Cleaning watch as he asked? Is that why no one got the warning about the Metz attack in Rose Square?"

The gangs keep a watch out for the Metz. It's part of an unwritten deal. We protect the people, warn them if it looks like a Cleaning's about to take place so they have time to get out. In return, they give us money and food. And don't complain when things occasionally get out of hand.

Anger flashes in his eyes. I've hit a nerve. "There was nothing we could do to warn people. Everything happened too quickly."

"No one was on watch, were they? Because Samson told you to take them off. How many people died today because of that?"

Jay takes a step toward me, his fists clenched at his side. "Samson knows what he's doing. He's working for the benefit of Outsiders." The words trip off his tongue as if he's repeating what someone's told him. Perhaps he is.

I glare up at him. "Really? So, what's he doing to stop the Metz?" I step forward and jab my finger into the firm muscle of his chest. It's a stupid move. I'm goading him to lose his temper. And when Jay loses his temper, he can get violent. But I'm so angry that I don't care. "You need to stand up to him, Jay. The people out there are angry, can't you see? Angry and afraid. And I bet once they've licked their wounds, they'll be wondering why none of the gangs warned 'em that the Metz were coming. It's our job to protect them!"

"Our job?"

A fleck of spit lands on my cheek.

"Our job? I don't see you doing anything to help. Just keep your nose out of my business, Aleesha. It's nothing to do with you anymore."

"But the Snakes ..."

"I don't remember you takin' that much interest in the gang before," he retorts. "Go and find another gang to tag along with, if any will have you. That's what you usually do, isn't it?

72

Switch to another gang when you get bored of one? So much for loyalty."

He gives me a shove and I stumble from the room. The door slams in my face.

I raise my fist to bang on it but manage to stop myself. Instead, I press my forehead against the cold wall and take a deep breath in an attempt to hold back the tears pricking my eyes.

He's right, of course. But how else was I supposed to survive out here? It was either that or be on the streets or at the mercy of the pimps who hang around down by the river. One run-in with them was enough.

I walk slowly down the stairs, tapping my fingers against the cracked grey wall. Jay's in deeper than I thought. And if the other gang leaders that Samson's got control over are the same, the gangs will do nothing to protect people from further Metz attacks. Perhaps this time the Chain have got it right. If you get rid of the Metz, the killing will stop. The Cleanings will stop. And the government will have to listen to the people.

* * *

I head for my rooftop via Rose Square. Metz officers guard the streets up to the square, stopping anyone from going past, and there's a faint smell of smoke in the air that reminds me of the aftermath of a Cleaning. I wonder if it's rubbish in the streets they're burning or bodies.

I wonder how many people have died today.

Hobies huddle in groups, keeping a wary eye out in case the Metz move in. A scruffy kid steps out in front of me, his hands held up and a sullen, pleading expression on his face. Out of the corner of my eye, I see a woman watching us. I pull the packet of pink pills from my pocket and place it carefully in his hand to hide the chit underneath.

"Vitamin pills. They're good for you."

The woman's eyes narrow. The boy gives me a shifty smile. "Thanks, missus." He pockets the pills then shoves his hand inside his thin jacket, apparently to scratch an itch.

I pat him on the shoulder and head off down the street, wondering if his minder will find the chit. Perhaps not. He seemed a smart kid.

Lost in thought, I wander down to the river. The tide is out and a few early flies flit over the stinking mud. In summer, the flies and the stench are unbearable, and only the scavengers who scrape a living from what the tide brings in come this close to the water.

You need to find this officer again.

Katya's words. Easy for her to say. Hundreds of Metz officers, all identical, and I'm supposed to pick the right one? With the small risk of them arresting me as soon as their scanners pick up who I am.

I realize my brows are knitted together. *Turn that frown upside down.* The corner of my mouth twitches. It had been one of my mother's favourite sayings. She would place a finger at each corner of my mouth and turn it up, or, if I was being particularly stubborn, tickle me until my frown turned into a laugh.

If we get rid of the Metz, the killing will stop. We need to find out more about them. How they work. Who they are.

Something is niggling at me. Some memory that's important. Something to do with the Metz. It lurks at the back of my consciousness in a pool of other thoughts and memories, but every time I try to tug it out, it sinks deeper into the murk. I close my eyes and let my mind wander, flitting from memory to memory and most definitely not focusing on that one. Then, like a boat brought in on the tide, it comes to me ...

I had been in the southern part of Four, scouting out the area around the concrete jungle: the big mass of rubble and junk that for some reason the government has never cleared. It's one of the rougher areas and usually pretty quiet. Even the hobies stay away. Rounding the corner of a street, I nearly ran headlong into the huge black figure of a Metz officer who was standing stock-still in the middle of the road.

I stumbled backward around the corner, my heart beating so loud I thought it would be heard a mile away. But the officer didn't seem to notice I was there. Which was odd. So, I hung around, straining my ears to find out what was going on.

"I have been ordered to bring you back. You must come with me." The gravelly tones of the Metz officer were almost a whisper.

"Please, just let me be. I promise no one will ever know." A man's voice. "Just tell them I'm dead. That you killed me while I was trying to evade capture."

A hesitation. Then the officer spoke again. "You will come with me."

"No!" A scream of pain. I turned to leave but something stopped me. The terror in the man's voice, perhaps, that made me think that whatever awaited him was worse than death.

I picked up half a brick from the floor and threw it at the officer. It bounced off his helmet, but he turned and began to move toward me, dragging a pale, whimpering figure along the ground.

"Stay out of this."

I stood my ground, but more because my legs were weak with fear than out of bravery. "No. Let him go."

The officer reached for its weapon, then paused. It released

75

its grip on the pale figure and turned its head, as if responding to a shout. But the street was silent. I bent down and picked up the other half of the brick. But the officer glanced once more at the man on the ground, turned and ran back up the road as if it were being chased by an army.

I crouched down by the man. He was wearing a long, ragged coat and a thermal hat. I reached out to grasp his shoulder, but he flinched and held up an arm to ward me off.

"Hey, it's okay. It's gone."

He looked up at me and I reeled back in shock. It was like the colour had been drained out of him. As if he were a ghost or something. His eyes were the palest blue and ringed by white eyelashes that were almost invisible against his skin. His eyebrows were white too, but he didn't look old. His skin was smooth and youthful. A pink blush infused his face with colour and he looked down at the ground.

"Thank you. I am in your debt."

The phrase was oddly formal. His accent wasn't from this part of the city either. More like an Insider's accent. The man tried to get to his feet but collapsed back to the ground, clutching his side with a whimper of pain. I reached down to help him up. "Come on, I'll see you home."

His home turned out to be the concrete jungle. I didn't think that anyone actually lived there, but he directed me to a small passageway that seemed to lead into the heart of the rubble.

"You live here?"

The man nodded and began to crawl into the entrance way. "Wait!" I called after him. "What's your name?"

His teeth flashed white in the darkness as he turned to look at me. "Giles."

A cawing seagull lands a few feet away, pulling me out of the memory. Dusk is falling, the sun hidden by thick cloud. No sunset tonight.

Giles. He knows something about them.

It's not far to the concrete jungle. I've only been here a couple of times since that night I helped Giles home. Once to call in the favour he owed me, when I got him to show me and Trey the entrance to the old underground tunnels, and again when we went back through the tunnels to break into the government headquarters.

The loose piles of concrete blocks and rubble are treacherous, and more than once I have to put out a hand to stop myself falling. At one point, I dislodge a small pile of stones that rattle down to the ground. The noise is loud in the still night air. Unlike most parts of Area Four, the jungle is strangely quiet. I guess no one really comes here.

Finally, I reach the rough square opening that I think is Giles's home. "Giles? Are you there? It's me, Aleesha."

But I'm met with silence. I wait a minute and call again. I'm about to venture into the dark when a hiss stops me short.

"Aleeeesha?" He sounds wary.

"Yes. Can I come in?" I glance back over my shoulder nervously. Perched on the edge of the rubble, I feel exposed to whoever may be looking.

There's a grunt, which I take as a yes. I scoot inside the entrance to the tunnel but it's so small that I end up with my back curled against one wall and my legs pressed against the other.

How can anyone live in a place like this?

A slight scuffle to my right is the only warning I have before Giles's white skeletal face appears in front of me. He leans in to inspect me and a shiver runs down my spine. *He is such a freak.*

I chide myself for the thought. No more a freak than any other person out here.

I fumble in my backpack and pull out the protein bars and some dried jerky I'd managed to buy on my way here. Parting with it is hard, particularly as my stomach is screaming out for food. But if this is what it takes to get Giles to talk, so be it.

His eyes widen. "For me?"

I nod but hold the packets away from his outstretched hand. "If you can help me with some information."

Giles rocks back on his heels and I realize that the part of the tunnel he's in is much higher. Although the entrance way is narrow, it must open up to a larger space.

"What information?" he asks warily.

"Information about the Metz."

There's a low hiss followed by silence.

"You know something about them, don't you? How they're controlled?"

Another pause. "Why do you want to know?"

I let out a breath. *He does know something. But how to get him to speak ...?*

"There was a huge fight in Rose Square today. I was with some kids and we were cornered by a Metz officer. He was going to take us in – that's what he was supposed to do. But instead, he let us go. And I remembered when I first saw you. When the Metz officer was attacking you—"

"He wasn't attacking me!" Giles's voice is sharp. Somehow, I've touched a nerve. "He was trying to take me back."

"To take you back where?"

He doesn't answer but I sense him moving closer to me. His leg brushes mine. I'd expect him to stink as much as any street hobie, but his odour is faint and slightly musky. Not at all unpleasant.

"What do you want, with this officer?"

"I just want to understand. I ... I've always thought they were monsters. But he bled, just like a man. So are they people? Or machines?"

Giles hesitates for a moment before speaking. "They are both. When a recruit passes the tests to become an officer, a chip is implanted in their brain. It dampens their emotions. They no longer feel hurt or pain, or love or joy. It means they can focus on their training. Their job."

"Their job? To kill people?"

Giles shakes his head. "To uphold the law." There's a wistful note in his voice. His eyes seem to glow in the dark as he stares past me at the tunnel wall.

"And the chip is what controls them?"

"When they put on the suits."

Suits? "You mean the armour?"

"Yes. The chip at the back of the neck connects to the suit. It's like a second skin, amplifying their ability to fight and move. And messages can be sent directly to officers from the captains."

"So the captain controls each officer's actions?"

Another hiss. I sense he is considering how much to tell me and whether he can trust me, so I sit and wait in silence until he is ready. It's odd. When he talks about the Metz, his speech becomes less disjointed and more ... normal. Less hissing too.

"Things happen instantaneously," he says eventually. "If I told you to do something then your ears would hear the instruction and send that to your brain, which would then process it and decide whether to carry out the action or not. Inside the suit, the instruction goes directly to the brain and the body acts. There is no pause for decision-making."

"So, they *are* like machines?"

A clawed hand grips my arm. His fingernails dig into my skin and I bite back a cry. I pull my arm away, but his grip is tight. "Not machines," he hisses.

"Okay, okay, not machines." *What's his problem?*

Giles appears satisfied and removes his hand. I rub my skin, trying to get the circulation back into my arm.

"So, if they can only be controlled when they're in the suits, what happens when they take them off?"

"They only remove their suits when in the main compound. It is forbidden to remove them anywhere else, and when you are in the suit you would not even think to remove it. When they take their suits off, all memories of what happened outside the compound are left behind."

I stare at him in amazement. "They don't remember anything of what happened Outside? They wouldn't remember if they'd *killed* people?"

Giles doesn't answer.

"So if this officer chose to go against the order to capture me and the children. If he decided to let us go, does that mean his chip is faulty?"

"Perhaps … Or perhaps he is stronger than the system. There were always a few officers who didn't respond fully to the implant. They sometimes retained memories of what happened when they were outside the compound."

Stronger than the system.

I can sense the tension the air. He wants me gone. But I have to know more. "How do you know so much about this? Were you … in the Metz?" My disbelief comes through in my voice. I can't imagine this small pathetic creature ever being as large and strapping as the Metz officers.

The question seems to anger him, and he pulls back further into the dark tunnel, hissing. "You should go now, Aleeeesha." He emphasizes each word in turn and elongates the vowels in my name.

"I-I'm sorry." I hold out the food to him. "Here you go." I stretch my arm out into the dark and feel a hand close around the bars.

His face appears, suddenly so close that I pull back in alarm. "Why do you want to know all this, Aleesha? Are you trying to hurt people?"

"N-no! We're trying to help people. If we can take down the Metz, that will help people."

He cocks his head to one side and looks at me sadly. "The Metz are people too."

"Who controls them? Who controls the Metz?"

But Giles is gone and I'm left talking to the empty darkness.

8

Trey

Bryn rushes into Abby's kitchen, his face thunderous. "What the hell have you done?"

I glance up in surprise, the plectrum falling from my hand to clatter on the hard, tiled floor.

"The news broadcast. It was you, wasn't it? Those files you found in the government basement?" Bryn strides over to me, his boots leaving a trail of mud on the floor. I shrink back as his piercing blue eyes bore into me, suddenly afraid. But he sighs and runs a hand through his dirty blond hair streaked with grey. "I'm sorry, Trey. Just … What were you thinking?"

My hands shake as I stand and gently rest the guitar against the wall. "We thought … I thought that if we told people the truth about what had happened, they would insist on change. The government may not listen to Outsiders, but they'd have to listen to Insiders."

Bryn walks over to the window and stares out. His fingers drum a regular rhythm on the pane like he can't keep still, even for a minute.

"Do you not think people already realize that there's something wrong with this society? But that they accept it?"

I stare at him in disbelief. "No! *I* didn't realize there was anything wrong. What we get taught in school—"

"What you get taught in school is a load of rubbish." Bryn thumps his fist against the pane. "Look, Trey, I know your parents kept you hidden away from all this. That you've not spent much time in London. But other people? People who live here? They're not blind or stupid. They're smart – they're genetically engineered to be smart. They can't *not* know that there's something wrong when a goddamn lethal barrier surrounds them."

"When you've grown up with something, when that's the way things have always been, do you always question it?"

I turn with a start. Abby stands in the door to the hallway, a pile of neatly folded bandages in her arms. "You have a different perspective on things, Bryn, because you've grown up elsewhere. You've seen what other societies are like. You're forgetting that we have no communication from outside London. Nothing is allowed in or out without the government's say-so. And it's been a couple of generations since the Great Flood. Most people don't remember that time, or if they do, all they remember is the bad stuff. The wars and the famine, everything that led to the Wall being put up in the first place."

I stare at her in surprise. "You know all this?"

Abby shrugs, puts the linen down on the kitchen table and opens a cupboard. She starts neatly stacking the piled bandages on a shelf. "I was the one who asked all the questions at school, Trey. I felt something was wrong, but I couldn't work out what it was. When I met Bryn and the others from the Chain, everything started to become clear. I didn't know all the details of this Population Regulation Act they're talking about, but it's not surprising."

"There you see!" I wave my arm in Abby's direction. "Some

people get it!"

Bryn throws his arms up. "Yeah, because everyone's like Abby. How many Insiders do you see who've given up everything to live a shitty existence Outside just to help people?" He glares at Abby as if his gaze could lift her up and plonk her back Inside the Wall. A faint blush rises under her olive skin, but she stares down at her hands, neatening the corners of a perfectly folded square of fabric.

Bryn takes a step toward her then pauses and returns to the window. He lets out a big breath. "Look, all I'm saying is that not everyone is like Abby. And once she got involved in the Chain, she had more information than most. She's right, people don't know what's going on outside this country. They don't know the situation is wrong because they've never experienced anything else."

"Isn't that why we should tell them?" I ask. My fingers curl into fists and I have a sudden urge to slam my hand down onto the table.

Bryn doesn't seem to hear me. "The government," he continues, "*they* know this situation is wrong. But they're the ones who've got the most to lose by changing it." He sighs. "Look, Trey. I know why you did what you did. All I'm saying is, you should have come to me first with this information."

"I did!" I'm shouting, but I don't care. Maybe if I shout someone will finally listen. "I *did* mention the papers to you and Millicent and Murdoch. And you told me they didn't matter. That they weren't *important*. Because your plan was so much *better*. Except it didn't work, did it?"

Anger flashes in Bryn's eyes. "Now wait a minute—"

"No, you wait! You keep telling me that the Chain is trying to create an equal society. That you're going to make things

84

right in the city. But when I actually have some information that could help with that, you just ignore me. You don't care about any of this, do you? You talk about doing all this stuff, but when it comes down to it you don't actually do anything!"

I lean on the table, panting.

"For god's sake, Trey! Will you stop being so naive? When it comes down to it, people are self-interested creatures. They may believe in what's right or wrong, but their first priority is self-preservation." He snorts. "Though you seem to be the exception to that rule. First, you throw away the future your father and I gave you. Then, rather than waiting for the fuss to die down, you just go and give the government another reason to come after you. Honestly, sometimes I wonder if you really *are* my son. You don't seem to have inherited my survival instinct!"

Tears prick my eyes and I gulp them back. It doesn't matter what he thinks. I don't care. He's not my real father anyway.

"You're wrong! You just think the worst of everyone. You don't even give people a chance to do the right thing." I push past him toward the back door.

"Trey, wait. I'm sorry—"

The door slams behind me, cutting off his words. Tears blur my vision as I stumble toward the back gate. *I just need to prove him wrong.*

* * *

I know the quickest way to the Wall by now. Once Inside, I walk quickly along the deserted streets, inhaling the clean air. I'd never really appreciated how lucky we were to have air that smells of, well, nothing. Or at least, nothing offensive. Though the foul-smelling air Outside doesn't choke me as much as it used to. Perhaps the stench of filth, rotting garbage and all the other unpleasant smells that linger in the streets have dampened my senses.

The screens that line the buildings are all showing the news. A crowd has formed in one of the squares and I tag onto the back of it to listen to what the President has to say. A light drizzle gives me an excuse to keep my hood up, hiding my face and hair from whatever cameras may be watching.

The newsreader is giving the President a grilling about the contents of the "secret papers", as they're calling them. But the President is dismissive. He seems to have an explanation for everything, and when it comes to the co-tronkpretine question, he just cuts the newsreader off mid-sentence, accusing him of sensationalising news to take attention away from the real work the government are doing to help people living Outside the Wall.

Around me, there are murmurs of agreement. People begin to dissipate and I move with them, not wanting to be left alone, staring at the screens.

Was Bryn right? Are they just going to ignore this? Do they want to be blind?

I wander the streets, searching the faces I pass for some sign that people are bothered by the news. That they're going to do something about it. But it seems like life Inside carries on as normal. That they don't know – or care – about the events Aleesha had described in Rose Square. That the world Outside the Wall doesn't exist to them.

Perhaps they're not the people I thought they were.

I perch on the edge of a narrow blue bench in a small leafy square lined with boutique shops and cafés. It's one of the more peaceful squares and I know it well. Ella used to bring me here when she was charged with looking after me. We would sit inside her favourite café and watch the people crossing the square, making up stories about their lives.

I lean forward, resting my elbows on my knees, and rub my eyes. I feel overwhelmed. There's too much going on. Things aren't going as planned. Bryn's mad at me, Katya's ignoring what we've done and has some crazy plan to take over the Metz, and Aleesha ... Our fight's been nagging at me ever since I returned to Abby's. I don't have anything to apologize for, but still, it feels like there's something ... unfinished. As if I've hurt her somehow.

A bird lands on the arm of the bench, cocks its head as if assessing whether I'm a source of food or danger, and hops down to the ground beside my feet. It pecks at some crumbs left by the previous occupant. It makes me smile.

There aren't any birds Outside, at least not ones like this. Its bright blue wings are folded back against its cream belly as it hops around unafraid. A lump grows in my throat. I miss living here. Inside. Miss the fresh air and the smell of the flowers. Even in winter, green plants and trees line the streets and hang down from the balconies of the many apartment blocks. Outside, everything is grey and muddy.

I jerk my head up at a familiar laugh.

Ella.

She's walking arm in arm with a tall, lean man with light brown hair that flops over his face. When they reach the coffee shop I've been watching for the past twenty minutes, she stops and says something to him. He bends down to kiss her lightly on the lips, then walks away as she pushes the door open.

Ella has a boyfriend?

But I guess she could have had a hundred boyfriends for all I know. Even before I went on the run, we'd only really spent holidays together. And in recent years, since Ella started work, they had been short holidays. Even though she's my sister, I know little about what goes on in her life.

I get to my feet and walk over to wait outside the café. A few minutes later, she exits, walking right past me, her heels clicking on the paving slabs.

"Ella?"

She freezes and turns around. But her eyes pass over me again. I sigh and step forward, pushing the hood back. Her face relaxes into a smile.

"Darwin!" Three neat steps and she's pulling me into a hug. "It's good to see you."

She steps back, frowning, and casts a worried look around the square. "But what are you doing here?" She lowers her voice to a whisper. "What if someone sees you?"

I pull my hood back up and shrug. "It's okay. I'm careful. Can you call me Trey?"

Darwin is my first name and, until recently, the name everyone knew me by. Darwin Trey Goldsmith. But Bryn told me to drop it. Said it made me sound like an Insider. Which it does, of course. I've got so used to Trey that it sounds odd to be called anything else.

Ella gives a wry smile. "Okay then, *Trey*." She holds out her cup to me. "Hot chocco. Would you like some?"

I nod and take a sip of the hot, sweet liquid. It explodes in my mouth and coats my tongue in a rich, creamy froth. "Mmm."

"Do you remember that time there was snow on the hills in Wales? And Martha made us hot chocco as a treat?"

I nod. It got cold in Wales during the winter – much colder than London. I'd spent most of the time I wasn't at school at our family's tumbling-down house that was nestled between steep hills and only accessible by pod. Martha was the nanny bot who'd looked after us when we were kids. Ella used to love tricking her and sneaking out of the house. I was young the year we had snow, but Ella had dragged me out into the hills. We'd spent all day outside and were freezing by the time we'd returning to a frantic Martha who was on the verge of activating her emergency protocol and calling in a search team.

"This is better than hers," I say, taking another sip and handing back the cup.

"They get the good stuff. It's *almost* real chocolate," Ella replies.

We turn and walk up the street. "How are they?" I ask. I don't need to specify who.

Ella sighs. "Okay, I guess. Father isn't great. He's working too hard. And we're having to move ..."

"Move?" My head snaps up. "Where to?"

"Just a few streets away. We can't afford the apartment since Father got demoted, even with my pay coming in. Fortunately, Mother knew a family looking for a bigger place and we managed to swap."

My fault. The lingering sweetness of the chocco turns sickly in my mouth.

Ella squeezes my arm. "It's not your fault, Dar— Trey," she says quietly. "Besides, the new place is quite cute really."

I stare at the ground. Guilt twists my gut. Of course it's my fault. If I hadn't been born, they'd all be a happy family. Dad, Mum, Anabel and Ella. Father would still be a government minister and Anabel wouldn't have been banished to another country.

"Is ... is Father around?" I ask.

"He's probably still at work." Ella checks the band on her wrist. "Actually, he may be just leaving. He tends to walk home nowadays. We can probably catch him if we hurry."

"Do you not need to go back to the office?" I glance at her in surprise.

"No. I was in early today and they probably won't notice I'm gone anyway."

She smiles and tucks her arm through mine. "Come on."

We walk for about twenty minutes until we get to an area I recognize, just around the corner from our home. *Or what was my home.* It all looks so familiar. Everything is just the same. As if nothing has changed. I guess in here, it hasn't.

"There he is." Ella points across the street. It takes me a moment to spot him. Bowed over, he looks shorter than I remember, and there's more grey than brown in his hair. As we walk over I notice that one shoe is scuffed at the front. *Is this the same man who refused to leave the house unless he looked immaculate? Can a few weeks change a person this much?*

He almost walks past us, seemingly oblivious to his surroundings.

"F-father?"

He starts and looks up, wild-eyed. "Darwin?" He peers under my hood.

I sigh. "Trey, Dad. It's Trey."

"You shouldn't be here!" he hisses, looking around as if a Metz officer could jump out from behind the nearest lamp post.

"I need to talk to you."

My father frowns and shakes his head. "Too dangerous," he mutters. "They may be following me."

"The graveyard just up the road," Ella whispers. "Let's meet there."

We reconvene five minutes later in a small, ancient graveyard nestled between tall buildings. Father seems to visibly relax away from the bustle of the street. Does the President have people following him or is he just being paranoid?

We sit in silence for a moment on a plastic bench that's seen better days.

My father breaks the silence. "Was it you?" he asks hoarsely.

"Was what me?"

He sighs. "You know what, Trey. The news reports. The President thinks you and that girl found something when you broke into the headquarters and went to the press."

I stay silent.

My father bows his head and clenches his fists in his hair. "What were you thinking, Trey? Going to the press was a stupid idea. You don't understand—"

"No, you don't understand!"

"Keep your voice down," Ella hisses, waving frantically.

"You don't understand," I whisper. "This city is built on lies, and someone has to stand up for the truth. People have the right to know what happened. We're a democracy, aren't we?"

My father's face twists briefly into an expression I can't read. He begins to massage his temples. "Releasing the information in that way was a bad idea. Now, Outsiders are fighting and Insiders are scared. No one trusts us. And if they don't trust us, how can we help them?"

Excuses. More excuses.

"The drug – tronk – is it still being used today?"

"I can't answer that."

I snort. "That's a yes then. But why would you keep feeding it to them? When you know what it's doing? The papers I found just mention the possibility of long-term side effects. There must have been studies done since then ..."

My father nods. "There's an ongoing monitoring program at

the labs. And yes, there has been evidence that co-tronkpretine has a negative impact on brain function over time."

I try not to think about what goes on at the labs. "So why hasn't it been banned?"

"It has been brought up occasionally. I even raised it myself, ten years ago, and put a motion forward that we should consider banning it and focus on engineering better quality food."

"And?"

"The President pulled me to one side and told me that if I didn't withdraw the motion, I would be out of a job. I suspect that anyone else who's raised objections got a similar response. There isn't enough real food to feed everyone. And the two businesses who control the factory-produced food have significant influence over the government."

This is news to me. "What do you mean?"

My father sighs. "I've told you all along, Trey, there are too many pieces of the puzzle you're not aware of. You think of our society as simple, with simple problems and solutions, but it's more like a multi-layered web: when you break one strand, you don't know what the repercussions will be. There are two companies who deal with the production of factory food. They make everything apart from the government rations. And they're the biggest employers in this city. They are more powerful than anyone. Even the government." He looks down at his hands twisting in his lap. "The President has to keep them sweet. So the government rations citizens are given are ... basic, to make people want to buy the better quality food that's for sale."

"But that's blackmail!" Ella's face is a picture of shock.

"Well, I'm not sure that word would go down too well with the President, but you're correct." My father smiles wryly. "And it certainly doesn't help Outsiders. But when they have the power to cut off the food supply to the city ..." He spreads his hands. "What can we do?"

"Open up the borders," I say slowly. "Why can't we open up the borders to trade with other countries again? I know we screwed them over by not warning them of the Great Flood but that was years ago."

"I honestly don't know, Trey. Foreign affairs weren't really discussed at cabinet meetings. But if we go to them, we need to be in a position of strength, not begging for aid. The real solution would be a time-bound strategy to take down the Wall and support Outsiders to improve their prospects. But no government is brave enough to commit to that."

"Why not?" I ask.

"Because we are a democracy." He blows out a breath. "Outsiders may outnumber Insiders ten to one, but they don't vote. If the government set out such a plan there would be a revolt. Many people – important people – wouldn't stand for it. And I'm afraid they're more influential than a handful of Outsiders."

I press my palms into my forehead. "So how is anything ever going to change?"

"I gave up asking myself that a long time ago."

We sit in silence. Finally, Ella speaks. "I don't think all Insiders would be happy if they knew this. Your generation perhaps, Father, but not ours. There's so much hidden under the surface of what we're told ... so many lies."

My heart leaps and I smile at her. "Exactly! And you're shown nothing in here of what really happens Outside. If people knew about the Metz attacks ... that they murder children, babies, surely they couldn't ignore that?"

My father gives me a sad look and the hope that Ella's

comment inspired deflates like a popped balloon. "Insiders are just as scared of the Metz as Outsiders, Trey. And just having the conversation we're having is enough to get us all dragged off for a life of hard labour on the Farms." He glances up at the wall behind us.

Are they really watching us? Listening to us, here?

I lower my voice. "So if the Metz didn't exist, people might act?"

"What are you thinking, Trey?" Ella sounds troubled. "You can't get rid of the Metz. No one can."

"Of course not." My mind races. I lick my dry lips. "W-who's in charge of them anyway?"

"In charge of who?"

"The Metz. There must be a commander in charge. Or a government minister?"

My father gives me a suspicious glance. "Why do you want to know?"

I look down at my hands. "Just curious. They've been chasing me for weeks. No one knows anything about them. Even whether they're human or … well, something else. But they seem to behave as a pack, as if there's a central person controlling all their moves. Like in a VR game or something."

"That's very perceptive, Trey." He looks impressed and a rare shiver of pride runs through me. "There are different layers of command, of course, but ultimately they lead back to the Metz Commander. He reports to the Secretary of State."

"I've never heard of the Metz Commander," Ella says.

"You won't have done. He stays out of the spotlight. Completely out. Even when I was in charge of some of the Metz operations, I didn't get to meet him. Only the Secretary of State and the President himself know who he is."

"You were in charge of Metz operations?" *Another thing I didn't know about my father's work.* But then, I guess I had never asked.

"A long time ago. I worked in the department when I was a junior minister. Though I think things are run differently now." He frowns. "Back then, ministerial authorization was required for any operation of significance. Now, I believe the Metz have a lot more autonomy. And the Metz Commander more power."

"So, if no one knows who he is, I guess he must live in the compound then?" I say slowly.

My father gives me a sharp glance. "What do you know about the compound?"

I shrug. "Only that it's more heavily guarded than the government headquarters."

"That it is. And don't get any ideas about trying to break in, Trey. At some point, your luck is going to run out." His shoulders sag and he seems even older. "Please, just look after yourself. We can't take any more …"

Guilt twists my stomach as he trails off.

At some point, your luck is going to run out.

9

Aleesha

I look up as the gate to Abby's back yard swings open. Trey walks through and carefully closes the gate behind him. He turns and freezes when he sees me.

His face is a carousel of changing emotions. Delight. Relief. Annoyance. Wariness. I get to my feet, my backside cold and numb from having sat too long on the stone step outside Abby's kitchen door. It's been two days since I stormed off and left him in the street. Two days of waiting for him to come and find me to apologize. Two days before I realized that he wouldn't know where to start looking.

"Uh ... you're here ..." His voice trails off.

I look down at my hands. They're gripped together, my fingers twisting around one another, clenching and unclenching.

Come on. This doesn't have to be hard.

I take a step toward him. "I was just coming to see Abby. Check that the kids got back to their father okay."

Trey glances away. "Sure."

"Well, I'll be going." My feet carry me toward the back gate.

No! You came here to apologize. Don't wimp out now.

I pause and search for something to say. Anything to put off the moment. "You found your way back here okay, then? The other day?"

I wince inwardly.

Trey nods. "I'm getting to know some of the streets at least." He reaches out a hand, then pauses and lets it fall back to his side. "Look, I'm—"

"You're getting to know your way around pretty good," I interrupt. *Why? Why interrupt? Why just not let him speak?* "Umm … for an Insider."

That's it, make it worse why don't you?

There's a silence. I clear my throat. "Sorry, I didn't mean it to sound like that."

I close my eyes and take a deep breath. When I open them, Trey is smiling. "It's okay," he says with a shrug. "I am still an Insider. Though in time, maybe I'll become a hybrid."

"A hybrid?"

"A mix of the two. Like you, right? Your mother was an Insider, so you're at least part Insider, but you've spent all your life out here, which makes you an equal part Outsider."

"Hmm." I hadn't thought of it like that. Hybrid. I turn the new word over in my mind.

We fall into silence. Trey takes a step forward and opens his mouth as if to speak, but then closes it again. We're only a few paces apart now. One more step from each of us and we would be close enough to touch.

You were the one who left him. You were the one in the wrong.

"I—"

"I'm …" He blushes. "You first."

Hesitantly, I step toward him and take a deep breath. "I'm sorry about the other day. I shouldn't have stormed off on you like that. Or shouted at you. I was just upset, because of what happened in Rose Square. And the kids …"

I stare at the worn stone underfoot. A solitary weed is trying to force itself up through a crack.

"I'm sorry too," Trey says quietly. "I shouldn't have had a go at you. I still think what Katya did – taking that woman's chip – was wrong, but I can also see why she might think it necessary."

I glance up at him, but he's staring down at the weed too. "So … friends again, then?"

He lifts his head and smiles at me. My stomach flutters. "Friends."

I let out a sigh of relief and smile weakly. "Great."

Another awkward silence.

"Has Abby gone out?" Trey asks finally.

"N-no. She's in there with Bryn. I didn't want to interrupt them. It sounded like they were having a bit of a heart to heart."

Trey raises an eyebrow. "You mean? Um …" He blushes again.

I smile. "No, they weren't kissing or anything. But from what I could hear through the door, I got the impression they didn't want to be interrupted. They definitely like each other though, right?"

"I think so. But Bryn's as stubborn as an ass, and I think Abby's worried he'll run off again if she gets too close."

"As stubborn as a *what*?" *Did I just hear that correctly?*

Trey laughs. "An ass. It's a kind of donkey, I think. Though really, it's just a phrase. A figure of speech. Anyway, Abby told me that they'd had a thing years ago. But then Bryn met my mother and fell in love with her instead …" The smile falls from his face. "If only he hadn't. He and Abby might have had their own family. It's obvious she wanted one – she loves kids. And my parents would have had a normal family too. Without me messing things up."

There's a trace of bitterness in his final words and I reach out to touch his arm. "Hey, you can't change what's happened. Besides, I can't see Bryn being the sort of person to settle down. If it hadn't have been your mother, it would have been someone else."

He sighs heavily. "I guess so. So, what have you been up to anyway? Any news on the rogue officer?"

"Not exactly." I smile. "But I've managed to find out more about the Metz."

We perch on Abby's back step and I update Trey on my conversation with Giles.

"The albino guy? You think he was a Metz officer?" Trey stares at me and I can almost read his thoughts.

"Not an officer, no. He's not big enough. But he must have had *something* to do with them to know how they're controlled."

"By the Commander …" Trey's voice trails off and he stares out across the yard.

"The Commander?"

"The person who controls the Metz." Trey turns to look at me. "I went to find my father." He hesitates for a second and a flash of pain crosses his face. "He said it's all secret. No one in government really knows what the Metz get up to. Only the Secretary of State and the President himself know who the Commander is. Which is kind of odd, don't you think? That the cabinet don't insist on knowing more?"

Not if they don't want to know. But I don't say this. He'll think I'm just being cynical again.

"How is your father?" I ask cautiously.

"Not good." That flash of pain again. "H-he looks as if he's aged fifty years. They're having to leave their apartment and move to a smaller one. They can't afford it anymore with his drop in wages. But it's more than that. He just seems … lost.

Like he's given up on everything. And Ella … well, she's still Ella, but I can tell she's worried about him too."

"Ella's your sister, right?"

Trey nods. "Well, one of them. The one I grew up with. Anabel's my older sister – the one I didn't know existed."

It strikes me then what Trey's gone through in the past few weeks. He's been hunted by the Metz for being an illegal citizen, found out that his father isn't his father, and his actual father is a commitment-phobic spy, that he has a sister he never knew existed and had a rather rapid introduction to the world Outside the Wall. And despite all that, he chose to risk his life and stay here rather than leave and go back to his old life.

"I—"

The door slams open behind us. "What are you two doing here?" Bryn looms over us.

I stand and stretch. "Nothing."

"Just chatting," Trey says at the same time.

Bryn looks at us suspiciously. "Well, come in then. There's no need to freeze your butts off out here."

He sounds positively jovial – for Bryn.

"Would you like tea?" Abby smiles at us as we walk into the kitchen, her hand poised over the kettle. Her dark hair is brushed neatly back from her face, rather than being messily pulled into her usual braid, and her skin glows in the warm light of the lamp.

Well, something's changed.

"Sure, tea would be great," Trey says, walking over to sit down at the table. I join him and nod at Abby when she raises her eyebrows in my direction.

"The children got back to their father. There's a neighbour he mentioned who knows the … situation and is happy to help out."

It feels as though a weight has lifted from my shoulders; one I didn't know I was carrying. "Thanks, Abby." I smile at her. "I went to Underwood Road, to see if I could find their house, but I didn't want to ask around, in case, well ... you know." *In case I gave them away.*

"Their father came back yesterday. He left this for you." She reaches into a cupboard and places an apple in front of me. A real apple. I pick it up and run my fingers over its smooth skin. There are a few wrinkles and it's slightly soft, but it still has that wonderful sweet smell.

It must have cost him a fortune. And when he needs all the money he can get for the kids.

The thought causes tears to prick at my eyes, though I'm not sure why.

"You're supposed to eat it, not inhale it." Bryn sounds amused. I open my eyes and catch him staring at me.

"Yeah, sure." I almost drop the apple back on the table.

"Here you go. If you want to eat it now, that is." Abby slides a knife across the table to me.

My stomach definitely wants to eat it. It's gurgling away as if there's a four-course meal in front of me, not one apple. Carefully I cut the apple into quarters and place one in front of everyone. It takes a *lot* of willpower.

"No, Aleesha, it's yours." Abby tries to push her portion back, but I stop her.

"Eat it. It's not often we get fruit out here, right?" I lift my quarter up but they're still staring at me and suddenly my stomach feels tight and uncomfortable and not like it wants to eat at all. "Please," I whisper. "I don't often get to give something back."

I stare down at the table so they can't see my cheeks flush.

"Thank you," Trey says quietly. I hear the crunch as he takes a bite. "Mmm, it's delicious. We had apple trees at the house in Wales, you know."

I appreciate his attempt to move the conversation on. Abby picks up on it, asking what they did with them, and Trey talks about apple cakes and juice and something called cider until everyone's eyes are off me and I can eat my apple in peace.

I lick the last of the sweet juice off my fingers, trying to memorize the taste.

"Have you seen anything of your rogue officer, Aleesha?" Bryn's voice breaks into my thoughts. I don't bother asking how he knows. Trey must have told him. Or Katya, perhaps.

"No." I hesitate. "Though I managed to find out some more about how the Metz work."

"Oh?"

I repeat what I told Trey on the step outside. Bryn's forehead furrows and he stares at the wall behind me, seemingly lost in thought.

"Interesting," he says finally. "Very interesting." He turns to me. "And you don't know anything more about this Giles fellow? Who he is or where he comes from?"

I shake my head. "There are rumours about him in Four. That he's an outcast from Inside. A mutant. That something went wrong with his genetic enhancements."

Bryn snorts. "What, because he's an albino? That's just a chance occurrence – it's a genetic abnormality, but a natural one. You come across a few of them in every country."

"The poor man," Abby says. "People here wouldn't understand that."

"Of course, because you have no understanding of the world

beyond Britannia. No communication with other people or cultures ..." He checks himself and smiles wryly. "Sorry, you'll get me started again."

"What I don't understand," I say slowly, "is how this chip thing works. Is it like the chips in your arm? But how can it be used to make you forgot what you've done? Or to stop you feeling?"

Trey frowns. "We were taught something about it in class. Not about the Metz, obviously, more about the principles of how technology can be used to repair damaged brains. Like when people have strokes and stuff." He looks shamefaced. "I'm afraid I don't remember much of it though. It was pretty technical."

"Well, I'll update Katya tomorrow." Bryn glances over at me. "Unless you want to tell her yourself?"

I shake my head. The further I can stay away from her the better.

Outside, the light is starting to fade. The days are getting longer, but winter doesn't want to release its grip on the city just yet. A gentle patter starts up on the window. Rain. Great.

"You'll stay here tonight, Aleesha." I jerk my head up but Abby smiles, softening the statement. "I'm afraid Bernie's still in the front room – he's not well enough to go home – so you'll have to bunk in with Trey again."

"Fine."

I can almost feel Trey blush beside me.

"I'd better go and see how Bernie's doing, actually. He seems to be pulling through, though I'm not sure how – I thought that stomach wound would see him off for sure." She picks up a bowl of hot water and heads for the door.

We spend the evening talking and eating. Bryn tells us some stories of the countries he's been to. He's a good storyteller, and if I close my eyes I can almost imagine the spicy smells of the markets in Morocco and the snow-topped peaks of the Alps. They sound part of a different world.

Abby plays the guitar for us and I'm surprised to find that Trey can play too. His fingers fumble on the strings a little, and he's not as practised as Abby, but the music is so beautiful that it stirs something inside me and makes my throat tighten so much that I can barely breathe, and I have to leave the room and plug my ears with my fingers to block it out.

Later, as I lie in Trey's narrow bed, staring up at the cracked ceiling, I realize what that feeling was. It's not a feeling I have a word for, but it's the comfort and happiness you get from being in a place that feels like home, mingled with the sadness that comes from the knowledge that it's not, and never will be, home.

Outside, the rain is hammering on the window, and I'm glad I'm not up on my roof tonight. It would be cold and miserable up there. Alone.

Don't get used to it. It won't last.

I sigh. As if reading my mind, Trey's voice trickles up from the floor. "Where have you been staying, these past nights?"

"On my roof."

"Your roof?"

"I'll show you tomorrow."

Now, why did I say that? I've never taken anyone up there before. Apart from Lily. And that was only because there was nowhere else for her to stay.

A pause. "Aleesha, can you teach me how to fight?"

To fight? I prop myself up on one elbow and look down at him. "Sure, I can try. But why?"

His face is pale, but it's too dark to read the expression on it. "I need to learn. In case you're not around to babysit me."

I can hear the smile in his voice.

"Okay, well when you're aching and bruised all over, remember, you asked for it."

I fall back on the pillow and close my eyes, tiredness suddenly overwhelming me.

"Night, Aleesha."

"Night, Trey."

10

Trey

The streets in Area Four are ankle deep in water. My boots are waterproof, thank heavens, but I tiptoe through, trying not to splash any of the filthy water up my legs. Aleesha seems less concerned. I make a mental note to speak to Bryn about getting some knee-length boots.

Any dry patch of land is occupied. Hobies crouch in doorways and on benches and old fountains, but there isn't enough space for all of them. The unlucky ones stand, huddled beneath thin cloaks and blankets. Occasionally, someone reaches out a skeletal limb toward us, begging for food, money or tronk.

In the end, I just look straight ahead. The thin porridge Abby had given us for breakfast sits heavy in my stomach and guilt creates a tight lump in my throat that makes it hard to breathe. If I don't look at them, part of me can forget they're there.

But that's the problem, isn't it? People don't want to see them, don't want to know they're there. I'm as bad as any other Insider.

I nearly run into Aleesha's back when she stops abruptly. "Wh—"

She waves her hand to shush me. I follow her gaze to a young man who's swaggering up the street, his arm looped over the shoulder of a pretty brown-haired girl a year or two older than me. His hair is cropped close to his skull and he's well-muscled, for an Outsider.

The girl says something to him and he laughs and smiles down at her. Then he spots us and the smile twists into an ugly frown. My mouth goes suddenly dry and I take a step back.

"Let's go," Aleesha mutters under her breath.

But the street is narrow here and the depth of the water forces us into the middle, toward the couple. Aleesha stops again. She folds her arms and adopts a casual slouch, but as her arm brushes mine I can feel her trembling, though whether it's from fear or anger I don't know.

"Aleesha," the man says.

"Jay."

Oh, so this is the ex-boyfriend. I look at him again, more warily this time. Pale scars crisscross the black tattoos that wind up his arms and around his neck.

"Who's your friend?" Jay smirks and the hairs on the back of my neck bristle.

"None of your business," Aleesha snaps. They stare at each other for a moment and I'm reminded of two dogs circling each other, deciding if it's worth their effort to fight. "Are you going to let us pass?" she says finally.

Jay seems slightly taken aback. "Yeah, whatever." He steps to one side, tugging the girl after him. She narrows her eyes but doesn't say anything. As we walk past them, I feel a splash of water hit my leg. I turn to see Jay give me a mocking grin.

I attempt a scowl but suspect I just look stupid. Turning, I follow Aleesha down the street.

Five minutes later, Aleesha turns into a narrow alleyway and pauses. "Here we are."

I look up. The building in front of us is one of the tallest around. "How do we get up?"

Aleesha flashes me a smile. "Follow me."

She hoists herself up through an empty window frame and reaches down a hand. I take a deep breath. *Got to learn to do this for yourself, boy.* Besides, climbing is one of the few physical activities I'm half-decent at. I curl my fingers over the crumbling concrete lip and pull myself up and over, into the building.

The route up to the roof is convoluted. We go up a staircase that seems half-derelict for a few floors, then through an empty apartment and out onto a small terrace. Then up a ladder, in through another window and up another staircase until we appear to reach a dead end. Aleesha pulls over a rusted chair and stands on it, reaching up above her head. A moment later, she pushes open a trapdoor and hoists herself up.

"This way," she calls down.

I pull myself up, my muscles protesting at the effort, and sigh as I see her already waiting by another ladder on the far side of the roof.

"Fasten it behind you," Aleesha says before starting up the rusted rungs.

Finally, we reach the top. A flat roof stretches out, about thirty metres long and twenty-five wide. In the centre is a small, ramshackle building with a corrugated iron roof that looks like it's seen better days.

"What do you think of the view?" Aleesha calls. She spreads her arms wide and spins around, gazing up at the sky.

I rest my hands on my knees, panting. No wonder she's fit if she comes up here a lot. When I've caught my breath, I stand and look about. We're above most of the surrounding rooftops, which are littered with black solar panels and lightning rods. The Wall looms behind them, and from up here you can see the tops of the tall glass towers Inside peeping over it.

"It's amazing!" I walk to the stone parapet that lines the roof and force myself to look down. I immediately regret it. Miniature people move along the narrow streets far, far below. Closing my eyes, I swallow and take a step back.

"Careful." Aleesha grips my shoulder. "The parapet isn't all that solid in places."

I stumble backward and open my eyes. Ten paces away, part of the parapet has crumbled away completely.

"Come on." Aleesha walks over to the small building. There doesn't appear to be a door, which is odd. Why build something you can't get inside? The roof extends on one side, creating a sheltered area between the brick walls, at the back of which is a small pile of folded blankets and clothes.

I stop dead. "You've been *living* up here?"

"Sometimes," she replies defensively. "It's safe up here and not too cold. In the summer," she adds as an afterthought.

A gust of wind rattles the iron roof. I don't know what to say. Given the alternative – joining the hobies on the street – I can see why she would come up here, but to spend cold, wet nights up here alone … *I really lucked out, finding Abby.*

"You're the first person I've brought up here, apart from Lily," Aleesha says, almost shyly.

Lily? "You brought Lily up here?" I look back toward the ladder leading down from the roof. "How?"

She laughs. "It wasn't easy. But she was a tough little thing." She waves at the floor beneath the overhanging roof. "Would you like a seat? Or shall we get started?"

I eye the dusty concrete floor. "Let's just start, shall we?"

"Sure." She kneels and rummages under the blankets.

"Do you miss him?" The words spill from my lips before I can stop them. I bite my lip, instantly regretting my outburst.

What if she says yes?

Aleesha freezes. "Who? Jay?"

"Yes."

"I don't know. At first, I did a bit. Not so much now." She stands and turns to face me, a rolled-up piece of fabric dangling from her hand. A smile curls the corners of her lips. "Why, are you jealous?"

Heat rises to my cheeks. "N-n-no, of course not." *Damn that stammer.*

She pushes past me back out into the open. "Ah, come on, I'm only kidding you. What about you, Trey? Any crazy ex-girlfriends you left behind at that school of yours?"

"What, at St George's? Britannia's premier school for boys?" I try to keep my voice casual as I stride out to join her.

No reason to tell her I've never had a girlfriend. Just play it cool.

Aleesha twirls the rag in her hand. "Ready?" She raises an eyebrow.

"Sure." I blow out a breath. "Let's do this."

Aleesha starts by having me run a couple of laps of the roof. Then she makes me do a series of exercises, so she can "see how I move". I'm not sure if I'm doing them right or wrong, but I feel pretty stupid all the same.

After that, she joins in, and we use the rolled-up fabric to do resistance exercises. Squats, bicep curls, tricep curls. She's smaller and lighter than me, but stronger, so we balance out. By the end of that session, I'm dripping with sweat and my muscles feel like jelly.

We walk over to the shelter and she hands me a half-full bottle of water. I gulp it down, only stopping when it's pulled from my hand.

"You have to learn to ration it. Sometimes you'll need to go thirsty." She frowns and takes a single sip from the bottle, which I realize, with a flash of guilt, is almost empty.

"Your legs are weak," she continues. "Do sets of squats daily to build them up. And press-ups and pull-ups for your back and arms."

"Anything else?" I ask.

"Well, your stomach could do with some work too." She prods me in my belly button and I double over. "See?"

I glare up at her. "I asked you to teach me how to fight, not give me a workout."

Aleesha folds her arms. "You need to get into shape to be able to fight. Skill will only get you so far. I'm lucky – because I'm small and a girl, guys underestimate me. But you won't get such an easy time of it."

I grunt in reply and she rolls her eyes. "Come on then, let's fight."

Back out on the roof, we turn to face each other. Aleesha takes a step back. "Keep your distance as much as you can. More distance gives you more time to react. And keep moving." She begins to circle me. "Move!"

I start and shuffle around on the spot. If I keep doing this, I'm going to get dizzy. I step out into her path and bring my fists up.

"Good!" She points two fingers at my eyes and then back to hers. "Always look at their eyes. The eyes can tell you what they're planning to do. That's why fighting the Metz is so hard. You can't see anything behind their masks, so you get no warning."

She continues moving, so graceful she looks like a dancer on the stage. Her long, dark braid swings gently behind her. "W—"

A flash of movement. I raise my arm but am too late. My cheek stings under the force of her palm.

"Keep your eyes on your attacker!" Aleesha scowls. "Stop getting distracted."

"Well, stop being so distracting then," I mutter under my breath.

"What was that?"

"Nothing." I massage my jaw. "Sorry. Eyes. Eyes."

We continue circling each other. The next time she strikes, aiming a low blow at my stomach, I manage to dodge enough so it catches my side instead. *Nearly.*

We carry on this strange dance. Eventually, I get brave enough to try an attack of my own, but my arm finds only thin air, throwing me off balance. I stagger to the left and trip backward over something. The concrete roof knocks the breath from me and I gasp, black spots dancing at the edges of my vision.

A weight lands on my chest, forcing the air from my lungs. I lash out instinctively, and the weight shifts downward, first to my stomach, then lower. I close my eyes and lean my head back, gulping in air. An attractive, sweet smell wafts across my nostrils and I open my eyes to find Aleesha's face barely six inches from my own. Suddenly, it becomes difficult to breathe again.

"Are you okay?"

I nod, still unable to speak. She looks relieved. "Sorry, I forgot how hard the floor is here. It's better practising throws and stuff on a padded floor."

A padded floor. That sounds better.

She reaches forward, and her fingers begin to explore my head, prodding behind my ears and around the base of my skull. "Did you bang your head?"

But I can't answer. Just the feel of her hands on me sends a thrill of excitement tingling through my body. My heart begins to race and the thought of speaking to her, saying anything at all, makes my mouth go dry.

Aleesha frowns. "We should probably call it a day."

She begins to push herself up, but I reach my hands up to her hips and she freezes.

What are you doing?

But my brain isn't functioning properly. It's being pushed to the back of my mind, being crammed into a smaller and smaller space as something else takes over. Heat rushes through me and the air between us is suddenly thick, like before a storm on a hot summer's day.

Her face softens into a smile. One of those real, genuine smiles that's so rare for her.

"So, if you haven't had a girlfriend, that means you've never been kissed, right?" she murmurs, leaning fractionally closer. There's a wicked glint in her eyes that makes me shiver.

"I didn't say that."

Aleesha raises one eyebrow. "You didn't have to."

Oh great. So much for playing it cool.

My hands wrap around her back of their own accord, my fingers running up the bones of her spine. She inhales sharply.

I jerk my hand away. *Was that wrong?* But her face is closer now and I can't think. I don't *want* to think. I just …

Her lips brush against mine, sending another surge of heat pulsing through my body. They're soft and warm, pressing lightly on my own. Unconsciously, I part my lips slightly and feel a flicker of movement dart inside my mouth. It's odd … but nice.

Strange feelings surge through me. Feelings that I'm unfamiliar with. Uncomfortable with. A thousand butterflies playing on my skin. An iron fist clenching my stomach tight. An overwhelming need to pull her closer to me.

My hands roam their way up Aleesha's back, out of my control now. I stroke her hair, that beautiful, smooth hair, and pull her head down to mine so that our lips are crushed together.

I feel her pull back, her head pressing against my hand. Coherent thoughts are trying to push through the fog in my brain, but I don't let them through. I just want to stay in this moment.

But her lips are gone. My hand is pushed away. She's pulling away. Panting slightly, I open my eyes and look up at her, the blood rushing to my cheeks.

What did I do wrong?

She looks away. "Sorry, I took advantage. I shouldn't have—"

"No, wait!" I grab her arm as she moves to get up. "I-I mean, it's fine. You didn't ... it was nice." I cringe inwardly.

It was nice?

Aleesha rolls back on her feet and grabs my arm to pull me up with her. She glances down and smiles, raising an eyebrow. "Nice, huh?"

Oh no. No, no, no.

My cheeks burn. Finally, my brain pokes through the desire that's slowly draining from my body. *Perhaps I should just jump off the roof now? You bloody idiot. What must she think of you? You can't even control yourself. It was just a kiss.*

"Hey, stop that blushing." Aleesha's finger taps my chin, and reluctantly I lift my eyes to hers. She smiles impishly. "It wasn't just nice. It was great." She drops her hand and turns away, walking back over to the shelter. "Shall we do some warm down exercises before heading back?"

I clear my throat. "Sure." My voice comes out half strangled. I take a deep breath, feeling the cool air quench the heat in my body. "Sure, let's do that," I repeat, more firmly this time.

Come on, snap out of it.

But even as I start jogging around the perimeter of the roof, her words come back to me.

It was great.

I turn my head so she can't see the grin on my face.

11

Aleesha

Over the next few days, things get worse. The riots continue, not at the same scale as the massacre in Rose Square, but every day more wounded people fill the streets. The rumours about the tronk in the food supply have turned into wild stories about the government rations, each more horrific than the last. One thread connects them all: the government is poisoning us.

Shops are cleared out of food as people spend, beg and steal to avoid having to eat the government rations. Prices go up. Then the hunger strikes start.

People surround the government food depots, sitting in front of the gates, chanting and cursing. I doubt it bothers the guards much. They fly in and out by pod and the gates only open to allow trucks out to deliver rations and medical supplies. The Metz come in to disperse the crowds, but they seem quite half-hearted about it. They're probably happy that the people are starving themselves to death. Saves the hassle of killing them.

It almost makes me laugh: people going on hunger strike when there isn't any food to begin with. Almost.

Trey spoke to his sister, who said this is happening all over the city, not just in Area Four. There are riots and protests in almost every area. Except the rich ones. The gangs from Four and Five have started moving up into Six, looting shops for food.

Things have got a bit weird between me and Trey since our training session up on the roof. I've thought about suggesting another session – he needs the practice – but I think he might get the wrong idea. Sometimes I catch him looking at me when he doesn't think I'm watching and the look makes me uncomfortable. Like we're a couple or something.

I should never have kissed him. But when he ran his fingers up my back, I couldn't help but give in to the feelings that surged through me. Now I've confused things. Confused myself. Trey's not just some guy. He's my friend. The only friend I've got. And I don't want to lose my friend when things blow up. And they always do blow up, eventually.

To take my mind off Trey, I've been stalking Metz officers. Trying to find Rogue, as I've named him. It's a dangerous game and one I can only get away with because I know this part of the city far better than any Metz officer ever will. Even then, there are a couple of times when an officer catches me by surprise and I barely escape being shot or tasered.

It's a hopeless task. Like trying to pick out a single ant in an army of them. I sometimes wonder if perhaps I imagined the whole thing. Maybe he's no different to the rest of them. I wish I'd thought to somehow mark his uniform, so I'd have a better chance of finding him.

But it turns out that's not necessary. Because *he's* looking for me.

It happens on the fifth day. A group of four officers are patrolling one of the main roads in Four. They patrol in bigger groups now they're more likely to get attacked. People grudgingly make way for them. The odd person shouts or throws a bottle as they pass, but most are still too terrified to move. They keep their heads down and silently pray for the officers to pass them by.

Something about the movement of one of the officers catches my eye. It lags behind and marches slightly out of sync with the other three. Rather than keeping its gaze locked on the street ahead, its head pivots occasionally, as if it's looking for something.

I drop down from my perch in the empty window frame and position myself carefully on the edge of a group of hobies with my back to the approaching Metz officers, so they can't scan my face. Their footsteps beat a regular rhythm down the street.

The first two officers pass me by, walking side by side, almost close enough to touch. The third walks past alone. I turn and look straight at the final officer. Its head turns fractionally toward me before returning to a neutral position. But it doesn't pause, not even to scan me. It just keeps on walking down the street.

I let out the breath I've been holding and am about to return to my window seat when a flicker of movement catches my eye. The final officer in the group slowly and deliberately moves its right hand behind its back and extends a single finger to the left.

I freeze, staring at their retreating backs.

Did I imagine that?

"What's up, eh?"

My attention snaps to the scraggly haired old man in front of me. "What? Oh, nothing."

He grunts in response and licks his lips. His eyes run down my body. *Time to go.*

I force my legs to move and follow the officers down the street, keeping a safe distance. It's easy enough, they can't exactly get lost in the crowd. About a hundred metres down, where a narrow side alley appears on the left, they pause and appear to have a conversation, though I can hear no words. Three of them move off, but the fourth – one who'd made the mysterious hand gesture – turns into the alleyway.

I reach the entrance to the alleyway and press my back against the wall. *It could be a trap.*

But I know this alley. It connects two main streets. No dead ends. I risk a peek around the corner. The officer's standing part way down, motionless like a statue.

I take a deep breath and, before I can think about how stupid a move this might be, step out and walk toward it. I stop when I'm two paces away. Close enough to see the tiny number imprinted in the armour.

ML486. It's him.

We stare at each other. At least, I'm staring at him. Who knows what's going on under that helmet.

"You came to find me?" I ask eventually. My muscles are tense, my hand resting on the knife concealed against my leg.

"Yes. For answers."

"Answers?" I'm stalling. Giles said the chip at the back of their neck connects to the suit. So if I could get him to take his helmet off, perhaps that would break the connection between him and whoever's commanding him.

"I let you go. You and the children. It was against protocol. But I felt ..."

The words sound odd, coming out in the standard gravelly neutral voice. It feels like I'm talking to a machine.

"You felt what?"

His shoulders rise in a shrug.

"Did you feel like it was wrong to arrest us?"

"Yes. No. I don't know. I felt odd … inside. This isn't normal."

Giles said the chip dampens their emotions.

"You felt emotions?"

"Emotions?"

"Feelings. Like being happy or sad. I think … I think you have something in your brain that stops you feeling emotions when you have this suit on." I take a deep breath. "If you can take off your helmet, that may break the connection and we can talk properly."

He shakes his head. "It is an offence punishable by termination to remove any part of your armour when outside the compound," he intones.

I shrug. "Well, I can't help you then."

Will he take the bait?

Another silence. "*Can* you take the helmet off?" I ask finally. Maybe Giles was wrong. Maybe once they're in the suit they're locked in, unable to release themselves.

"I don't know," he admits. "In the compound, everything is removed for us. We are not designed to take it off ourselves."

I purse my lips and look up at him. There's a faint join that runs across the shoulders and dips down in a curve at the front of the armour. If it does come off as a separate piece, there must be a catch somewhere.

"Can I try?"

The officer takes a step back. "No!"

The shout bounces off the walls and I freeze. A spike of adrenaline courses through me. *Surely the other officers must have heard that?*

But nothing happens, and after a moment my muscles relax.

"It's the only way." My fingers itch to run along that join, to find the catch and remove his helmet. To finally see who, or what, lies underneath. I reach a hand up toward his neck, but a gloved hand grasps my wrist in an unyielding grip.

"What if I can't survive out here? Outside the compound?" His words are at odds with the calm, monotonous tone that carries not a trace of fear.

"Is that what they told you?" I whisper.

"I don't remember … But I've never been outside the compound. Not without this."

Can that be true? If so, what sort of creatures are they?

I drop my hand. "Well, okay, but I'm not sure if I can help you then."

Another silence. I wonder what he's thinking. If he is thinking.

"How do you know this will work?" he says finally.

I lick my lips. "I don't, not for sure. But someone told me it might."

"Someone?"

I curse inwardly. Whatever Giles had to do the Metz, it's pretty clear he is hiding from them.

"Look, I'm not even sure that I *can* take it off. But I could try? And if at any point you want me to stop, then just say so."

"How do I know I can trust you?"

"You don't." I gaze up at the expressionless mask. "You can either choose to trust me, or not."

I glance back over my shoulder. *How long until the others come back?* I don't think Rogue will hurt me, not now, but I doubt he'll stop the others if they identify me. I'm still a wanted criminal, after all. I shift my feet, rustling the litter underfoot.

"Fine. You try."

I reach up again, then realize the next problem. Rogue must

be over seven feet tall and, at five-two, there's no way I can get his helmet off easily. Looking around, I spot an overflowing trash can further up the alley and point to it. "I'll need to stand on that."

Rogue takes a couple of steps backward until he's standing next to the trash can. I grimace. Climbing on rubbish piles isn't my kind of fun. There's no telling what you may find. Gingerly I push down on the top and jump my legs up, so I'm kneeling on top of it.

"Turn around." I run my finger along the thin line that encircles his giant helmeted head, then rock back on my heels and bite my lip. "I'm going to get my knife out. Don't worry, I'm not going to hurt you. I just need to see if there's a catch inside."

He shifts warily but doesn't protest.

I draw the thin stiletto blade from my pocket and place the tip on the line at the back of his neck. But it's too narrow even for the slim blade.

Dammit. There must be a way in.

Then I spot another line, going vertically up from the back of the neck. About two inches up, it widens slightly. I place the tip of my blade in the opening and insert it carefully. There's a faint click.

I hold my breath, then let it out in a rush when nothing happens. *What were you expecting?* "Hold still."

Clasping the helmet with both hands, I give it a tug. My hands, slick with sweat, slip on the smooth surface. It doesn't budge.

I try twisting it. The helmet moves fractionally to the left. This time, when I tug the helmet up, it comes free and, with an effort, I pull it up and over the officer's head.

The weight of the helmet throws me off balance and I lurch

forward, crashing into Rogue's hard, broad shoulders. Quickly I push myself back on top of the bin, clutching the helmet to my chest, panting. I blink and stare into the wide, fearful eyes of a man.

Not a machine. A man.

His head is on the large size, but I guess that's in proportion to his body. Dark blue eyes flick from side to side, the pupils dilated. Brown hair cropped short. Strong jawline, straight nose. Just how you'd design a perfect man.

His face begins to redden, and his cheeks puff out. My heart lurches. Maybe I was wrong. *Can he breathe without the suit?*

But the expression of disgust on his face suggests something else. "You're going to have to breathe at some point," I say, laughing.

The tension in the air eases. His breath comes out in a rush and his nose wrinkles as he breathes in and out.

"Are you okay?" I ask cautiously.

He looks around and then down as if checking all parts of his body are intact. "I-I think so. Does it always smell this bad?"

His voice takes me aback. It's gentle and smooth, rising and falling with his words. Normal. He takes a deep breath, which sends him into a coughing fit, and he bends over, spluttering.

"Yes. It stinks, but you get used to it after a while."

"It looks different." He leans forward to peer at my face and I shrink back reflexively. "*You* look different."

I tense. "What do you mean?"

He pulls back. "Everything is grey."

I turn the helmet over in my arms and peer inside. There isn't much to see. It's lightly padded and moulded to the shape of his head. There's a section of brushed metal where the base of his head would rest, and I wonder if that's something to do with the chip in his head. I lift the helmet up over my head and look out through the visor.

"It looks just the same to me."

They are my words but in the gravelly voice of the Metz.

My hands slip and the helmet crashes down onto my shoulders. I push it up, clawing at the slick material, but it won't move. I can't breathe. *Get it off!*

Robotic fingers push mine aside and the helmet pops up over my head, leaving me gasping and sucking in air.

"The helmet changes your voice. That's why you all sound the same," I say eventually.

"Yes. When we are out here, we are not individuals. We are one entity."

I stare into his eyes. They look ... normal. Friendly even. "Who are you?"

A faint crease appears on his perfectly smooth forehead. "What do you mean?"

"What's your name?"

"ML486."

I roll my eyes. "No, not your number. Your *name.*"

He looks confused.

I sigh. "I'm Aleesha. You know that. That's my name. What's yours?"

"I don't have a name. ML486 – that's my name." The tremble in his voice betrays his uncertainty.

"You must have had a name once? And a family?"

"The Metz are our family." He lifts the helmet and peers into it, as if might hold the answers to my questions.

"You don't remember anything of your life before you were in the Metz?"

"Our life is the Metz. The Metz are our life. Upholding the

law is our privilege."

A snort explodes from my mouth and I hastily wipe my sleeve over my lips. *He's brainwashed. The lot of them must be completely brainwashed.*

Rogue frowns. "What's wrong?"

"Um, nothing. Look, I can't call you ML486. It feels wrong. I'm going to call you Rogue, okay?"

"Rogue." He tests the name out. "Why?"

I shrug. "Because you're different. Not like the others. A—" I check myself. *A rebel.* I have a feeling that if I mention that particular word, the helmet will be slammed back down again and Rogue will turn back into officer ML486.

"So, what do you do when you're not out murdering people on the streets?"

He scowls. "We do not *murder* people. We are law-keepers, not criminals."

Right, so if we kill, we're murderers. If you kill, it's upholding the law.

I jump down from the trash can and brush myself down, stamping my feet unnecessarily hard on the ground to shake off some imaginary dust. *Don't rise to it.*

"Right, because a six-year-old girl is a criminal who deserves to die?"

Oops.

"What?" Rogue frowns.

"What about the compound?" I change the subject. "What's it like in there? What happens?"

"In the compound? We sleep and eat and train."

"That's it?"

"What else is there to do?" The frown deepens. "You told me you could help me understand these feelings. These …

emotions."

I hesitate. "Do you feel different without the helmet on?"

He nods. "I feel ... confused? I don't know what I'm supposed to do." He looks down at the helmet again. "It's uncomfortable."

I try a different tactic. "When you get back into the compound and take your suit off, do you remember what happened outside?"

"Not usually." He looks wary. "We're not supposed to remember. But sometimes, recently ..." His voice trails off. "Since I started having these feelings, I remember more. Is there something wrong with me?"

"Not something wrong, something right." He looks puzzled. I take a deep breath. "What you're feeling, this is normal. What normal people feel. Look, can you remember what happened the day you first saw me? With the children? Tell me what you remember."

"That was a long time ago."

"Only a few days." I try to keep the annoyance out of my voice.

Rogue's eyes glaze over as he stares into the distance. "We were on a routine patrol when we were called to deal with a disturbance. Criminals fighting each other. We managed to apprehend the individuals involved and were leaving when my scanner picked up a wanted individual. You. I followed you into an alleyway. There were some children ..."

"The children. What did they look like to you?"

"I don't remember. They were children." He shrugs. "They were laughing, I think?"

My stomach lurches and my shock must show on my face because Rogue gives me a puzzled look.

"What?"

"They weren't laughing," I say, fighting to control my voice.

126

"They were crying."

"Crying?"

"Crying. They were distraught because their mother was dying. Her body was on the floor next to them. And they were frightened. They were scared of you."

His eyes widen. "Of me? Why?"

"Because you, or another officer, killed their mother," I say carefully.

"No. We do not kill."

His vehemence takes me aback. *He really believes that.*

I take a deep breath and force myself to place a hand on his arm. His face is so young. So innocent. It's hard to believe he's a trained killer.

"You know you said things look different without the helmet on? Well, maybe it makes what you remember different too? Maybe *they* don't want you to remember what really happened."

"They?"

"Whoever controls you. Who do you report to?"

"We have unit captains. They get their instructions from the Commander."

My hearts skips a beat. "And who is the Commander?"

"He's in charge of protecting the city. A hero." Rogue stands a little straighter. "He's a—"

He stops suddenly and gives me a suspicious look. "Why do you want to know?" He lifts the helmet up to place it over his head.

"Wait!" I step forward until we're almost touching. "I'm just trying to understand why you're different from the others."

A flash of anguish and indecision passes across his face. "I don't want to understand," he says finally. "I just want to do my job."

"But they're lying to you!" The words burst from my lips before I can stop them. "You're not helping people, you're killing them!"

He pauses, the helmet hovering above his head. "We *do not* kill!"

"Come back here." I reach out and place my hand on his chest. "Come back, and I will show you what it's really like out here. Then you can decide for yourself what the truth is."

He hesitates for a second, then lowers the helmet over his head.

"I'll wait here for you. Every day at noon. I'll wait ..."

My voice dies as the helmet clicks into place.

"I must go. They are waiting." The gravelly, inhuman voice is back again. All trace of the man underneath the suit has gone. He turns and trudges up the alleyway, scattering litter in his wake. I wonder if he'll remember any of this when he returns to the compound.

I stand there, lost in my thoughts, until a faint rustling noise causes my ears to prick up. An earthy scent mingles with the background smell of decay.

Uh oh.

"Aleesha." Samson smiles as I turn around. He looms up, almost as tall and bulky as Rogue, and I take a step back. The more distance I have between us the better.

How does he manage to sneak up on me like that? He's too big to move that quietly! And how much did he see?

"I didn't see you as the type to be making friends with the Metz." His voice is completely neutral.

"Friends?" I force a laugh. "Why would I be *friends* with the Metz?"

He looks amused. "I saw your exchange, just now. Good work managing to get his helmet off. I'm not sure anyone's had the

128

audacity to do *that* before."

Audacity? What does that mean? I curse inwardly. I hate not knowing things.

"Though I'm surprised you didn't just take the opportunity to put a knife through his neck." Samson raises an eyebrow. "Seems more your kind of style."

I fold my arms and draw myself up tall. I'll be damned if I'm going to let him intimidate me. "Well, maybe you don't know me as well as you seem to think."

He steps toward me and I step back before I can stop myself. *Stand your ground! He's just doing it to make you scared.*

But, as much as I hate to admit it, it's kind of working.

"Perhaps you're right. But why, Aleesha? What are you trying to get out of him? What have you been *told* to get out of him?"

His voice is hypnotic and I feel my mouth open to speak before I've even worked out what I want to say.

"I ... He let me go, once," I manage. "He could have captured me, or killed me, but he let me go. I-I wanted to know why. If there were others like him."

Samson's eyes widen for a split-second and his jaw goes slack. But in a heartbeat, his face is hard again and his eyes narrow suspiciously.

"It's true!" I protest.

"Interesting ... a rogue officer. I didn't know such a thing was possible." His eyes flash again. "So the Chain want you to figure out why? To see if you can get a spy inside the hive?"

"The hive?"

He flicks his fingers impatiently. "The compound. That's their plan? To try to infiltrate the Metz?"

I meet his eyes and force my expression to stay neutral. "I don't know what the Chain are planning. They don't trust me with their secrets."

"And the new leader? This woman who's in charge now – who is she?"

I shrug. "Sounds like you know as much about her as I do."

His huge hands close around my shoulders. I can feel the strength in them, strong enough to crush my bones.

"Don't mess with me, Aleesha."

His fingers tighten and I wince as a flash of pain shoots up my neck.

"Her name is Katya. She's from out of town. That's all I know." I glare at him. "Now let me go."

The pressure on my shoulders eases, then disappears completely. I roll them back, trying to loosen off the tense muscles.

"Remember what I said, Aleesha, about their motives. They do not have Outsiders' best interests at heart." He takes a step back and his face drops, his eyes, for a moment, almost sad. "I hope you'll realize that. Before it's too late."

"I—"

He whirls around, and the tips of his long dreadlocks whip across my cheek. Before I can retort, he's striding off down the alley and I'm left alone again, more confused than ever.

12

Trey

I'm walking back to Abby's after another trip Inside to see Ella when I run into Bryn and Aleesha, hurrying in the opposite direction. The frown on Bryn's face clears when he sees me.

"There you are, Trey. Good timing."

"Where are you going?" I ask. Aleesha is alert, her feet dancing on the street, resenting the pause.

"Meeting at HQ." He lowers his voice. "To see where we're at. Figure out if we can get into the compound. Katya asked for both of you to be there."

I sigh and put off the idea of lunch for a little longer.

We're the last ones to arrive and as we enter the large room on the first floor of the Chain's headquarters, Katya closes the door firmly behind us. Murdoch's sitting at the large wooden table. To my surprise, Milicent sits opposite him. Next to her is a geeky looking man with glasses who I vaguely recognize. He's toying with a black box.

Katya motions to the table. "Take a seat."

We sit down and Katya takes the chair at the head of the table. She looks at Aleesha. "Any luck finding your rogue officer?"

Aleesha nods. "I managed to get his helmet off."

There's a moment of shocked silence. "Go on," Katya says finally.

I've already heard the story, so I tune out while Aleesha repeats it. "Do you think he'll come back?" Murdoch asks when she finishes.

"I don't know. It depends how much he remembers when he gets back to the compound. He still believes the Metz are doing the right thing, but now he knows that what he sees through the helmet isn't what's really there ..." She shrugs. "He'll be back."

"How about you, Trey? Bryn mentioned you managed to speak with your father." Milicent looks at me expectantly.

I nod and report back on what little I know, surprised that Bryn hasn't already updated them. "This Metz Commander sounds like he's in charge of everything. The government doesn't have much to do with the operations anymore. He must be powerful."

"He is." Katya holds her wristband up to her mouth and mutters something. A holo of a man appears above the table. He's frozen in the act of speaking, unaware that his image is being captured. I've never seen him before in my life but something about him sends a shiver down my spine.

"This is the Metz Commander," Katya says.

"Nice looking chap, isn't he," Bryn comments, his voice laced with sarcasm.

I glance sideways at Aleesha. Her face is expressionless, but I notice her shift uneasily in her seat.

The man is younger than I'd thought he'd be. In his forties, perhaps, or early fifties. Black hair is slicked back from a widow's peak and his face is long and thin, matching his nose and colourless lips. His whole face is twisted on one side, as if someone's put a screw into his cheek and turned it, dragging the skin around. But even that, on its own, isn't what frightens me.

It's his eyes. So dark they're almost black, they are both piercing and empty. As if behind them there isn't a person but an empty void.

"He's a tough one." Katya's voice quivers and she visibly shakes herself. "Almost inhuman himself. And very secretive. He rarely leaves the Metz compound. I have managed to find out a few things though. Firstly, as we expected, security at the compound is tight, tighter even than the government HQ. Most staff who work in the compound never leave, and the officers only go out on patrol."

She pauses to take a breath. "Secondly, at the moment, they can only control officers' movements from within the compound. They are given their orders there, but once outside, it's difficult for the Commander to give fresh orders if the situation changes. They *are* working on a mobile control solution, but he seems to be having a raging internal conflict over this. Part of him likes being holed up in the compound – I'm not sure if that's because he feels safe there or just because he doesn't like people – but part of him wants to be closer to the action on the ground. Or, as he put it, to be able to 'see them bleed'."

Katya closes her eyes and a shudder racks her body. "As I said, not a nice man."

The room falls silent.

"How did you find out all that?" I ask. *Perhaps I underestimated her*.

Katya gives me a withering look. "He may seem inhuman, but in many ways, he's still a man."

Oh. I feel the heat rise in my cheeks and stare down at the

table. *No more stupid questions.*

"What about your rogue officer?" Milicent looks at Aleesha. "Can we get him to spy for us?"

Aleesha shakes her head. "He doesn't trust me yet. He needs to see for himself that what the Metz are doing is wrong. That they've lied to him and the other officers."

"What are you suggesting? That we set up a Metz attack so he can observe?" Murdoch sounds dubious.

"No. That would be way too risky. People would end up getting killed." Katya looks thoughtful. "But they must keep records of operations. True records, I mean, not what the officers see."

"If we could get access to their records database, I know the name of the operation my mother was killed in," Aleesha says. "If we were to show him that—"

"Why not just show them the footage of what happened in Rose Square?" Bryn narrows his eyes.

Aleesha glares back at him. "'Cos at Rose Square, Outsiders *were* attacking Metz. My mother was unarmed. And she was one person against a hundred Metz – there was no reason for them to kill her without a trial."

Milicent barks a laugh. The sound is so unexpected, and unlike her, that I turn to stare. "Show him what happened in the Rose Rebellion then, if he wants to see death without trial."

Something in her voice makes me think she's not talking about the events of last week. "Rose Rebellion?"

"They didn't teach you about *that* in your history lessons then?" There's pain and hatred in her eyes and her mouth is pinched.

I shake my head, wondering what she's talking about.

"The Rebellion was a long time ago, Milicent," Bryn says gently. "Many people don't remember."

"Well they *should!*" Her eyes glisten, and the perfectly polished nails on her lined hands dig into the wooden tabletop. "It is never too late for justice."

There's an awkward silence.

"Well, we can't access the system from outside the compound anyway," the guy in glasses says eventually. "We've already tried that."

"So we figure out how to get in." Aleesha leans back in her chair and folds her arms. "What? That's what you really want, isn't it? And once we're in, we can see where they're at with the mobile control device thing the Commander mentioned."

Geek brightens. "If we could find out how far they've got, we may be able to figure out where I'm going wrong with this one." He looks dolefully at the black box.

"You're overlooking one important point. There's no way in."

"Come on, Bryn. You of all people should know that there's *always* a way in." Murdoch's Irish lilt is mocking.

Katya raises a hand to forestall Bryn's protest. "Let's talk through the options. Ground level entry *is* next to impossible. The only time an entrance opens is when the Metz shifts change, twice a day. They get their supplies delivered to an underground basement, but the supplies are searched thoroughly before being taken up. How about the tunnels?"

Murdoch shakes his head. "We scouted out the underground tunnels but they're all blocked. Besides, if there were any way in from below, I'm sure they've got extra security on it now after we got into the government headquarters that way. They're not stupid."

"The Commander believes the compound to be impenetrable," Katya says.

"That in itself is a weakness," Bryn comments.

"What about new recruits? They take in older kids as well as babies." Milicent has composed herself, her face once again emotionless. "Couldn't we grab a couple of their latest intake and give their chips to Aleesha and Trey?"

I bite my lip to stop myself shouting out. *How can they think it's right to just take someone's chip?*

But Katya shakes her head. "They only have one intake a year of kids their age – after they've finished school. It'll be another six months before they come in."

Another pause. I search my memories of what my father had said about the compound, trying to find something that may help us, but all I can remember is him telling me to stay away.

"Well, if we can't go in at street level and we can't get through underground, there's only one option remaining," Bryn says, rocking his chair back. "Go in from above."

Milicent looks surprised. Katya looks thoughtful. Murdoch looks pissed – but then I imagine he'd react that way to anything Bryn suggests. "Impossible," he dismisses with a flick of his fingers. "Even if we could access a pod, there's a no-fly zone around the compound."

"Yes, but perhaps we can do something about that," Katya says slowly. She turns to the guy with the glasses. "Jameson, the Commander gets in and out by pod. Anything you can do to scramble the codes?"

He nods enthusiastically. "That shouldn't be hard. We experimented with it a while back and it seemed to work. We'd need to time it right, of course."

"We can do that," Katya smiles wryly. "He's keen for us to meet again."

Bryn looks at her sharply. "You have a way of getting in touch with him?"

"Not directly," she admits. "We leave messages at one of the hotels Inside. A rather antiquated way of doing things. He thinks it's romantic. You wouldn't have long though. Perhaps an hour or two at most."

"It might be enough." Murdoch furrows his brow. "I could take Matthews in—"

Aleesha coughs. A loud, deliberate, unnecessary cough.

"What do you mean *you're* going in? I doubt you can just break in from the roof. We'll need someone to let us in from the inside. And I'm the only one Rogue's seen, let alone trusts."

There's a silence. Murdoch glowers at her.

"She's right," Katya says reluctantly. "But Jameson, you'll need to go with her."

"Me?" The man lurches forward and his glasses almost drop off the end of his nose. He pushes them up with a shaking finger. "I-I can't go in there!"

"You're the only one who understands how the device works."

"Which is why you need me here." He presses his finger into the table for emphasis. "You lot are useless with anything to do with technology. If I get captured, there'll be no one to fix your comm units or hack devices!"

"He's got a point, Katya." Murdoch sighs.

The room falls silent.

"I could help, perhaps?" I reach for the black box and turn it over in my hands. "Show me how it works, what the setup is inside and where you think the issues might be." I push it back across the table. "I know the basics of electronic systems and programming. Enough to ask the right questions if we do find someone in the compound to help."

"No!" Bryn bangs his fist on the table and glares at me. "We are *not* sending them in alone again. They barely escaped with their lives last time."

"And proved their capabilities," Milicent intercedes.

Bryn glares at her. "They were lucky. I'm not having you risk their lives needlessly again."

"We're not risking *anyone's* lives needlessly," Katya soothes. "They may be the only ones who can get in, but we're not going ahead with this until we've worked out every detail of the plan. The last thing we want is to make the government suspicious of our ultimate goals."

Ah. And for a moment I thought she actually cared about us.

She looks at Aleesha. "Once inside, you could pretend to be recruits. You'll need to find out from your officer if he can help you get around without arousing suspicion. I don't know what level of access recruits have."

"I can't imagine they have access to the main information system and records, particularly those the Metz and government want to keep hidden," Milicent says acidly. "Besides, it seems unlikely that this officer will just let them into the compound, however rogue he seems to be."

A flicker of annoyance crosses Katya's face. "Let's see what Aleesha can find out. Hopefully the rogue officer will be curious enough to try to find her again soon. If not, then we'll have to rethink, but we don't have much time. The Metz aren't used to people fighting back, to losing officers. At some point they'll put a stop to it."

The words hang in the air.

"What do you mean?" I ask eventually.

"They can't let this go on much longer. They rule by fear, and that fear is starting to diminish now people have got desperate and have seen that it's possible to take them down. I don't know for sure, but I suspect they're planning something already.

They'll bring all their forces together to stamp down their authority once and for all. And kill anyone who gets in their way."

My breath turns sour in my mouth. Has there not been enough killing? An image of the wounded lining Abby's kitchen appears in my head. The blood and screams of pain. This wasn't the peaceful uprising and protest I'd imagined when I took the government documents to Theo's dad.

This wasn't what we planned.

But if there's some way we can put it right, we have to try.

* * *

I stay behind as the room empties. Jameson takes the black box apart and explains to me how it works. Some of what he says goes completely over my head, but I understand enough to realize that he doesn't know why it doesn't work. There's just something missing. His voice and posture speak of his frustration at not having this final piece of the jigsaw.

When I leave, Bryn's leaning against the stone pillar at the base of the steps leading up to the house. He falls into step beside me.

"You know your way around now," he comments.

"A little. Enough to get back to Abby's."

There's a pause. "How's your family?" He gives me a sideways glance. "I know you've been going Inside to see them."

I don't bother asking how he knows.

"They're ... Dad's not doing so great. They've had to move to a smaller apartment, but I don't think that's it. It's something to do with his work. I think he just feels powerless to change anything. Like he's given up on everything."

Bryn stops and rests a hand on my shoulder. "It's been a tough few months for him, Trey. Any man would be affected by it."

I sigh. "I wish he could just go away, to the house in Wales. He's always loved it there. But then there would be no money to pay for the apartment or anything else."

"And your mother?"

"I've only seen her once. She looks older, but I think she's coping with it better. Ella's worried about both of them but ..."

I hesitate. I'm not sure how much I should tell Bryn. He could pass the information on.

"But what?"

I turn and start walking again. "She thinks the government are wrong. She won't say so in front of Dad, but her boyfriend and his friends are forming a group – a coalition, they're calling it – to protest against the government's actions."

"Isn't that what you wanted? Insiders to protest?" Bryn asks evenly.

"Yes, but ..."

"But what if the Metz find them?"

I nod and bite my lip. The images of the riot in Rose Square leap into my head, but this time it's not some unknown Outsider being bludgeoned by the Metz, but Ella. I grab Bryn's arm. "Don't tell the Chain about them. Please?"

Bryn nods. "Okay, I won't." I must look worried as he pats my hand. "I promise. Is anyone listening to them?"

"Some people, I think. Younger people, students." Suddenly, I don't want to talk about it anymore. "Where did Aleesha go?"

Bryn shrugs. "She rushed straight out as if she'd just remembered something important."

Oh.

"Have you two had a fight?"

"No, nothing like that." *Just that she's been avoiding being alone*

140

with me. I can feel a blush rising to my cheeks and look about for some distraction. "Err, this is a shortcut, isn't it?"

I dive down a passageway on the left. It kicks us onto a busy shopping street. I glance inside a food store as we walk past and see that the shelves are nearly empty. Outside one of the government rations stores, a crowd of people sit, blocking the entrance, while the distributor looks on, annoyed but powerless to do anything about it.

"I know you don't like her, but she's not as bad as you make out," I say eventually.

"It's not that I don't like her." Bryn moves up to walk beside me. "But she's damaged, Trey. It's not her fault, god knows she's had a tough life, but that doesn't change the facts."

"What do you mean the facts?" I snap, turning sharply onto the road that leads to Abby's house. I quicken my pace, not caring if I leave him behind, but Bryn matches me stride for stride.

Who is he to lecture me about relationships anyway? It's not as if he's a good role model.

He grabs my shoulder, yanking me to a halt. "Ask her, Trey. Make her talk to you. Ask her how many men she's slept with. If she can even remember."

The tight ball of anger inside me explodes into a blind fury. Spots dance in my vision as my arm swings through the air. At the last minute, Bryn turns his head, so my fist connects with his jaw rather than his nose. The impact reverberates down my arm, making my elbow tingle.

He stumbles back, clutching his jaw. For a moment, both of us stare at each other, frozen in shock. Then Bryn throws back his head and laughs.

"I guess I deserved that." He stretches his jaw and winces.

"You've got it bad, lad." I turn to go but he grabs my arm. "No, wait. I wasn't insulting her. I'm speaking the truth." He steps forward and grips my shoulders. "She's a pretty girl. If she'd been born ugly, she probably wouldn't be alive today. Do you get what I mean?"

I shake my head, confused.

Bryn sighs. "Out here, with no way of getting food or money, she's only got one thing to sell. Herself."

"You're wrong!" *How dare he call her a ... a whore!* I raise my arm again, but he's quicker than me and grasps my wrist.

"She's smart enough to trick most of the Outsiders down there." Bryn jerks his head in the direction of Area Four. "And perhaps that worked for a while. But there are some bad men out there. Those in Three and Four, they're some of the worst in the city. They see a pretty girl and they just think of one thing. And they'll take what they want by force if it's not given willingly."

"You mean she was raped?" I stare at him.

He shrugs. "Maybe. Or maybe she bargained with them. For food or shelter. Protection against other men. Only she knows."

"But she was just a kid when her mother left," I whisper. My brain stands still.

"And she's what, eighteen now? Still practically a kid." Bryn's face softens. "No one should have to do what she's done to survive. No one. But that kind of thing doesn't go away, however much she tries to hide it inside. She doesn't know *how* to have a proper relationship." He sighs. "All I'm saying is, don't go getting involved with her until you know more. You'll just end up getting hurt."

He gives me a searching look. "Though I suspect it may be a bit late for that. You've already fallen for her, haven't you?"

Anger rises in me.

"Because you're a great one to give relationship advice, aren't you?" I put as much sarcasm into the words as I can. "The man who's *never* been able to make a relationship last." I wrench my arm free of his grip. "Get your own life in order before you interfere with mine."

I stride down the narrow alley behind the row of terraced houses, expecting to hear Bryn hurrying to catch me up. But the only noise to break the silence is the sound of my own footsteps.

I throw open the back door and storm past Abby, who looks up in surprise from the sink. "Tr—"

Whatever she was going to say is cut off when I slam the kitchen door. I take the stairs two at a time and, closing my bedroom door on the world, collapse back on the bed.

It smells of her.

How dare he say that stuff about her! He knows nothing about her life or who she is. How dare he presume to know what I feel? Fallen for her, indeed …

I sit up and cradle my head in my hands, my fury ebbing away.

But you have, haven't you? Fallen for her.

And when I think about it, he's right. I don't know much about her at all.

13

Aleesha

E ven during daylight, the concrete jungle is deserted. I lean against a crumbling, boarded-up old shop and scan the open area that separates the jungle from the surrounding buildings. A bit like the dead zone that lies between the Wall and the buildings on either side.

I wait.

A faint ray of sunshine breaks through the clouds and glints off something in the rubble. I look closer. The same flash of light, between two slabs of concrete. A mirror? Or a spyglass?

I'm not the only one keeping watch.

A trickle of cold sweat runs down my neck. The people who live in the concrete jungle are outcasts. Forced to scrabble together a measly existence in the ancient pile of rubble. Many have a fearsome reputation.

Even Giles was scared of the Boots Brothers.

Coming here during the night is one thing, but walking across that broad open area, in full sight of anyone looking out for easy prey, is quite another.

Needs must. I have to find out how to get to the operations records in the compound and Giles is the only lead I have. We can't wait any longer.

I wipe my palms on my trousers and pull out the new knife Bryn had given me this morning. I'd been surprised at the gesture, but he'd shrugged it off, saying he'd seen it and thought I'd have some use for it. It's a good blade and perfectly balanced for throwing.

In my left hand is one of the knives Jay had given me. Not as good, but a blade's a blade. The stiletto knife is hidden in my boot. I'm hoping I won't need it.

I move quickly across the empty space. It's surprisingly clean. The rain seems to wash most of the dirt away down to the river. Yellow weeds reach up through the cracks, strangled by their concrete collars.

The mountain of rubble looms in front of me. Ideally, I'd walk around it to reach the point where I know a safe route up to Giles's home. But if anyone is watching, they'll then know exactly where I'm going. Better to lose myself from sight in the rubble.

Cautiously, I make my way up through the tottering pile of concrete, metal and stone. The larger blocks are mostly wedged in place but trusting the smaller blocks between them is riskier.

I'm about ten metres up when there's a flash of movement to my right. I whip around, one arm already poised to throw.

A man perches on top of a slanted slab five metres away. He grins, revealing a hotchpotch of rotten teeth.

"Now wot's a pretty girl like you doin' 'ere?"

He jumps down from the slab and takes a step toward me. There's a breath of wind and a foul stench wafts toward me, catching at the back of my throat. Greasy, lank hair hangs to his shoulders and the patched fabric of his clothes looks stiff as if the stains have never been washed out.

I try not to think about what stains they might be.

"Stay right there!" I raise my knife, ready to throw. At this range, I bet I could hit him in the eye.

"Ooh, she's armed." The voice comes from behind and above me.

Shit. Two of them.

"D'ya think she knows 'ow to use that blade?" the voice says again.

I step carefully to the side, not letting the first man out of my sight until the second man appears in the corner of my vision. My mouth goes dry as I realize he's been crouched right above my head.

"I reckon so, brother," the first man replies.

I take a couple more steps backward until they're both in front of me. One high, one low.

The second man is a mirror image of the first. Same slight, weaselly build. Same dark, lank hair and pasty, pock-marked face. They're twins.

The Boots Brothers.

My heart sinks further. I can sense them eying me up, assessing how much of a danger I am. They're cautious though, not yet committing to the attack.

They're scavengers. They go for easy targets or the pickings left behind after a fight. I need to hurt them enough to scare them off but not too much … If I kill one, the other has nothing to lose.

The taste of iron fills my mouth. I've been chewing my lip. I push my shoulders back and try to sound confident. "I don't want to hurt you, but I will if you don't leave right now."

But my plan doesn't work. The first man pulls a knife from his belt and steps toward me. He moves delicately, knowing without looking where to place his feet on the shifting rubble.

"She's a bit skinny, brother," he says, cocking his head to one side. His eyes are bright, and a dribble of saliva runs from the corner of his mouth. "But we 'aven't had meat for so long."

"Not for days, brother," the second man gibbers. He capers from side to side on top of the slab. "She looks fun t'play with." His jaw drops in a gaping smile.

Nausea twists my gut and I take a deep breath.

Time to take one of them out of the picture.

They'll assume I'm right-handed, so I throw with my left. The knife buries itself into the shoulder of the man on top of the slab. He screams and falls backward, out of sight.

One knife down.

"You bitch."

I turn back to the first brother. His face twists in anger as he moves closer, and with a sickening feeling I realize I've underestimated him. He knows how to move, how to fight.

The blade he's holding out is long and dirty, coated in rust. Although, perhaps it's not rust. I tear my eyes from it and meet his.

Always look at their eyes.

"Take your brother and go and I promise I won't harm you or come after you. He needs your help."

My voice is calm and steady in contrast to the wailing pleas of the injured man. But my words do no good. He keeps coming.

He makes the first move, lunging forward. I parry it easily and step to the side, careful not to get cornered in by the blocks of concrete surrounding me. Immediately, he attacks again, and this time I not only dodge his blade but skim my own across his cheek.

Blood bubbles up from the shallow wound and he hisses. His dark eyes narrow to slits.

"I told you. Best to leave. Now."

He eyes me warily but doesn't move. I take another step to the side but my foot lands awkwardly on a small block that rocks, sending me stumbling backward.

In an instant he's on me, slashing his blade toward my face. I lean back and raise my arm, feeling the sharp sting as his knife cuts through my top and skin.

My foot skids on loose gravel and he lunges forward. I strike out and, more by luck than anything else, the two blades clash in mid-air.

For a moment, we press against one another. His rotten breath is almost enough to make me pass out. He leans into me and I'm forced back. Cold, rough concrete brushes my back.

A low rumbling sound makes him hesitate. It gets louder, and over the man's shoulder I catch sight of rocks and stones tumbling in a landslide down the slope toward us.

The noise makes him turn, and as soon as his attention wavers I grab his wrist and twist it, hard. The knife drops from his hand and clatters between two blocks. I bring my knee up between his legs and wrap my arm around his neck. My sharp new knife presses into the fold of skin on his neck.

The rumbling subsides. The blocks come to rest in their new positions.

"One final time. I suggest you get your brother and leave. Okay?"

He nods.

"I didn't hear you." I grit my teeth, trying to avoid breathing in his odour.

"Okay, okay. Don't kill me!" He scrunches up his face and the acid smell of urine adds to the stench in the air. I force myself not to pull away from him. I don't think he'll follow me now, but I need to move quickly.

I remove my arm from his neck and push him hard. He falls to his knees. Then I'm off, running across the blocks, jumping from one to another even as they shift under my feet.

After five minutes I pause for breath and look about to get my bearings. Going by my position relative to the buildings I can see across the wasteland, I'm not far from the entrance to Giles's tunnel. I pick my way slowly across the rubble and, to my surprise, see him sitting on a low block.

He gives me a wave as I approach.

"You were expecting me?" I ask.

He doesn't answer but stares at my arm. The black fabric is soaked in blood. "I, um, ran into some trouble." I turn my arm to inspect the damage. The cut isn't deep, but I dread to think what that blade had on it. "You don't have any antiseptics, do you?"

To my surprise, he nods. "You did well. Taught the Boots Brothers a lesson." He giggles to himself.

"You saw?" I narrow my eyes. "The rockfall. You caused that?"

Giles shrugs and smiles again.

"I ... I came to ask you something. Ask for some help."

"I thought you might come back, Miss Aleesha." He turns his head to the side and looks at me with his pale blue eyes. "Best come inside."

Inside?

I crawl into the low tunnel entrance after him, following more by sound than sight as my eyes haven't adjusted to the dark. My uneasiness returns the further I get from the sun. *Have I escaped one trap just to walk into another?* The rumours about Giles are almost as bad as those about the Boots Brothers.

Though I haven't heard anything about him eating people.

The tunnel slants down and, about ten metres in, Giles

whispers a warning. "Watch the drop."

I feel carefully ahead and find the edge of a large block. Twisting around, I lower my feet down. Without Giles's warning, I'd have plunged head-first over a metre down.

There's a flash of light ahead and Giles stands silhouetted in a doorway. I get to my feet, the tunnel tall enough to stand in here, and take the curtain he's holding out. My hand brushes his and he pulls away.

I stand in the doorway, blinking in the unexpected brightness, and look around in amazement. If I'd ever pictured what Giles's home was like, this wasn't it.

Dozens of lights create a soft glow and the room is warm, which is odd given it's underground. Richly coloured fabrics drape across almost every surface, hiding the concrete and rubble that must lie behind. A pile of soft cushions on one side of the room sits next to a set of crates that are filled with books. My eyes are drawn to them. So many books! My fingers itch to pull them out, smell their musty, ancient smell and feel the thin, delicate paper between my fingers.

The tops of the crates are scattered with a handful of seemingly random objects. A long counter lines the right side of the room, with a hotplate and a hole in which sits a bucket. A couple of pans hang from the wall above. Under the counter are shelves with a few utensils and some bottles of water. No sign of food.

Giles gives a mock bow, trailing his fingers through the air. "Welcome to my sanctuary."

"It's wonderful," I say. And it is. Puts my roof to shame. It feels a bit like Abby's house. A real home with a real person living here. I look at the pale, hunched figure dressed in rags and struggle to connect this man with the bright colours and cosiness of the room. I'd kind of imagined him living in a dark pit.

"Where do you get the electricity?" He must use a lot of it.

"Solar panels." He points a finger at the ceiling.

"And you built all this yourself?"

He nods, and there's a gleam of pride in his eyes.

I step further into the room. Giles shuffles awkwardly and I can tell me being here makes him uncomfortable. "Why do you live here? In the jungle?"

"I had to disappear. And no one comes here. The few that do think I'm a ghost. Or a freak." He smiles. "Not a person worth bothering with. Which is fine by me."

He speaks normally. No hissing. I wonder if that's part of the act. To make people leave him in peace.

I walk over to a small table that's piled high with boxes, tools and bits of wire. Giles reaches out an arm, then quickly pulls it back. "Don't touch!"

I raise my hands in the air. "Fine." It all looks like junk to me anyway. "Why did you have to disappear?"

It's a casual question, but from his reaction, you'd think I asked him why he eats babies for breakfast. He turns on me, his eyes scrunched up and his face twisted into a distorted mask. "No questions!" he hisses.

"Okay, okay, sorry." I take a step toward him and reach out a hand, but he flinches away from me. "Sorry."

He shrugs and turns his back to me.

What a strange guy.

I turn back to the table and a pair of black boxes catch my eye. One looks like a work in progress, a tangle of wires and metal chips, but the other looks complete.

"What are they, Giles?" I point, careful not to touch anything on the table.

Giles turns. His eyes brighten, and he straightens and walks over to me with quick, light steps. "They're combined control units. This one is a completed version, but there's a glitch in it." He lifts the black box to show me. "But I'm working on a new prototype." He indicates the tangle of wires and launches into a technical explanation. At least I assume it's some kind of explanation – I barely understand a word of it and find myself tuning him out.

Trey would know what he was talking about.

There's a pause in the flow of words and I catch Giles staring at me. "That's amazing. You must be smart to know how to use all this stuff." I wave my hand vaguely at the table.

Giles ducks his head in embarrassment. "There is so much to learn, to discover," he murmurs.

"Giles, I need to ask you something," I say carefully. "You remember the Metz officer I told you about? The one who remembered me?"

Giles nods cautiously.

"Well, we managed to get his helmet off. He … what they see through the helmets is different, isn't it? It's not what we see?"

Another nod.

"I think he's a good person. Not the sort of person who wants to be killing people. And I thought, if I could show him what *really* happens on Metz operations, it might change his mind and he'd help us. I don't think he can come outside without his suit, can he?" I don't wait for an answer. "He wouldn't be able to get out of the compound. But I'm sure they have records of their operations inside the compound. And if I could get in and show him what really happened, then he'd have no choice but to believe me."

I pause and hold my breath, waiting for his reaction.

"You want to go inside the compound?"

I nod. Giles throws his head back and laughs. It's a high-pitched, manic laugh that makes me shiver and take a step back. Then he jerks his head back down and snaps his lips shut into a smile. Or at least, I think it's supposed to be a smile. It looks more like a grimace.

"And they call *me* crazy."

"But if I could get in, then would you know how to access the computer system? The records of past operations?"

"If you could get in? How are you planning on doing that? The place is impenetrable!"

"You got out."

It's a shot in the dark, but from Giles's reaction I know I've hit close to home.

"I had help," he says, drawing himself up. He's not as short as his usual hunched appearance makes him look.

I'm itching to know more, but don't want another "no questions" closing off our conversation. "Let's just assume I can get in. How can I get around the place?"

Giles shrugs. "They'll pick up your chip within ten metres of the place. You won't even get in. Unless ..." He looks at me slyly. "Unless you don't have a chip, of course?"

I stare back, my expression neutral.

"Interesting," he muses, drumming his fingers on the black box he's still holding in his hand. "Well, you could pretend to be a recruit, if you can get hold of a suit. Most officers don't know who the recruits are. But this officer of yours would need to take you everywhere. You wouldn't be able to access different areas without him."

"Wouldn't they recognize me? I ... err, I'm on their wanted

list at the moment."

"Not if they're not in their suits. They won't know who you are, or that you need to be arrested. That's how it works. Once they're out of the suits they don't usually remember anything they've done. How else do you think they can live with themselves?" He gives me a sharp look. "And perhaps it is best that they don't know what they've done."

What does he mean by that?

I push the thought to the back of my head for later.

"And how would we access the records of past operations?"

"From the training room. Though he'll only be able to access certain versions of the operations."

My heart sinks. "The versions *they've* created?"

"Yes."

My fingers twitch in frustration but I'm careful not to show it.

"And to access the real versions of what happened, you'd need some kind of passcode or authorization?"

Giles's face twists into a smile and he nods.

He knows some way in.

"Is there a back way into the system? If you don't have the right code or pass?"

Giles considers this for a moment, then shakes his head.

"And my rogue officer wouldn't be able to get this code?"

Giles shakes his head. *He's enjoying this game.*

I chew my lip and consider the options. Given Giles's reaction to any suggestion of hurting the Metz, I can't believe he'd suggest taking the access code by force. Though it may come to that.

"Do *you* have some way of accessing the system? From here?"

A sharp intake of breath. "Not from here." The words came out almost reluctantly.

"But you have a way of accessing it from inside the compound?"

He cocks his head toward me, then gives a reluctant nod.

Okay, he has something. But I have to keep playing his game.

I glance around the neat room, which is seemingly at odds with the clutter piled on the table. Though perhaps it just looks like clutter to me. I walk over to the crates full of books and bend down to examine them. Some look to be technical manuals but others are story books. They must have cost a fortune. *Where did he get the money?*

"I lost my mother when I was six," I say, running my finger across the spines. "I never knew my father, though I believe he was driven out of the country before I was born. My mother loved me, played games with me, gave up everything for me."

I can sense Giles listening, but I'm careful not to look at him. He seems to prefer it that way.

"One day she went out to meet someone and never returned. Twelve years I've spent wondering what happened to her, and a few weeks ago, I found out." I stand. "She went to Rose Square, to meet someone. My father, I think, but he wasn't there. Instead, she was surrounded by Metz, hundreds of them. They beat her, trying to get information out of her, but what did she know? Nothing. So they shot her. Left her to bleed in the dirt."

I fight to control the rising anger inside me and keep my voice neutral.

"A few weeks ago, a young girl saved my life. Lily. They killed her too – shot her without trial. She was six. What can a six-year-old do to deserve to die?"

I close my eyes and take a deep breath. *No emotion. Emotion scares him.*

"I know they were ordered to do it. Controlled, even. That they probably don't even remember—" My voice breaks.

Calm.

"Whoever ordered it is to blame. Whoever controls them. We need to find out who that person is. Remove them from the system."

"But the system is set up around them."

His voice in my ear makes me jump and my heart skips a beat. I hadn't felt him creep up on me. I turn to find his face inches from mine.

"Then we have to take down the system," I whisper.

Finally, he looks at me. In his eyes I see indecision, fear and sadness. Then he pulls back and reaches for a small vase that sits on top of the book crates. It's painted in a crude design that gives it a cheap appearance.

When he turns back, he's holding a tiny baton in his hand. He holds it out to me. "The key. Press the blue button and the code will display. It changes every minute. Perhaps they have changed the system, but I think not." He shrugs. "They believe I am dead. And besides, no one can break into the compound." He smiles wolfishly.

I think back to the last time we broke into a heavily secured building. How they knew we were there because we'd used a dead woman's identity. "Won't it be associated with you? Trigger an alarm?"

Giles shakes his head. "Not unless they've changed the security procedures. The senior Metz officers – the captains – have access to the real files and they sometimes use the training room to review past operations."

I reach for the baton, but he pulls back, his expression suddenly fearful. "You won't hurt them, will you?"

"Who, the officers?"

He nods. "It's not their fault."

"I know. I … I won't hurt them, and I'll do whatever I can to stop anyone else hurting them," I say carefully.

But can you really stop the Chain? And the people?

That's a problem I'll deal with later.

I reach out again, and this time Giles drops the device into my palm. "Think about what you really want, Aleesha." He cocks his head to one side and stares at me with those pale eyes. "When you let revenge define you, all you have is bitterness and regret. You must want more than that from life."

The comment takes me aback and I feel a sudden flash of anger. *How dare he presume to know what I feel?*

I hold the device up between my thumb and forefinger. "I'll look after it."

He ducks his head and turns away.

I walk over to the tunnel entrance and pull the curtain aside. Glancing back, I see him curled in a ball on the cushions, covering his head with his arm. The sight tugs at something in my chest.

Can he really be happy here, as an outcast?

"Giles?"

He raises his head to look at me.

"If you need anything, anything at all. Just let me know, okay?"

A flash of a smile and a nod.

I let the curtain fall behind me and crawl back down the tunnel, the darkness seeming all the colder compared to the warmth and light I've left behind.

14

Trey

Aleesha returns to Abby's that evening, subdued and thoughtful. When Bryn asks where she's been, she just replies that it's not important.

We've fitted into a routine on the nights she stays here, which is most nights now. Better here than her roof. I change while she's in the bathroom and then we switch places. By the time I come back in, she's wearing Abby's old t-shirt and shorts and is lying in bed with the sheet pulled up to her shoulders. Things are awkward between us now, since the kiss on the roof, as if neither of us knows what to do next.

Perhaps it was all a misunderstanding. Maybe she didn't mean to kiss me.

I sigh and splash some cold water onto my face.

When I return to the bedroom, Aleesha's sitting up in bed. I close the door and am about to switch off the light when she stops me.

"Wait. Is there somewhere safe you can hide something in here, where Abby won't find it? Something small?"

"What thing?"

"This." She opens her hand to reveal a small rectangular device. I lean forward but she closes her hand and pulls away. "What is it?"

She hesitates for a second before answering. "We may be able to use it to access the Metz information system."

I stare at her, but she shakes her head, smiling. "Don't ask me where I got it from."

"The rogue officer?"

She frowns and shakes her head. "No. Look, I don't want to risk carrying it on me and I can't leave it up on the roof as I may not be able to fetch it in time. Can we hide it here?"

I think for a minute then take down a carved wooden ornament, painted to look like a doll. Aleesha gives me a disparaging look. "Is that the best you can do?"

I twist the doll and the two halves come apart. Inside is another doll; a smaller version of the first. I open this to reveal a third doll. There are six in total. I pull out the smallest one and open it, holding it out to Aleesha. "Will it fit?"

She places the device in the base of the doll and I replace the top. It fits, just. Leaving the smallest doll out, I replace the others inside one another and put them back on the shelf. The smallest doll I tuck into a break in the skirting at the back of the wardrobe.

"Safe enough?" I ask.

Aleesha nods. I turn out the light and drop onto the mattress on the floor.

"You know Bryn's moved upstairs?" Aleesha comments in the darkness. "He's not down with Bernie anymore."

"You mean, he's sharing with Abby? Good."

Tentatively, I reach up, feeling around for her hand. "Aleesha ..."

But she pulls away and the mattress creaks as she rolls over. "Night, Trey."

I sigh inwardly. "Night, Aleesha."

* * *

At breakfast the next morning, I ask Aleesha if we can have another training session. "I think I've just about recovered from the last one."

"Sure. Have you been doing the exercises I showed you?"

Bryn splutters out a mouthful of tea. "Exercises?"

Aleesha looks at him evenly. "Squats, push-ups, stomach work. He needs to build some muscle. I'm teaching him how to fight."

Abby nods approvingly. "Good idea. You need to be able to look after yourself out here."

While we're eating, a boy arrives with a message from Katya. I don't understand the code written on the grubby piece of film, but apparently Bryn does. "She's arranged to meet the Metz Commander tomorrow night. She thinks we should have at least two hours from six thirty." He looks up. "Any chance of finding your officer and getting him on board before then?"

"Maybe." Aleesha shovels a spoonful of porridge into her mouth. "It depends if he returns to our meeting point."

Bryn sighs. "Well, let's keep our fingers crossed."

The early morning drizzle abates as we climb up to Aleesha's rooftop. We jog a few laps of the roof and do some warm-up exercises together in silence. Then Aleesha hands me one half of a broken chair leg she'd taken from Abby's. She keeps the other half.

I look at it dubiously. "What's this for?"

"Well, I figured it might be a bit risky to use actual knives. Besides, you don't use a knife unless you really want to hurt someone, and I kind of figure that's not really your style. You'll be too cautious."

I sweep the baton through the air in front of me. It reminds me of when Ella and I used to play witches and wizards as kids. "Fine."

We work through some drills. Lunging, blocking, dodging. "It's to get your body used to the movements. Builds muscle and helps sharpen your instincts," Aleesha explains.

"Aleesha," I say carefully, blocking her blow from above. "I was chatting to Bryn about you yesterday. He said you were ... damaged goods."

"Did he now." She stops my return parry deftly and steps to the side. Her voice is neutral, but her lips tighten.

"He said that growing up out here was tough. That you may have had to do stuff you didn't want to do. To survive. That you might want to talk about it."

She gives a harsh laugh and drops her arm to her side. "And what makes him think I want to talk about anything?"

"Maybe because you've never had anyone to tell before. Because it might help."

"Help with what? What's in the past is in the past." She moves forward suddenly and I'm not fast enough to dodge the baton that comes down hard on my thigh.

"Oww!"

"Never let your eye off your opponent." She scowls and walks over to the shelter. "I thought I told you that before."

She takes a gulp from a bottle of Chaz and holds it out to me. I take a sip of the fizzy liquid and hand it back. It's sickly sweet and I wonder why so many people out here drink it. There seem to be more bottles of Chaz than water on the shop shelves.

Aleesha replaces the top on the bottle and throws it onto the pile of blankets.

"What do you want to know? That I was attacked? Raped?"

161

Her voice is harsh and cracked. "Does that make you feel better? Make you pity me a little more?"

"No, I ..." I gently rest a hand on her arm, but she shrugs it off and strides over to the edge of the roof. A little *too* close to the edge for my comfort. She stares out over the rooftops.

"You don't understand. It's different out here ..."

"Try me," I say quietly.

Aleesha sighs. "I was six when my mother left. The first few days I waited at home. Then the people from the children's home came for me."

"Why didn't she take you with her?"

Aleesha shrugs. "Guess she thought it would be safer for me to stay behind. I managed to escape from the children's home once they realized I wasn't chipped and begged for food on the streets for a bit. There wasn't much going but I was quick and figured out I could get away with taking the odd thing from shops or a kitchen table without being caught. Until one day, my luck ran out. It was an apartment I'd been to before. The door was left open and there was food on the table. That should have warned me – no one leaves their door open in Four. When I crept in, the door slammed behind me and a man was looking down on me.

"He was kind at first. Fed me, offered to let me stay. I was able to wash for the first time since I'd left home. I didn't find it odd that he watched me while I washed and that sometimes, when he thought I was sleeping, he'd stand over me. Just watching."

She falls silent for a moment. "He didn't just watch for long. And I was old enough to know that what he was doing was wrong. So I ran away again. That's when I found this rooftop."

She was six! What kind of man ...

My gut twists, and I swallow to try and get rid of the sour taste

162

in my mouth, glad that Aleesha can't see the look of revulsion on my face.

I take a deep breath. "Y-you came up here when you were six?"

She smiles. "Yeah. There was a big flood. I nearly got washed away in it, but the water lifted me high enough to get in through that window. I just kept climbing until there wasn't anywhere else to go."

"And you lived up here, then?"

"Some of the time. But it was too cold in winter. And I couldn't carry much water up here."

I can picture her trying. A young Aleesha, doggedly hauling bottles of water up those endless flights of stairs. My heart aches for her. "Was there no one who would help you?"

She gives a harsh laugh. "There were plenty of men willing to help me. Some of them were even kind, for a time. But you get nothin' for free out here."

Silence again. Aleesha runs her fingers over the parapet. The stone crumbles under her touch.

I don't want to press her, don't want to ask the question, but I have to know. "Did they ... rape you?"

She casts me a swift glance. "Sometimes. If I couldn't get away in time. But most of the time I managed to avoid it by doing them other ... favours."

My stomach heaves and I struggle to resist the urge to turn and walk away. I'm not sure how much more of this I can listen to. "That must have been terrible."

"It was what it was." Aleesha shrugs. "And they weren't all too bad. One guy taught me to read. Another to fight." A smile briefly lightens her face. "Mind you, he wasn't very good at it. But I became better able to look after myself. Began to work out how best to survive. That's when I started tagging onto the gangs."

"That doesn't sound much better."

"Gang life is risky, sure. But if you're smart enough to stay out of the way of the fighting then it's not too bad a life. You get fed at least."

"So you joined the Snakes?"

She shakes her head. "Not at first. There was a smaller gang. The leader took a fancy to me, so I was with him for a while. He didn't even want to sleep with me. I think he preferred men but wanted a girlfriend for show. There was a big fight with the Snakes one day and that's when I met Jay."

"He looked like a bully," I mutter under my breath.

"He's not so bad." She looks out over the rooftops. I wait for her to continue, but after a short pause she straightens her shoulders and turns around to face me. "Ready for round two?"

I nod. Clearly, the conversation is at an end.

We practise some more with the batons, but my heart's not really in it. I guess Bryn was right, in one sense. She's not exactly the girlfriend I'd imagined having. But he's also wrong. She did what she had to do to survive. That doesn't make her a bad person.

After twenty minutes, Aleesha calls a halt.

"I can go a bit longer," I pant.

"It's nearly noon." She takes a swig from the Chaz bottle and hands it to me. "Finish it off."

"What's happening at noon?"

"I said I'd wait for Rogue at noon every day. In case he comes back." She turns to look at me. "Wanna come and see?"

"Sure." Though, really, I'm not sure at all.

* * *

The alleyway Aleesha leads us to is full of rubbish and smells even worse than Area Four usually does. There's an overflowing trash can about halfway down and a couple of closed doors. Aleesha kicks both the doors. One doesn't budge but the other creaks open revealing a dark room.

"Wait in here. You might scare him off if he sees you."

I wrinkle my nose at the acrid smell of urine. "Can't I just hide behind the trash can?"

"Nope."

I step gingerly inside and she pulls the door shut, leaving me just a crack to see through. I pinch my fingers on the bridge of my nose and try to take shallow breaths.

I press my eye to the gap in the door. All I can see is Aleesha leaning against the wall of the alleyway, tossing a knife idly. We wait.

I'm about to call it a day and pull open the door when Aleesha stiffens and pockets the knife. A moment later, she moves out of view.

By straining my ears, I can just about make out what she's saying. "You came."

"I want to know more." The gravelly tone makes my blood run cold.

"Do you remember what happened last time? When you got back into the compound?"

There's a pause. "Some of it. And a feeling. A feeling that something was wrong. That you might be able to help."

Another pause. "We should probably go somewhere more private. Do you have a torch?"

There's a grunt of assent.

They're coming in here?

I just have time to step back before the door swings inward

and Aleesha walks in. The Metz officer following her has to duck and twist to enter the narrow doorway. A beam of light flashes around the empty space and comes to rest on me.

"Wh—"

"He's a friend. I promise he won't hurt you."

I shield my eyes from the light, blinking at the brightness.

"Darwin Goldsmith," the voice rumbles.

"Um, can I take your helmet off?" Aleesha asks. "You're more human that way."

There's a pause. "Fine."

"Give the light to Trey." A heavy torch is shoved into my hands and I shine it up toward the officer's head. Aleesha's standing on her toes, reaching up with a long, fine knife. "Bend back a bit?"

The officer obliges and there's a click. "Now twist the helmet a fraction to the left and it should come off." It reaches up two massive hands and grasps the helmet tight. A moment later I'm looking into the eyes of a young man wearing an expression of disgust.

"That smell …" He looks around the room.

"Pretty bad, isn't it," Aleesha says.

The officer eyes the helmet in his hands as if he'd quite like to put it back on.

"Rogue, meet Trey. Trey, meet Rogue. Now, I've got an idea."

"Go on."

His voice is normal without the helmet on. Slightly gruff, but that could just be because he's trying not to breathe in the stinking air.

"You want to find out the truth about what happens on Metz operations?"

"I *know* what happens. I've been on them," he cuts in.

"You know what you see," Aleesha continues. "Which isn't the same as what's actually there, at least, not all of the time. But they'll be on your systems, right? The records of past operations?"

"Yes. We often access them for training."

Aleesha frowns. "All of them? You can access all the files?"

Rogue shakes his head. "Of course not. Some are restricted."

"There you go! The ones they don't want you to see. Look, you want to know the truth and I want to access one record. To know why my mother died."

Rogue's expression doesn't change. "Your mother died in a Metz operation?"

"Yes." Aleesha looks up at him and her eyes are bright with tears that glisten in the torchlight. "They killed her. I was six."

"What did she do?"

"Nothing!" Aleesha looks as if she's about to punch him but stops herself. "Nothing."

I stay silent, holding the flashlight in front of me, an awkward witness to this dance of wills.

"Please," Aleesha whispers. "She was all I had. Let me show you what happened to her."

"And how do you expect to get into the compound?"

"From above."

A look of surprise flashes across Rogue's face; the first emotion I've seen from him. "There's an exclusion zone."

"I know. Leave that to us."

There's a pause. Rogue looks as if he's fighting some internal battle.

"When?" Rogue asks finally.

"Six thirty tomorrow evening."

"No weapons?"

"No weapons."

"And only you?"

"And Trey. But no one else."

He casts a dismissive glance in my direction. Obviously, he doesn't consider me a danger. "Fine. Six thirty tomorrow. Most people will be eating then so it should be quiet. I'll wait at the entrance to the compound under the Commander's landing platform. It's on top of the east tower."

I close my eyes and let out a breath. *It's really going to happen.* A flush of nervous excitement courses through me.

"Thank you," Aleesha whispers. She places a hand on his arm. "You won't regret it."

"I sincerely hope not," Rogue replies stiffly.

"One more thing," Aleesha says as he raises the helmet to his head. "Will we need a disguise? To look like new recruits, perhaps?"

Rogue gives a brief nod. "I'll see to it."

The helmet clicks back into place. "Tomorrow," he says, grabbing the flashlight from my hands and twisting his bulk to get out of the door.

"Tomorrow," I echo.

We follow him out. The alleyway smells almost fresh after the stench of the enclosed room. "Do you think we can trust him?" I ask, gazing at his retreating back.

"Do we have a choice?"

Yes, I want to say, we do have a choice. We could choose to stay out of this mess. To be safe. Would anyone really blame us for not wanting to risk our lives again?

But I keep my mouth shut. If there's a chance that this could work, that we could find the key to controlling the Metz, to stop the killing, then the risk is worth it. Besides, Aleesha's face is set in that determined look I'm starting to recognize. No one will stop her going in.

And I won't let her go in alone.

15

Aleesha

The pod is smaller than I'd imagined. It's been hastily painted in Metz colours: black with yellow stripes down both sides. The paint glistens in the light. "It's not quite dry but we can't wait any longer," Murdoch says from the open door. "Let's go."

Inside, there's a bench running across the back of the pod and a small control panel up front. Trey follows me in and Jameson and Bryn squeeze in behind him. With five of us in here, there's barely room to breathe.

"You two sit at the back," Bryn instructs.

I perch on the bench next to Trey. The seat is obviously designed for one person and our thighs press together. I find the contact strangely reassuring.

Last night, I'd lain awake, going over and over our conversation on the rooftop. I'd regretted it then, telling him all that stuff, stuff I've told no one else before. In the dark hours of the early morning, the things we'd talked about, the memories that I'd managed to bury for so long came flooding back, and I'd curled up in a tight ball and trembled as they consumed me.

But I'd listened to Trey's light, even breathing as he slept on the mattress below me and inhaled the sweet smell of flowers that lingered on the sheet I clutched, and those two things, those two small things, helped me remember that I was safe now. That I wasn't alone anymore. I had a friend. And finally, as the sky outside lightened from black to pre-dawn grey, I had slept.

"Ready?" Murdoch's voice pulls me back to reality. He's at the control panel, his gun slung over his shoulder. Jameson's sitting on the floor next to Trey, holding a small rectangular device on top of his crossed legs. Bryn tucks himself up in front of him, his weapon pointing toward the closed door. Trey and I are unarmed. It was decided it was too risky for us to take any weapon in, even a knife.

"If they catch you, a knife's not going to help you," Bryn had said when I'd protested the decision. "This is a covert operation. Get in and out without them even knowing you were there."

Covert is a new word for me. Apparently, it's an old word used for top-secret operations, where spies went in undercover to enemy territory. Which, I guess, is exactly what we're doing now.

My body tingles with excitement and adrenaline. Trey's thigh twitches beside me and his face is pale and tight. He looks like he's regretting volunteering. I reach out for his hand and give it a squeeze, getting a weak smile in return.

"I thought pods flew themselves?" he asks Murdoch. His voice shakes slightly, and I wonder if he asked the question to take his mind off what's ahead.

"They do," Murdoch replies. "Fortunately, there's a manual override. No pod apart from the Commander's will fly itself to the Metz compound. You ready, Jameson?"

The man nods and the lump on his throat jumps up and down. *He's nervous too.*

"Let's go then."

I'm disappointed to find no windows in the pod. There's a narrow strip of what seems to be clear material at waist height, but it's so covered in paint that it's impossible to make out anything on the other side.

"Do people not want to look out?" I whisper to Trey.

He shrugs awkwardly in the small space. "They mostly just want to get to where they're going. And some people say it makes them feel sick, looking out."

"Jameson, you ready with those codes?" Murdoch must be able to see what's ahead if he's flying the pod. I wish there was enough room to peer over his shoulder, but I'd have to climb over Bryn and Jameson to get there.

"N-nearly." Jameson's fingers move in a blur across the interactive holo display that hangs in the air above the small box in his lap.

"Are we there already?" I ask. We've barely been gone five minutes. I didn't even feel us take off.

"Just approaching the no-fly zone," Murdoch mutters.

"Okay, just waiting for authorization …" Jameson pauses and taps his fingers on his knee. "Come on … We have it!" His fingers move across the display. "We're good to go."

"You sure?"

"One hundred percent."

"Okay then." Murdoch's voice is strained and the tension in the pod goes up a notch. I wonder what will happen if Jameson's code doesn't work and we're found to be impostors, but I decide it's probably best not to ask.

"We're in. Just coming down to land. Are you two ready?"

We straighten simultaneously. I glance over at Trey. His face is still pale, but his expression is determined.

"We're ready," I say.

Bryn checks his wrist. "We're right on time. Let's hope your officer is too."

I don't feel the pod land but a moment later the door slides open and a cold wind whips around the inside of the small compartment. Bryn jumps out first, his weapon cocked, and motions for us to follow.

"Comm check?" Jameson's voice sounds simultaneously through the bud in my ear and in the pod.

"Fine," I say, and Trey nods.

"Remember, we don't know if it'll work inside the compound. And if you're below ground level, I'm pretty sure it won't work," Jameson continues.

"Keep an eye on the time," Murdoch says, still staring straight ahead. "We'll be back in an hour and a half exactly. You must be here – we can't wait."

I push back my sleeve and glance down at the slim band on my wrist. It feels odd, even though it's moulded to fit. I hover my finger over it and a display flashes up. 18.30.

"Come on!" Bryn hisses. He's lit up against the night sky and the wind whips his hair around his face.

I step out of the pod. We're on the roof of one of the four corner towers of the compound. It's not a particularly tall building and the glass apartment blocks surrounding it tower over us. Yet it feels strangely isolated.

"Aleesha!"

I turn to see Bryn glaring at me. He's bent over by an access panel in the roof, his hand on a tiny red pressure pad. Looking closer, I see he's wearing a thin glove. *The Commander's fingerprints?*

The panel slides open. Bryn raises the gun to his shoulder, his finger hovering over the trigger.

A face appears in the space underneath the panel. *Rogue*. A flash of anger crosses his face as he looks into the barrel of the gun.

"That's him, Bryn," I say quickly, stepping forward so Rogue can see me.

"Get in then, quick," Bryn replies, not taking his gaze off the man inside.

I climb down the short ladder into a short, dimly lit corridor. Rogue pushes a package into my hands as Trey climbs down to join us.

"Here, change into this now. Give your clothes to your friend."

"Bryn? Hang on for five!"

I get a grunt in response.

Trey gets a similar sized package. "What is it?" He stares up at Rogue, who's looking around nervously.

"Recruit's suit. Standard issue. It moulds to your body, so you can't wear it over clothes – it'd look odd. There are boots too. I had to guess the size."

I take a couple of steps down the corridor and begin to strip off my clothing. Trey and Rogue turn their backs and stare resolutely at the wall, which makes me smile. I pull on the suit and select the smaller pair of boots. There are no pockets in the suit, so I curl my fingers around the small black device that Giles had given me. Reluctantly, I hand my boots and clothes up to Bryn.

"If *anything* happens to those boots, you're paying for a new pair." He shrugs off the look I give him.

"You're breaking into the Metz compound and you're worried about your boots?" Rogue asks. His voice is tinged with disbelief.

"They're good boots! Cost me an arm and a leg."

But these feel better. They wouldn't be any good Outside – they don't come high enough up to keep out the flood waters – but they're so comfortable and light that it barely feels as if I'm wearing shoes at all.

Like the suit. Rogue was right. It clings to my body, feeling snug but not tight, almost like a second skin. Looking up, I catch Trey staring at me. He blushes and turns away, fumbling his clothes into a ball. I look down again. It really does show every curve. Even my hip bones jut out, though they're less prominent than a few weeks ago. Abby's food is doing some good.

"Good luck," Bryn whispers hoarsely from above.

The panel slides shut, cutting off the noise of the wind and the city and leaving behind an awkward silence.

"Ready to go?" Rogue asks. His right eyebrow twitches and his eyes flick around nervously.

I nod. "Let's do this."

The comm bud in my ear crackles. "Do you copy?" Jameson's voice.

I brush the tiny microphone I'd transferred from my clothes to the neck of the tight suit. "Yes, I can hear you."

I glance over at Trey, who's looking guilty. He points at his neck and shrugs an apology. "Trey left his mic on his clothes, but he can hear you too."

"Great. We're out of the exclusion zone. We may fall out of range but we'll contact you again when we're close to pick-up."

The bud goes silent. Rogue opens the door at the end of the passageway. On the other side is a circular lift, large enough for six people, though I suspect only three Metz officers. Even without his armour, Rogue is over a head taller than Trey, with broad shoulders and chest. His suit is black, not grey like ours, but it clings just as tightly to his body. You can see the outline of every muscle, even his stomach muscles.

I catch myself staring and look away. *He really is a perfect man, from the outside at least.*

"This takes us down to the main level. The building above ground is mainly used for staff accommodation and dorms. We're currently in the Commander's tower."

"Did you have to get permission to come up here?" Trey asks. His back is pressed against the lift wall as if he's trying to get as far away from Rogue as possible.

"Not exactly. I am currently assigned to work for the Commander, so I have access to most parts of the tower. I told the duty officer that the Commander had forgotten something and asked me to take it up to the roof for him. That should cover your pod arriving and departing."

His voice is wooden. Almost emotionless, but there's a trace of something underneath. Fear perhaps? Or excitement.

"You work directly for the Commander?" *Why didn't he tell me this before?*

Rogue reaches past me to press a button on the side of the lift and I catch a whiff of his scent. Spicy and warm. The back of my neck tingles and I look down at my feet, secretly relieved when he pulls back, and the smell disappears. The lift plummets down.

"Yes. The highest achievers after your first two years on the street are assigned to his unit for a year. It is an honour."

"So, you're a high achiever?" Trey's lips twitch and there's a trace of sarcasm in his voice.

Trey? Sarcastic?

"Yes." Rogue doesn't appear to notice.

"Do you know where we can access the records of past

operations?" I say quickly.

"And wherever new technologies are developed and tested," Trey adds.

Rogue frowns at him. "The tech labs? What do you want w—"

"It doesn't matter," I interrupt. "Let's access the records first, then we'll see how we're doing." I shoot Trey a warning glance and get a sour look in return.

There's a bleep and the lift door opens. Rogue leads the way out.

"Remember last time," Trey whispers as we follow him out.

I roll my eyes and nod. "It's fine," I mutter back.

We need to get him on side first. He still doesn't believe. But he will.

Rogue turns and I smile brightly up at him. "So, the records?"

"We will go to the training rooms. Past operations can be accessed there, though I only have access to the basic level. Special authorization is required for confidential missions."

"What if we're stopped?" Trey asks.

"You are two first-year recruits. Normally first-years wouldn't have access to the training rooms, but you both excelled in your recent tests so I'm giving you a tour of them as a reward."

"Our tests?"

"Yes. You were top in strategy." He points at Trey, then turns to me. "And you were top in weapon handling."

The corner of his mouth turns up slightly. Is he smiling?

"Follow me."

He leads us through a door and out into a short corridor. We walk around a corner and through another set of doors into a much wider corridor. It stretches into the distance, with sets of double doors leading off at regular intervals. Circular cut-outs in the ceiling let in a strange green light. It's eerily quiet and even our footsteps barely sound on the hard floor. Rogue sets a quick pace and I have to hurry to keep up with him.

"Most people who aren't on patrol will be eating in the mess hall," he says.

I'm not sure what a mess hall is but that might explain why the corridors are so quiet.

Perhaps luck is on our side.

I chide myself for the thought. It's dangerous to rely on luck.

Twenty paces down, he pushes open a door on the left and we enter a narrower corridor, still dimly lit. "The training wing," Rogue explains.

On our left is a single long room with a door some way down the corridor. On the right, a set of smaller rooms, each with their own entrance. Rogue stops at one and pushes the door open.

"Do you not need a pass to get through?" I ask.

"They automatically detect your presence."

Through their chips, presumably. Which means the chances of us getting anywhere in the building without Rogue are next to none.

The room is larger than I'd first thought. It stretches back about twenty paces and is about ten paces wide. It's empty apart from a black cabinet in one corner. Rogue strides over to it and brushes his hand over the top. A holo appears in the air and a voice booms out "Training system activated".

I walk over. "Can you turn the sound down?"

"These rooms are all soundproof. No one can hear."

A set of options flashes on the screen. Rogue selects one and a long list appears. "This is the list of operations I have access to."

I peer at the words, running my eyes down the list, looking for Operation Nightshade, or any mention of LC100.

"It's not there." I pull back, trying to contain my disappointment. *They wouldn't let everyone access it – it was confidential.*

"Can you search the system?" Trey asks, coming over to join us.

Rogue nods and selects a symbol at the top of the display. "What do you want to search for?"

"Operation Nightshade," I say.

A few seconds later, a shorter list appears on the screen.

"Operation Nightshade report, Operation Nightshade reality training, linked documents," Trey reads out. "They're all marked as Level 2 access though. What does that mean?"

"It means I can't access them," Rogue replies. "Level 3 can be accessed by any officer, Level 2 by captains and Level 1 only by the Commander or a person he specifically gives access to."

I open my fingers, revealing the small black device. "This may give us access."

Rogue gives it a dubious glance.

"What's the reality training?" Trey asks.

"It recreates what actually happened on the operation so you can experience it."

"Try selecting that." I hear the words and it takes me a few seconds to realize that they came from my mouth.

"Are you sure?" Concern radiates from Trey's voice.

No, I'm not sure. Do I want to see my mother die? Would it be any worse than what I see in my dreams?

"It's asking for a code." Rogue's voice is still neutral. Either he hasn't noticed the tension in the air or he's ignoring it.

I swallow and look down, trying to focus on the small blue button on the device. It's embedded in the plastic, and I have to dig my fingernail in to push it. When I do, a set of eight numbers and letters flashes into the air. Rogue taps them into the system.

Another pause. I tense and look back at the door to the room. My ears strain for the first sound of an alarm and my legs are ready to sprint, though where we could go I have no idea.

"Authorization complete. Operation Nightshade reality training loading."

A progress bar appears on the display, slowly filling. Then my vision blurs. I blink and when I open my eyes, the training room has gone and I'm standing in Rose Square.

A light wind ripples the covers of the empty market stalls. They look abandoned, as if the owners have just dropped everything and run.

But no one would abandon their stall in Area Four, would they?

The square is eerily deserted. I've never seen it this quiet, not even late at night. There are always some hobies and usually a drunk or two passed out on the steps leading up to the monument.

I look around and see Trey and Rogue standing to one side. *This is the reality training, huh. Pretty realistic.* There's even a faint stale smell in the air, though it's not half as bad as the actual Rose Square.

A flash of movement on the balcony of one of the buildings catches my eye. It's a Metz officer, crouched down behind a stone column that doesn't quite disguise its bulk. I glance down and across to a side alley. Officers fill the narrow space. Waiting.

My heart begins to race, and I rub my clammy hands on the slick fabric of the suit. *This isn't real. They can't hurt you. Can they?* Perhaps we should have checked that with Rogue before this started.

I'm about to open my mouth to say something when I see her running into the square toward me.

"Mama," I whisper.

Her hair streams in the wind. A smile lights up her face and my heart aches so much I think it might burst. I am six years old again and my feet move toward her.

But I freeze as the expression on her face turns from joy to fear. She looks around the square, brushing dark tendrils of hair from her face. Her lips move in soundless words. A few more steps toward the statue.

Fear radiates through me, freezing the air in my lungs. All the memories I'd faced in the dark hours of the morning return, along with others that were buried even deeper, as if each memory I face unearths another one. Wave after wave of emotions wash over me. Anger, shame, desperation, defeat.

I push back against them, fighting for control of my body. She is here. And she doesn't know what's about to happen. But I do.

I take a deep breath and air rushes into my lungs. The dizziness passes, and my feet are no longer frozen to the floor.

"Mama!" I run toward her. "Go!"

Did I just say that? My brain is confused. Part of me knows this isn't real, but it *feels* so real.

Almost as if she can hear me, she turns and begins to run back to the Town Hall. But it's too late. Suddenly we're surrounded by Metz. They seem to appear from nowhere, from every direction. Out from side passageways and houses, up from behind market stalls, jumping down from balconies.

They swarm around me, but somehow don't knock me down. Shouts fill the air. Warning shots. But my mother just keeps on running. Time seems to slow as I see an officer pause, lower its weapon and fire.

My mother screams and falls to the floor.

"No!" I run toward her, pushing through the crowd of officers.

Pain shoots through my kneecaps as I drop to the ground beside her.

There's the hiss of a taser. Her back arches and she cries out in pain.

"Where is he?" An officer looms above us. "Where is he?" it repeats.

A baton is raised. I throw myself in front of it, but it passes straight through me. There's a sickening crunch as it connects with my mother's elbow. Another scream of agony.

Frantically, I press my hands to the wound on her thigh, which is streaming blood onto the floor. "Hold on, Mama," I beg. But I can't help her. My hands pass straight through her leg. Her blood flows through my palm as if I were invisible.

And then it hits me. *I pushed through the Metz. Literally pushed through them.* I'm not really here. It's like the footage on the big screens. I'm watching something I can't be part of.

And somehow, that makes it so much worse.

I rock back on my heels, barely noticing that the officers around me have pulled back. I can't tear my eyes from her face, stricken with pain. But there's a fire in her eyes that I recognize. I see it in my own eyes sometimes, in the glint of a polished blade.

Hands grab my arms. Real, solid hands. They try to pull me away. I lash out. My fist connects with flesh and bone, and the hands drop away.

"Where is he?" The officer is still standing over us.

My mother raises her head slightly. The tendons in her jaw tighten, showing the effort it costs her. "You ... will never find him," she gasps.

The officer raises his arm and the barrel of the gun points toward us. "You will not tell us?"

"No!"

My cry carries over my mother's whisper and I curl my body over hers, knowing I can't protect her from what is to come but wanting to hold off that moment for as long as possible. Wanting to have this precious moment with her. I reach to brush the hair from her forehead and look into her eyes. And for a second, I can feel her soft skin, her shiny straight hair that she was so proud of. And in her eyes, I see only love. For me.

The shot explodes in my ears.

The bullet passes through my head, exiting between my eyes, and slams into her forehead.

Such a small hole to cause such damage.

"Mama," I whisper.

But her eyes stare sightlessly through me.

Everything goes quiet. The square fades. My mother disappears from under my hands and I'm suddenly back in the empty training room, disorientated and lost.

I curl up on the floor, wrapping my arms over my head, as if by doing so I can make the whole world go away.

Why did you go, Mama?

An arm wraps around me and I breathe in a familiar smell. *Trey.* He doesn't ask if I'm okay, just holds me, as my tears slow and the sobs that wrack my body turn to hiccups. I ache all over and feel strangely exhausted, as if all the energy inside me was focused on this one thing and it's now gone, carried away by my tears.

"You're ... crying?" Rogue sounds puzzled.

I pull away from Trey and wipe my eyes. "It's an emotion thing."

I get to my feet and turn to face him. He's clutching his chest and his face is a maze of emotions, chief among them confusion and fear.

"I have an ache. Here." He points to his chest and frowns. "Inside."

"Sadness." My voice is hoarse.

"She was your mother?"

I nod.

"She was beautiful. Like you."

Trey stiffens beside me and opens his mouth to speak, but I give him a nudge.

"Why did we kill her?"

"That's what we're here to find out," Trey says tightly. "Let's look at the operation file."

My mother's face is still there in my mind, a small hole in her forehead. Sightless eyes. A wave of nausea rushes up from my stomach and I bend over, closing my eyes and breathing deeply.

"Aleesha?"

I wave a hand at him. "I'm fine."

I force myself to straighten and walk over to join them at the computer. It's strange. My body feels exhausted and numb, like I just want to wrap myself in a blanket and sleep, but inside me, deep inside, a spark of anger is growing.

The anger I've always held against the Metz.

Except it wasn't their fault, was it? They were just following orders.

But whose orders?

Trey's frowning at me, concerned. "Are you sure you want to know?" he asks gently.

I shake myself. "Of course." I stare as Rogue opens the file, but the words blur in front of me. "Can ... can you read it to me?"

Trey nods. He begins to read off the screen and the words flow into my mind, slowly piecing together a picture of what had happened that day.

The Metz had had a tip-off that LC100 was in town. They still referred to him as that, in the file. Their information source said he was there to meet a woman, someone important. That's all they had. They didn't know if he was alone, or if he had other people with him.

"Wait," I interrupt. "Say that bit again?"

"It is suspected that LC100 has associates – that means friends – across the city who he could call on for aid. This visit to meet a woman could be a cover for his continued revolutionary activity. It must be assumed that he will not be alone. The only way to guarantee capture is through the use of overwhelming force."

Overwhelming force.

Trey pauses and looks at me. I nod for him to continue.

The next bit of the report talks about the preparations for the raid. General preparations, as they didn't know where or when they'd meet. It talks about papers for the government, the need to get approval for an operation "of this size".

Then, their information source came back with the identity of the woman. Maria Ramos. Confirmation that LC100 was planning to meet her at Rose Square in just an hour's time. A hurried call to the government while troops were already spilling out of the compound, moving to get in place.

And then Rose Square. The account of the actual event is brutally short. They were in place just a few minutes before Maria Ramos turned up. There was no sign of LC100. She refused to talk and was too badly wounded to bring in for questioning. A search of the surrounding streets and buildings turned up no sign of the man they were after.

"There's a 'lessons learned' section," Trey says.

"Lessons learned?" My voice is tinged with disbelief.

"Yes. Mainly the need to double check information sources. And to avoid rushed operations. They … they think he may have spotted the Metz approaching. That it scared him off."

No shit.

"Then it just gives some facts about who was involved. The captain who led the operation, the number of casualties, the government official who authorized …" Trey's voice trails off.

"Who authorized what? The operation?"

Whoever ordered it is to blame.

Isn't that what I'd said to Giles? It wasn't the Metz. They were just controlled. It was whoever had ordered the operation to go ahead. There's a fluttering in my stomach and my mouth goes dry.

Finally, I will know.

"Who was it?"

Trey stares at the screen, not appearing to listen.

"Trey, who was it?" I walk over to him impatiently.

But it is Rogue who reads the name from the screen, in his wooden, emotionless voice, as Trey turns to me, his face stricken with horror.

"Andrew Goldsmith. Junior minister, State Department."

16

Trey

Andrew Goldsmith.

The words are emblazoned on my eyeballs. I blink to make them disappear, but they're still there goading me. My father. The murderer.

I worked in the department when I was a junior minister. Back then, ministerial authorization was required for any operations of significance.

Rogue is eyeing me with an odd expression on his face. I want to look at Aleesha, but I can't.

"Open the file on LC100," she says in a tight, brittle voice.

Rogue obliges, and the operation file is replaced by another. It's an extended version of the files on the Personax database: a biography of the person and a holo image.

Aleesha grips the sides of the cabinet and leans forward until her face is just inches from the image of the man.

This is the man she believes to be her father.

When she pulls back, I examine him. The holo is of a young man, barely old enough to have a child Aleesha's age. He's handsome, with dark hair that curls at the base of his neck and piercing blue eyes, and he wears clothes that might have been fashionable twenty years ago. When we saw the holo of Maria

Ramos on the Personax database, I could see at once that she was Aleesha's mother. Her resemblance to her father – if he is her father – is less clear, though there's something in the shape of her face – her jawline and nose – that resembles the man hanging in the air. Or perhaps I'm just imagining it.

I scan the file, trying to memorize everything the Metz know about LC100. His name is Ricus Meyer, but his place of birth and parents are marked as unknown. It mentions an aunt who's listed as a guardian, with a London address that I recognize as being Inside the Wall.

The file goes on to state that authorization for his residence in Britannia was given by the Secretary of State. He arrived in London after the death of his parents, when he was thirteen, to live with his aunt. I do a quick calculation in my head. That would make him ... forty-one or thereabouts.

Whereas the section on his education and employment is almost bare, the section on his criminal record more than makes up for it. Arrested for spreading dissent against the government but released without charge. Suspected involvement in an attack against the President. No evidence. A raid on the food factories in Area Six.

The list goes on. Suspected involvement in a whole host of crimes. But no proof. *Why was he never charged? Or dragged off to the Farms? Unless the Metz were more lenient in those days.*

I shake my head. Unlikely. Perhaps this aunt of his intervened to protect him.

Aleesha's face is twisted in concentration as she reads. "Does this say he was in charge of a gang?" She points at a section toward the end of the criminal record section.

"Founder of the London Equality Movement." I scan the paragraph. "It seems to be a student group set up at the

188

university ... campaigning for equal treatment of Insiders and Outsiders. It was shut down by the university due to subversive activity."

I read further down. "Look, this is interesting. Under the 'deceased' heading it just says 'contact lost'. 'Ricus Meyer is believed to be alive but no longer in Britannia.'"

There's a pause. "That was just before I was born," Aleesha whispers. "My mother must have been pregnant at the time."

"What do you think 'contact lost' means?"

"I dunno. Perhaps he got rid of his chip?"

I glance down at my right forearm. It's covered by the tight material of the suit, but I can picture the pink scar underneath. It still itches sometimes. Abby said the scar would stay with me forever.

"He's recorded as coming back to the city twice," Rogue says. I'd almost forgotten he was there. "The second time was when Operation Nightshade took place."

"So, as far as the government are aware, he's no longer in London. They don't even know if he's alive—"

"He has a scar, just by his left eye," Aleesha murmurs. She reaches out a hand to touch the man's face, but when her fingers connect with the display, it flickers and disappears.

"Get it back!" Her hand hovers in the air uncertainly.

"We need to move on, Aleesha. There's no more information on there." I check the device on my wrist. 19.20. "Time's running out."

Her head whips around. "Why? Are you worried about what else your father has done? Who else he's *murdered?*"

I swallow. Her tone bites, but what hurts even more is that she's right. *What else has he done?*

Rogue has taken over the display. The words in the air blur as he scrolls through file after file, his expression getting grimmer with every passing minute. Suddenly, he pauses.

"This one mentions you. A raid on Dellom Street a few weeks ago." Another pause. "Some criminals were rounded up and an illegal girl was shot. The crowd attacked a group of officers." His finger hovers in the air. "Do you want me to activate the VR?"

"No!" Aleesha lunges forward, pulling his arm down and holding his hand in both of hers. She takes a deep breath. "I-I don't want to go through that again."

Rogue's face twists into an odd expression as he looks at the screen then down at his hand.

I glance at my watch again. 19.31. "Aleesha, we really need to move." My voice is harsh, though I'm not sure why. I try to soften it. "The device."

She drops Rogue's hand and wipes her eyes with the back of her sleeve. Tear tracks stain her cheeks. Then she straightens and is all business-like again, as if she's flipped a switch inside.

"You've seen what really happens on Metz raids?" She turns to Rogue. "That wasn't what they tell you, right?"

Rogue stands like a statue, staring at the holo display. Lines of text and images appear as he scrolls down. I wonder if he's even reading the words.

"They didn't tell us we would be doing this." His bottom lip quivers. "We are supposed to protect people. That's our job!"

"You should be able to make your own decisions about what's right or wrong," Aleesha says quietly.

"Yes, I mean ..." Rogue shakes his head. "I don't know." He jabs at the holo and the display disappears. "The captains make the decisions. We trust them. You've seen enough? Let's go."

"There's one more thing," I say. "You say captains make the

decisions at the moment. We have reason to believe that's going to change. Are your tech team working on something new?" Aleesha catches my eye and shakes her head a fraction. "Would we be able to talk to them?"

Aleesha rolls her eyes. But sometimes, being direct is the best way.

"You could speak to the professor." Rogue sounds uncertain. "He runs the labs here and oversees the medical program."

Aleesha flashes me a quick glance and I nod. Sounds like the right place. "Great. Will he mind us bothering him?"

"No. He likes visitors."

Rogue leads us back out into the large corridor with the eerie green lighting. It's cooler out here, but I only feel it on my head and hands. The suits are heat regulating, keeping our bodies at an even temperature.

"This way." Rogue stops at the next set of doors leading off the corridor and places his palm on a pad.

Not automatic access then.

I follow Aleesha through the doors and into a brightly lit corridor. It feels like a medic unit: spotlessly clean and minimally furnished with a lingering smell of antiseptic. Like the training wing, the corridor is a light grey, with a double strip of yellow running along the wall at waist height. A sign hangs from the ceiling, pointing to another set of doors on the right. Emergencies.

On the opposite side of the corridor, there's a double door labelled "General Assessment". Rogue walks straight past this and pauses outside an unmarked door further up the corridor. He presses a button and a buzzer sounds from inside the room.

There's a pause, then a voice crackles out from a small speaker. Rogue says something in a low voice, and a moment later there's a click and he pushes the door open.

The room inside is large and dimly lit. It looks like a laboratory; large workbenches separated by slim partitions. A large spotlight focuses on one of the nearby benches, which is part holo unit, part workbench. Electronic chips and wires are scattered on the bench next to a soldering iron that's glowing red.

An elderly man in a white coat steps back from the bench and comes to greet us. "Come in, come in. It's not often we get visitors here." He stops suddenly and runs a hand through his frazzled iron-grey hair.

"Thank you for agreeing to see us, Professor." Rogue gives him a formal nod. "These are the recruits I mentioned. They came top of their class in the recent assessments and I'm giving them a tour of the compound as a reward. They were interested in finding out more about your work."

"Excellent!" The man beams. "I've always said recruits should be told more about the process before they become officers."

I find myself staring at his left eye. There's something odd about it. It takes me a second to put my finger on it: the pupil is strangely dilated compared to the right eye.

"Oh, sorry, I forgot to switch my magnifier off." The eyelid closes for a second, and when it reopens the eye looks normal. "It's an implant. Very handy for detailed work." He sweeps his arm back toward the bench. "Of course, bots do most of it, but I find tinkering around helps me think."

I glance over at Aleesha, who gives me a nod. My lead, then. "What are you working on at the moment?"

"Have you been taught how the Metz operate yet? How they do their job?"

My mouth goes dry and I swallow nervously. *What are we*

supposed to know? Out of the corner of my eye, I catch Rogue giving an almost imperceptible shake of his head. "Um, not really."

"Well the thing that sets the Metz apart from law enforcement in the pre-Flood era is their ability to work together and instantly – or almost instantly – respond in a coordinated manner to a threat."

I sense the professor moving into lecture mode and school my expression into one of interest. Aleesha steps subtly away and walks over to the other side of the lab.

"So how does that work? Is it something to do with our chips?"

"Yes, well, sort of. You have just the one implant at the moment – the one you received when you arrived here that replaced your citizens' chip. When you graduate and join the officer ranks, you will be given a second implant. This implant links each officer to their captain and is only activated when they are wearing their helmet. We call it the master implant. When the captain instructs an officer to take an action, their body interprets that as a direction from the officer's brain. As there's no hesitation or thinking time, this means a group of officers can operate precisely as a unit."

"Like machines."

The professor nods. "Exactly."

"But what if the captains think random thoughts? Like that they need to scratch their nose or something?"

The professor throws back his head and laughs. "They did in the beginning, I believe. Before the process was refined. But not anymore. Part of the captains' training program is learning to focus their thoughts, so only relevant thoughts are directed to the implant and out to the officers. That's part of the reason the program is so long, and why only a certain percentage of those who begin it actually graduate."

"What happens to those who don't succeed?"

Rogue takes this one. "They return to their teams as normal officers. It's not often that captain vacancies come up, but when they do, the top performing officers are selected for the trials," he explains. "There are various stages and at each stage, officers are released back to their teams."

I consider this for a minute. "But if they want people to respond and act like machines, why don't they just use bots?"

"Good question, a very good question." The professor nods enthusiastically. "The need for the Metz arose at a time when the bot technology wasn't sufficiently developed. Human instincts and decision-making were vital to their role. The technology used then was just an extension of existing technology being used to equip special forces. Of course, bot technology is much more advanced now, but *politically* ... well politically, *they* don't like the idea that an army of bots is marching the streets. They prefer having humans in that role."

The corner of Rogue's mouth twitches. I suspect I know the professor's views on the matter. Behind him, I catch sight of Aleesha on the other side of the room, waving and pointing at her watch. We're nearly out of time.

"So, what are you working on at the moment?" I indicate toward the pile of electronics on the bench.

The man's brow furrows and he lets out a deep sigh. "This is a long-running project. But I think we've nearly cracked the final part of the problem. Under the current system, captains get their orders before they leave the compound and then transmit them to the officers in their team when they're out in the field. This generally works well, and it gives the captains some room for improvisation, but a couple of aspects are less than ideal.

194

Firstly, the range of the implants is limited. This isn't usually a problem in the field, as the team are within a limited distance of each other, but it means that the Commander often isn't able to *directly* instruct a captain once they've left the compound."

He pauses and looks at me. "What do you think the second thing is?"

I think for a minute. "Everything relies on the captain," I say slowly. "If you lose the captain, then you've lost control of the officers?"

"That's right!" The professor looks pleased. "There's a single point of failure, which is *never* good in a system. That's why the captains look identical to every other officer, so they can't be picked out. And why the top priority of every officer is to protect their captain, whatever the cost. But that's what this little device is designed to help with." He picks up a small black box from the bench behind him. It looks like a smaller version of Jameson's device but with an engraving on the front. A helmet with two yellow flashes on either side.

"What does it do?" Aleesha pads back over the room toward us.

"At the moment, the officers in each team are linked to a specific captain. This can be changed here in the compound. For example, if an officer is injured and another needs to take his place, we simply switch them over on the system. That's one of the beauties of the implant system. The officer doesn't need to spend time training with the new team. But they have to come back to the compound for the switch to take effect."

The professor presses his finger against the black box and a list of codes appears in the air above it. He scrolls down with his finger. "This is a mobile version of the main system. The Commander can use it to reassign officers to a different captain or control individual officers or groups of officers personally.

"It also contains a booster, extending the range in which the Commander can communicate with the captains. He'd still need to be out in the field to use it, but he could be holed up in a safe environment and control the operation directly, rather than relying on the decisions of his captains. He can even use it to access each captain or officer's helmet cam." He places the box down on the table and the display disappears.

"Of course, for most day-to-day work, this isn't necessary." He sighs and looks suddenly sad. "But there have been so many disturbances of late that—"

I lose the rest of what he says as there's a crackling in my ear, like a fly buzzing around. My hand moves instinctively to the side of my head before I catch Aleesha's warning glance and realize what it is.

A voice comes through, but the words are hard to distinguish through the static. "Com ... land ... minutes."

They're coming in? Now? How long have we got?

My hearing clears and I catch the professor looking at me expectantly. "Um, sorry, could you repeat that?"

He frowns. "I was just asking if you had any further questions."

"Oh. Err ..." I scrabble to get my thoughts together. "You said you're still working on it. When will it be ready?"

The professor opens his mouth to reply but Aleesha suddenly explodes into a fit of coughing. "Are you alright?"

She nods and gestures to her throat and the door. "Water ..." she gasps, her face reddening.

"Of course." The professor hurries to open the door. "There's a fountain on the right. Just press the buzzer when you want to come back in."

Aleesha gives me a look and hurries out. *Nice decoy.*

"As I was saying, we're not far off. We almost had it perfected years ago, then we suffered an unexpected setback. An important piece went missing. But we've managed to work out how to use the unit to control individual officers when inputting a text or voice command. It's linking that to the Commander's chip that's proving problematic. And the boosting is a challenge. Particularly in a city like this. So many tall buildings."

The bud in my ear crackles again.

"And how does it *work?*" I peer closer at the box.

"Well, obviously most of it is confidential. I'm not really allowed to talk about it with the officers or captains, let alone recruits." The professor gives me a sympathetic glance.

The door buzzes and Rogue moves to open it. Aleesha slips into the room and flashes her fingers at me.

Ten minutes.

I school my expression into one of disappointment. "No, I guess I can understand that. It's fascinating though."

"It is indeed!" The professor beams and claps me on the shoulder. "Well if for any reason you fail the Metz tests, get them to send you over to me. I'm always looking for more assistants." He gives me a wink.

Over the professor's shoulder, I catch Aleesha whispering something to Rogue. He nods and straightens. "We should be going, Professor. Thank you for your time."

The professor turns and smiles at him. "Not a problem, not a problem. Always nice to see some new faces."

He ushers us out and the door clicks shut behind us.

Aleesha checks her wrist. "I managed to delay a bit, but they can't wait any longer. The Commander's heading back any minute."

"It's not far to the tower. It will only take us five minutes to get up there." Rogue's voice is calm and controlled.

We walk down the corridor toward the double doors that lead back out into the wide corridor with the strange green lighting. But before we reach them, they're thrown back and a man strides in. Rather than pushing past us, he stops, letting the doors swing shut behind him.

Beside me, I feel Rogue tense.

"Problem?" Aleesha mutters quietly.

"Yes," Rogue whispers. He stands to attention and salutes. "Sir."

The corner of the man's mouth twists up in a cold half smile. "ML486. I wasn't expecting to see you here. And who are these two ... recruits?"

I can almost feel the seconds ticking by. Seconds we don't have.

17

Aleesha

Rogue seems lost for words. Then, finally, he collects himself. "I was on my way to mess when I received a request to escort these two recruits on a tour of the officer side of the compound. A reward for their performance in recent tests."

The officer's eyes scan us, and I get the same uncomfortable feeling that I get in Samson's presence. Or the President's. Like he can see right into my head and read what I'm thinking.

"Look up!" The man frowns. "Haven't you been taught to keep your eyes straight ahead when in the presence of a senior officer?"

I flush and raise my eyes, focusing on a point slightly above and to the side of his shoulder. "Yes, sir!"

"Better." He walks over to me and stops. Now I'm staring at his chest.

"And what did you excel in?"

"Weapons handling ... sir!"

He moves to stand in front of Trey. "And you?"

"Strategy, sir."

The man steps back and folds his arms. "And have you finished the tour?"

"Yes, sir. I was about to escort them back to the recruits' area."

"Very well. You'd better hurry if you want to eat. The mess hall is closing early tonight to allow medicals to take place before bed. You'll receive instructions shortly."

"Yes, sir."

Rogue steps to one side, pushing me back against the wall to allow the officer through. The man walks down the corridor and enters a room on the right.

"Let's go." Rogue pushes open the double doors and we emerge into the wide corridor with the strange green lighting. "Time?"

I check my wrist. "Five minutes."

He grunts. "We'll have to detour via the recruits' area. He may check my chip."

"Who was that?" Trey asks. There's a tremor in his voice and his feet trip over one another as he tries to keep up.

"My captain."

The man who controls you.

I glance behind me at the door we've just exited. Part of it is misted up as if a face has been pressed against the glass.

The corridor ends in a set of forbidding doors, as tall as two Metz officers. Rogue presses his hand on a pad on the right door and, with a click, it slowly swings open.

They're thick enough to be bombproof.

We enter a narrow corridor that's almost identical to the others we've been in except the strips on the grey walls are orange, not yellow. Rogue takes a sharp left and after ten paces stops at a round lift.

"Quick." He ushers us in and jams his thumb on the button.

The lift whooshes up and a moment later we're deposited in another corridor. Rogue leads us a short way down, then through a couple of pairs of doors to another lift.

I check my watch. "One minute."

The lift feels like it takes forever to arrive. Trey taps his foot and I want to tell him to stop, but I'm just as much on edge as him. I swallow hard. *Come on.*

Eventually the doors open, and the three of us cram inside. "Does this take us to the roof?" Trey asks in a cracked voice.

Rogue nods.

"Will you be okay? You won't get into trouble?" I ask, turning to look up at him.

He smiles down at me. It transforms his face from a wooden mask to something more … well, human. He reaches a hand up and, before I can stop him, gently smooths my hair. "I'll be fine."

I stare up into his deep blue eyes, my feet frozen to the floor. There's a gentle ping and the doors swish open behind us.

"Aleesha? Let's go." Trey stands, holding the door to the corridor open.

I start and tear my eyes away from Rogue's. At least the dim lighting hides the heat rising to my cheeks. I follow Trey down the short corridor and glance down at my wrist. It's time.

Above us, the hatch begins to open. A cold wind rushes in. I glance back at the door behind us, half expecting a hundred Metz to burst through, but there's just Rogue, standing with his arms folded.

Bryn's face appears in the opening. Backlit by the pod headlights, his hair glows like a halo around his head. His face is taut. "Quick."

He reaches down a hand and half pulls Trey up through the hole. I barely have time to turn and mouth a quick thank you to Rogue before Bryn pulls me up too. A gust of wind hits me as I emerge onto the exposed rooftop and I stagger to one side, the breath whipped from my mouth.

"Come on, we're short on time." Bryn grabs my arm and steers me into the open door of the pod, pressing in after me, so I can't turn around to look back.

The door closes, and I sense the pod lift off the ground. I climb over Jameson and Trey's legs to perch on the narrow bench. Jameson hunches over the device in his lap, beating a rhythm on his leg with the fingers of one hand.

"And we're out." He leans back and runs his fingers through his hair.

"Just in time," Murdoch comments from up front. "That's the Commander's pod over there. I hope to hell he's not looking this way."

The pod turns sharply, and I nearly fall off my seat. Curling my legs up, I wrap my arms around them and rest my forehead on my knees. *We made it.*

"Good job, you two. We're going to head straight back to headquarters for a debrief." Bryn murmurs something else to Murdoch under his breath. The atmosphere in the pod lightens, as if everyone has given a collective sigh of relief.

I feel the adrenaline begin to seep out of my muscles, leaving them weak and limp. A dull ache from my knees. *Perhaps they'll come after us. Perhaps they'll be waiting when we touch down.* Not that I want a fight. Just something to keep the adrenaline pumping. To put off that moment when the memories of the training room spill into my head, forcing me to relive her death again and again.

Maybe it's not such a bad thing, to have an implant that takes away your emotions.

"You okay?" Trey asks quietly.

It was his father who ordered her death.

I nod, not trusting myself to speak. I don't want to shout at him. At least, not yet.

* * *

Back at the Chain headquarters, Katya is waiting. She paces the room, dressed in a sleek strapless dress with a long slit up the side that offers a flash of thigh every time she turns. Her face is pale under her makeup and she twists her hands over and around each other as if wringing out a cloth.

She starts when we enter the room and waves a hand toward the table. "Sit. Report."

Trey speaks first, describing our journey through the compound and the training room. He skips over the report of Operation Nightshade and starts talking about the lab, but Katya holds up a hand to stop him.

"And did you find out more about your mother's death, Aleesha? What was her name again?"

I start. "Maria. Maria Ramos."

Beside me, Bryn stiffens. Katya's eyes flick to him and they exchange a look I can't read.

"What? Did you know her?" I stare at Bryn, but he stares at the table, his brow furrowed. He sighs and shakes his head. "No, I'm sorry. The name just reminded me of someone. But the Maria I'm thinking of was in another city. In Spain. Hearing the name took me by surprise. Go on." He flashes me a smile, but it doesn't reach his eyes.

Another one of his lady loves?

"Okay, well she was killed by mistake." I take a deep breath and close my eyes for a second to try and supress the emotions churning inside me. *Stay calm. Just tell the facts.*

"They were after the man she was meeting. His codename was LC100. The operation was big enough to be authorized by

203

a government minister—" My voice breaks, but I cover it with a cough. "They were determined to capture this man. The Metz sealed off Rose Square. Lay in wait. But there was a mistake. When she ran into the square and saw how empty it was, she realized something was wrong and turned to leave. The Metz moved in and it descended into chaos from there. When my mother refused to answer their questions, they … they shot her."

I pause to take a breath. "That's why the mission was confidential. It was a failure."

Murdoch snorts. "Nice to know even those monsters get it wrong sometimes."

"Yes, it seems so," Katya replies shortly. "Did the file say which minister authorized the operation?" She glances over at Trey and the ravaged expression on his face gives her the answer.

"Andrew Goldsmith," I say quietly.

I look down to see a set of curved indentations on the back of my hand, and I realize I've been digging the nails of my other hand into my skin. Strangely the pain calms me. Gives me something to focus on. Stops me doing what I really want to do right now, which is to fly at Trey and demand to know *why* his father killed my mother. Instead, I close my eyes and dig my ragged fingernails deeper into my skin.

"I see. Thank you, Aleesha. Now, Trey, what were you saying about the lab?"

Trey explains what the professor told him about how the system works. I half listen while focusing on keeping my emotions in check.

Andrew Goldsmith. His name pops into my head, accompanied by an explosion of anger that surges up my throat. The saliva in my mouth turns sour.

This isn't working.

I focus instead on what Trey is saying. "They're developing a mobile solution to the main command system. So that if one captain gets taken out, they can reassign the officers to another without them having to go back to base. Or the Commander could link directly to an officer or group of officers to give them instructions."

"Did he say how it worked?" Jameson interrupts. "Is it a direct implant-to-implant transmission from the Commander?"

"I-I think that's what they're trying to get to. But he said they're still working on it." Trey screws up his face. "He said ... that they've managed to get it to work from the device to an officer. So, they can instruct the officer using a text or voice command. But they're still working on the direct link to the Commander. And the boosting – he said that's an issue because of all the tall buildings."

"If you were high enough up, that wouldn't be so much of a problem," Bryn murmurs, half to himself.

"No ..." Jameson's voice trails off. "And he didn't give any details about the design of the device?"

Trey shakes his head. "No, he said it was confidential. And then we had to leave in a hurry."

"Was there anything else you saw in the lab?" Katya looks over to me. "Anything you noticed that might be important, Aleesha?"

I drag my eyes upward to focus on her. There was something. "I had a quick look around the lab while Trey was talking to the professor. It was mostly just desks and electronic stuff but there was a sign at the far end that pointed to some double doors. The doors were marked as 'authorized personnel only'." I pause.

"And the sign?" Katya asks.

"It said 'Subjects' Quarters'." I frown. "Do you think they have other people in there? That they ... test things on?"

Katya sighs. "Probably. But that doesn't help us for now." She turns to Jameson, who squirms under the intensity of her gaze. "Does what Trey said help at all?"

"Perhaps ... Text control could be a solution." But he doesn't sound at all certain.

Katya raises a fist but instead of slamming it down on the table, she keeps it clenched as her knuckles turn paler and paler.

"We need to be certain," she says eventually. "They're planning something big."

Bryn's head snaps up. "Who? The Commander?"

"The Commander, the government ... I don't know. But he – they – feel the situation is out of control. He talked about an overwhelming show of force. To get back the respect of the people. Create order out of chaos." Her voice is calm, but her hand is almost totally white.

Bryn frowns. "Their authority is weakened. People have never attacked the Metz before, but now they're having to patrol in larger groups because of the danger. And they've lost some officers. They need to strike back."

"Do you think they're planning a Cleaning?" I ask. A familiar dread seeps through my body at the word.

Bryn shakes his head. "A Cleaning won't be enough. They need something bigger. Something that will stamp their authority once and for all."

Katya nods grimly. "Something that people can't fight back against."

Bigger than a Cleaning?

"When?" My voice comes out in a whisper.

"Soon."

* * *

I trail Bryn and Trey back to Abby's house. It's raining, but inside the recruits' suit I'm still wearing, I'm warm and dry. Still, it's not a good night for being up on the roof.

But tonight, more than ever, I want to be alone.

As we reach the entrance to the back alley that runs behind Abby's house, I come to a decision. But as if he can read my mind, Bryn turns and grabs my arm.

"Come in," he says quietly. "There's a storm coming. And you shouldn't be alone."

But I want to be alone.

There's a rumble of thunder and the rain gets heavier. A few drops seep inside the neck of my suit.

"Please?"

It's the first time I've heard Bryn say the word, to me at least. And for once he's not looking at me with disgust or disapproval. So I follow him down the back alley to where Trey's waiting by the kitchen door.

The three of us stand, dripping on the stone floor, while Abby fetches towels, pours tea and fusses over us. Trey and Bryn sit at the table, but I take my tea and curl up in the large rocking chair in the corner. Perhaps they'll forget about me here.

"So, Aleesha, did you find out anything more about your father?" Bryn asks.

No such luck.

"The man who *may* be my father." I'm not sure why I bother to correct him. LC100, or Ricus Meyer, as I guess I should call him, is my father. I just know it.

Bryn flicks his fingers impatiently. "Whatever."

"You do look like him a bit," Trey comments. "Except your colouring. You take after your mother with that."

"What made you an expert on my genetics?" I mutter under

my breath. Only Abby's close enough to hear me and she gives me a sharp glance. I wrap both hands around my mug and take a sip of the liquid. It's hot and tasteless.

"So, what did he look like? Did the file say anything about his whereabouts?" Bryn prompts.

I sigh. "Dark hair, blue eyes. *Very* blue eyes. Could describe anyone right? His name is Ricus Meyer. Or at least, that was the name on the file. I guess it could be fake. He wasn't from London originally but moved there as a kid. He organized a lot of protests and stuff against the government." I think for a moment. "He must have been a couple of years older than my mother. They don't know where he is now or if he's even alive."

"He looked young in the holo," Trey says into the silence that follows my words.

"Yeah, because that was taken years ago. He'll be in his forties now," I snap.

Trey looks hurt. I stare down at the flakes of green leaf floating in my tea.

"He'd still have that scar though, wouldn't he? That wouldn't disappear?"

Shut up, Trey. Does he not get that I don't want to talk about it?

There's a creak as Bryn rocks back on the legs of his chair. Abby frowns at him.

"What scar's that?" Bryn asks.

"He has a scar here," I point at the corner of my left eye. "Kind of S-shaped."

There's a crash followed by a string of curses as Bryn's chair collapses. I jerk, spilling hot water in my lap. Abby stands up and folds her arms, a smile playing at the corner of her mouth.

"Dammit!" A hand appears on the edge of the table, and a

moment later Bryn pulls himself up, rubbing the back of his head. He bends down and picks up the broken handle of his mug. "Sorry, Abby."

"I'm not going to say I told you so ..." Abby says, turning and reaching for the brush.

"But you told him so," Trey said.

"But you told me so," Bryn said at the same time.

They look at each other and laugh.

A happy family picture.

My chest tightens, and I push myself up out of the chair and stumble from the room. I expect to find Bernie sleeping on the sofa in the front room, but it's empty. He must have gone home. *Or died.*

I wrap myself up in one of Abby's blankets and lie down, staring at the faded pattern on the sofa cushion. When the door opens half an hour later and Trey comes in to ask if I'm okay, I pretend to be asleep.

* * *

I'm woken by the sound of footsteps on the stairs. Tentative footsteps, as if someone is being careful not to be heard. The grey half-light of early morning filters through the window.

Silently, I push back the blanket and pad across the floor to the door. I ease it open a crack just in time to catch a blur of movement as someone rushes past into the kitchen. But their scent lingers in the air for a second longer. Fresh water and pine trees. Trey.

What's he doing up this early?

I dress quickly and pull my boots on in the empty kitchen. I hear the gate to the back yard swing shut. The cool morning air sharpens my senses as I set off down the back alley. Wherever

Trey's sneaking out to, I want to know.

18

Trey

The streets are quiet at this early hour. Hobies huddle in doorways or anywhere else there's shelter. Children nestle under the protective arm of a parent. Wary eyes glint from the depths of a shapeless mound of blankets.

Last night's rain has blown over but the mud lining the streets is still slick and I slip and slide as I hurry toward the Wall. I've a long way to go on the other side and I don't want to miss him. A couple of times I get the sense that there's someone watching me, but when I turn, there's no one there.

You're getting paranoid.

Once through the Wall, I pull my hood up to hide my face and set off at a fast walk. The odd house or apartment has its lights on; early risers getting ready for a day at work. Inside a small bakery, a young woman is stacking loaves of bread on the shelves behind the counter. The smell makes my mouth water. My stomach feels hard and empty. But there'll be time to eat later.

I'm tired but feel strangely alert. I didn't sleep much. Every time I closed my eyes I saw Aleesha's face. Her expression of hurt. Hate. Contempt. I know when she sees me, she thinks of *him*. That this will always hang between us.

Which is why I need answers. For her. And for me.

I hurry past the great dome of St Paul's Cathedral, overshadowed by the modern apartment blocks that replaced the historic stone buildings destroyed during the dark times that followed the Great Flood. In the park surrounding it, pop-up tents, like the kind used for street festivals, have been set up.

Finally, I reach the street where Ella had brought me to meet him. I lean against a wall to catch my breath, hoping that I'm in time. Father always used to go to work early – he said he enjoyed being first in the office when it was quiet – but perhaps now he has fewer responsibilities he doesn't need to work quite so hard.

I wait for twenty minutes, moving up or down the street occasionally so I don't catch the attention of the cameras. The street becomes busier; a one-way flow of people in blue suits heading to work in the government buildings just down the road.

Then I spot him. A thin, hunched figure shuffling down one side of the street in a light raincoat. A pang of pain lances through my stomach and a hard lump develops in my throat, making it hard to swallow. It's like someone has sucked all the energy and life from him, crumpling his body up.

My fault. This is all my fault.

He doesn't notice me as he walks past and doesn't even look up as I fall into step beside him.

"Father?" I murmur out of the corner of my mouth. "I need to talk to you."

His head jerks up at the sound of my voice, but he manages to keep looking straight ahead.

"The graveyard up ahead," I say.

He nods slightly, and I speed up, turning into the small gated park without looking back.

A few minutes later, he joins me on a low bench overlooking a pond full of golden fish.

We sit in silence for a minute. "You are well?" my father asks eventually.

I nod. "Mother?"

"She's alright. Bearing up better than I am."

He gives a short, hoarse laugh and his hands twitch in his lap. "How's the job?"

I immediately wish I hadn't asked. He stares sadly out. "Tedious. Dull. People mostly ignore me, and I ignore them. Do my hours and leave." His fingers twitch again. "But there are no late nights or working at home. I don't think I've spent so much time with your mother for years."

Another silence. "What do you remember about Operation Nightshade?" I ask eventually.

My father turns and looks at me in surprise. "Operation Nightshade?"

"You don't remember it? It was years ago, when you worked in the State Department. A woman was murdered. Maria Ramos."

He frowns. "Operation Nightshade is confidential. Why do you want to know about it? How do you even know it exists?"

"Maria Ramos had a daughter. A daughter who grew up never knowing what happened to her mother. That she was murdered by the Metz. That *you* gave the order for her death." The metal slats of the bench dig into my hands, but rather than loosening my grip, I tighten it.

"Her death was an accident, Trey."

A snort escapes me. "An *accident*? I've seen the footage, Father, I've been there. They shot her down, like she was some kind of animal to be slaughtered!"

213

"Where did you access these files, Trey? What have you been doing?" There's a tremor in his voice.

I ignore the questions. "You remember her then?"

"I remember the operation." He glances across at me and gives a short laugh. "What, you think I just signed it off without even looking? That I don't remember when a citizen died because of an order I gave?" He shakes his head sadly. "Believe it or not, Trey, I was good at my job. One of the reasons I worked such long hours was because I read every report, questioned my briefs and did whatever research was necessary to make the best possible decision."

"But you got this decision wrong. You screwed up."

"No, I didn't." He raises a hand to cut off my protest. "Let me speak. The decision was the right one, it was the execution that went wrong." He winces. "Sorry, poor choice of words. The brief I had on Operation Nightshade was that we had good intelligence to indicate that a known criminal who posed a threat to the government was in the city. He arranged to meet this woman and in the process of doing so, he revealed himself to our spy. The proposed plan was sensible: to clear the surrounding area so no citizens would get caught up in a fight, wait for him to arrive and then close in and capture him."

"But he didn't turn up."

My father sighs. "No. Perhaps he got word, perhaps our man had been turned, we don't know. Maria Ramos should never have been killed. But she should have been taken in for questioning—"

"And that would have had the same outcome, right?" Sarcasm drips from my lips. I'm hurting him. I know I am. But I don't care.

"Perhaps." He massages his temples with his fingers. "She was associated with *him*, after all. I doubt she was entirely innocent."

"But she had a daughter!"

"Who we knew nothing about! And that in itself is a crime."

We stare at each other until, finally, my father gives in and looks away.

"And this daughter. She's a friend of yours?" he says finally.

"Aleesha. Yes. She was six."

"Aleesha." He frowns. "The girl you broke into the headquarters with?"

I nod.

"Be careful who you trust, Trey. I know you feel you've been let down by us and by the government. But that doesn't mean the Outsiders you meet are any more trustworthy. They—"

"All my life you've taught me to trust the government. That what they're doing is right when it's so blatantly wrong! And now you dare to tell me where to put my trust?" I push myself up off the bench and glare down at him.

"Everyone has their own agenda, Trey." His eyes flash as he stands and draws himself up to his full height. Suddenly he is the father I knew again. The man I respected. The man I tried so hard to please. "And if you've got any sense, you'll figure out what that agenda is before trusting someone implicitly."

How dare he imply that Aleesha's untrustworthy just because she's an Outsider. Because she's not one of us.

My hands ball into fists. I can feel the ridges on my skin left behind by the metal slats. "I spent years blindly trusting you only to find out you were telling me lies. I think it's about time I figure out for myself who to trust." My throat tightens, choking off my words.

My father's face sags and he looks like an old man again. "I'm sorry you feel that way. I've always tried to do my best for you all. Given you everything you could need or want to get on in the world."

"While screwing over everyone else?" I wave my arm around. "But hey, I forgot. Outsiders don't matter, right?"

"Of course they matter, Trey. I've tried to do my best for *everyone*, but if you ever have a career in politics, you'll realize how impossible that is! When you're in a position of power, you have to weigh up every decision and put your own feelings aside to work out what the best course of action is for the people you represent. Not for you. For them. Nothing is ever black and white. There are always shades of grey. Unknowns, things that you have to take a judgement call on."

His face softens. "One day, perhaps, you'll be in a similar position yourself. Then maybe you'll understand." He reaches a hand out to my shoulder, but I bat it away.

"I think I already understand what's right and what's wrong." I clench my jaw. "Something *you* seem to have spent your whole life ignoring!"

I push past him, and he stumbles and falls back onto the bench. "Trey, wait!"

But I don't wait. I don't even look back. I run from the graveyard and plunge through the stream of people heading to work. Heading to their government jobs where they pretend to make our city a better place. I push past them, ignoring the shouts of annoyance and anger that follow me.

Then I'm out the other side and I keep walking, faster and faster until I'm far from the government buildings. My feet lead me to a familiar square where a wave of dizziness overwhelms me and I collapse onto a bench and rest my head in my shaking hands.

* * *

216

"Trey? Are you alright?"

A hand on my shoulder jerks me out of my stupor. *Ella.* Of course. This is her square, the one with the coffee shop.

"You look like you're about to keel over." She sits down next to me and grabs my head, turning it so I'm forced to meet her gaze. "What's wrong? Are you here to see me?"

I shake my head. A sweet smell rises up from a paper bag on her lap. She follows my gaze. "Are you hungry?"

She doesn't wait for an answer but breaks off part of the pastry and hands it to me. I hesitate for a second, then grab it. I rip a large piece off and shove it into my mouth. It's still warm.

"Guess so, huh."

I stop chewing and heat flushes my cheeks. "Th-thank you," I manage.

She glances around and lowers her voice. A lock of her brown hair falls down from the loose bun at the nape of her neck. "What's going on, Trey? You can tell me."

But I can't.

I finish the pastry. It feels heavy in my stomach, but the sugar surges through my system. "It's just a little crazy out there at the moment."

"Outside? I've heard." Her smile drops.

I glance at her in surprise. "You have?"

"Some of my friends live in Six. Or at least, they did." She sighs. "They've joined the other refugees."

"Refugees?"

Ella frowns. "Wasn't that what you were talking about? You must have seen some on your way over here. Six has become a war zone. Sammie was trapped in her apartment for two days before they moved onto an easier target. She and her parents left as soon as they could to come Inside. At least they have

217

Sammie's aunt to stay with. Most people aren't so lucky. The government are setting up some emergency centres to house people and help get them off the streets."

"I didn't realize things were so bad," I whisper.

Ella glances at her wrist. "Look, I'm going to be late for work." She hesitates. "Are you sure you're alright? If you wait here, I can come and meet you at lunch. We can talk more then."

I shake my head and manage a weak smile. "No, I'm fine, honest. I need to get back."

"Okay, little bro." She leans forward and gives me a peck on the cheek. "You take care of yourself. Oh, and eat the rest of this. I'm not hungry." She pushes the rest of the pastry into my hand, then turns, her heels clicking across the square.

The pastry gives me strength. I walk slowly in the direction of the Wall, going further north than normal and detouring to one of the larger squares where the screens alternately blare out news and advertisements. But the news headlines only confirm what I can see with my own eyes.

There's the usual crowd of people walking to work and taking children to school. But weaving between them are people laden with canvas bags, pushing hover floats with more bags and oddly shaped packages strapped to the top.

In one of the parks, a small group of people have set up makeshift tents, lines strung between the trees. An elderly woman perches on a spindle-legged chair, clutching her cape and looking disapprovingly around her.

Like upper-class hobies.

As I get nearer to the East Gate, the stream of refugees increases, as does the number of pods flying overhead. I wonder where they're all going to go.

Most of the people who live in Six consider themselves

Insiders. When they ran out of room to build more apartments Inside, people started spilling out, created a new enclave for themselves. But even those who have relatives Inside wouldn't be able to stay with them for long. Few people have spare rooms in their apartments.

You did this. If you hadn't insisted on that information going out, none of this would have happened.

I try to push the nagging voice in my head away. It's not my fault Outsiders acted irrationally. They should be attacking the government, not other people.

My father's words come back to me, wheedling their way into my head. *Nothing is ever black or white.*

I turn sharply, nearly running into a couple with a baby. Their float butts into my leg and I push it to one side, causing it to swerve into a wall. Ignoring their exclamations of annoyance, I break into a run and head for the Wall.

You caused this. You need to fix it.

"But how?" I whisper to the blue swirls of colour in front of me.

But neither the Wall nor the nagging voice in my head have an answer.

19

Aleesha

I press my back to the stone wall as Trey rushes out of the graveyard gate. His face is drawn, and he barges through the crowded street without looking back. I couldn't get close enough to hear their conversation, but I could tell from their body language that they were arguing.

Peeking through a small gap in the black patterned gate, I spot Trey's father slumped on a bench with his head in his hands. He looks older than I'd imagined. Less powerful.

Should I confront him here?

No. There'll be cameras everywhere and it's a long way back to the Wall. Besides, I still need to figure out what to do. I need to plan, not just act. Acting without thinking always gets me into trouble.

I walk away from the government buildings, my feet leading me down to the river. The tide is in and waves lap gently against the high wall that protects this part of the city from flooding.

Wouldn't do to dirty their streets.

The remnants of bridges that once straddled the old river stand proud of the muddy waters. There were so many of them. It's hard to imagine that they were all necessary. The one to my left seems to have been created entirely from metal cables and leads to a huge, ugly brown building with a tall tower that's slowly crumbling away. Specks of white fly on and off it. Birds. There seem to be lots of birds on the southern side of the river, taking over the places where people used to live. Not so many on this side. They've probably learned it's not safe over here. Too many hungry Outsiders.

I wonder what my father thought of this place, when he first came here. How different it was from his home.

Ricus Meyer. I turn the name over in my mind. Pair it with my mother's. Ricus and Maria. Maria and Ricus. I guess they kind of fit together. Ricus, Maria and Aleesha.

The information in the file filled in some of the blanks surrounding his life. His identity. I have a name. A holo image imprinted on my mind. But I'm still no closer to finding him. In fact, I feel further away than ever.

The niggling thought comes back to me. *He may not even be alive.* But I banish it quickly. He is alive. He just lives in the world outside this city. Of course he's alive.

Because if he isn't, what do I have to keep me going?

Inside me, emotions strain at their cage. As a child, I pictured it like a birdcage. With strong bars. A place for me to hide the unpleasant feelings and memories; those that make me angry or sad. I mentally pushed them inside and locked them away until I feel ready to deal with them.

But the cage is getting full. The emotions are leaking out through the wrought iron bars, pushing against the locked door.

The market stall covers blowing in the wind. A stale smell. Shouts. Screams. The thud of a baton. The crack of a shot. Mama.

I couldn't warn her. Couldn't save her.

They weren't even after her. So why kill her? But the Metz didn't think for themselves, did they? It must have been in their orders. The orders from the government. Did she know they would be waiting for her? Is that why she didn't take me to meet my father? Why she gave me the amulet before she left?

But she had been happy when she left. Not like someone who thought they could be going to their death.

My thoughts turn to Andrew Goldsmith. Why did he do it? The man Trey has spoken about doesn't fit the model of someone who'd give the order to murder an innocent woman. But it was a long time ago. People change.

That doesn't bring her back. If it wasn't for him, I wouldn't have been forced onto the streets. Forced to do all the things that Trey despises me for. I'd have had a normal life.

I slam my fist into the wall, feeling my knuckles crack.

No men. No tronk.

Just the word sends a wave of dizziness through me. Saliva builds in my mouth. My nerves tingle and my fingers twitch with an unexpected urgency.

Need it. Where is it?

My feet carry me halfway up the street before I force them to stop. I put my hand out and lean into the wall, gulping in air, as if by doing so I can flush this desire from my body.

This is his fault. He ordered her death. He killed her.

I focus on the anger, letting it flow through me. Anything to get rid of this craving. Thank god I'm Inside. Because if there was tronk in front of me now, I wouldn't be able to resist. And I promised her. I promised Lily.

They took her away too. The only two people I have ever loved and they took them away. Murdered them. Trey talks about justice, but who brings the people in power to justice? Who holds the government to account?

I rest my forehead against a window to stop my head spinning.

The Plexiglas is cool under my skin. The anger runs its course, leaching the strength from my body. It leaves behind clarity.

The only one who cares about them is me. I promised Lily I'd avenge her death. Now I make the same promise to my mother.

You will have justice, Mama.

Andrew Goldsmith may think he is safe from justice Inside the Wall.

He is wrong.

* * *

I slip back through the Wall and into Area Four close to the place where Jay had pushed me off the rooftop, the first time I fell through the Wall. I'd thought that I was about to die. No one survives contact with the Wall. Except me and Trey. Surely, we can't be the only ones?

The thought niggles at me, as much as I try to push it toward the back of my head.

If we could figure that out, there would be no barrier.

"Aleesha."

A deep, booming voice stops me in my tracks. *Damn.*

I take a deep breath and turn around. "Samson."

He steps out from the narrow passageway he'd been hiding in and looks me up and down. I don't think it's coincidence that he's here. Nothing is coincidental where Samson's concerned.

"What do you want?"

"Who says I want anything?"

I fold my arms. "Well, you're not really a chit-chat kind of person, are you?"

He looks faintly amused. "Not really. I was waiting for you."

My stomach tightens. "And how did you know I'd be here?"

At least my voice doesn't give away my nerves. I grip my arms so that my fingers can't shake. He feels uncomfortably close but taking a step back would show him that it bothers me. I force my feet to stay exactly where they are.

He ignores my question. "Have you changed your mind about working for the Chain yet?"

"Have you been following me? Inside?" I search his face, but his expression is a blank canvas. "You can go through the Wall?"

His eyes widen slightly, then he throws his head back and laughs. I'm not sure what's so funny. "No, at least, I've not tried." His face turns serious. "And I'm not about to. I have my own ways of getting Inside. But you're getting predictable. I just had a few people keeping an eye out for you."

"Fine," I snap. "So, what do you want to talk to me about?"

He glances around, then pushes me into the narrow passageway. I stop in front of a mound of trash that's piled almost as high as me.

"They're following you too, you know. Murdoch's team. They don't trust you."

"Can you blame them, given *you* keep bothering me?" *Damn idiot, blowing my cover.*

"I'm *trying* to warn you," he says through gritted teeth.

"About what? You don't *tell* me anything. Just keep dropping all these stupid hints that make me feel like a complete dumbass for not understanding." I slam my palm into his chest. He doesn't budge an inch. "You expect me to trust you instead? The guy who's admitted he's working with the government. Who says he's helping Outsiders but stands by while they get slaughtered by the Metz." I hit him again. The guy is like a damn brick wall. And he's blocking my way out.

I raise my fist again, but Samson closes his iron fingers around it. "The Chain don't care about London. At least, not all of them." His voice is low and fierce. "They want to take down the government, kill the President, destroy the Metz. But they're not interested in what comes *after* that. How society is rebuilt."

I stare at him in disbelief. "Then why are they doing all this?"

He releases my hand and it falls to my side. "That is the question you should be asking them." He half turns to leave, then seems to remember something. "Oh, and that officer you found? The one who helped you?"

I nod, my heart pounding.

"There's no need to worry about him. I mentioned it to the President. All Metz officers have had their chips reset. Your rogue officer won't be rogue anymore." He flashes me a smile.

"What do you mean?" I whisper.

But Samson has gone.

* * *

Samson was right. Murdoch does have people trailing me. A scrawny kid who I spot right away and an older guy, dressed as a hobie, who's less obvious. But I manage to lose both of them by heading to the rooftops. I crouch down by a solar panel array and try to figure out what to do next.

According to Katya, the Metz are planning something big. And that kind of makes sense. They're not used to people fighting back. And they're losing officers. Surely, it's only a matter of time before a captain gets taken down and they lose control of a whole bunch of them.

An overwhelming display of force. The ultimate Cleaning.

How many Metz officers are there in the compound? I should have asked Rogue. A lot, for sure. And they have pods. They could land in different places, maybe even fire down from the air.

The question is, will they wait for the professor to finish the device, or will the Commander decide to attack without it? The professor had said it was nearly ready ... Wouldn't it make more sense to wait?

A shiver runs down my spine. Whether they wait or not, an army of Metz officers descending on Area Four will end in disaster. Images flash through my mind like a newsreel. Blood, fighting, screaming. Slick cobblestones underfoot. The stench of sweat and fear and death.

I lean forward and retch. There's not much in my stomach to bring up but it leaves a bitter taste in my mouth. I get unsteadily to my feet, trying to will the images out of my mind. But they won't go away.

I need to warn people. But who will listen?

The Chain knows. Samson has control of the gangs, but he won't listen either.

My heart sinks as the only other option becomes clear. Jay. I can't imagine him listening to anything I say either. But the Snakes are the biggest gang in Four. People listen to them, and they listen to Jay. It's worth a try.

I climb down to street level and check to make sure I'm not being followed. But even if I am, it's not as if I need to make a secret of where I'm going.

Jay's apartment is empty. Or at least, no one responds to my banging on the door. I sigh. Snakes' HQ it is. But I'll be damned if I walk in there to be sneered and laughed at.

I'm approaching the back entrance to the HQ building when Jonas walks out. He says something to a greasy-haired young man slouched against the wall who straightens and mutters something in response. Jonas pats him on the shoulder and walks away.

I step out into his path. "Hey."

Jonas stops dead. A smile flashes across his face but it's quickly replaced by a frown. "Are you supposed to be here?"

"Why, has Jay banned me from the Snakes now?" I try to keep my voice light.

"Not exactly. But y'know, *she's* in there." He looks uncomfortable.

A pang of jealousy. I take a deep breath. "That's okay, I don't want to go in. But I do need to speak to Jay. Can you ask him if he'll come out?"

Jonas runs a hand over the shaved side of his head. "Sure." As he raises his arm, his jacket lifts and I catch a glimpse of the gun at his waist.

He turns to leave, then checks himself. "Is everythin' okay?" He frowns again, but this time it's a frown of concern. "Did you find somewhere to live?"

I nod.

He smiles weakly. "Good." There's a pause. "If you need anything ..."

"I'll let you know." I smile. It's odd. He seems to genuinely want to help me. Or perhaps he just wants Jay's cast-offs. The thought sours my mood.

But he has a gun ...

"Actually, Jonas, there is something you could help me with." He raises an eyebrow.

"Would I be able to borrow your gun? I'll bring it back later, I promise," I add quickly, noticing the flash of alarm that crosses his face.

"Is someone botherin' you?"

I shake my head. "Not exactly. I just ..." My voice trails off as I realize I'm not sure what to say. I can't tell him the truth, but I don't want to lie to him either.

Jonas pulls the gun out and reluctantly hands it over. "Just be careful with it, okay? And don't tell Jay. He'd have my head."

I flash him a smile and tuck the gun into my waistband, so it's covered by my jacket. "Thanks, Jonas. I'll bring it back later. Can you get Jay now?"

Jonas starts. "Oh yeah, sure. He might not want to speak to you though."

"I know. Tell him it's urgent. About Samson."

Jonas raises one eyebrow and then turns and walks back into the building. I lean back against the wall of the alleyway and nod to the guard. He ignores me and continues to chew on his gum.

Five minutes later, Jay emerges, tailed by Jonas. He grunts at the guard and pulls me back down the alleyway.

"Whaddya want?"

By his surly look, I don't have much time. "The Metz are planning something big," I say quickly. "Don't ask me how I know, I just know, okay? I wanted to warn you."

"Thought you wanted to talk about Samson." Jay's forehead creases in a frown.

"Samson won't listen. Look, since the broadcast went out on the news about what the government has done, people have been fighting back. But the Metz won't stand for it. They're going to crack down. I'm not sure what exactly, but it'll be big. Think a Cleaning, but bigger. And Samson has told you not to fight them, right?"

"Right." Jay nods slowly. I can almost feel the effort he's putting into trying to process what I'm saying. But there's no time.

"Samson's wrong." I hold up my hands as he opens his mouth to protest. "I know you don't believe me. I'm not going to argue.

I just want you to be ready. Be prepared. Because if the shit that I think's coming down on us does, then it's going to be like Rose Square but a thousand times worse."

There's a pause while Jay thinks. I glance at Jonas, who gives me an apologetic smile. *Would he help me?* Perhaps. But his loyalty to his leader is stronger than any feelings he has for me.

"So what d'ya expect us to do about it?" Jay says eventually.

"Warn people. Get prepared. I don't know, even look at places to hide away. Make sure people who can't fight are safe. Set up some traps. Just don't run at them head-on. They're bigger and stronger and have better weapons than us."

"But you're talking about whole neighbourhoods, Aleesha. There's nowhere for people to go!" He waves his hand around vaguely. "Are you sure about this?"

I nod. "It makes sense. They have to knock us down. Prove they're in charge. Look, I found out something important. Each group of officers is controlled by a captain. They look just like all the other officers, but if you take the captain out, the officers are leaderless. They'll have no orders coming through to them." I hold a finger up. "One captain."

"So how are we supposed to know which one's the captain if they all look the same?" Jay looks confused.

"They'll be the best-protected officer. In the middle of the group, I guess. All the others will sacrifice themselves to protect the captain."

Jay wrinkles his nose. "Are they bots then?"

"No." I sigh. Trying to explain the detail will just confuse him more. "Just remember. Look for the captain. Take it out."

"Captain. Take it out." He nods and takes a step toward me, lowering his voice. "Look, why don't you come back in. We could use your brains. Beth's great but she's not a fighter. Not

229

like you."

And you can't figure things out by yourself, right?

I swallow down the bitter taste at the back of my mouth. "I can't. I have something else I need to do."

I look up at the towering warehouse behind us and the blue painted snakes that wind their way around each other and feel a pull in my chest.

"Look after them, Jay."

I turn and walk back down the alleyway. First thing's first. I have a date with Andrew Goldsmith.

20

Trey

The back door to Abby's house is locked. I retrieve the spare key from its hiding place, punch in the number code on the door pad and let myself in. I top up the water in the kettle and flick the switch on the hotplate. Nothing happens.

Damn electricity. I'd been looking forward to a cup of tea. I roll my shoulders back and wince. Everything aches. What would I give for a relaxation chamber. Ten minutes in the hot steam would ease some of the tension in my muscles. The model they had at school had a built-in massager to knead away knots and lactic acid.

And out here, I can't even get a proper shower.

I stretch out my back and rub my neck. I push the thought of massages away and lift Abby's guitar off the wall. Sinking into a chair, I begin to strum a tune Abby taught me. My fingers move instinctively over the neck and strings, remembering by touch what notes to play, and I let my mind wander to other things.

Why are Outsiders attacking their own people? Surely it's the government they should hate? But the government are too far removed. How can they attack the government when they can't go Inside? They've tried blocking the food depots and stores. But they're

the ones who suffer if the food doesn't get out, not the government.
The strings vibrate, digging into my skin. I switch to a simpler four-chord repetitive tune. Harder and harder I strum.

Instead, they attack the people they see as benefiting from the government policies. Insiders. Or those Outsiders who are practically Insiders.

My fingers slip on the strings and a harsh discord cuts through my thoughts. I stop strumming and the final chord echoes in the room.

The Wall. It all comes back to the Wall. While that stands, the government are safe and protected. They don't care if Outsiders fight among themselves. It just proves their point – that they need to be controlled.

Footsteps sound in the back yard and a moment later, Abby walks in.

"What are you doing playing in the dark?" She reaches for the light switch. "Oh. Electricity off?"

I hang the guitar back on the wall and take the bags from her. At first, I'd thought Abby was just old-fashioned and refused to install technology in her house. All-in-one home systems have been around for decades and even the most basic apartments have automatic lighting, heating controls and security systems. Or at least they do Inside. Out here, it's only the newer apartments and those who can afford to install the technology. And half the time, the solar panels seem to be broken and there's no electricity to power anything.

Outside, the clouds part momentarily and a shaft of sunlight brightens the gloomy room. Abby stretches her arms above her head and basks in it. "Oh, for summer to come," she murmurs.

"Don't you find it too hot?" I ask. The height of summer was the one time I was glad not to be in London. The heat was slightly more bearable out in Wales, though my mother constantly worried about the risk of wildfires. We always had a pod on standby to escape if needed.

"Sometimes. But anything's better than this dreariness. Still, at least the constant rain keeps the water tanks topped up."

I peer inside the shopping bags lined up on the table. "What have you been buying?"

"Supplies." She sighs and turns away from the window. The clouds close and the room is plunged into gloom again. "Bryn said the Metz are planning something big. And with the incident at Rose Square, most of the supplies I stockpiled over the winter have gone."

She pulls a small bunch of green fragrant herbs from one of the bags and carefully hangs them above the counter alongside some withered, dried plants. I unpack the bag in front of me, stacking white fabric and gauze neatly on the table.

"They go in the cupboard." Abby lifts down a pair of narrow-necked jars and places them on the table.

"Do other people grow the plants you need, then?" I ask as I move the bandages to the cupboard behind the counter.

"I get a few that way – mostly for cooking. But I got these from a shop up in Six. They're one of the only suppliers of fresh food Outside. Real food from the Farms or smaller growers outside the city. Normally I'd never be able to afford his prices, but he's had next to no business for the past few days. People are either locking themselves in their homes or abandoning them to go Inside. He'd already been looted once and was packing up to take as much as he could carry with him. I got these for next to nothing." She nods at a small jar on the table. "Even managed to get some honey – I'd never be able to afford that normally."

"Is it really that bad up there?" I'd thought Ella had been

exaggerating, but perhaps not.

Abby nods and tucks a loose strand of hair behind her ear. "It's bad. I-I've never seen anything like it. People are just locking up their homes and leaving with next to nothing. They're terrified." Her face drops. "And others ... people from outside the area, I guess, are just running around smashing windows and breaking down doors. Running into shops and just clearing the shelves."

"Did you recognize the people looting? Were they from around here?"

Does it matter?

"Some of them were street hobies. And you can hardly blame them, really. When you're starving and you've got nothing, you'd take any opportunity to get food ... But the ones who were breaking into people's homes, they weren't hobies. Some of them were from the gangs in Three or Four. They had the symbols." She gestures to her neck. "Tattoos."

"And they were just taking advantage of the opportunity," I say bitterly. "Why can't people look further than their own noses? If they worked together then everyone could be better off – including them!" I slam my fist on the table. A narrow-necked jar wobbles and falls over.

"They see people in Six as Insiders." Abby picks the jar up. "To some people, they're as much the enemy as the government." She smiles at me. "You've only been out here a few weeks, Trey. You're still an Insider at heart. You haven't had to grow up with nothing, fighting for survival. To them, this is logical."

Her words hurt me, though I'm not sure why.

I reach for the next bag of bandages and pull it toward me. Rolls of white fabric unroll themselves across the table. I make a grab for them, but one falls onto the floor. "Aren't the Metz doing anything to stop the looting?"

"That's the strange thing." Abby's hand shakes as she tries to push a handful of herb stems into one of the jars. "They're nowhere to be seen. It's like they're just leaving people to fend for themselves."

I stop rolling the bandage in my hands. "Or perhaps they've been called back to base. To wait."

"But why?" Abby gives up trying to stand the stems in the jar and drops them onto the table.

I reach over, pick up the herbs and place them in the jar. She gives me a watery smile.

"The streets feel different," she says finally. "Like there's a storm building."

A silence descends. I finish re-rolling the bandages and slump back into the rocking chair, tugging at a loose thread on the hem of my t-shirt.

There's a ping from the hot plate.

"Oh great, the electricity's back on. Would you like some tea?"

I nod silently, staring at the mosaic of floor tiles.

"You were up early this morning. Did Aleesha go out with you?"

"No." I look up. "Was she not here when you got up?"

Abby shakes her head. "No. I'm pretty sure she spent the night here, but she was gone when we ... when I came down." She turns away but not before I catch the faint flush in her cheeks."

Her embarrassment makes me smile.

"Where's Bryn?"

"I'm not sure. He said he had to go and report to the Leader and that he might go to the headquarters after that."

"I thought Katya was in charge now?"

Abby sets the kettle on the hotplate to boil, turns around and rests her hands on the narrow counter behind her. "She's in charge here. But Bryn's independent. You know he doesn't like taking orders." She rolls her eyes. "I think perhaps he's keeping an eye on Katya and the rest of them. Reporting back."

The kettle whistles and she reaches up for a mug. "There was something bothering him last night, but he wouldn't tell me what. I don't think it was just the Metz gearing up for the raid, it was something else ..." She sighs. "I thought he was finally opening up, that we were getting somewhere. But then he shuts up tight again."

She hands me a mug of hot water. "How are things between you and Aleesha?" Her voice is artificially casual.

I blow on the water to cool it. "I don't know," I admit. "I thought things were going okay, but then, well, you know what the file said? About my father authorizing the raid?" Abby nods. "Last night, she was looking at me differently. Or rather, she wasn't looking at me at all. I don't think she said a single word to me all evening. And when I went in to talk to her before bed, she pretended to be asleep." I stare down into my mug. "I think she looks at me and thinks of my father. And what he did. Like I somehow had something to do with it."

Abby takes a sip from her own mug. "It's difficult for her, Trey, you must see that. I'm sure she doesn't blame you, but seeing her mother die ... even if it happened a long time ago, must have brought up a lot of emotions. Maybe she just needs some time alone."

"Maybe." I pause, wondering how much to confide in her. "Abby, do you think I can trust her? I thought I could, but then Bryn said something and now ... I'm not sure."

Abby considers this for a moment. "I don't know," she admits finally. "I think it would depend on what it was you were trusting her with. She's quite protective of you, in a way. And she's brave – recklessly so. I think she'd look after you in a fight. But if you got in the way of something she really wanted, or her own survival ... well, I don't know." She smiles sympathetically. "But perhaps I'm being too harsh. I do think she has a good heart and, underneath it all, she's a good person."

I smile weakly.

"Nobody's perfect, Trey. It's our faults as much as our strengths that make us who we are. My grandmother used to say that life can break us, but it's what we do with the pieces that matters." Abby turns back to the table and begins to chop up some of the herbs. "She was a wise person, my grandma."

It's what we do with the pieces that matters.

"She told me a bit about her past. What men did to her." I take another sip of tea. The mug clatters on my teeth. "It sounded horrendous. Is it normal out here? For girls to be ..." I can't say the word.

"Raped?" Abby finishes. She nods briskly and transfers the chopped herbs into a small bowl. "In Area Four, yes. Five, less so. What you probably didn't realize when you lived Inside is that Outside isn't just one place. Each area is different. People who live in Six think of themselves as Insiders. Those areas nearer the river – Four and Three – well, they're where the poorest of Outsiders live. And those who are trying to lie low and keep away from the Metz."

"Illegals."

"Yes, I imagine most unchipped citizens end up there. Or in similar areas around the city. Area Four has one of the lowest employment rates in the city. In fact, it's even lower than Three. A lot of people who live in Three work out on the docks."

She glances up at the sound of footsteps and smiles. "Ah, Bryn's back."

The door opens and Bryn steps into the kitchen. He frowns when he catches sight of me, but his face quickly clears. "Did you manage to get everything you needed?" He nods at the empty shopping bags on the table.

"Pretty much," Abby replies. "I just hope I won't need it all."

"Best to be prepared," Bryn says grimly. "Things are getting worse in Six."

Abby nods. "I saw. Any update on Metz movements?"

Bryn grimaces. "Just that they're not moving. From our reports, it seems like they've all been pulled back to the compound, which suggests that something is going to happen imminently."

"What about the Commander?" I ask.

"Not a peep." Bryn shrugs. "Jameson's working as fast as he can to update the controller and get it ready to test. He asked if you'd be able to go over and give him a hand, actually."

"Me? I'm not sure I can be much help." I stand and walk over to the sink to rinse my mug. The gloom I'd been feeling lifts slightly.

"Well, sometimes just having another person there to bounce ideas off helps." He checks his wrist strap. "Let's have a bite to eat and then head on over."

"There's some bread and stuff in the cupboard." Abby indicates with a nod of her head. She lifts a messenger bag off a hook on the wall and begins to pack it with bandages, packs of disposable gloves and jars of green paste.

I fetch the dry bread, cut it up and smear it thinly with some fake meat paste. It looks as unappetizing as it tastes. What I wouldn't give for a burger.

Don't start that again.

"What's that for?" Bryn asks with a mouth full of food. His

eyes narrow. "You're not planning on going out there are you?"

Abby continues to pack the bag, but a faint blush tinges her cheeks. "I'll go where I'm needed."

"You're needed here." He scowls at her. "Injured people know where to find you. There's no need to put yourself in danger."

"What if they can't make it here?"

"Then they probably won't survive anyway." Bryn puts down the sandwich and walks around the table. He gently pulls her hands from the bag. "Please, Abby, it'll be a shitstorm out there. I can't protect you and do my job."

Abby pulls her hands from his grasp and straightens. "I've been taking care of myself perfectly well all these years, Bryn McNally."

Bryn flinches and his eyes harden. For a moment they stare at each other and I feel awkward, like I should step out of the room, except that even that movement would draw attention to my presence. Finally, Abby drops her gaze.

"I'll be careful, I promise. I just want to be prepared, that's all." She smiles and reaches out to pat his arm. "Don't worry about me."

"Just stay here. If what we think is going to happen happens, you'll have a queue of people out the door before you know it."

"If that's the case, send Aleesha along to me," Abby replies brightly. "She's much better at helping with the gory stuff than you two."

Bryn grunts and grabs the rest of his sandwich from the table. "Ready, Trey?"

I nod, stuff the remaining bread into my mouth and pull my boots on. The hurried departure sends my heart racing and I choke on the crumbs, my mouth suddenly dry.

It feels like a tide is about to turn. A storm surge is coming.

And Jameson's device might be the only thing that can stop it.

21

Aleesha

I wander up and down the street just up from the entrance to the government headquarters where Trey's father works. *Not Trey's father. Andrew Goldsmith.*

Thinking of him as Trey's father complicates things.

Metz officers guard the gate in the shimmering grey barrier that surrounds the headquarters buildings. There are cameras everywhere, but it's lunchtime, so people are flowing up and down the road and in and out of the cafés that line it. I keep my head covered with a bright scarf and find a spot to wait at the top of some steps where I have a good view down the street.

I'm not expecting to see Andrew Goldsmith until later in the day. He seems the type who'd stay in the office and work through his lunch break. But about fifty minutes after I arrive, a familiar stooped figure emerges from the gate and shuffles up the street toward me.

My mouth is dry, and I wish I'd taken more of a drink at the last fountain I passed. My body feels tense and ready for action, like the moment just before we landed on the tower of the Metz compound. Time slows, and for a second that feels more like an hour, I'm poised on the crest of a wave. I could fall back, go back to my place Outside the Wall and let Andrew Goldsmith walk away. Or I could ride the wave, knowing that it will crash down and things will never be the same again.

If I do this, Trey will never forgive me.

If I walk away, how will I ever forgive myself?

Mama.

How can I live knowing that justice was within my grasp but that I let it slip through my fingers? Will I wake every night with her face in front of me, twisted in pain? Will the shots ring out in my sleep, a constant rat-a-tat-tat in my head? Will every dream remind me of her? Until that one memory of her washes away all the happy memories of my childhood? Until I forget what it was like to be loved and held and tickled until I laughed out loud?

Hot tears burn my eyes.

I'm sorry, Trey.

I plunge down into the mass of people, weaving through them toward the spot where Andrew Goldsmith had been standing.

When I reach it, he's no longer there.

My hearts stops. I scan the faces in front of me, taking care not to meet anyone's eye. None of them are his.

I tug the scarf a little further down over my face and turn to make my way back up the street.

And then I see him.

He's standing outside a café, holding a half-eaten sandwich and looking up at a news screen. He's in the way of the crowd, but he doesn't seem to notice or care. He just stares up at the screen. When I follow his gaze, I see why.

On the screen is a picture of Trey. And me.

I duck my head and move quickly through the sea of people toward him. When I reach him, I grab his arm and use my momentum to pull him forward.

"What—?"

I turn to look at him and his eyes widen in recognition. I take advantage of his shock to lead him to the side of the street into a small niche behind a stone pillar. I think it's a camera blind spot, though I'm taking no chances.

"You need to come with me now. It's Trey. He's in trouble." I look up into his eyes, trying to convey urgency and concern.

He tenses, his eyes flicking around as if he knows someone is watching us. "What's happened? What kind of trouble?" He glances back toward the news screen as if that will provide the answer.

"There was a run-in with some Metz officers," I lie. "They were trying to take him in. He managed to get away, but he was injured – badly injured. Abby's doing her best, but ..." I let my voice trail off.

His face whitens, and for a second I think he's going to pass out. But he composes himself and his eyes narrow. "So why are you here? Where's Bryn?"

"Bryn got hurt too. He was with Trey and managed to defend them both and get away. He got hit in the leg." I draw a finger across my thigh. "Abby says he won't be able to walk for a week."

Andrew Goldsmith reaches out and grips my shoulders. "How bad is bad? Why haven't they taken him to a medic?"

I push his hand away. "You know we can't take him to a medic. He got shot in the stomach and chest. He ... he's struggling to breathe." I look away, unable to meet his eye.

This is wrong. I wrap my arms around my stomach. My heart's hammering in my chest, so loud that he must be able to hear it. He'll know I'm lying and walk away.

Then I won't have to do it.

But when I finally steel myself and look up at him, he just

nods at me. "Let's go."

We move out into the crowd of people heading up the street toward a large square. Andrew stops. "We should take a pod – it'll be quicker."

I falter and look at the small white pods taking off and landing on the other side of the square. He's right. But the pods must have cameras. They may not even let me in without a chip.

But if Trey really was dying, you'd take the risk.

Besides, I've never flown over the city before. I don't count the trip to the compound. I couldn't see anything then.

"Okay, fine." I pull the scarf down lower over my face and follow him across the square to join the short line of people waiting for a free pod. A solitary Metz officer guards the station, but it seems more interested in scanning the crowd than checking the people waiting in line.

My nerves tingle as we get to the front of the queue. Andrew Goldsmith presses his hand to the door and it swishes open. He waves for me to enter.

Cautiously, I step inside, glancing around for any sign that this is a trap. My fingers twitch to pull out a knife.

Not yet.

The door closes.

"Where's the nearest pod point?"

I think fast. The nearest pod points are in Six. Too far away. "Don't land it Outside. Any pod that lands is being attacked. It's crazy out there. Land somewhere near the East Gate. It'll be quicker."

He nods, seeming to accept the explanation, and gives the pod the destination.

I could do it here.

My hand slides down my leg, feeling the slight bulge of my

concealed knife.

It would be easy. There's no one around.

I shake my head. There's not enough time. I need to question him first. Get answers. And there will be cameras in here for sure.

"Are you alright?"

I start. He's frowning at me. "Yeah. Just worried."

The inside of the pod is opaque apart from a thin strip a couple of feet off the floor. I crouch down to look through it and stifle a gasp.

We're already high up, speeding over white rooftops tiled with black solar panels and weaving between the taller glass towers. It's like looking down from my roof, but we're moving so fast that the people on the streets below appear and disappear in a flash.

A minute later, the pod slows and begins to descend. It settles on a rooftop, six floors up.

"We're here?" I ask, standing up.

"Yes. Most pod points in the city are on rooftops. There's not enough space at street level."

The door opens, and he steps out. I follow and grab at my headscarf as a light breeze catches it, blowing it back off my face.

We're at the end of a line of pods. It's a busy station, with people milling around, and no sooner have we stepped away from the pod than someone moves to take our place. A hand on my shoulder pushes me toward a large lift at one corner of the rooftop.

I keep my head down as people crowd in around me, trying to make myself as small and inconspicuous as possible. I look out as we descend. The Wall rises up, just a few streets away.

I could leave him here. Walk away without another word. He would know what that meant. I could go back to Abby's and find Trey and tell him …

Tell him what?

The lift stops, and people begin to spill out. And instead of walking away, I wait for Andrew Goldsmith and instruct him to go through the East Gate, to take the first right and wait for me outside an old boarded-up electronics shop.

Only then do I turn and walk away.

Once through the Wall, I tug off the bright scarf and bind it around my waist, under my jacket. Insider to Outsider. Just like that.

If only things were that easy.

I'm not kept waiting long. He hurries down the street, conspicuous in his unease and blue government suit. I realize I haven't thought this through properly. He'll get mobbed before I can take him anywhere wearing that thing.

I could do it here.

No, it has to be in Four. He has to see.

"Aleesha," he says, hurrying up to me. His face is drawn but alert. "How far do we have to go?"

"Not too far."

I pick the quietest route I can through the back streets, but we still get some odd looks. I make him take off his tie and swap his jacket for a hobie's long cape. The hobie is delighted. Andrew Goldsmith not so much, but I silence his protests with a look.

The street that separates Five and Four is busy and I pull him across it, hoping his knowledge of the areas Outside the Wall is a flimsy as Trey's.

"Wait, I thought Abby lived in Area Five?"

As if reading my mind, Andrew pulls his arm from my grasp

and stops, looking around at the dirty grey apartment blocks and the boarded-up windows of the shops below. Further down the street, a fight breaks out between two hobbies and a crowd gathers to watch.

"We're nearly there," I say in a low voice. "Just, let's keep moving, okay?"

Already eyes are starting to turn to us. A street kid loitering up ahead seems to be watching us, but as I catch his eye, he turns and runs off. I feel eyes bore into the back of my head, but when I whirl around, I just catch the vacant glances of hobies.

You're being paranoid.

Or perhaps not. The first tendrils of doubt curl in my stomach. My uncertainty is mirrored in Andrew Goldsmith's eyes.

Now is not the time to get cold feet.

I grab his arm and steer him into a side alley. "It's not far."

We walk past a body of a man staring sightlessly up at the grey sky and I have to use all my weight to pull Andrew Goldsmith on. We pass another two before we emerge onto the street, but these look as if they've been dead a while and dumped here out of the way.

"Why haven't they been moved?" Andrew whispers to me as we emerge onto a busy street. He casts a panicked eye around. "Where are the Metz?"

I snort. "I was hoping you could tell me that. They've all but disappeared from the streets. Rumour has it they're planning something big. Know anything?"

He shakes his head. "I'm not involved in any of the big decisions anymore," he says sadly. "Though even in my previous position I didn't have much to do with the Metz or security."

"But you worked in the Secretary of State's department once?"

He gives me an appraising look. "Yes, a long time ago. I was a junior minister there. But a lot of what was going on ... it didn't sit right with me. So I asked for a transfer."

I almost laugh out loud. *Didn't sit right with you? Murdering innocent people?* I bite my lip and turn sharply left at a crossroads. The mixture of anger and adrenaline is a toxic cocktail that surges through my veins. I quicken my step. Nearly there.

"Aleesha. I wasn't expecting to see you here."

My head jerks up at the familiar voice.

"Hi, Jay." I glance to his companion. "Jonas."

"Who's this?" Jay eyes Andrew Goldsmith, who's hovering nervously behind me. "Looks like an *Insider*." He frowns as if trying to place him.

"Jay, remember I said I had something to do?" I lower my voice. "This is that something. You need to focus on getting ready for the raid."

His eyes narrow. "Yeah, and mebbe you just said that to get me out of your way. To protect your Insider friends." He raises his knife so the tip hovers in front of his mouth.

Oh, if only he knew ...

"Jay, we don't have time for this." I give Jonas a pleading glance. His eyes narrow and he opens his mouth to speak but before he can say anything, a voice comes from over my shoulder.

"She's right. The Metz are coming."

I curse inwardly.

Jay flashes a wicked smile. "And what would you know?"

"I came to warn you." There's a slight – a very slight – tremor in Andrew Goldsmith's voice, but Jay doesn't seem to notice it. "They're massing at the East Gate."

Jay glances from him to me and I can sense his uncertainty. He doesn't *want* to believe him, but he still trusts me.

"Fine," he says reluctantly, lowering the knife. "But if I see you again, we're going to talk."

He steps to one side and we hurry past.

"Who was *that?*" Andrew mutters to me as I direct him left up Pearson's Passageway.

"One of the gang leaders."

Ahead of me is open space and grey clouds. Rose Square. My heartbeat quickens, and I have to fight to keep my breathing calm. I stop abruptly at the end of the passageway and brace myself as Andrew Goldsmith barrels into my back.

The market holders are packing up their stalls. People walk across the square, some stopping to look up at the news screens, but most have their heads down, focused on their own business.

"Do you know this place?"

"I-I'm not sure ..." His voice trails off.

"It's Rose Square." I glance sideways, looking for a reaction, for a sign that he knows why he is here, but there is nothing. His face is pinched as if he's trying to figure out what I want to hear.

"There was a massacre here a few days ago," I continue, conversationally. "The Metz stormed in, lots of people got killed."

My left hand stretches down my leg and fondles the handle of my knife. The good one that Bryn gave me.

His face clears. "Ah yes, I saw that on the news ... a tragedy." His hands twitch. "Look, can you just take me to Trey, please?"

I force a smile onto my face. "Of course, this way." I motion for him to go back down the passageway. "Take this right, it's a shortcut back to the main road."

He stops. "Look, what's going on? I'm starting to b—"

The point of my blade presses into the small of his back. "Just go right," I whisper.

249

His body stiffens. "Go on," I prompt, turning him gently around to face the entrance to the narrow alley, barely a metre across, that leads back behind the buildings. "I'm right behind you. But don't run. I'm fast. And I'm pretty good at throwing this too." I let the blade scratch his skin.

He stumbles forward. Energy courses through me. I feel strong. Powerful. It's intoxicating.

After ten paces, the alleyway opens up into a small courtyard. There's a small lean-to structure in one corner that by the smell is a compost toilet. Litter covers the ground, and in the far corner another narrow passageway leads back to the main street.

I push Andrew Goldsmith forward until his nose is pressed against a brick wall. Then I bend down and stretch out with my free hand to rummage in the pile of trash that's piled up next to us.

Please still be there.

My hand closes around the cold handle of Jonas's gun and my knees feel suddenly weak. I take a step back and my breath catches in my throat as tension rushes from my body.

You could have done it with the knife.

But I couldn't. A knife is too personal. Besides, I want to be able to look him in the eye when he tells me why he ordered my mother's death. It's easier to control the situation with a gun.

Of course. That's the reason.

I take a deep breath and shove the knife roughly back into my pocket. Closing both hands around the handle of the gun, I lift it in front of me.

"Turn around." At least my voice sounds more confident than I feel.

Sweat beads on the back of Andrew Goldsmith's neck. His

whole body trembles. He raises his hands and turns slowly, his eyes widening as he catches sight of the gun.

"Kneel down."

He obeys, still holding his hands high.

"Trey ... please, where is he?" His eyes flick about the court-yard as if his son could jump out at any moment.

"He's fine. I don't know where he is."

My hands shake. I take a deep breath, pushing Trey out of my thoughts.

"Thank god," he whispers, closing his eyes for a moment.

He's being held at gunpoint and looks relieved?

But the look passes.

"You lied. To get me to come out here."

"Yes. Do you know why?"

Andrew Goldsmith doesn't ever look surprised. "Your mother," he says flatly. "Operation Nightshade. Trey said you were her daughter. I d—"

"Shut up!"

He clamps his lips together.

"Rose Square was where it happened." My aim is steadier now. I have control of my body again. "Where they shot her down. On the day she disappeared."

I hold the gun in front of his face, just out of his reach in case he tries anything stupid. But he won't. Andrew Goldsmith is not stupid.

"I was six. She was my world. Everything!"

Anger and grief battle to escape from my cage of emotions but I force them back down.

Stay calm. Stay in control.

"Do you know what it's like, being alone out here? No mother, no father, no one to look out for you? Not even a chip to get food with. No chance to go to school. No medicine when you're sick. Do you know what it's like?"

"No," he says quietly. "I don't know."

His gaze is unnerving me. Even though I know he's not Trey's real father, I can't help but see part of him in Andrew Goldsmith's eyes.

"Why did you authorize the operation?"

"It was my job."

"Did you never question whether it was right?"

He considers this for a moment, his eyes never leaving mine. "Of course. I question everything. The operation was intended to capture a known criminal. A criminal who was considered a danger to society. So yes, on balance, I did think it was right."

"On *balance*. For *Insiders*."

"For Insiders *and* Outsiders. No one benefits from conflicts like this. People just get killed. He was a troublemaker."

"Because he stood up for people? For what he thought was right?" My hand begins to tremble again.

Control. Control.

"Why was he meeting her?"

"I don't know. The only reason he would have been in London was so he could stir up rebellion. We presumed she was one of his contacts here – part of a plot against the government."

His voice is so calm and reasonable. It makes me want to punch him. I flick the safety catch off.

"You presumed," I say flatly. "You didn't know?"

He goes to shake his head, then stops. "No. You rarely *know* anything with intelligence. It's a balance of probability. Of judgement."

"And you judged her guilty," I whisper.

"No, that's not what I meant." He looks up at me, but I don't want to listen to his excuses anymore. I put a fraction more pressure on the trigger.

"My mother did nothing wrong. She deserves justice."

Fear flashes in his eyes. "And is killing me justice? It won't bring your mother back. Or help save anyone else."

The sound of shots rings in my head. Her scream. Suddenly it's her in front of me, her who I'm pointing the gun at. Her eyes pleading for mercy. My aim falters and I lower the gun, my whole body quaking.

Andrew Goldsmith doesn't move.

It's not her. You're just seeing things.

I blink, and the memory is gone. Though her scream still echoes at the back of my mind.

"I will give her justice. Avenge her death." My voice cracks and hot tears prick my eyes. I take a deep breath. I can do this.

"Is that what she would want, Aleesha?" His voice is soft and quiet. "Is revenge all you want?"

"Shut up!"

His poisoned words. He's trying to manipulate me. That's it. I take a deep breath and raise the gun again. "Any final requests?" My tone is deliberately ironic. *She* didn't get any.

Andrew Goldsmith's face pales. "How about mercy? Mercy can be more powerful ..."

His voice trails off and he stares at my finger tightening on the trigger.

No more talking. No more hesitation.

"They didn't show my mother any mercy."

22

Trey

The wide road that separates Areas Five and Six is crammed with people queuing to get through the East Gate and looters carrying their spoils back to whichever area they came from. Occasionally a fight breaks out when someone sees their belongings being carried away, but it's usually over quickly; the owner of the items either backing down or being silenced.

In the distance, the Metz frame the East Gate, visible over the heads of the crowd. I count six of them. They ignore the violence erupting at intervals down the street and part of me wonders if they've just given up on us. Perhaps there's no pullback, no big raid planned. They've just decided to abandon the areas Outside the Wall and let people fend for themselves.

We cross the street and plunge into Six. The normally clean and tidy streets are littered with broken furniture and the remains of smashed food parcels. Decorative window shutters hang half off their hinges. Acrid smoke hits my nostrils, carried on the wind from a shop further up the street.

"Makes you wonder if we really should be trying to help them, doesn't it?" Bryn mutters. "Look out!" He yanks me toward him as something comes whizzing through the air. A chair crashes to the ground. I glance up and see a guy with a shaved head and dragon tattoo down his arm leaning out of an apartment window. He gives an unrepentant shrug.

"This is what happens when the Metz disappear?" I whisper.

"This is what happens when there's no discipline," Bryn corrects. We turn down the narrow alley that leads to the Chain headquarters. "Those guys back there were part of the Dragons. An Area Five gang. Their leader should be reining them in, not sending them looting." He shakes his head. "So much for the Brotherhood uniting the gangs."

The old building looks even more dilapidated than usual. The lower windows are boarded up and purple graffiti is scrawled on the brick walls.

I stop at the foot of the stairs. "You've been attacked?"

"Na," a man with tight braids pulled back from his face grins. "It's just for show. Make it look like the place has already been raided." He twirls a knife between his fingers.

The guard on the other side of the steps leading up to the entrance snorts. "Any excuse for you to get out the spray paint, Zane!"

"Too right," Zane replies. His teeth flash white against his caramel skin. "Go on up, you're expected." He jerks his head toward the front door.

Once inside, we head to the conference room on the first floor. Angry voices spill from the open doorway.

"I *know* the consequences, but I can't do any more than I'm doing!"

Bryn pushes open the door and we walk in. The expression on Jameson's face turns to one of relief. "Trey! Come over here. I wanted to ask you about a text command link."

I walk over to him, eying Katya warily. She's pacing the

255

room like a caged animal, her body tight with anger. The black controller box is set out on the table next to a small robot. Scattered tools, wires and electronic chips are spread out across the wooden surface. Matthews sits on the opposite side of the table. She gives me a sympathetic look as I sit down.

"I've managed to get the text command function working when it's directly linked to the Metz chip. But tapping into the chip remotely is problematic. That's what we struggled with last time." He brings up a text display and types in a basic command. The robot turns to the left and walks five steps across the table.

"You've got a Metz chip in that?"

Jameson nods. "We managed to get one out of an officer who went down during that incident in Rose Square. It makes testing much easier." He blows out a breath. "I'm missing something ... I just need to work out what."

Behind us, Katya and Bryn are arguing in low voices. Matthews goes across to join them.

"I'm just saying we should get further clarification before doing anything rash," Bryn says more loudly.

"We've *had* clarification. Just because you don't agree—"

There's a slight pause then Katya continues, but her voice is too low for me to make out what she's saying.

"Any ideas?"

"Huh? Oh, sorry, what did you say?" I flush guiltily.

Jameson looks crestfallen. "I was wondering if you had any thoughts on how to intercept and replace the communications between the captains and the officers."

I think for a minute. "I don't think there's an easy way. Either you give the captains a demand that overrides the orders they were given at the compound or you take out the captain ..." I try to remember what the professor had said. "But then you're stuck with the same problem they've got: how to reprogram the chips of a group of officers to respond to a different captain when they're out in the field."

"What about if you physically had their captain's implant?" Matthews walks over and points at the black box on the table. "Could you connect that chip to your device and control it that way?"

Jameson's face brightens. "That could work ..." He purses his lips. "In fact, that would make things much simpler. The only issue then is to get our text command to work through the chip. But that *should* be doable."

"Will the chip work outside of the host? It won't have some failsafe where it shuts down if it's removed from the body?" Matthews asks.

Jameson's shakes his head. "I don't think so. The last one we got seemed to work fine." He waves toward the robot. "It's just a communication chip at the end of the day."

"But isn't it implanted in their brains? Wouldn't it kill them if we try ..." My voice trails off. They're giving me that patient look the teachers used to give me at school when I'd asked a stupid question.

"I imagine so. *You* were the one who was talking about taking out the captains." Matthews cocks her head toward me, a faint expression of amusement on her face.

"But I didn't mean to kill them! I just thought—"

"That you could make them go to sleep or something?" She shakes her head. "The Metz are too dangerous to mess with, Trey. If we take one out we need to be a hundred percent sure they're *out*. Otherwise, someone will end up getting killed. It's them or us."

I stare down at the table, chewing my lip. *Them or us.*

"If we had a medic unit and surgeon here and knew exactly where the implant was in their head, then perhaps we could take it out without killing them, but we don't have that luxury." She squeezes my shoulder. "Just remember, *they're* why you're out here."

"And if we can get control of them, then we can turn them back *against* the government," Jameson adds, his voice rising in excitement. "The machines will be under our control."

"They're not machines," I mutter under my breath. "They're *people*."

Matthews shakes her head. "Not while they're under the control of the government they're not."

I stare at the black box. I'd not really thought about what the Chain would do once they had control of the Metz. The plan in my head had only got as far as stopping them hurting Outsiders. Not using them as an army.

"We need to get hold of one to test," Jameson murmurs to himself. "I can set up something that might work but we'll never know until we test it."

A crash from downstairs makes me jump. Katya takes three quick steps over to the window and looks down onto the street. Footsteps pound on the staircase. Whoever it is, they're taking the stairs two at a time.

The door bursts open and Murdoch runs in, his face flushed and chest heaving.

"Aleesha ..." he pants, leaning forward and grabbing at his chest. "Down in Four ... She's got him ..." He glances up and for a second our eyes meet and his face blanches. Then he looks away.

"What? You're not making sense." Katya strides over to him, frowning. "What's she done?"

Bryn walks over to join them. Murdoch coughs and tries to catch his breath. He mutters something too quietly for me to hear, but I see Bryn's face tighten.

I push back my chair. "Is Aleesha in trouble?"

"No," Bryn says sharply, glancing over at me. "Sit down, Trey." But I don't like the look on his face.

Something's wrong. There's something he's not telling me.

Katya pulls back from the huddle and begins to pace the room again. Neat, quick steps. One arm is folded across her chest and she taps her fingers on the opposite arm as she walks.

"This could work. Yes, this could actually work better."

I'm not sure if she's talking to herself or expecting an answer. It seems no one else does either, as the room falls silent.

"If she does it, that may carry more weight. Her grief. Her revenge. Yes, it will bring people together. It will ready them for the fight."

A sick feeling develops in the pit of my stomach. I glance at Bryn. His face is taut and he's refusing to meet my eye. "What's happening, Bryn? T—"

Katya turns suddenly. "Murdoch, is there a team ready to go?" He nods. "They'll be waiting for us at the border to Four."

"I wasn't anticipating moving this soon, but she's forced our hand. It may work out better this way. Draw the Metz out." She looks over at us. "Jameson, get that device working. Matthews, get him whatever he needs to make it work."

"Wait. This is too hasty." Bryn grabs her arm. "Murdoch may be wrong. Aleesha may just be talking to him ..."

Katya stiffens and looks pointedly at her arm. Bryn takes a step back and releases his grip.

"We have our orders, Bryn. We've already discussed this. We need to focus people's attention. Stop all this stupid looting and remind them who the real enemy is."

Bryn looks unhappy. "But—"

"No buts. That's my order. That's *his* order." Her eyes flick to me. "Stay here. Look after Trey."

I don't understand. Why would I need looking after?

"What's going on? What's Aleesha done?" I push my chair away, but Matthews grabs my arm and gives a slight shake of her head.

"This isn't about the city, you know that." Bryn gives Katya a cold look, but she just raises one eyebrow and stares back at him. They're like two dogs facing off and waiting for the other to back down. Matthews shifts nervously beside me.

"*I* don't question our leader's decisions." Each word is like a pin prick in the silence. "And you can be certain that he'll be hearing about *your* questioning once this is over." Her words make me shiver.

Bryn's eyes narrow. "Don't threaten me, Katya. I've been around a lot longer than you."

She leans forward until their faces are just inches apart. "Then I'd have thought you would know better than to rebel, Mr McNally. No one is irreplaceable. Remember that."

She pulls back and turns to leave. "Murdoch, come with me. The rest of you, stay here."

Bryn takes a step toward the door, but it slams in his face. He curses and slams his fist into the wood. "Dammit!"

I look from Bryn to Matthews and back to Bryn again. "What's going on? Why won't anyone tell me?"

But they won't meet my eye. The only sound in the room is Jameson humming to himself and tinkering with his stupid box.

Bryn leans back against the wall and closes his eyes. His face is lined with anguish. "I'm sorry, Trey. I can't."

"What do you mean, you can't?" I wrench my arm from Matthews' grasp and stride over to him. "If Aleesha's in trouble, I want to know."

"She's not in trouble. At least, not yet," Bryn says tightly.

"Then why can't you tell me?"

Bryn leans forward and massages the top of his nose with finger and thumb. "Because you can't do anything to stop it. Trust me, Trey, it's better this way."

"Can't do anything to stop w—" Then it hits me. The thought slamming into my brain like a hammer. And everything suddenly makes sense.

Ice shoots through my veins and I step backward, reaching a hand out to the wall to steady myself. "My father," I whisper. "She's gone after him, hasn't she?"

Bryn stares down at the floor. The room spins around me.

"Trey, why don't you sit down?" Matthews sounds concerned. There's a tug on my arm but I bat her away.

"Tell me, dammit!" Anger flares in my belly. I push off the wall and go to stand in front of Bryn. "Look at me and tell me what the hell is going on."

But still he refuses to look me in the eye.

I clench my fist. "What is she doing to him? What are *they* doing to him?"

Silence.

I slam my fist into the door to the side of Bryn's head. It feels good, so I do it again. "Tell me!"

"Trey, stop." Rough hands grab my wrists, forcing me back. "Stop!"

I stare up at him. Blue eyes, just like my own. I guess that's where I get them from. "Just tell me what's happening," I whisper. "Please."

He looks away and drops my hands. "Sit down."

I move on autopilot and sit on the chair that Matthews pushes toward me.

"We had an order come through yesterday. From the Leader. He feels things are getting out of control. That some event is needed to bring Outsiders together. A trial of a prominent government official."

"A trial?"

I'm struggling to think clearly. My mind is fogged, each thought swimming through a thick soup, unable to find other thoughts to piece together what's happening.

Bryn grimaces. "A nominal trial. More of an execution."

"An execution?" Two pieces click into place and my stomach plummets. "Dad. They're going to *execute* him?"

I'm on my feet and have taken two paces before my brain catches up. But Bryn is quicker. He grabs me, throwing me back into the chair. "I said to sit!"

I stare at him in shock, too paralysed to speak.

"I'm sorry." He wipes his forehead with the back of his hand. "This is all such a damn mess."

"We ... we have to stop it."

Bryn looks at the floor and shakes his head. I look at Matthews. "Please, we have to stop it. He's not done anything wrong!" I grab her hand and stand, tugging at it. "We can stop it, if we go now."

But she pulls her hand away. "I'm sorry, Trey, really I am."

I run to the window, but Katya and Murdoch are already out of sight.

How long will it take them to get there? If it's a trial, that will take some time to pull together, right? They'll need to find him. Find Aleesha.

My head snaps back to Bryn. "What's Aleesha got to do with this?"

Bryn continues staring at the floorboards and sighs. "Nothing. Except that she seems to have had the same idea."

"The same idea?"

Bryn doesn't answer.

She wouldn't ... would she?

I think back to the training room. The look on her face when Rogue had read out my father's name. I'd been too stunned to take it in. There had been grief there. But also determination. And hate.

She saw her mother die.

"No," I whisper into the silence.

"Murdoch may be wrong." Bryn lifts his head and takes a pace toward me. "Perhaps she just wanted to talk to him, ask him some questions."

"She could have done that Inside." The fog in my head clears now. Too late, I finally understand. "We have to go." I push past Bryn's outstretched arm and pause with my hand on the door. "Will ... will you help me? He's not a bad man. You know that."

Bryn's face is a mask of indecision. I pull open the door and run toward the stairs. Whether he's coming or not, I don't have time to wait.

As I reach the front door, heavy footsteps pound the stairs behind me.

"Trey, wait!"

I wrench the door open and run down the steps. He catches me at the bottom and I turn to face him. "Do you know where they'll take him?"

Bryn nods grimly. "The same place Aleesha will. Rose Square."

23

Aleesha

Trey. *My mother's smiling face. Andrew Goldsmith. My mother's terrified face. Her body juddering as the bullets hit. Trey.*
The images play through my mind like a spinning wheel that gets faster and faster until the faces blur into one.

Trey. Mother. Trey. Mother.

My hands are shaking. I need to get a grip. Why is it so hard to kill someone? All I need do is tighten my finger on the trigger. One small movement and it will all be over.

Andrew Goldsmith stares up at me, his eyes silently pleading with me to put the gun down. He looks old – older than I remember from the screens when he stared down at us as the Minister of Education and Health and told us what he was doing to help us. He looks a different person now.

He has lost too. Lost his job. His son.

Dammit, I've already thought this through. Decided that he deserves to die.

But I reached that conclusion when he was far away on the other side of the Wall. Now he's a living, breathing person kneeling in front of me.

You have to do it. She deserves justice.

I steady the gun, aiming the barrel between Andrew Gold-smith's eyes. For a moment, I think he's going to beg for his life and I'll have those words ringing in my head for the rest of my days, but he just swallows and looks down at the ground.

I take a deep breath and slowly let it out as my finger closes on the trigger.

No!

I wrench the gun away as the shot fires, the bullet embedding itself in the brick wall. I stumble backward, my arm falling to my side.

We stay there for a moment, our gazes locked, both of us wondering what happens next. My heart races so fast I feel as if I've sprinted two street lengths. A bitter taste lingers in my mouth.

"Go," I manage eventually, the word escaping in a hiss between my gritted teeth.

But he doesn't move, still frozen with his hands in the air.

"Go!"

What more does he want me to do?

I march over to him and yank his arm. Finally, he seems to get the message. He staggers to his feet, blinking and looking around.

"You're letting me go?" he whispers.

I shove him toward the narrow passageway that leads back out to the main street. "Down there. At the street, turn right. Follow it up to Area Five. You should be able to get to the East Gate from there."

"Why?"

"Why what?" My body feels weak from adrenaline and I want to slump down right here, in this stinking courtyard, and close my eyes.

"Why are you letting me go?"

I scowl at him, wishing I knew the answer to that myself. "Just go. Before someone else catches you here."

"Thanks." He offers me a weak smile then, to my relief, turns and stumbles down the passageway.

I sag back against the wall, the gun falling from my hand. *Dammit. I had him! The man who was responsible for her death. And I was too weak to do it.*

My eyes seek out the bullet hole in the far wall. People will have heard the shot. I should get out of here.

I pick up the gun and flip the safety catch on before shoving it into my belt and wiping my hands down my legs. I'll go back to my roof, chill out for a bit. Figure out what to do next.

But I don't get the chance. As I emerge from the alleyway, a commotion further up the street catches my attention. A crowd is gathering around a small group of people who are pushing their way toward me. There are shouts and jeers.

I push myself against a boarded-up shop window to let them pass. A flash of blond hair catches my eye and panic surges through me as Katya looks directly at me. A smile of satisfaction crosses her face.

A moment later, Murdoch's pulling me through the crowd to a small group at the centre. My heart sinks when I see Andrew Goldsmith, blood streaming down his forehead, being held up by his arms by two of Katya's heavies. He glances up and gives me a wry smile.

"You know this man, Aleesha. Andrew Goldsmith. The man who authorized Operation Nightshade." Katya sounds jubilant.

I stare at Andrew Goldsmith. He shakes his head. Just a fraction.

"We're taking him to Rose Square. To be tried by the people."

I tear my eyes away to look at Katya. She is immaculate as always, not even a smear of dirt on her face.

Finally, I find my voice. "What do you mean?"

Katya waves a hand at the baying crowd. "They will decide his fate. As he decided theirs. But I think we can both guess what their judgment will be."

I stare up at her. "No," I whisper.

"Yes." She smiles coldly. "He will be executed. And you will be the one to do it."

* * *

A crowd has already gathered in Rose Square by the time we arrive. I stumble along with my head bowed, being carried as much by the press of the crowd around me as by my own legs. Murdoch's hand is heavy on my shoulder. He squeezes it occasionally, just to remind me that there's no escape.

I try to get my brain to work, but it's fogged, and every thought is as hard won as a street fight. My muscles are heavy, the adrenaline in my system drained away to leave only acid.

Think. There must be a way out of this.

"Aleesha?"

Rough hands pull me up the worn stone steps of the monument and push me unceremoniously against the stone pillar. The noise of the crowd is a dull hum, as if I'm listening to them from underwater. Their faces are angry. Fists pump the air. Was it only a few days ago the news was broadcast? Did that cause all this hatred and fury? Or was it buried in these people all along, just waiting for a release?

Katya's face appears in front of me. She brushes a tendril of hair off my sweaty forehead. The gesture is almost motherly. "Are you okay?"

I see her lips form the words, but I can't hear them. I close my eyes and shake my head, stretching my jaw to try to pop my ears and clear whatever it is that's stopping me from hearing.

Get a grip. Breathe. Think.

My heart rate slows. The noise of the crowd engulfs me. I open my eyes.

"Are you hurt?" Katya looks concerned but this time her words sound in my ears.

I shake my head.

She looks relieved. "I know this must be a shock to you, seeing him here."

It takes me a moment to remember who she's talking about. I glance over at the man kneeling on the edge of the stone steps. He's not even struggling now.

"He's the man who ordered your mother's death. Now you have a chance to make him pay."

Make him pay.

Images of my mother flash through my mind again, as I stare out at the square. "This was where it happened," I whisper.

This is where she was chased down. This was where she died.

Inside me, something stirs. A burning ache in my stomach.

"Yes. But that's not all. He was responsible for the health and education of Outsiders. For population control. It's because of his laws that you and so many other people are classed as illegal. That you're forced to scrape out a life on the streets. *He* could have done something to change the system. He *should* have done something."

"He should have done something," I repeat, staring at the spot where my mother died. The gathering crowd doesn't reach back that far. If I blink I can almost picture her crumpled body. Her dark blood staining the cobbles.

My fists ball at my side and the embers burning in my gut spring into flames. They burst the cage door open, releasing years of memories. Memories I had locked away. The cold nights shivering on the street or up on my rooftop. The pain when the kind hobie woman had warmed my wet, frozen feet. The shopkeeper who had turned me away, but pressed food into my hand when he thought no one was looking.

I remember the times I'd got sick, but had to wait it out, not knowing if I'd survive or not, unable to go to a medic for help. Stealing books and trying to remember the letters my mother had taught me. Gazing with envy at the children lined up at the school gate. The children who were allowed to learn.

"It was because of him. All because of him."

Her words trigger more memories. Begging on the street. The first time I tasted tronk and the man who sowed the seeds of that addiction. The men who raped me. The men who I let rape me because it was that or starve.

The fire rages inside me. It consumes me.

More recent memories. Lily. My beautiful Lily. The Gollin children, huddled over their mother's body as the Metz officer loomed closer.

Hot tears blur my vision and stream down my cheeks. The fire burns me up inside and drives the water from my body. Something is pressed into my hand. A gun.

A gentle shove from behind causes me to stumble forward. The kneeling man turns to look at me, and as his eyes meet mine my resolution falters. They are not like Trey's to look at, but there's the same expression of hurt and resignation that I saw last time we parted. I take a step back and lower my arm.

Can I take away Trey's father? Because he took away my mother?

"It is your right, Aleesha," Katya whispers in my ear. "You

269

must avenge your mother's death. It's the only way you can be whole. The only way to heal the wound."

I shake my head and wipe my arm across my eyes. *Damn tears.* "No. I ... it's not right. It shouldn't be this way."

But I don't know what's right anymore. Tears cloud my vision and anger clouds my thoughts.

Maybe if he dies, the government will listen. Maybe then things will change.

"Look around. The people are demanding it. They want justice. They trust you to make the right decision."

I open my mind a crack to let the shouts of the crowd in and take a step back in shock.

"Aleesha! Justice! Aleesha! Justice!"

They're calling my name. Mine. I scan the faces. I recognize some of them – a lot of them. My people. They don't deserve to be starved and poisoned. To have their children taken from them. We may not be smart or beautiful, but we deserve better.

"Aleesha!"

They're looking to me. Not in fear or disgust, but in admiration.

They trust you to make the right decision.

How can I let them down?

I step forward. I'm behind him now, he's kneeling in front of me. A criminal awaiting execution. I raise the gun and point it at the back of his head.

His blood will be on your hands.

My hand wavers.

They want justice. They trust you.

My finger grips the trigger and a strange feeling passes over me, like I've been here before.

You let him go, remember?

But it's so hard to think over the baying of the crowd.

Why? Why did I let him go?

And then it comes to me. Giles's words. And Bryn's. And Trey's. *Revenge is not the answer.* Because if I kill him now, how does that make me any better than him? Than *them*?

I can kill if I have to, if my life depends on it, but not like this. Not when he's kneeling helplessly in front of me. This isn't justice.

I lower my arm. The gun drops from my hand and clatters down the steps.

"No," I whisper.

The crowd falls silent. There's a murmur of unease.

"What are you doing?" Katya hisses in my ear.

"I-I can't do it ..." I turn to her. The tears on my cheeks feel cold now. "Not like this. This isn't a trial, it's a mob."

Her face hardens. "It's the only justice there is out here." She pushes past me and pulls her own weapon from her belt.

"Andrew Goldsmith. You have been judged by your people – the people you were elected to protect – and have been sentenced to death."

There's a scatter of cheers from the crowd.

No, this isn't right.

I turn and reach out for her arm, but I'm pulled backward by two of the guards. My fingers claw at empty air. A movement at the back of the crowd catches my attention. It's Trey. He's running toward us, but he's too slow. He's not going to make it in time. I redouble my efforts to get free but the men holding me are too strong.

"No!" My cry is lost in the cheering of the crowd.

This wasn't supposed to happen.

Katya lowers her gun until it's resting against the back of

271

Andrew Goldsmith's head. His body trembles and his lips move with unspoken words. A prayer perhaps?

"This is their justice."

The shot rings out and the crowd falls silent.

For a second, Andrew Goldsmith remains kneeling. Then he slowly topples forward and falls face down on the steps. Blood spills from the wound on his head. The noise of the crowd swells. Shouts of anger and jubilation.

Blood. Always blood.

I tear my eyes away and search the crowd for Trey. He's staring blankly at the place his father had been kneeling, his mouth open. If he's screaming, I can't hear it over the cheers and shouts of the crowd. He strains against Bryn, who's holding him back, his arms wrapped tightly around Trey's thin body. As I watch, he pulls Trey's head into his shoulder, as if by doing so he can hide him from the horror of what's just happened.

His eyes flick from Trey to Katya and a look of revulsion passes across his face. Then he turns and begins to pull Trey away, the two of them stumbling together from Rose Square.

My legs finally give way and I fall to my knees. When I close my eyes, all I see is Trey's face, ravaged with grief and horror. And in the ashes of my heart, I know that I have lost him.

My only friend.

* * *

I slump with my head in my hands on the steps at the base of the statue. Trey's face is frozen in my mind, overlain on a sequence of images that replays again and again. The shot. Andrew Goldsmith falling to the ground. The blood. Except in the image, it's me holding the gun. Me shooting him.

Someone sits down beside me and there's a light touch on my

shoulder.

"Hey."

Katya. I jerk my head up and pull away.

"What now?"

"Nothing. Just thought you might want to talk." She rests her elbows on her knees and looks out at the square. The crowd have dispersed. The spectacle is over.

"What will happen to ..." I can't finish the sentence.

"The body?" She glances at me. "We'll make sure it's returned to his family. Milicent will help with that."

Of course. Milicent.

"I'm not a monster, you know," Katya says, staring out. "I don't like killing people and I don't do it needlessly."

Even now, she can't leave me alone.

"Really." She begins to pick at an invisible thread on her sleeve. "I was like you once, you know."

I snort. "I doubt that!"

There's an awkward silence. I wish she would just go away. I'm barely able to move; all the energy has drained from my body. But she seems determined to talk.

"I was born in Moscow." She gives me a sideways glance. "That's in Russia. My father was an important man. Like here, genetic enhancements for embryos are reserved for the rich and powerful. My sister and I were given everything. Beauty, brains, athleticism. The full package. When I was eight, my father was assassinated."

She glances at me again, but I keep looking straight ahead.

"A friend of my father's smuggled me, my sister and my mother out of the city. He took us to a secret cabin in the wilderness. He was the only person we saw for three years. My mother was an amazing woman. She kept us alive and taught us so much.

Our society at the time was dominated by men. But you could succeed as a woman if you picked the right men to approach … if you knew how to use them. Perhaps the same skills you learned growing up here."

I swallow hard. *Like the gangs. We rise and fall with our men. Or because of them.*

"One day, when I was eleven and my sister, Anya, fifteen, a group of soldiers stormed the cabin and arrested us. They offered no explanation, but they must have caught Stavros and tortured him into revealing our existence. He didn't care for us kids much, but he loved my mother. Self-interest all the way. That's men for you. We were taken to a Gulag. It's where they send people who don't fit into the society the government want. You have to be strong to survive the Gulags and most people give up. In Russia, our winters are harsh. Many freeze and starve."

A shiver runs down my back and I wrap my arms around my knees. The memories of cold nights and frozen feet play through my mind.

"It doesn't get that cold here, does it? You don't even get snow. In the Gulags, it buried the ground for half the year. But worse than the snow was the wind. It blew from the north, cutting through you as if you were made of paper and whistling through the gaps in the hut where moss wouldn't stick. Even today, the whistling of wind through a crack takes me back.

"My mother caught the attention of the camp commander on the first day. She was so beautiful. He invited her to dinner, but of course, it wasn't *just* dinner." Her fingers play with the loose thread, tugging it from her sleeve. "Every night she came back broken, until one day something in her snapped. We knew when she went to him that night that she wouldn't be coming back.

She was too spirited – it wasn't in her nature to be submissive. The next day, they made us watch as her body was fed to the camp dogs."

My stomach turns, sending a rush of nausea up my throat. I close my eyes, but it doesn't help.

"Anya also got singled out," Katya continues, as calmly as if she were discussing the weather. "I was still plain, skinny and flat-chested, but she was beautiful. Like a china doll. The camp guards weren't supposed to interfere with the occupants, but it didn't stop them. One Christmas Eve, the guards were having a party. They came and took her away. They were drunk on vodka, but not drunk enough." Her tone turns bitter and she spits out each word in turn. "They raped her. Again, and again, and again. Sometimes more than one at a time. She was thrown back into our hut in the early hours of the morning and died later the same day. I held her in my arms and promised I would avenge her. Avenge them both."

I swallow. "So how did you escape?" I just want this to be over.

Katya jerks out of her daze. Tears shimmer in her eyes. "I was lucky. The women in my building looked after me. Made sure I was kept as grubby and ugly as possible. One day, a few years after Anya died, a man was brought in with the latest batch of workers. He was different to other people in the Gulag. Intelligent. A fighter. And handsome – he must have come from a wealthy family. At first, he ignored the scruffy kid who latched onto him, but I was the only person who could remember Moscow – if only faintly at that point – and have a proper conversation with him. He taught me how to fight and together, we figured out a way to escape.

"Back in Moscow, I chose the highest profile gang, walked up to its leader and persuaded him to take me as his companion."

She smiles across at me. "My mother taught me well. Three years later, I hunted down and killed the camp commander and guards from the Gulag. I built connections in the government, kept digging until I found out who had arranged for my father's death. Then I killed her too."

She turns and takes my hands in hers. Her skin is smooth and soft, unlike my cracked hands and torn fingernails. "We have both had to fight for survival, you and I. We have both lost our parents. And I can see it inside of you – the need to avenge your mother's death. Only then will you be able to move on. To accept what has happened and build your own life."

Her gaze locks me in, but for once, I don't feel threatened. I understand now, why she is the way she is. Why she placed that gun in my hand.

But she is wrong.

When you let revenge define you, all you have is bitterness and regret.

Giles was right, even if I didn't want to listen to him.

I pull my hands away gently. "I'm sorry, but I'm not that person. I can't do it. I'm not as strong as you ... I can't kill someone in cold blood, even if they hurt me. There has to be another way."

"There is no other way, Aleesha," Katya says softly. "At least, not in this society as it is now." She pats me on the knee and gets to her feet. "Think about it. And when the time comes – when you're ready – I will help you face your demons."

She says something to one of the other men and they walk away, leaving me alone. I stare down at my feet.

Justice and revenge. I had thought they were two words for the same thing. But I was wrong.

24

Trey

The world spins. I push against the arms that hold me. Whose are they? It doesn't matter.

Nothing matters.

I let myself be carried away, my feet stumbling obediently along the rough street. There's a thick fog in my head that stops me thinking. Something bad's happened. But my brain has shut down.

I feel like that time I got lost in the snow in Wales and lay down to sleep. It was cold, so cold, but after a while the cold went away and I just felt numb. Like I was floating on air.

The arms push me down. My knees bend and I half fall onto a stone step.

"Trey?"

Trey. That's me.

I'm shaking, so hard that my teeth rattle in my jaw.

"Trey! Talk to me!"

The voice cuts through the fog in my head. I shake my head. My ears clear and I flinch as I'm suddenly assaulted by noise.

"W-what?"

I look around. A narrow street. People walking by. Bryn kneeling in front of me.

Bryn.

I focus on him. There are deep creases on his forehead and his eyebrows have moved so close together that they look like one. He mouths some words that I don't catch.

"I-I ..."

But I don't know what to say. Something bad has happened. I can feel it. Something b—

It comes back to me, slamming into the forefront of my thoughts like a sledgehammer.

Father.

The gun.

The shot.

An image appears in my head. He's kneeling at the top of the steps surrounding the statue, his hands cupped together in front of him. His face is pale but his eyes, when they meet mine, are not fearful but resigned. He opens his mouth to speak, and somehow I know his words are addressed to me. That he had something he wanted to say to me. But at that moment, the gun fires and his face freezes.

I was too late.

I didn't see where he fell. The baying crowd blocked my vision. I wonder if anyone reached out an arm to catch him. Or if they just let him fall, face down, on the ground.

Was it quick? It looked quick.

I shake my head, trying to rid myself of the thought. But the sequence replays itself, again and again.

"Trey, please talk to me! We need to get out of here." Bryn's voice is anxious. Afraid.

Bryn, afraid?

I force myself to focus on what's here, what's happening now. Bryn's tugging at my arm. But my limbs are so heavy.

"Go away," I mumble, leaning back against the wall.

"Trey, I know you've had a shock and I'm sorry. But we have to go *now*." Bryn leans closer and I can smell the mint on his breath as he whispers to me. "They know you're his son."

"What?"

I force myself to sit up and look around. A small group of people stand in a huddle a little further up the street. They're muttering to each other and occasionally one of them looks in our direction. The man nearest us holds a serrated knife down by his thigh. He strokes the blade with one finger.

Do they want to hurt us?

It's so hard to think. I look the other way. Two guys my own age are walking up the alley. They each have a snake tattoo that encircles their necks, choking them.

They're coming for us.

Bryn pulls me to my feet. But it's too late.

"Yer that boy on the screens, aren't you? *His* son." The guy jerks his head back up the street. "An *Insider.*"

"We're just going," Bryn says, pushing past him.

But his friend steps forward to block our path. "Don't think I know you. Yer not from around 'ere, are you?"

"I'd suggest letting us past." Bryn's voice is low and dangerous. "You'll regret it if you don't."

The first guy chuckles. "Are you threatening us, old man?"

Bryn takes a step back toward me. Without taking his eyes off the guys with the snake tattoos, he mutters under his breath, "When you see a break, run for it, okay? I'll hold them off as long as possible."

"When we see a break, we *both* run for it," I whisper back. My legs still feel too weak to run.

If they kill you, would it really matter?

The thought lingers unpleasantly at the back of my mind.

"Keep your eye on that group behind us." Bryn sounds nervous. They're walking casually toward us. Four of them: three men and a woman. "They're coming."

"Afraid, old man?" the guy taunts. "It's the boy we want. Leave him and we'll let you go."

I force myself to keep watching the group of four. There's a blur of movement in the corner of my eye and a yell of pain followed by a string of curses.

"Go!" That's Bryn.

I glance over my shoulder. One guy is lying on the floor, clutching his thigh. Blood leaks from between his fingers. The other is holding his knife out in front of him but his hand trembles and his eyes twitch. Bryn lunges forward and he dodges to one side, but not before Bryn's knife slits a line through fabric and skin.

A gap opens up.

I run.

A hand clutches at my top. My feet are wiped out from under me and I crash to the floor.

Instinctively, I roll away. A dark shape looms over me and I roll to my knees, raising my arms above my head.

But the expected blow doesn't come. The shape resolves itself into a man. He staggers backward, bleeding from a wound to his head.

Bryn crouches in front of the remaining two men and woman, a knife in one hand and a baton in the other. He's clearly the best fighter, but the three of them are closing in on him. Worse, they're standing between him and me.

He catches my eye over the shoulder of one. "Run!" he mouths.

But I can't. I don't think my legs could move that fast even if I wanted them to.

I glance around, looking for something I can use as a weapon. The street is littered with trash, but most of it is plastic wrappings and other soft materials. A reddish object, half hidden under the rubbish, catches my eye.

A brick, broken in two.

I pick up the two halves. At the same moment, a muffled yelp of pain comes from behind me.

Bryn.

They have their backs to me and are only a few metres away. I don't have to throw far. The first brick hits the side of one man's head, not enough to take him down, but enough to distract him and give Bryn an opportunity to land a punch to his nose.

He stumbles back into a wall, blood gushing down his face.

I raise the second half brick. In front of me is the woman. I hesitate.

I can't hit a woman.

She turns toward me, her eyes filled with hate. There's a flash of metal in her hand but I catch the movement in her eye and step to the side. Quick enough to avoid the blade plunging into my stomach but not quick enough to avoid it altogether.

A flash of pain shoots up my side. I bring the brick down toward her head. Her reactions are slow – the brick connects with her skull with a thickening thud. Her eyes roll back in her head and she crumples to the ground.

I back away. A hand grabs me from behind. I whirl around, brick raised, and lash out instinctively. It connects with the thug's shoulder, but he doesn't budge. Blood trickles down the side of his face from Bryn's earlier attack. The tip of his serrated blade tickles my chin.

"Gotcha now, boy," he breathes. The rotten stench of his

breath makes me gag.

Something whizzes past my ear. The man's face freezes in shock. A small knife protrudes from his eye. I stare in horror as he falls back to the ground.

Bryn grabs my hand. "Come on."

We stumble down the street and onto a larger road. People give us strange looks as we pass but no one tries to stop us. Maybe it's the blood-stained knife in Bryn's hand. Or the murderous look on his face.

Streets pass in a blur. Somehow my legs keep moving until Bryn stops and doubles over, releasing my hand and pressing it to the side of his chest. I look closer as a grimace of pain crosses his face. A wet stain darkens his jacket. "You're hurt."

"Let's just keep going."

He sets off up the street before I can protest.

When we reach the gate to Abby's yard, Bryn leans against the wall to catch his breath.

"How are you holding up?" He scans my face anxiously.

"Okay," I lie.

He nods and opens the back gate. I can see Abby through the kitchen window, standing at the table surrounded by dried plants and herbs. She glances up and the smile falls from her face.

I help Bryn inside. His skin is cold and clammy.

"What's happened? You're hurt?" Abby looks from Bryn to me and back again.

"Trey's hurt," Bryn gasps.

Abby assesses us quickly. "So are you, and you're worse. Trey, sit down over there." She nods to a chair and I sink into it, a wave of dizziness washing over me.

I stare blankly across the room as Abby switches to nurse

mode. Quick, efficient and emotionless. Almost emotionless. She heats water, cursing at how long the hotplate takes to boil it, and makes Bryn strip and lie down on the table. There's a long, deep slash on his right side. I take one glance at it then look away as my stomach heaves.

"Yarrow for the bleeding," Abby murmurs, walking past me to pour hot water into a bowl.

She cleans and examines Bryn's wound. He winces but doesn't cry out as she prods around. From the scars on his chest and back, he's used to injury.

"It's pretty clean and not as deep as I first thought," Abby says, straightening up. "If it doesn't get infected, it should heal fairly quickly."

She sticks some small pieces of tape across the cut and smears it with a thick paste before bandaging it up. "There you go. Please, take it easy for a few days?"

Bryn eases himself off the table. "I'll try."

A smile twists the corners of Abby's mouth. "Liar."

She empties the bowl of bloodied water and refills it. "Let's have a look at you, Trey."

Gingerly, I peel off my long-sleeved top. I flinch as Abby reaches out to me. She gives me a sympathetic smile. The cloth is warm and soothing, but it needles at the cut on my side and I clamp my teeth together to stop myself crying out.

"Ah, it's barely a scratch," Abby says reassuringly.

I steel myself and glance down. A thin line of red tracks across my pale skin. She's right – compared to Bryn's wound, it is only a scratch. From how much it hurts, I'd expected something more impressive.

Abby wraps a thin bandage around my waist. "We'll leave this on for a day or two just to protect it but then you should be fine to take it off."

I lean back into the chair and close my eyes. My body feels heavy and my head throbs. My mind replays the same scene, over and over again.

The crack of the gunshot reverberates in my head.

Blood clouds my vision.

"Trey, come over here." Abby pulls me from the chair and leads me over to the large rocking chair in the corner. She gently pushes me down and tucks a blanket around me. A warm mug is pushed into my hands. "Drink this."

My hands are trembling too much to hold it steady, so I rest it on my knees. It has an odd smell: sweet but slightly medicinal.

"What is it?"

"A herbal drink. I added a little honey," Abby replies.

"And a tot of something stronger," Bryn adds.

"Alcohol?"

"It'll help with the shock," he replies.

Cautiously, I take a sip. It's got a kick to it, but the honey is sweet. I feel suddenly more alert. "It's good."

Bryn and Abby move to the far side of the room and start talking in low voices. I tune them out, focusing on holding my mug steady enough to drink.

The back door bangs open and the room falls silent. I look up.

Aleesha stands in the doorway. Her hair is dishevelled, pulled half loose from the tight braid she wears it in. Dirt smears her face and a thin line of dried blood runs across her chin. She sways slightly and Abby steps forward to catch her as she half falls into the room.

Her eyes find mine. "You're okay? I heard ..." Her voice trails off as her gaze switches to Bryn.

Abby tries to sit her down, but Aleesha pushes her away. She leans on the table instead. "It's gone a bit crazy. They want a fight. It's like ... bloodlust or something. I don't know—"

She clamps her mouth shut.

Bryn looks as if he's about to speak but stops himself. I feel three pairs of anxious eyes on me.

"Why are you here?" My voice sounds odd. Cold and controlled.

Aleesha looks down at the table as if the grain of the wood may hold an answer. "I don't know. I think ... I wanted to explain." She gulps and scrubs her sleeve across her eyes.

"You were holding a gun to his head." They're my words but they sound as if they come from someone else. It's like I'm separated in two, watching my body think and speak.

"Yes."

"You wanted to kill him."

"No!" She takes a deep breath. "At first I did. I-I wanted to know why he did it. Why he killed my mother. And I wanted justice for her." She looks up and takes a few steps toward me, still leaning on the table. "But I couldn't do it, Trey. I let him go. Told him how to get back to the East Gate. I thought he would be safe!"

I stare at her fist, clenching and unclenching, and place the mug on the floor. Inside me, anger builds. I let it grow.

"What did you say to him?" I lift my eyes to hers. "How did you get him Outside?"

Aleesha looks away. "I-I told him you were hurt. That you were asking for him."

"Ha!" A bitter laugh. A bitter taste in my mouth.

Was that me?

"You used me to draw him out?" My hands propel me up out

285

of the chair. "To lead him to his death?" I stagger toward her, reeling like a drunk.

"I didn't know!" Aleesha backs away from me. "Trey, I let him go. But he ran straight into Katya a—"

"And what did you do to stop her? I saw you in the square. The gun was in your hand!"

I step forward, shrugging off the hand on my arm that tries to pull me back.

She used me to get to him. If it wasn't for me, he'd still be alive. If I'd left London as he asked me to, he'd be alive.

"The gun was in *your* hand," I repeat.

A sob catches in her throat. "They made me, Trey. I didn't want to. I refused!" Her eyes glisten. Her face, for once, an open book.

Why did I ever trust her?

My hands ball into fists.

"Trey, let's just stay calm, okay?"

I ignore the voice like I ignore the quieter voice in my head that tells me to stop. The anger drowns it out.

"It's your fault. You brought him out here. You—" A sob rises in my throat.

"I'm sorry." Tears spill from her eyes, weaving light tracks on her dust-covered cheeks. "I'm so sorry, Trey."

Her lips move again but I don't hear what she says. That strange sensation hits me again, like I'm floating away from myself. All I can hear is the pounding of my heart. All I want to do is hurt her. Like she hurt me.

You always knew she was a killer. How could you have let yourself care for her? Love her! You fool.

The muscles in my right arm twitch.

"You killed him."

286

"No, I ..."

"Look at me, damn you!"

She draws her eyes up slowly. I want her to see the hate flowing through me.

This is how much you've hurt me.

She flinches and steps back.

"Bryn was right. You are damaged goods. No wonder you have no friends. No wonder no one wants to be with you. You're broken. Trash."

There's a flash of anger in Aleesha's eyes and her face changes to that cold, expressionless mask that I remember from the first time I met her. "I shouldn't have come. I just wanted t—"

"To what? Apologize? Pretend like you care?"

She glares at me. "I do care!" Her voice breaks and she draws a deep breath. "He ordered my mother's death, Trey."

"Your mother was about to run off with a criminal!"

"Trey." A warning hand on my arm. I lash out behind me and hear a grunt of pain.

"Maybe that's why your mother left you." My voice rises. "You never thought of that, did you? Why didn't she take you with her if she was meeting your father? Perhaps it was because she didn't *want* you."

She stiffens and turns away, but I don't want her to turn away. I haven't finished yet. I grab her shoulder, pulling her roughly around.

"Trey, stop!" Abby's voice comes from a distance.

My arms rise in front of me, fists balled like a boxer. I can see her hands clench at her sides, but she refuses to raise them. Refuses to fight.

I grab her right arm and yank it up in front of her, but when I release it, she just let it fall to her side. She gives a harsh laugh.

"What are you going to do, Trey? Hit me?"

I let my fist fly.

The blow catches her on the chin, jerking her head to one side. The shockwave tingles up my arm. I raise my arm again but strong arms close around me. I fight against them, but I'm dragged back.

"Enough!"

Then I'm flying into the wall. My head smashes back and sharp needles rain down on me as I slump to the ground. Bright lights dance in front of my eyes.

What happened?

I'm back in my body again, blinking at the room in front of me. Bryn stands over me, his chest heaving. His fist is drawn back, and I cower in anticipation of the blow.

It doesn't come.

Under his arm I see Abby pass Aleesha a wadded-up piece of cloth, which she presses to the trickle of blood running from the corner of her mouth. She's looking straight at me, her face a picture of shock.

I did that?

Her lips mouth the words "I'm sorry".

Guilt floods through me. My chest tightens, and I feel like I'm about to be sick. I lurch to my knees.

"Aleesha, I—"

But she's already at the back door. Abby says something to her, but Aleesha shakes her off and yanks open the door. Without a backward glance, she staggers out into the yard.

25

Aleesha

I stumble away from Abby's, away from Area Five. My jaw throbs and the coppery taste of blood lingers in my mouth. But that is nothing compared to the look Trey had given me. A look of pure hatred.

What did you expect?

He was right. I am broken. Every word he spoke was true. If it wasn't for me, Andrew Goldsmith would still be alive. Trey's mother would still have a husband. Trey and his sisters would have a father.

There's a dull ache at the back of my throat. My chest is tight and it's hard to breathe. But my stomach feels empty. As if everything I had held back for years behind the bars of my cage has rushed up to escape my body, leaving behind an empty shell.

Maybe that's why your mother left you. Perhaps it was because she didn't want you.

Trey's words bite deep. Was I always like this? I had thought it was life on the streets that had made me tough. Forced me to think only of myself. But perhaps it's part of me, like my dark, straight hair and snub nose. Some bad thing inside me that makes me hurt the people I love.

My feet carry me down through familiar streets. Someone

shouts my name, but I ignore them, lost in my own thoughts. Finally, there is nowhere left to go.

Is it a coincidence that my feet brought me here, to the place where Lily's body burned? The stone I laid her on is still there, though the last of her ashes have long since been blown away by the wind. I run a finger across the cold, hard surface.

I miss you, Lily.

Tears well in my eyes.

I let you die. I let him die. Why can I never do the right thing? Why did I think killing him would help anything?

A cold wind whips in across the water. Hard drops of rain patter onto the concrete slab in front of me. I shiver and wrap my arms around my chest. It's cold down here. I should find shelter, get out of the rain. But I don't feel like going to my roof. It reminds me of Trey now. Reminds me of our kiss.

I was right not to encourage him. I knew I'd only hurt him. I just didn't think it would be in this way.

I brush my fingers across my lips, remembering the tingle of his mouth on mine. It had felt so … right.

Will he ever be able to forgive me?

But I know the answer to that. Every time he sees me, he will see his father dying.

If I could only go back and change things. Find some way of making things right.

I turn and walk along the waterline, shoving my hands deep into my pockets. The wind whips the tears from my eyes and salt mingles with the blood on my lips. My fingers close on a small, hard object. I pull it out. The security device to access the Metz system.

Perhaps there is somewhere I can go. Someone who will understand.

At the next street, I turn inland. I let my feet carry me on. The rain has set in and the daylight's fading as I reach the edge of the jumble of concrete blocks. I climb quickly, hauling myself up the larger blocks until I find the entrance to Giles's home.

I crawl into the mouth of the tunnel. The rain has seeped through my clothes and my teeth are beginning to chatter, but at least in here I'm out of the wind.

"Giles!"

There's no answer.

I call again and am about to set off down the tunnel when I hear a familiar hiss.

"Aleeeesha?"

A pale shape appears out of the dark. "What do you want?" He sounds suspicious.

"I've bought the device back. If you want it." Silence. "Um, can I come down?"

Another hiss. The pale outline backs away into the tunnel.

I take that as a yes. I feel my way through the tunnel until I reach the heavy curtain. Blinking, I step inside the brightly lit cavern and let the curtain fall back behind me. Giles stands watching me. I shiver. It's warmer in here, but rain and exhaustion have chilled me to the bone.

Giles silently picks up a blanket and hands it to me.

"Thanks." I wrap it around my shoulders. It's thin but surprisingly warm.

I dig the small black device out of my pocket and hold it up for him to see. "Do you want it back?"

No answer. I walk over to the small table that's still piled high with electronics and look for a free space to put it down. There isn't one, so I place it on top of a shiny black box.

I freeze, my hand still holding the plastic baton. There's a symbol etched into the black surface, half hidden by a metal lockbox placed on top of it. I push the lockbox away, revealing the symbol: a helmet with flashes of yellow on either side. The symbol of the Metz.

I look up at Giles, who's shifting uncomfortably from foot to foot. "You got this from the compound?"

He frowns. "What are you doing here, Aleesha? You didn't come just to give me that back." His eyes flick to the small baton in my hand. "Keep it."

I pocket the device and step away from the table, suddenly aware that I'm dripping water everywhere. Using a corner of the blanket, I squeeze the water out of my hair.

"I ... I didn't have anywhere else to go." My voice is small, and I have a sudden urge to curl up and bury my head in my arms. "Everything's gone wrong."

Giles cocks his head to one side, his face expressionless. He indicates the pile of cushions behind me. "Sit."

They look inviting. But I'm soaking wet. There's a small crate off to one side, so I sit on that instead. Giles crouches in front of me like a street hobie.

"You went to the compound?"

I nod. "That's where it all went wrong."

"How did you get in?"

"Through the roof. A pod disguised as the Metz Commander's."

He considers this for a moment, then nods. "That would work," he admits. "If you had someone inside the compound to let you in. And then?"

I tell him about accessing the Operation Nightshade files. Finding out that Andrew Goldsmith had authorized the operation to kill my mother.

"I wanted to kill him. To avenge her death." I stare down at my hands, remembering how they felt on the cold metal of the gun.

"You wanted revenge." His tone is placid.

"Yes."

"But revenge is not the same as justice."

"No." I look up at him. "Why didn't I see that? Until … until it was too late?"

He looks thoughtful. "The two are easily mistaken. Justice helps puts right a wrong. But revenge balances one bad act with another. Two wrongs don't make a right. And neither can bring back what was lost."

"Katya said I needed to avenge my mother's death. To move on with my life. That's why they killed him. For me." My throat tightens, and it becomes hard to breathe.

"Who's Katya?"

"The leader of the Chain … the organisation I've been working with. I-I let him go. I was going to kill him. But I let him go. Then *they* captured him. Said I had to execute him. But I … I couldn't do it. So, she took the gun and shot him herself. For me."

Giles shakes his head. "That doesn't make sense." He frowns. "Why would she kill him for you? There must be more to it than that."

I press my knuckles into my forehead. My head throbs and my eyes are sore from dirt and tears.

If only I could go back and have this day again. Everything would be different.

"Can you put it right?"

"What?" I look up into his pale eyes. There's a kindness in them that I haven't seen before. I always thought they were icy and cold. Or crazy.

"You have done something wrong. You need to balance the scales."

"I—" Dust catches in my throat, triggering a cough. "Do you have ... water?" I gasp in between fits.

Giles stands and walks to the other side of the room. My coughing subsides, and I wipe my eyes so he doesn't think I've been crying. A few minutes later he hands me a steaming mug. I take a sip. It's surprisingly sweet.

"What's in it?" I ask.

"Honey. Good for coughs." He gives me that odd half-twisted smile of his.

Honey? How did he get hold of that? It costs a fortune. I wave my hand around the room. "Where did you get of all this? It must have cost—" I bite my lip.

"You help people, they help you."

I eye his skeletal form. "Maybe you should sell some for food. You could have got a week's food for this honey."

"Maybe. But honey reminds me ..." His voice trails off and his eyes darken as he stares into the distance.

Of what? I want to ask. But I don't.

"I don't think I can ever put this right," I say quietly. "The way Trey looked at me ... it was as if he never wanted to see me again."

"He probably doesn't. At the moment. This isn't about doing something for him. It's about doing the right thing."

"I don't understand."

Giles turns and walks over to the table. "You said you wanted to take down the system." He starts tidying, closing and neatly stacking boxes of chips, metal and other junk.

Did I?

"The system is broken," Giles continues. "It was set up to be broken. The Metz were designed not to keep order, but to create fear. If you remove that fear, the system begins to collapse."

"And that's a good thing?" I ask uncertainly.

"No, that's a very bad thing!" Giles says vehemently. "That would bring chaos!" He slices his arm through the air, sending a pile of books crashing to the ground. "You need to *change* the system. To fix it." He bends down and picks up the books.

"And how do I do that?"

"Alone? You can't."

"So, you're telling me to do the impossible," I say flatly. Silence.

I blow out a breath. "There's a more immediate problem. The Metz have pulled back. They're not on the streets anymore. Everything is getting … crazy. But the Chain think they're planning something big. Like a huge Cleaning or something. To crush the uprisings."

A pause. "It's happened before. Have you heard of the Rose Rebellion?"

I shake my head, but the name sounds familiar. "I don't think so."

"It was a long time ago. I found the reports buried in the secure files. That's how Rose Square got its name. It all began with a love affair between an Insider and an Outsider. Such things were banned at the time. They were caught, and she was publicly executed. He started a rebellion in her name. Insiders and Outsiders came together. They plotted to overthrow the government. But they were betrayed."

He pauses.

"And what happened?" I prompt.

"They were killed. All of them. Half the city got set on fire and in the confusion, they were rounded up and shot. Many more died in the flames. The government blamed the rebels for the fires, but the files held the truth. They were set by the Metz." He turns and shrugs. "It worked. There hasn't been a rebellion of that scale since."

I swallow. "Until now."

And we caused it. By releasing the information.

Giles is holding something in his hands. The black box with the Metz symbol.

"Giles, when we were in the compound, we spoke to a professor," I say carefully, watching him closely. His nostrils flare. "He mentioned a remote command device," I continue. "Something that would allow the Commander to better control officers outside the compound."

A pause.

"The professor said they'd nearly perfected it years ago, but a vital piece went missing."

Another pause.

"It did," Giles says finally.

I glance at the box cradled in his hands. "What was it? The piece?"

Giles's jaw gapes in a parody of a grin. "Me."

I stare at him. "You?"

Giles looks down, turning the box over and over in his hands. "I created the device. I'd nearly perfected it when I left."

"You left because of it?"

Giles nods. "I realized what it would mean. Without it, the captains are given orders in the compound, but in the field they can make their own decisions within certain parameters. But with this, one person would be able to control them all. That is too much power. I tried to explain this to the professor, but ...

he didn't listen." He sighs. "He was a mentor to me. But he was also flawed."

"And is that a replica?" I ask, nodding to the box in his hands.

"Yes. It's not exactly the same. I've made a few modifications." He looks down at the box. "It's controllable by voice and has to be programmed to the user. And you can … you can use it to turn off their implants."

"What?" I rub my forehead. My head throbs and I'm finding it hard to think.

The faintest tinge of pink colours Giles's cheeks. "I don't know if it'll work. I haven't been able to test it properly, but the theory is sound. It should block any signals coming into the control chip and effectively switch it off. Like removing the chip, but without having to cut it out."

I frown and massage my temples. "So, the officers would be human again?"

"They *are* human."

"Okay, sorry. What I meant was … they couldn't be controlled? Would they get their memories back?"

"Yes, their memories are still there, at least those from the time before they had the chip implanted. The chip just makes them forget. After that … I'm not so sure." He frowns. "I suspect the memories of their time as officers may be gone, but I don't know."

"And they couldn't be controlled?" I repeat.

"The government may have a way of resetting the chips. That's quite likely, in fact. But the officers would need to return to the compound for that to happen."

My brain is spinning. "Wait, I'm confused. This device can be used to both control officers and release them from control?"

Giles nods. "Yes. Two different settings. But you can't just switch between the two. Once you've turned off the chip, there's no going back. The officers will be able to make their own decisions."

I try to absorb this. *The Chain want control of the Metz to use them against the government. But the government wouldn't send all the Metz out at once, that would be dumb. If we only controlled some of them, then they would end up fighting each other. Killing each other.*

The thought makes me feel sick. That's not the answer. But if we could switch the chips off then perhaps we could persuade the freed officers to help us.

I eye the black box in Giles's hands. "That thing is valuable. Is that how you've paid for all this stuff?"

"Other bits of technology, yes. But not with this." He pats the box fondly.

"You could sell it for a lot of chits."

"Of course. A lot of people would want it. But the question is, what would they do with it?" He gives me a searching look. "It could be very dangerous in the wrong hands."

I imagine Katya's face if she got her hands on it. What she'd do with it.

"So, you said it's programmed to only work for one person?"

Giles nods.

"Would you ... would you come out with me? To test it out if the Metz attack?"

"No!" Giles shrinks back. The tall, confident man disappears. Hunched over he seems small and weak, as if he's folded in on himself. He looks down at the floor as if ashamed. "No."

I take a deep breath. "Would you let me take it? To protect Outsiders, if the Metz attack." I take a step toward him. "I won't hurt them."

Giles's eyes flash. He curls his arm protectively around the box and hisses at me.

"I'm not going to take it from you. Not if you don't want to give it to me." I let my arm drop back to my side.

Giles mutters something under his breath. He backs away to the far side of the room and sits on the edge of the unmade bed, looking down at the box and mumbling to himself.

What's he doing?

I stare up at the brightly coloured fabrics that drape over the ceiling. I'm not sure what to make of Giles. Whether I can trust him. Whether he trusts me.

When I look back he's standing in front of me.

"You can stay here tonight. I will decide in the morning."

26

Trey

The grey light of dawn filters through the cracked glass window. I seemed to toss and turn all night, and when I finally did fall asleep, my dreams were so full of blood and violence that it was a relief to wake up.

I am weary. So, so weary. Not just from lack of sleep, but like all the energy and life has been drained out of me. I swallow, trying to soothe my raw throat, and close my itching eyes, wondering if there's any possibility I'll fall back to sleep. But the memories of yesterday won't let me rest.

The daylight gets stronger and there are sounds of movement from the other bedroom and footsteps on the stairs. Still, I can't bring myself to get up. It all seems too much effort.

Perhaps half an hour later, I hear the back door click shut and footsteps sound on the stairs. There's a tentative tap on my door. I grunt, and Abby takes that as assent to crack open the door.

"Trey? Do you feel like getting up?"

The smell of mint tea wafts in. I stare at a thin crack in the ceiling.

"I'll just put it down here for you then," Abby says after a moment.

The door clicks shut.

I want to chide myself for being rude, but the truth is, I don't care. I don't care about anything anymore.

The tea is half cold by the time I can bring myself to sit up and drink it. A short while later, the door opens again.

"I've brought some hot water up to the bathroom," Abby says, looking in. "Go and have a wash. You need it."

Oh, thanks very much, Abby.

I sniff under my arms and decide she's probably right. My limbs are stiff and sore, and I stifle a groan as I hobble to the bathroom. A steaming bowl of hot water is waiting, a bucket of cold beside it.

A steamy relaxation chamber, it is not.

I wash quickly then plunge my head into the basin and scrub at my hair, checking in the old mirror on the wall that I've got all the soap suds out. The boy in the mirror looks older than I feel. There's a haunted look in his eyes and tiny wrinkle lines at the corners of them.

I run a hand through my hair. I'll have to ask Abby to cut it. The remains of the black dye she'd used to disguise my white-blond hair linger on the tips as if someone's had a go at me with a paintbrush. I dress and make my way downstairs, feeling slightly more human.

Bryn walks into the kitchen just as I'm sitting down. I stare at the bowl of grey watery porridge that Abby's pushed in front of me. There's a sprinkling of sugar on top. Sugar is a luxury – this is her way of trying to make me feel better.

A heavy hand on my shoulder. "How are you feeling?"

I shrug it off. *How does he think I'm feeling?*

"I've just been to talk to Katya," Bryn continues. "To find out" – he clears his throat – "to find out what happened to your father's body."

I stir the porridge and watch as the crystals of brown sugar dissolve into it.

"Trey?"

"I heard."

I put a spoonful of porridge in my mouth. Tasteless, as always. I choke it down. My brain is telling me I need food, though my stomach is tight.

I look up, just in time to catch Bryn and Abby exchanging a look over the top of my head.

"They managed to keep his body safe from the crowd. It will be taken to your mother today." He sounds pained. But then he knew my mother, of course. I wonder if he'll go with the body, to comfort her.

I jerk my head up. "They've moved. Recently. How do they know—"

"They know, Trey," Bryn says gently.

Of course. Milicent. She'll know.

There's a bitter taste in my mouth. "Mother. Does she … do they know?"

"Not yet," Bryn says quietly.

I push the porridge away and get to my feet. "I should tell them."

"Eat something first?" Abby pushes the bowl back toward me. "Please, you need it."

I ignore her and cross the kitchen to the back door. "I have to go to her." I turn the door handle.

"Trey!" Abby calls. I turn, and she gives me a sympathetic smile. "Your boots."

I look down at my bare feet.

Oh.

Bryn puts an arm around my shoulder and leads me back to the table. "Sit. Eat. Then I'll take you to the Wall myself."

I force down the tasteless mush. Memories crowd my head, as much as I try to push them back. My father's sad, worn face burns in my mind. The final thing I'd said to him had been to accuse him of ignoring what was right and wrong.

I hadn't told him I loved him. And now, it was too late.

Salty tears fall onto my spoon. I scrub the back of my hand across my eyes to brush them away.

If only I could go back and change things. I should have known Aleesha would do something. I should have recognized what that hard expression on her face meant. I could have stopped this.

Should have. Could have.

But then, am I any better than her? I lashed out too ...

I hand the empty bowl back to Abby. "Aleesha ..." I hesitate. "She hasn't been back, has she?"

Abby shakes her head and turns to place the bowl in the sink.

I flush and look down at my hands. *How could I have lost control like that?*

"Any updates on the Metz situation?" Abby asks quietly.

"No," Bryn replies. "But the atmosphere on the streets is tense. Everyone's waiting for something." He shakes his head. "I don't think they'll leave it much longer."

Abby twists a towel around the bowl to dry it. "What about the device Jameson's been working on?"

"He was up all night on it. Thinks he's got something that should work, but, of course, there's no way of knowing until he can test it." Bryn grimaces. "We're hoping that they won't all come at once. If we can find a small group of officers, alone, then we can test the device properly. Before ..."

The word hangs in the air.

Before it really matters.

I lean my head on my hand and yawn. Perhaps I'll go back to bed.

"Do you think they—" There's a banging on the door and Abby falls silent. Bryn opens it and a boy of about twelve falls inside. He's red-faced and panting hard.

"They're coming," he gasps. "Metz ... East Gate ..."

"How many?" Bryn asks, pulling the boy roughly to his feet.

The kid looks up and the fear in his eyes makes my breath catch in my throat.

"Many," he whispers. "I-I didn't stop to count 'em. But they were still comin' through when I left to come here. More than I've ever seen in me life."

"Where were they going? Down into Four? Along to Three? Up here?" Bryn's voice is harsh.

"Everywhere," the boy pants. "They were going everywhere."

Bryn lets go and the boy stumbles back. "Good work." He pulls something from his pocket and presses it into the boy's hand. "Make sure you stay away from it, okay? Go up to Six. Find somewhere to hide out and wait until it's all over."

The boy nods, wide-eyed, and stumbles out of the door.

"This is it?" Abby asks.

Bryn nods. "This is it."

"You don't have to go." Abby's face is pinched and tight. "After what they did ... to Mr Goldsmith ... you don't owe them anything."

Bryn closes the distance between them and plants a soft kiss on her forehead. "It's my job," he says quietly. "Only Katya has seen anything like this before. They need me."

Abby gives the slightest of nods. "Come back?" she whispers, turning her head away.

"I promise."

"I'll be getting things ready, then," she says, unhooking the bag of medical supplies from the wall.

"Stay here, Abby," Bryn warns. "People will be coming to you soon enough. At least here you have water and shelter."

Abby shrugs and nods. "Sure."

My legs suddenly come to life and I lunge forward, reaching for my boots. "I'm coming with you."

Bryn turns, his face angry. "No, you're not. Stay here, Trey."

"But I can help—"

"No, you can't." He walks over and grips my shoulders. "And I can't be worrying about you. You'll be too much of a distraction. Stay here and help Abby."

He hesitates for a second, then pulls me into an awkward hug. "Take care of her for me, okay?" he whispers in my ear.

He pulls back and stares down at me. I give a half nod and he pats my shoulder and turns to pull on his boots. "If the fighting reaches here, barricade the doors and get upstairs. If the worst happens, escape out of the skylight in the loft onto the roof."

Abby's head snaps up. "You think they'll come this far north?"

Bryn shrugs. "I don't know. It depends whether people in Four run or fight. How far they want to take this. How much resistance we can provide."

Abby moves around the table. "The Chain … you do have a plan, right?"

"If Jameson's box works then we have a plan." Bryn pulls open the door.

Abby grabs his sleeve. "And what if it doesn't work? What then?"

Bryn gently strokes her cheek. "Then we're in for a fight."

The door bangs shut behind him.

Abby stares at it for a second then shakes herself and returns to the table. Her hands tremble as she unpacks then repacks the medical bag, her lips moving as she silently checks off supplies in her head.

This is it.

My stomach churns with indecision, the porridge turned sour in my gut.

Staying here, out of the way of the fighting, feels cowardly. I glance at Abby and reach again for my boots. She'll be safe here.

"Don't do it, Trey." Abby doesn't look up. "Bryn was right. You don't know how to fight. You'll just get yourself killed." She glances up. "It's not worth it. Think of how your mother would feel, to lose her husband *and* her son."

Irritation surges through me. More emotional blackmail. Part of me knows she's right. But I push that part of me down.

"I'm going upstairs," I say through gritted teeth.

At the top of the stairs, I lean forward and rest my head against the rail.

They killed my father. Katya's face and the cries of the mob still ring in my head.

Why should I help them?

Because not every Outsider was part of that mob. There are people who need protecting. People who can't fight.

Like Abby?

I feel a pang of guilt. But Abby will be safe here. They'll target Area Four. Three, maybe. Bryn's always a pessimist.

I pad silently across the floor to Abby's bedroom. The door is slightly ajar, and through it I see a pile of Bryn's clothes, scattered on one side of the bed. Gently, I push the door open and step inside. It feels wrong to be in here. Intruding on their personal space. But I need a weapon. I rifle through Bryn's clothes, searching for a knife. He seems to have a never-ending supply of them – he can't have taken them all with him.

But my hands come up empty.

I'm about to leave when something on the side of the bed catches my eye. A leather sheath, strapped to the leg of the bed. A thin handle protrudes from it.

Within reaching distance should someone disturb them in the night.

Bryn, the pessimist. The six-inch blade gleams in the light. I press the tip of my finger lightly to the edge of it and winch as it breaks the skin. At least it's sharp. After replacing the knife in its sheath, I unstrap it from the bed and wrap the leather cord like a belt around my waist. Then I tiptoe back out of the room.

I wait in my bedroom until I hear Abby's footsteps on the landing and the bathroom door click shut. Then I run lightly down the stairs, missing out the step that creaks, and into the kitchen. Adrenaline surges through me as I pull on my boots and reach for the door handle.

It's locked. *Damn her.*

The key is missing off its usual hook. I search the kitchen to no avail. Finally, my eyes alight on the medical bag, still sitting on the table. I open it and dig inside the small front pocket. My fingers close around a metal key.

Footsteps on the landing. I run to the door and fumble with the key.

"Trey? Is that you?" Abby's voice comes from the stairs.

The key turns with a click and I yank open the door just as Abby walks into the kitchen.

"Sorry." I pause in the doorway. "Stay … stay safe."

Then I slam the door behind me and run down the path to the yard gate.

* * *

I come across the people fleeing first. Men and women, already bloodied, limping in search of safety. Mothers clutching children to their chests. Unlike the refugees from Six, these people don't carry anything with them.

A young woman, supporting an older man who's bleeding heavily from his head, passes by me and I grab her arm. "What's happened? Where are you going?"

She stares at me with wild eyes. "The Metz. They just came … One minute we were in the kitchen and the next, everything's gone crazy. Like a Cleaning, but with no warning." She glances at her companion. "Is there a medic round here?"

I hesitate and glance at the man who gives a weak moan. "There's someone who may be able to help." I give her directions to Abby's house.

"Wait!" I call after her. "Where's the fighting?"

The woman pauses and turns to look at me. "Everywhere."

At the road that marks the boundary between Areas Four and Five I hesitate and pull back, wondering where to go. My heart's pounding and my limbs feel jittery.

Calm down. You'll be no good in a fight if your hands are shaking.

I close my eyes and draw in a slow breath. My nose wrinkles as an acrid smell hits my nostrils. Smoke. The pounding of my heart intensifies. Except it's not just my heart. Nothing can beat that loud.

I peer out onto the main street. A haze of smoke hangs in the air, but through it I can just about make out the outline of the Metz officers filling the street. They move steadily toward me, lashing out with their batons at the people who run across in front of them, trying to escape to the relative safety of Five.

My breath turns sour in my mouth. Screams and shouts

echo between the tall buildings across the street. There's the occasional shot, but more often it's the dull thud of a baton or the clash of metal against metal.

I take a step back. Bryn was right. I'm not a fighter, not really. If I went back to Abby's, I could help her with the wounded. Except I'm not much good at that, either.

If Jameson's box works then we have a plan.

But their plan has a single point of failure. Jameson is the only one who knows how to use the box. Apart from me. And it doesn't have much range. They'll have to get it to the heart of the fighting.

The thought makes me sick.

You wanted to help, didn't you?

I pull out Bryn's knife, take a deep breath and launch myself across the street.

Just as I reach the other side, a man lunges out in front of me. His hair is lank and matted and the knife he holds in front of him is dark with blood.

I tense, readying myself for a fight, but he just pushes past me. I walk further down the street, but a scream makes me turn around, just in time to see a Metz officer raise its baton and bring it down with a sickening crack onto the man's head. He crumples to the ground. The officer steps over the body and turns to look straight at me.

I run.

Everywhere I turn, it feels like there's a Metz officer waiting. Twice I get fired at; the second time I feel the air move as the bullet passes by my ear. I lose track of where I'm heading. The fighting is all around me.

Just keep moving.

The smoke is thicker here. Flames leap from the window of a

ground-floor apartment. The dull thud of an explosion sounds from a few streets away. I glance up and see faces pressed against the windows of apartments higher up, their occupants trapped by the fire.

There's a whoop from a side street. A Metz officer is on the ground being beaten by a group of young men. People are fighting back. But most of the time, they're not winning.

"Get down!"

The voice is familiar, though the words aren't aimed at me. I skid to a halt and look around.

"Slowly now …"

I backtrack up the street to a narrow alleyway. It opens up into a large courtyard a few metres down. Murdoch has a gun pointing at someone out of sight. As I walk up the alley, he raises his hand. "Now!"

There's a crash and he darts forward. I run out into the courtyard and just have time to take in the Metz officer prone on the floor when a gun is pointed at my face.

"Trey?" Murdoch scowls at me and lowers the weapon.

"Did we get it?" Zane leans out of a third-floor window, smashed open.

"Yup!" one of the men on the ground shouts up.

Murdoch wipes his hand over his forehead, smearing dirt with blood. "We think it might be one of the captains." He looks back at me. "What are you doing here?"

"I-I came to help. Did Jameson get the device working?" I look around. "Where is he?"

"I damn well hope so," Murdoch growls. "He's holed up in an apartment block through there." He nods to an archway. "Turn right and it's a few doors up. Blue snake on the wall."

He turns back to the officer. "Right, let's see if we can get its helmet off."

The archway leads to a wide street. Glancing up it, I see the apartment Murdoch mentioned. The painted snake along the wall is just visible through the grime that extends up to the ground-floor window. On the fifth floor, a child's face is pressed to the window. As I watch, a woman pulls her away and glances anxiously down at the street.

A shot rings out and I pull back, pressing my back against the wall. There's the sound of running feet and I catch a glimpse of Katya's retreating back, her long blonde braid whipping out behind her.

I peer out again. The coast is clear. I run across the street to the entrance to the apartment block and press the intercoms for the apartments at random until the door buzzes and I can push it open.

Once inside, I close the door behind me and sag against it in relief.

"Trey?"

I look up at the voice. Matthews looks down from the first landing. Her brown hair is grey with dust. "Get up here before you're seen."

I follow her into a room that looks onto the street. There's a bed on one side of the room and a table and a couple of chairs against the opposite wall. Jameson is hunched in a corner, the box in front of him. His eyes are red-rimmed with dark circles underneath.

There's a slight crackle and Matthews puts her hand to her ear. She nods at Jameson. "They think they've got a captain down. Try it now."

Jameson brings up the display and types something into it. "Has that done anything?"

Matthews crosses to the window and looks out. "No. They're still fighting. Shit!"

"What is it?" I join her at the window. A mass of Metz officers comes into view. They walk three abreast and I count ten rows back. They're marching toward us.

My stomach tightens. "H-how can there be so many of them?" I whisper.

"They must have emptied the compound," she says grimly. "Jameson, now would be a great time to get that device working."

"I'm trying." But his voice is tight with fear and his hands tremble as he types in another command.

There's a flash of movement overhead. A black pod shoots down the street. I catch sight of Murdoch standing in the archway, looking up at us. Matthews shakes her head and he pulls back.

The marching officers pause outside the apartment block and Matthews yanks me back from the window.

"Do they know we're here?" My voice cracks and I swallow, trying to get some moisture into my mouth.

"Come on, come on!" Jameson mutters. "Stop, damn you! Why won't you stop!" He slams his hand down on the device and closes his eyes.

There's a pounding on the door downstairs.

"Trey, go and check the back window," Matthews says quietly. "See if there's a way out. Jameson, get ready to move."

"This should work ... I don't understand," he mumbles, not appearing to have heard her.

I walk over to a door that leads into the back room of the apartment. There's a small window and a door leading out onto a fire escape. The door's locked, but when I press my hand to a security pad on the inside, it clicks open.

There's a crash from downstairs. Heavy footsteps on the stairs.

"Jameson, we're going. Now!"

I run back to the doorway. "This way!"

But it's too late. The door to the room explodes inwards. Matthews turns, already firing, but a spray of bullets hits her in the chest, her body jerks and she slumps down the wall.

Jameson huddles in the corner, clutching the black box to him. For a second his eyes meet mine. Then the Metz are on him, dragging him up. He screams in pain as a bolt of energy from a taser jerks his body.

I stumble backward. My brain's screaming at me to move, but my legs don't seem to have registered the command. My foot scrapes on the floor and, slowly, one of the black figures turns.

I duck and slam the door just as the bullets hit it. They whizz through the air above me.

Of course a door won't stop them.

Reaching the back door, I yank it open and run onto the fire escape. But there's no way down. The ladder has been pulled up. A bullet whistles past my cheek as I climb over the rail and drop to the ground.

The impact knocks the air from my lungs and shoots pain through my knees, but I manage to roll behind a small outbuilding. Somehow, I force myself up and stumble away.

Matthews is dead. Jameson, as good as dead. And the control device – the control device has failed.

27

Aleesha

When I awake, Giles is watching me from the other side of the room, the black box clutched protectively to his chest. I wonder if he's been like that all night, not daring to fall asleep.

My limbs feel heavy and I stifle a yawn. It doesn't feel as if I slept much. Whenever I closed my eyes, Andrew Goldsmith appeared in front of them. Kneeling in front of me. Talking to me about mercy.

I shake my head in an attempt to dispel the image.

The lights in the room brighten and Giles walks over to the counter. I push myself up off the soft cushions and massage my neck. Must have slept awkwardly.

"Here." Giles holds out a mug.

I take a cautious sip, but the drink isn't too hot. I gulp the rest down and a surge of energy courses through me. I look up in surprise.

"A stimulant?"

Giles nods. "I use them occasionally, for late nights." He holds out a pair of protein bars. "Yellow or red?"

I take the red bar, rip it open and chew hungrily. The drink helps with the cardboard-like texture.

Giles opens the other bar and chews it slowly. "What would you do if you were in charge of this city?"

The question takes me aback. "You mean if I was President?"

"Yes. If you could do three things, what would they be?"

I think for a minute. "Legalize all citizens classed as illegal and give them a chip. Allow Outsider children into Insider schools and move some Insider kids to Outsider schools. Open big kitchens where people can get food – real food – for free. And make all Insiders go on a compulsory tour of Area Four."

"That's four things."

"Yeah, well, I couldn't decide."

"You wouldn't bring down the Wall?"

"That would be my fifth thing. After the others."

"Interesting." He takes another bite of the bar. "Why?"

I shrug. "Take the Wall down and the Outsiders will just raid the homes of Insiders. Same thing as what's happening in Six. Insiders need to see what life is like for Outsiders. *Really* see. They need to care that Outsider kids get the same education as their kids. And Outsiders need to know they're not a threat. Then you can take the Wall down."

Giles appraises me with those pale eyes. I wonder what answer he was expecting from me.

"And if you had control of the Metz? What would you do then?"

"Deactivate their chips and try to persuade them to keep the laws. But proper ones, protecting everyone," I say promptly.

"And if they refused?"

"That's their business. They can go and get another job."

I finish the bar and toss the wrapper in the bin.

"Here." Giles holds out the black box.

I stare at it for a second, wondering if this is a trick. "I can take it?"

He nods. It seems I have passed the test.

I reach out and take the box from him. It's heavier than I'd expected, and the surface is so smooth it almost slips from my hands. I turn it over. "How do I use it?"

"First, I need to reprogram it. When I nod, say your name. Like this." He reels off an oddly formal phrase then, taking the box back from me, brings up the display.

"I, Giles, relinquish control of this device to Aleesha." He nods at me and points to the holographic display.

"I, Aleesha, accept control of this device and promise to use it only for good." It feels a little strange making a promise to a black box.

"Change of control accepted." The monotone voice makes me jump.

Giles hands the box back to me. "Now it will only respond to you. If you need to transfer control, you need to repeat the procedure." He frowns. "Though please don't. Remember what I said."

"It could be dangerous in the wrong hands." I nod. "Um, what do I do with it?"

It turns out the box is surprisingly easy to use. There are two settings: control and deactivation. "Deactivation is simple," Giles explains. "You just select the chip you want to deactivate and give the command."

I select the control setting. An image of Giles's room appears above the box. The objects and us are outlined like a pencil sketch. Giles shows me how to zoom in and out. "I haven't fully tested the range, but it's likely to be fairly limited."

A pulsing dot flashes in a corner of the room. "Is that a chip?"

He nods. "It's one I've been using for testing. Select it."

I press my finger to the dot and a command box appears.

"Now you just tell it what you want to do. Keep things simple though – one command at a time. You can select multiple chips by keeping your finger on this part of the box." He demonstrates. "Then you can give one command to all of them."

"What about the captains? Will they show up any different?"

Giles nods. "They'll show as red dots. That's their second chip. You can control their actions using this, but I'm not sure if you can replace the directions they're giving to the officers. So, to be sure, you'll need to deactivate them." He hesitates. "Just ... make sure they're somewhere safe, okay? Deactivation will be a disorientating experience for any officer. They'll be vulnerable."

I nod and draw in a breath. "Okay. Thanks." I give him a weak smile. "I'll take care of it."

He hands me a strap so I can hang the box around my neck. I tuck it inside my jacket. It creates an awkward bulge but at least it's out of the way.

As I turn to leave, a thought strikes me. Something Samson had said, that I'd forgotten about until now.

All Metz officers have had their chips reset. Your rogue officer won't be rogue anymore.

"Giles, what happens if the officers have their chips reset? Back at the compound?"

He glances up at me. "It means any memories they've retained since the last reset will be wiped. Sometimes they'll reset chips if they think there's a fault."

"How about the officer I mentioned? The one I talked to. If he had his chip reset ... he wouldn't recognize me?"

Giles shakes his head. "Probably not."

He walks over to the thick curtain blocking the entrance to the tunnel. "Good luck, Aleesha. And remember, *they* are people

317

too."

I step through into the dark tunnel and the curtain closes behind me. The box hangs heavy around my neck as I crawl toward the light.

* * *

To my surprise, when I emerge from the tunnel entrance, it's already late morning. I must have slept for longer than I thought.

Immediately, I get the sense that something is wrong. The air tastes of smoke. There's often smoke from hobie fires, but this is different. Besides, even hobies tend to stay away from the concrete jungle.

I step out from behind the concrete blocks that hide the entrance to Giles's tunnel and stare. Black smoke rises from fires across the city. Sounds of violence carry on the breeze. More violence than normal, that is. On the wasteland that separates the jungle from the rest of the city, people lie as if asleep.

Except they're not asleep.

I scramble down from my vantage point, scanning the area for any sign of danger. A flash of movement catches my eye and I duck behind a low block, then peer around it. A figure darts out from the rubble and moves between the bodies on the ground, patting them down. I recognize the slight build and the capering movement. It's one of the Boots Brothers.

Raiding the dead? No surprises there.

He moves closer to the Wall. There are a couple of bodies right up against it and I wonder if they were pushed into the Wall or ran into it willingly to avoid something worse. It seems the Metz have finally made their move.

The man pulls the first body away from the Wall, dragging it along the rough ground by its feet. He doesn't see the Metz officer emerging from a dark alleyway, but someone else does. There's a shout from the rubble. The man looks up and begins to run. But he's too late. There's a crack as the officer fires, and the man falls to the ground screaming and clutching his leg, his body convulsing as an electric shock ripples through him.

I hesitate for a moment. *Leave him. The Metz would be doing everyone a favour by getting rid of them.*

But this seems as good an opportunity as any to test out Giles's device. If it doesn't work, I can retreat back into the rubble pile and rethink.

The officer walks over to the man who's screaming for his brother. I wonder what his brother will do. Whether he'll go to his twin's aid or stay hidden and save his own skin.

A knife whistles through the air and bounces off the officer's helmet.

You'll have to do better than that.

I creep a little closer and tuck myself behind a concrete block out of sight of the Boots Brothers and the officer. I pull the black box out of my jacket and activate it as Giles had shown me.

An image of the surrounding area appears in the air. It's a little tricky to get the hang of moving the hologram around but I manage to zoom in on the officer looming over a writhing figure on the ground. They seem to be near the limit of the range, perhaps a hundred metres away. A green dot pulses on the back of the officer's head.

I select the dot and the command box appears. The outline of the officer raises its weapon and points it at the man on the ground, who raises his arms to ward off the blow.

319

"Lower weapon," I whisper.

The words appear in the command box, and a fraction of a second later the officer lowers its weapon.

It works!

I try again. "Turn around and take two steps forward."

There's a slight delay while the device registers and passes on the command, then the black figure slowly turns and takes a couple of steps toward me. My pulse quickens, and I feel a rush of adrenaline.

Another figure emerges from the rubble. I watch on the display as the man crosses the space to his brother, then turns and creeps up behind the Metz officer, a knife raised above his head.

At the last minute, the officer turns, swiping at the man's arm. The knife flies through the air and the force of the blow knocks the man to the floor. The officer stands over him, impassive.

I bite my lip. Why did he attack? Perhaps there's some built-in defence mechanism.

"Stay still. Do not defend yourself." I peer around the concrete block. The second brother gets to his feet, eying the officer cautiously. He retrieves his knife and, without warning, launches himself forward and brings the knife down on the officer's back.

This time the officer does nothing to defend itself. But the knife scrapes harmlessly down the impenetrable armour. The man throws himself at the figure again, but his weight is barely enough to make the officer rock on its feet.

"Taser attacker in the leg," I murmur into the command box. Best put the Boots Brothers out of action for now.

The officer raises its weapon and the man falls to the ground wailing. I step out from my hiding place and walk over to them.

There's a flash of recognition in the first brother's eyes.

"You!" His thin lips twist into a grimace as he reaches for his knife.

"Point weapon at men."

He freezes as the barrel of the officer's gun is aimed at his head. His eyes flick to me and back to the officer. "You control it?"

"Seems like it," I say with a smile.

The command box flashes, confused by the command. *Damn, this thing needs a mute button.*

I chew my lip, wondering what to do. I don't want to deactivate the officer here, but I also don't want it wandering around Area Four.

"Return to compound," I instruct.

The black figure turns and begins to walk away.

I turn back to the twins. "Remember, you owe me one," I say, hoping I've made the right choice. Perhaps it would have been better for everyone if I'd just let the officer kill them both. But if there's one thing I've learned from life, it's that it's always worth being owed favours.

I tuck the box back into my jacket and walk toward the sound of fighting.

At first, I wonder where everyone is. Fires rage out of control, fuelled by the piles of rubbish that litter the streets. There are a few bodies and a couple of people who are too close to death to help, but everyone else seems to have disappeared.

The sound of sobbing catches my attention. I follow it and find a young woman, hunched over, her arms wrapped around a young child. She looks up in alarm at the sound of my approach, but her face relaxes as she catches sight of me.

I crouch down beside her. "What happened?"

She looks up at me and opens her arms to reveal the bloodied face of a young boy, perhaps two years old. His face is peaceful, as if he's sleeping, but his skin is pale and his chest still.

"The Metz. They came so quickly ... We had no warning. We tried to run but they were everywhere."

She's bleeding too, from a shallower wound on her forehead.

"We got caught in the middle of a fight. Everyone was fighting each other to get away from them." This triggers a fresh bout of sobbing.

"Where did they go?" I ask, looking up and down the street.

"I-I don't know. They were everywhere ... and then they were gone. Everyone was gone, like they'd been herded away."

My blood chills. I pat the woman's shoulder and stand, quickening my pace as I move further north and east.

I need a plan. I can't just stop them one at a time. And sending them all back to the compound is no use. We need to take them out of action. But without hurting them.

I duck into a side alley and come face to face with Jay. His face is smeared with dirt and fresh blood leaks from a slash on his shoulder. Jonas is two steps behind him, along with another member of the Snakes whose name I can't remember.

Jay doesn't look pleased to see me. "Aleesha? Wh—"

"What's going on?"

He scowls at me. "Metz raid. A big one. We barely got ten minutes warning and we only got that because I went against what Samson had said and upped the Cleaning watch."

You mean you took my advice.

But, of course, he's not going to admit that.

"What about the other gangs? And Samson – what's he been doing?"

Jay looks angry. "That—" He bites his lip. "He told us not

to fight, but what could we do? They raided the headquarters. They've never hit us that hard before. We've been fightin' back, tryin' to protect people, but they're just too hard to take down."

"I have something that can stop them," I say quietly.

"We need more weapons. Guns. Do you think the taser bullets they use would work on them?"

Jonas gives him a dig in the ribs. "Err, Jay. She said she can stop 'em."

Jay gives me a disbelieving look. "You what?"

I pull the box out from under my jacket. "This is a control device. It overrides the instructions the Metz get."

Jay reaches out a hand, but I pull back. "I'm the only one who can use it. It's linked to my voice."

His eyebrows knit together. "How does it work?"

"It would take too long to explain." *Especially to you.* "But I need to get through to where the most Metz officers are. It'll take me too long to pick them off one at a time. I need your help."

Jay considers this for what feels like an age. I tap my foot and glance at Jonas. He shrugs sympathetically.

"Fine," Jay says eventually. "They've been through this part of Four and down to the river. Far as we can tell, they're sweepin' up north. Toward Rose Square."

Rose Square. The irony doesn't escape me.

I take a deep breath. "Okay, let's go."

Jay's eyes flick to a point just over my shoulder and widen.

"Go where?" Samson enquires from behind me.

Someone is cursing me today.

I turn to face him. "We're going to stop the Metz." I fold my arms awkwardly across the bulge in my jacket. "Let's talk on the way."

His eyes narrow and flick to my chest. I lower my voice. "Please? I'm on *your* side. Kind of."

"Let's go," Samson says authoritatively, as if he'd just made the decision. "Jay, find the best way through. I need to speak with Aleesha."

Jay doesn't look happy about being ordered around but he mutters to the others and they move off. I walk after them, forcing Samson to follow me.

"What are you playing at? And what are you carrying in your jacket?"

My neck prickles at his proximity. If I were taller, I'd be able to feel his breath on my neck. The thought sends a shiver down my spine and I feel a flash of anger that he can still intimidate me with just his presence.

"So, this is how your plan for protecting Outsiders played out?" I spit. "Do you even care how many people have died so far today?"

"I care," Samson says tightly. "More than you will ever realize."

I stop and turn to face him. "You could have stopped all of this!" I jab a finger in his chest. "If you and the President are so close, why didn't you stop it?" I swallow and try to draw a breath, but it catches in my throat.

He brushes my hand away. "Don't you think I tried?" His eyes tighten. "I asked him for more time, so I could try to get the gangs to cooperate."

"If you hadn't ordered them not to fight, to take people off Cleaning watch—"

"Would it really have made that much difference against an army?" he snarls. "Don't be too quick to accuse, Aleesha. You're hardly blameless yourself."

I take a step backward. He rises above me like a shadow, the whites of his eyeballs the only light in the dark. It feels as if the air is snatched from my lungs.

He's right. I should have done more.

I clutch at my chest, but my hand closes instead around the square box.

"Are you comin' or not?" Jay shouts from further up the alley.

I tug the box out with trembling hands. "There is a way to stop it. It's a control box. Don't ask me where I got it from. And I'm the only one who can use it – it's voice activated. I've tested it. I can control the Metz. Or shut them down altogether."

Samson's eyes widen. "You can override their orders?"

"Yes. But I need to be in close range. We need to do one group, then move on to another." I bite my lip. "I-I need your help."

His brows knit together. "To get you in there?"

I nod. "And protect the Metz."

"What?"

It's the first time I've seen real surprise on his face. In fact, any expression other than annoyance or anger.

"Guys!" Jay again.

I turn and begin walking. Samson follows. "If I stop them attacking Outsiders, they'll be defenceless. People will butcher them. You need to make sure people don't attack them once they're inactive."

"Let me get this straight. You want *me* to protect the *Metz*?"

I glance up over my shoulder at him. "Yes."

"Why?"

"Because they're people. Just like you and me. At least, not exactly like us ... but without the suits and the chips in their heads, they're people. We can't just kill them."

We walk in silence for a minute. The sound of fighting gets louder and the streets get busier, mostly with people running away.

"And why did you think I would help you with this?"

"Because you said you cared about helping everyone. Insiders and Outsiders. And there's no one else," I say flatly. "If you won't help them, I'll have to send them back to the compound. Back into *their* hands."

Another silence. "Okay, I'll help." He sounds reluctant. "But they'll need to be together. In one place, ideally inside."

There's a shout from up ahead. We've found the Metz.

"Rose Square," I say over my shoulder. "Just get me to Rose Square."

28

Trey

I run blindly from street to street, jumping over prone figures and dodging fights. Smoke stings my eyes, blurring my vision as tears leak out and run down my cheeks. Shots ring in my ears, but I'm not sure if they're shooting at me or someone else. Or perhaps it's just the echoes of the bullets that peppered Matthews' chest.

I stumble down another alley. An alley that leads to nowhere.

Slumped against a door, I stare at the brick wall in front of me and gasp for breath. My lungs burn and my hand shakes as I raise it to wipe my eyes. But I'm still holding the knife. Somehow, I've kept hold of it all this time. I almost have to prise my fingers off it to replace it in the sheath.

I stare down at the ground. Matthews and Jameson are dead. The box didn't work and is probably smashed to smithereens now anyway.

"What happens now?" I ask aloud.

But I'm alone in the alleyway, not even an old hobie around to give me an answer.

Then we're in for a fight.

Bryn's words come back to me. But how can you win a fight against an enemy that's almost impossible to kill?

Maybe we can't win. But we can still fight. Dad said I'd never be able to break Aleesha out of the government headquarters and that if I tried to rescue her, we'd never escape. But I did it.

Dad.

My chest constricts, and my throat goes tight. *Did the Chain get his body home before all this started? Or is he lying alone in a room somewhere, waiting for someone to return for him?*

I push the thought away. I can't think about that now. Except that the harder I push, the more vivid the image becomes in my head. Without really thinking, I walk back to the entrance to the alleyway and peer out. The street is empty. Doors hang off their hinges, boarded-up windows have been smashed open and a thin trickle of smoke weaves from a burned-out shop. But there are no Metz around.

I'm alone. In a place I don't belong. I close my eyes and lean back against the wall. *Maybe I should just go home. Tell Mother what happened. Find Father's body and take him home.*

Abby was right. I'm no fighter. And why should I help these people? They wouldn't help me. I shuffle up the street. In the distance, the top of the Wall rises above the dilapidated apartment blocks. Once through it, I'll be safe.

Not really safe. They'll still be after you Inside.

Maybe. But not today. Not when *this* is going on.

Further up the street, a group of hobies are clustered around a body on the floor. I'm reminded of the first time I came through the Wall, all those weeks ago. When the hobies had attacked me and stolen my coat.

Nothing changes.

I cross to the opposite side of the street, ready to run if need be. But their demeanour is different. They're not pawing at the body, searching it for chits or food. They're ... stroking it? Two of them are crying. Rough, angry sobs, as if they're embarrassed about it.

One of them looks up at me. The side of his face is bruised, and when he holds up a hand I see a bloody piece of cloth roughly wrapped around it.

"They killed 'im," he says shakily. "Why do they do it? He ain't done nothin' wrong."

He pulls back, revealing the body of his friend. Though the dead man's hair is lank and filthy, they've smoothed it away from his face and laid him out with his hands crossed on his chest. One of the men spits onto a grey cloth and wipes the blood off his fallen friend's face.

"We were going to take 'im to the river. But they're swarming down there." He looks down sorrowfully. "Can't even give the dead some dignity, can they?"

I shake my head. "I-I'm sorry."

"You lost someone, lad?" an old woman asks. At least she looks old; she's probably no more than forty.

I nod, tears pricking my eyes. "Yes."

She stands and walks over to me. A stench of body odour and rotten food washes over me and I have to force myself not to recoil. She reaches out a dirt-crusted hand and gently pats my arm. "You should head that way." She points to a road further up the street. "Bill said they're heading to Five, but if you can get past 'em up to Six, mebbe you'll be safe there. They'll likely be round 'ere with the cleanin' bots once they've finished off the fightin'."

I look down into her bright eyes, and behind the tiredness and grief I see a spark of determination. "We stick together out 'ere. They might be 'shamed of us and want rid of us, but we're tough to kill off." She glances back sadly at the body on the floor.

"'Ee went down fighting."

The lump in my throat gets thicker. *And I thought they were going to attack me. Presumed they were raiding the dead, not mourning a friend. What kind of person does that make me?*

I place my hand over hers. Her skin is warm and rough. "Thanks for the directions. But I'm going that way." I glance back down the street to where I last heard the sounds of violence.

The woman's face wrinkles in concern. "But that's where the fightin' is."

I pat her hand gently. "Exactly."

A toothy smile splits her face. "Careful, lad. You look like a smart one. Yer not big enough to take 'em down, but mebbe you'll think of some other way."

I hurry down the street. The box may not have worked but there may be another chance to change the tide of the fight. One I bet the Chain won't have thought of.

Rogue. He'll be out there somewhere. I just have to find him.

As the noise of violence grows louder, my heart begins to race and adrenaline powers my legs. Dizziness washes over me. I think back to my lessons with Aleesha. What had she said? *You have to control your breathing. Control the adrenaline – don't let it take you over.*

I slow my pace slightly and try to breathe evenly. The dizziness passes.

A man staggers past me, bleeding heavily from a wound on his leg.

"Where are the Metz?"

"They seem to be heading to Rose Square. Dunno if they're trying to herd people there or what."

"How do I get there?" I call after his retreating back.

"Right, left, then right again. But it's a bloodbath. I'd stay away if you want to live."

A bloodbath.

I run into the first Metz on the next street. There are three of them, fighting a group of about ten men and women. One guy has managed to wrestle a gun off one of the officers, but as I watch, he gives up trying to figure out how to fire it and takes to beating the officer over the head.

I skirt just close enough to check the officers' codes. None of them are Rogue. I duck left down the next alley and follow it up to another street. Finally, I'm somewhere I recognize. I'm pretty sure this road runs parallel to Rose Square.

There are lots of Metz on this street, some searching houses and dragging people out from hiding, others engaging with Outsiders. But for every person they shoot down or throw aside, another person steps forward to take their place. It's like they're trying to overwhelm the officers with sheer numbers.

My step falters. *How am I ever going to find Rogue in this lot?*

I'm jolted to one side by a man backing away from a looming dark figure. His face looks familiar. Half of his head is shaved, and the other half is braided to his neck. I step back as he raises his arm and deals the officer a blow on the hand with a nail-studded club.

The Metz officer pulls back, dropping its weapon. The man stoops down to retrieve it, revealing a snake tattoo that winds around his neck.

There's a shout from above followed by a crash. The black figure sways from side to side then slowly topples to the ground. A scatter of cheers erupts from the surrounding Outsiders who swarm over the figure, tugging weapons free from its belt.

"Damn thing won't work," the man in front of me mutters, turning the device over in his hands.

I step forward. "It may be programmed to only work for them."

The man looks up and frowns. "Do I know you?"

"I, err ... know Aleesha."

Recognition dawns on his face. "Oh yeah. I'm Jonas. You with that Chain lot?"

"Not exactly. Have you seen Aleesha?"

Jonas nods. "Yeah, she's over there. Says she's got something that can stop 'em. The Metz, that is. We're tryin' to get her up to Rose Square."

My heart leaps as I follow his gaze. But I can't see Aleesha, just a crowd of people who seem to be trying to force their way through a line of Metz officers to a narrow street. They look more coordinated than most groups of Outsiders. A huge black man – almost as big and bulky as the Metz officers – seems to be in charge.

What has she got?

"Coming?" Jonas asks.

I nod, but he's already taken off, running toward the crowd, gun in hand. I wipe my sweaty palm on my pants and pull the knife from my belt.

Be brave.

But my legs are shaking as I set off down the road. The crowd of people has broken through the line. They're running up the street. I walk faster, then break into a run. But when I'm about ten paces away, the line of officers closes up again and I skid to a halt.

One of them raises its gun. I stare into the barrel.

"Don't move," a voice says quietly in my ear. "If you don't attack they probably won't shoot."

Probably?

I take a step back and feel hot breath on my neck.

"There's an alley on the left. Ready to run?"

I nod, not trusting myself to speak.

"Run."

I run.

Bullets whizz past me. There's a sharp pain in my shoulder, another from my ear, but I keep running. The crack of the gun drowns out all other sounds. A weight hits my back, propelling me forward into the shelter of the alleyway. There's a crash from the street and a volley of shouts. People run toward the line of officers, brandishing weapons.

The young man who'd fallen on me lies face down at my feet. I crouch down and roll him over. He's younger than I'd thought, perhaps thirteen, with dark hair cropped short. A dark stain on his chest slowly spreads outward. I touch it and my fingers come back covered in blood. A familiar wave of nausea turns my stomach.

The boy's eyes flutter open and he lets out a low moan. For a second our eyes meet, and he opens his mouth, trying to communicate something. Then his eyes roll back and his head falls to one side.

I reach out and gently close his eyelids, then pull his body to one side of the alley and place his hands on his chest. "I'll come back for you," I whisper.

If I survive.

Then I turn and run up the alley to Rose Square.

Smoke rises from the south part of the square, the black skeletons of the market stalls just visible above the crowd. The rest of the square is a sea of black, but at street level it's impossible to see what's going on.

I kick down a door into the building to my right and run two floors up. Numbered apartments lead off the landing, but one of the doors is slightly ajar. I run inside and over to the window.

The guy with the leg wound had been right. The Metz are herding people into the square. They're lined up in the far north corner: men, women and children, ringed by Metz officers. Guns pointing in.

On the opposite side of the square lie the wounded and dead. Anyone who can't stand. That's where most of the screams are coming from. Across the rest of the square, more people are being herded in. There are pockets of fighting but too many Metz for it to make a difference.

Except in one area.

A group of Outsiders are slowly but surely making their way toward the statue. The front line holds makeshift shields in front of them. Metal doors, trash can lids and what look to be pieces of Metz armour. They use them to push the Metz back. Behind them, others fire guns or throw bottles filled with some kind of explosive.

The Metz shoot back. Some of the Outsiders fall. But still they keep going.

At the centre is the tall black man with the dreadlocks. He seems immune to the bullets whizzing around him as he shouts orders and throws impossibly large missiles at the officers. Following in his shadow is Aleesha. She's hunched over, clutching something to her chest.

I turn to leave, but a movement near the wounded people catches my eye. A woman with long dark hair is pushing through the line of Metz, a familiar dark green bag slung over one shoulder.

Abby.

I run for the stairs. Something tells me the Metz aren't going to take kindly to anyone interfering with their plans.

I burst through the door, but I've barely taken two steps when someone barrels into me, knocking me to the ground.

"Trey?"

I gasp, the air knocked from my lungs by the impact.

A hand grabs my arm and pulls me to my feet. I lurch to the side, somewhat unsteadily. Bryn's face looms into view.

"I thought I told you to stay out of this! You're bleeding. Are you hurt?"

Bleeding?

I reach my hand up to my ear and it comes away wet. "I'm fine. Abby—"

"Where is she?" The colour drains from Bryn's face and his grip on my arm tightens.

"With the wounded." I point across the square. "I think they're—"

But Bryn is already off. I run after him, trying to follow in his wake as he ploughs between Metz officers, pushing them and Outsiders aside in his haste. A man tumbles to the floor and I jump to avoid him but my foot catches on his leg and I'm sent flying.

I crawl to my knees, but the gap ahead of me has closed.

A foot catches me in the stomach. I gasp for air, stars dancing across my vision. Then I'm being dragged along the ground.

I barely have time to figure out what's happening before I'm tossed like a limp doll onto a pile of bodies.

Underneath me, somebody groans.

"Gerroff!"

Feeble hands roll me over and I hit the dirt again.

"Sorry," I gasp.

A cry of terror rips through the moans of the wounded. I

twist around, just in time to catch sight of Abby, her hands outstretched as if to ward off the huge black figure in front of her, a trailing white bandage unravelled in her grip.

I scramble to my feet, knowing I'm already too late, that there are too many people between me and her. I lurch forward, jumping over prone figures in my haste.

"Abby!"

Bryn's voice, coming from the right. He fights his way past the Metz lining the square. Two officers lie on the floor in his wake, clutching at their knees.

Abby turns at the cry and, at that moment, the officer brings the butt of its gun down on her head and she crumples to the floor.

No!

I try to move faster but there are just too many people. I glance down to find my footing, and when I look up Bryn is almost there. Another officer intervenes. Bryn lashes out but the officer swipes at his arm and I catch the glint of steel as his knife cartwheels through the air.

Abby lies motionless on the floor beside a gibbering man who looks like he's praying. That or begging for his life. The officer hovers its gun between him and Abby as if unsure who to shoot first.

It decides on Abby.

Time seems to slow. I'm still ten metres away.

It takes aim.

Bryn launches himself at the officer's arm.

The shot goes wide, bouncing off the helmet of an officer a few feet away who staggers back. Bryn falls to the ground, almost landing on top of Abby. The officer swipes at him, dealing a hard backhand that whips his head around with a crack.

Five metres. Three more prone figures.

The officer lowers the gun, pointing it at Bryn, who shakes his head, dazed.

Three metres.

Somehow the knife is still in my hand. *Throw it?* No. I'm no Aleesha. I'd probably hit Bryn or something.

Bryn tries to get to his knees. To shield Abby's body with his own.

"Stop!"

The officer's head turns a fraction toward me. Bryn launches himself forward, but the officer throws him to one side.

I leap over the final man and run into it. Literally. It stands there placidly as I wheeze, then it reaches out a hand to shove me aside.

"Wait! Let's … talk about this."

Talk about this? What are you doing?

I need a plan. I have no plan.

Then I catch sight of the number on the officer's chest. ML486.

"Rogue?" I whisper.

The figure doesn't move.

"Rogue, it's me, Trey," I say more urgently.

He knows who I am. Doesn't he?

"Trey, get out of the way!" Bryn staggers to his feet.

"No, you don't understand. This is th—"

A gloved hand connects with my cheek. Pain lances through my jaw and my legs collapse underneath me.

I look up into the barrel of a gun. Behind it a blank mask. The hope that had surged through me dissolves into fear.

I close my eyes and wait for the shot to be fired.

29

Aleesha

They crowd around me as we move across Rose Square. My arms are pressed tight to my side, and though I stumble occasionally as we push through the tide of Metz officers, the press of people around me means I never fall. My protectors.

They're a mix of people. Some are Samson's – the core members of the Brotherhood – the rest are Snakes. I know them all by sight, if not by name. Which makes it all the harder when they're cut down.

I want to help fight but I don't even have space to draw my knife. Even if I did, I'm too short to throw it over the heads of the people surrounding me. I clutch the box to my chest to protect it from the buffeting and wonder if I can get it out here, to stop the Metz who are standing in our way. But it's too chaotic. I doubt I could even bring up the display, let alone select the small dots representing the chips.

We have to get to the monument. There I'll have some space to see.

At one point I glance up and catch sight of a figure standing in a window looking out over the square. They must have a good vantage point. *I should have thought of that.*

I shake my head. No, Giles said the device had limited range.

I must take it to the centre of the fighting.

Our arrowhead is breaking through the ranks of officers. We're pressing forward. Not far now.

Samson looms over me, shouting orders and throwing wire baskets of stones passed up by the people behind. It seems the Metz guns don't work against them, so taking them out by sheer force is the only option. Relieved of their burden, the carriers step forward to replace the people who fall or are swept aside by the black army.

"Statue!"

The shout comes back from the front of the column. The point of the arrowhead has made it.

"Surround it!" Samson bellows.

We surge forward and I almost trip as my feet hit the lower steps leading up to the statue. The steps where Andrew Goldsmith met his death less than twenty-four hours ago.

I shake my head. I can't think about that now.

You have a chance to right the wrong.

From the top of the steps, I survey Rose Square. The south part of the square is swarming with Metz. In the north part lie the dead and wounded. Across from them, people are lined up in rows as if awaiting execution. The Metz have a plan, and it looks as if we don't have much time.

"We'll hold them off as long as possible." Samson draws a pair of long-nosed guns from his belt. "Be as quick as you can. We're exposed."

A quick glance around confirms this. We're in full sight of the Metz. And their guns.

I activate the device and an image of the surrounding area appears in the air above it. It extends almost to the boundaries of the square. Dots flash everywhere, mostly green with a few red ones sprinkled among them.

The captains. I'll take them out first.

But it's easier said than done. The dots are so closely packed that I have to zoom into an area to separate them out and select individual ones. It's painstaking. And I can't tell if stopping the captains has any effect on the officers they control.

I'm dimly aware of Samson on one side of me, firing across the heads of the Outsiders ringing the foot of the statue. On the other side, Jay and Jonas hold makeshift shields up to protect me.

I change my tactics. Take out the immediate threats to us first, then get the rest. Zooming in on the area around the statue, I select ten of the closest flashing dots and activate the command box.

"Stop fighting."

I move to another area, select another ten and repeat the command.

There's a shout of surprise from someone on the other side of the statue.

Is it working?

A bullet whizzes past my ear. I look up, trying to spot where the shots are coming from. More black figures seem to be converging on us. They must be able to see the holo. Do they know what I'm doing?

I search for the red dots. They're spread out, but I go through them one at a time, each time repeating the command to stop fighting.

There's a puff of dust as a bullet ricochets off the stone step beside me. I try to focus on the display but it's hard. My heart hammers in my head, mingling with the sounds of screams, gunfire and clashes of metal.

Samson ducks down beside me. "Can you get them to go away?" he gasps. "They may not be fighting but they're stopping us getting to the others behind."

He stands and shouts something to the people on the other side of the statue. Looking up, I see he's right. The Metz officers immediately surrounding the statue look as if they're made of stone themselves. A couple of the Snakes attempt to push them back but it's like trying to move buildings.

A yell of pain makes me look up. Jonas is bent over, shielding his shoulder. His face is twisted in pain. Jay shouts at him and he turns toward me. For a second our eyes meet.

"Jonas, y—"

"Just stop them." He manages to smile through his pain and there's an odd look in his eyes that I don't recognize. "Please." He pushes his shoulders back and raises the thick, battered piece of metal he's using as a shield. At least one bullet has passed straight through it.

I swallow and turn my attention back to the display. I'm the only one who can stop them. I just need to work faster. I select the flashing dots immediately in front of us.

"Line up in the south part of the square."

The black figures turn and begin to push back through their companions. Adrenaline courses through me as I pull together the next group of officers. "Stop f—"

A heavy weight lands on top of me, knocking me over. The edge of a step digs painfully into my ribs. The box lands with an ominous crack on the step below. "Command not understood. Please repeat," it intones.

Stars jump in front of my eyes as I push myself up, twisting to throw the weight off my back. I stare in horror as Jonas's body flops limply down in front of me. Blood spills from gunshot wounds to his shoulder, chest and leg. But the one that killed him is right in the centre of his forehead.

The shield he'd been using to protect me – leaving him exposed – is still clutched in one hand.

"Aleesha!"

Jay's shout jolts me out of my shock. He rests the bulletproof window shutter he's using as a shield on the step beside me. It looks heavy. His body trembles with exhaustion and blood runs down his arm and over the gun in his hand. He jerks his head out over the crowd. "Stop them!"

I nod dumbly and pick up the box with shaking hands. The display flickers and then goes steady. It's too time-consuming to match individuals on the ground to the shapes on the display, so I just zoom in on the general area where the shots are coming from and select as many of the flashing dots as possible. "Stop fighting and line up in the south part of Rose Square."

Almost immediately, the dots begin to move off. I repeat the procedure.

"Can you not just turn them off?" Jay yells.

I shake my head but the nagging voice in my head chides me.

If you deactivate them, they'd be disorientated and lost. Easy to take down.

And my friends are dying.

But I promised Giles.

My fingers fly over the display, selecting officers and sending them over to the south part of the square. It's almost like the VR games some of the Snakes play. At least it would be if the consequences weren't so real.

The sound of fighting eases and I take the opportunity to stand up and look around.

Rows of officers are lined up in the south part of the square as if awaiting inspection. Some Outsiders are prodding them, but most people are still embroiled in fighting the officers I haven't managed to stop yet.

There are still so many of them.

"Abby!"

The cry rings out over the sounds of clashes and gunshots. I know that voice. *Bryn!* I whirl around, scanning the square for him.

I see Trey first, stumbling across a pile of bloody bodies, and my breath catches in my throat. The Metz guarding the area have raised their weapons. He'll be caught in a crossfire. My hand shakes as I find the officers on the display unit and tell them to turn around.

Then I spot Abby, standing with her medic bag, her hands warding off the black figure looming over her, gun raised. Bryn's trying to get to her, somehow barrelling through the officers like a one-person tornado.

"Aleesha, the next lot are coming!" Samson shouts from the other side of the statue.

I follow his gaze. The officers surrounding the lined-up Outsiders are filtering off and coming toward us.

I glance back to Abby and hesitate.

Which to do first?

"Aleesha, now!"

A barrage of shots rains overhead. Samson lets out a yell of pain. There's a sharp prickling sensation on my shoulder.

I select a load of the marching dots at random and tell them to turn around. *That should slow the rest of them down.*

A shot rings out from the other side of the square and my heart stops.

No!

Abby is motionless on the floor. Bryn's beside her, clinging to the officer's arm as it tries to shake him off. Trey's still moving but a couple of officers have spotted him and are raising their guns.

I have to stop them.

My fingers are already on it, picking the officers just as they begin to fire. "Stop fighting." No time for anything else and I seem to have lost the ability to string words together anyway.

Bryn is thrown to one side and Trey's standing in front of the black figure. Just ... standing.

I zoom in on them and stab my finger at the green flashing dot. But my hand's shaking so much that I miss.

Damn.

The barrel of his gun is pointing at Trey's head. *Move, you idiot!*

I try again. This time my finger connects and the command box pops up.

"Stop fighting!"

A shot fires.

I stare at the display, then up across the square. The officer is motionless, the hand holding the gun hanging by his side. In front of him kneels Trey, swaying slightly, his eyes wide in shock. Bryn writhes on the ground, clutching his shoulder.

I reach a hand to my own shoulder, mirroring his action. It burns, a steady, throbbing pain that radiates out. Blood leaks from my torn top. The bullet must have skimmed the surface.

Later. Think about it later.

I push the pain away and focus on the display in front of me. I work more methodically now, trying to block out the noises around me and focus on selecting groups of officers and sending them down to the south part of the square. I lose track of time and what's happening around me.

Samson slumps down beside me. "Nearly there." He pulls a dressing from his pocket and tears it open with his teeth. "Good work." He presses the dressing over his arm and winces. "Damn Metz guns don't work for us. Must be configured to the user, like your box."

"Guess so." I find the last few fighting officers and order them to join their silent, still companions. I lean back and scrub the sweat from my forehead. My throat is so dry I can barely swallow and my eyes sting. I close them, but Abby's motionless body appears in my mind, and I can't deal with that right now.

"We've still got to get the ones outside the square."

Samson nods. "But this has to be most of them, around this area at least."

Jay stumbles over to us. His clothes are dark with blood and he's swaying unsteadily on his feet. "Is it over?"

"Not yet," Samson replies. "But soon. Here, eat this." He pulls a small bar from his pocket and hands it over.

Jay looks at it uncertainly, then rips it open and takes a bite. Samson pulls some more dressings from another pocket and holds them out. I take them from him and start to patch Jay up.

"What's that pod doin'?"

"Pod?" Samson turns sharply to follow Jay's gaze. "Damn."

"What is it?" I press the final dressing into place and turn to look.

A pod is flying in, so low it's almost skimming the rooftops. It's black with the distinctive yellow stripes of a Metz vehicle but much smaller than the usual troop carriers. And all in a rush, the adrenaline leaves my body and my legs collapse under me.

The Commander.

What saliva is left in my mouth takes on a bitter taste that coats the back of my throat. This is it then.

Samson looks to Jay. "Any bullets left? I'm out."

Jay pulls a gun from his belt and promptly drops it. It clatters down the steps. Samson reaches forward to retrieve it. I pull Jay down to sit on the step beside me. "Just eat the bar." He nods obediently. I wonder how much blood he's lost.

Defending you.

The pod swoops lower, coming in over the square. For a moment, I wonder if it's going to land but it's coming in too fast for that. Samson opens fire, but the bullets bounce off the pod as if they're nothing but pebbles. Something drops from its belly.

Then the world explodes.

There's a dull ringing in my ears and it feels as if time slows. My throat constricts as I wheeze, trying to draw in air. It's thick with dust, coating my mouth and throat and choking my lungs. I'm suffocating. My muscles spasm as I panic, my whole body fighting for oxygen. Spots dance in front of my eyes and a growing blackness threatens to overwhelm me.

I try to take a breath. A normal breath. And air finally makes it down to my lungs. The humming in my ears fades and running footsteps approach.

A hand pats me on the back. "Relax."

I manage to breathe in a bit more air. The choking dust and smoke have gone and the coughs wracking my body subside. Tentatively, I take a deeper breath.

"Drink." A water bottle is shoved into my hand and I gulp at it greedily.

Wiping my eyes, I look around. Katya is standing in front of me. Dirt is smeared across her face and a rough bandage is wrapped around her left arm, but somehow she still manages to look beautiful.

Murdoch is behind her. And behind him, looking down at his feet, is Trey.

I look away. "What happened?"

"They dropped explosives," Murdoch said. "We've been running around the streets for the past half hour trying to take the pod down, but the damn thing stays just out of range."

There's a small crater in the ground not five metres away. The top half of a man hangs out of it. The bottom half is missing. My stomach does a huge flip-flop and I tear my eyes away. But that wasn't the only bomb. The second hit the group of Metz officers neatly stood in rows, knocking them to the ground like toy soldiers.

"They hit their own people?" Samson frowns. His dark skin is grey with dust.

Katya shrugs. "Better lose them than hand over control to us." Her voice is hard. She glances at the box around my neck. "That's not Jameson's device. Where did you get it?"

I open my mouth to reply but Trey interrupts me. "It's coming back!"

Katya pulls something from her belt and glances at Murdoch, who nods. "If it comes that low again ... Clear this space," she orders.

I stare at the object in her hand. It's coil of silver cable with a looped padded handle at one end and what looks like a metal claw at the other. "What are y—"

"Don't argue, just get down!" Murdoch shouts.

I stumble backward down the steps. The pod has circled around and is coming back down from the north. Katya hands one end of the cable to Murdoch and crouches on top of the steps, her eyes never leaving the pod.

It drops low, clearly planning to make another run. Katya murmurs something under her breath to Murdoch, who nods.

The pod swoops toward us. Katya stretches her arm back and launches the metal hook into the air. The cable reels out behind it. The belly of the pod opens just as the hook curls around one of its landing rails.

"Now!" Katya yells.

Murdoch darts to the statue, the silver cable trailing from his hand.

The world explodes. But this time we're expecting it. My hands clamp down on my ears and I hold my breath, waiting for the dust to settle.

The cable begins to tighten. Murdoch's wrapped it twice around the base of the statue and is pulling back on the handle.

"It's slipping," he gasps, his feet skidding forward.

"Let me." Samson appears behind him and grasps the handle. He braces his feet against the base of the statue and heaves back.

From somewhere in the cloud of dust comes a sickening crash. The cable goes slack.

For a moment, we all just stand there. Slowly, I make my way down the steps, my sleeve pressed to my mouth. I cross the square, past the first crater and the body of the man who lost his legs. Past more still forms of men, women and Metz officers.

I follow the silver cable into the dust until the outline of the pod appears. It lies on the ground, half crumpled like a broken egg. I stop in front of it, wondering if whoever is inside can look out.

Katya comes to stand beside me. Samson moves to my other side.

I wonder how we can open it. If there's any way of getting in.

I'm not left wondering for long.
There's a hiss from the pod and the door begins to open.

30

Trey

The pod is half crushed into the ground. If anyone inside has survived, it would be a miracle. I peer over Aleesha's shoulder as the door slides open. I'm not sure what I'm expecting to see. A Metz officer?

The huge man with the long dreadlocks raises his gun and points it at the opening. The door sticks for a moment, and through the gap I see a thin man collapsed over a dashboard. He's dressed in one of those skin-tight suits and is clearly dead.

The opening widens, revealing a second man who's hunched in a half-crushed seat. Katya inhales sharply as the man turns his face slowly to us.

He's in a bad way. Blood pours down one side of his face, and the right side of his body appears to be trapped in the twisted metal of the pod. But I recognize his scarred face and those dark, malevolent eyes.

Recognition flickers in his eyes and his face twists into a snarl of rage. "You ..."

"Yes, me." Katya's voice is hard and cold.

The Commander tries to speak again but all that emerges from his mouth is a dribble of bloody saliva. His chest heaves with a shuddering breath and his head rolls back against the side of the pod.

"Wait!" Katya holds out an arm to stop Murdoch moving forward. She holds out her hand to the man with the dreadlocks. "Can I have that?"

"No way." He scowls at her. "But I'll check for you."

He steps forward and gingerly pokes the man in the chest, then the cheek, with his gun. He presses his fingers against the Commander's neck. "He's gone."

My breath comes out in a rush. I close my eyes and feel my body sway.

It's over.

We stand there in silence for a minute. Me, Aleesha, Katya, Murdoch, Jay and the black man. A gust of wind blows away the final traces of smoke and dust, and around us, people begin to stir. A ragged cheer breaks out from somewhere behind us, but the voices are quickly hushed.

It doesn't feel like a victory. Just an end.

A muffled crash comes from one of the streets leading off the square. "I should go and fetch the rest of them in," Aleesha says to no one in particular. Her voice is tired. She looks a wreck.

I look over at the Metz officers standing in file. There must be a hundred of them. Maybe more. Most Outsiders stay away, but some are prodding and poking them. Waiting to see if they'll fight back.

The man with the dreadlocks bends down to speak to Aleesha. "We need somewhere safer to put them," he says quietly. "Once people realize they're not going to wake up, it won't be long before they start trying to take them apart. I can't protect them out here."

Aleesha nods. She turns to Jay. "What about the headquarters? It's the only place I can think of that's big enough."

Jay looks in an even worse state than Aleesha, a far cry from the cocky man we'd bumped into on the street. Blood leaks through the dressings plastered over his body and he holds his right leg awkwardly. He runs a hand unsteadily over his stubble and gives a hoarse laugh. "Sure, I guess so. It's not as if there are many of us left to use it." He looks uncertain. "Not for long though, right?"

"Wait." Katya steps forward. She smiles at the tall black man and holds out a hand. "I don't believe we've met."

"We haven't." The man ignores her outstretched hand. "Though I may have run across some of your colleagues." His eyes flick briefly to Murdoch. He inclines his head slightly. "My name is Samson."

Oh. So, this is the leader of the Brotherhood. The man who betrayed me to the President.

And yet, Aleesha now seems to trust him. More than Katya and the Chain anyway. I wonder why.

"I'm Katya."

"I know."

They stare at each other like kids daring each other not to blink.

Aleesha brings up a display above the box. It's an outline image of the square, every figure sketched in detail. She zooms in on an area of flashing dots and begins tapping on them. It takes me a minute to figure out what they are. "The dots are the officers' implants?"

She nods but otherwise ignores me. When all the dots are selected, a command box appears. She murmurs something into it. A few seconds later there's a panicked shout from the far end of the square followed by a dull thumping sound.

The Metz are moving.

The display vanishes. "I told them to follow Jay to a large warehouse and line up inside." She frowns. "I tried to keep it as simple as possible, but perhaps I should go with them. I can pick up more of them on the way."

"Yes, you should." Jay's copper skin visibly pales at the thought of a hundred Metz officers trailing him along the street. *I don't blame him.*

Katya turns and holds out her hand. "I think you should give that device to me, Aleesha. You've done a good job. Thank you. But it's time for us to take over."

Aleesha tucks the box inside her jacket. "No can do. It only works for me. Besides, what would you do with them?"

Katya's eyes narrow. "We can use them against the government. Give them a taste of their own medicine."

"And then? If you do take the government down? What next?"

"I don't think I quite understand you." Katya's voice is like ice.

"What happens? Who takes charge? Who decides what happens to them?" Aleesha gestures toward the officers who have lined up in a trail leading halfway across the square.

Katya steps forward and lowers her voice. "We can discuss that later. Now just give me the box."

She reaches out but Aleesha takes a step back and folds her arms across her chest. "No. I ... I'm not going to let you treat them as machines. They're people."

Katya gives her a strange look. "*You're* protecting them? After what they've done to you? They killed your mother, remember? All your life they've hunted you." Her voice is low and intense. She gently places a hand on Aleesha's arm, and this time Aleesha doesn't pull away. "You need closure. You need to face your demons."

Something passes between them – something I don't understand, and I don't think anyone else does either. Then Katya's face falls and she lets her arm drop.

"I will face my demons in my own way," Aleesha says quietly. "Not by killing. There's been enough death here today."

Katya straightens. "Then I need to take that device off you. I'm sorry, Aleesha, but you don't understand the stakes here. It is too valuable a weapon."

Aleesha shifts slightly on her feet. I recognize her posture from our training sessions on the roof. She's getting ready to fight. "No," she says calmly.

Katya's eyes narrow. "Murdoch."

Murdoch gives Aleesha a sympathetic shrug and moves to grab her. Instead, he runs straight into Samson, who's somehow inserted himself in front of Aleesha. He moves fast for a big guy.

Murdoch sidesteps, but Samson blocks his path again. "I don't want to hurt you, but I will if you try anything." His voice is deep and menacing. It sends a shiver down my spine. Murdoch looks torn.

"It *is* a valuable weapon." Samson turns to Katya. "And whoever designed it has entrusted it to Aleesha. We should respect that."

Jay clears his throat. "Um, can we sort this out and go? They, err … seem to be waitin' for us." He waves to the Metz officers.

"Fine," Katya says through gritted teeth. "We've got enough to do today clearing this mess up. But we will meet to discuss this tomorrow." She glances at Aleesha. "I expect you to be there."

"I'll call the gang leaders together. We'll lay out the dead and do our best for the wounded." Samson's eyes are heavy and his shoulders slightly hunched, as if he's carrying a great weight. "Jay, I'll come and find you at your headquarters later. Don't leave anyone else in charge of the Metz."

Katya looks around and seems to notice me for the first time. "Ah, Trey. Have you seen Bryn?"

"He's over with the wounded. With Abby ..." My throat constricts, and I think if I say anything more I will start to cry so I clamp my teeth together. My eyes start to brim with tears, and I close them and breathe deeply through my nose.

When I open my eyes, Aleesha's staring at me, her face stricken. "Is she ...?"

I shrug, unable to speak. Part of me wants to run over to them now. But another part of me doesn't want to face what I'll find.

A young boy runs up and skids to a halt in front of Samson. He glances suspiciously at the rest of us. "They're pullin' back, boss. The rest of the Metz are headin' back up to the East Gate."

I close my eyes and the tension in my throat and chest eases slightly. *It really is over then.*

"And there's a man called Bryn and a dark-haired woman askin' for you," the boy continues. My eyes snap open. He's looking straight at me. "Yer Trey, right?"

I nod. "She ... she's alive?"

The boy shrugs. "Looked like it. Never seen dead people talk."

"Thank you," says Samson. "Now, I've got another job for you." He pulls the boy to one side and lowers his voice. The boy gives a couple of nods and runs off again.

I hesitate for a moment and a hand squeezes my shoulder. "Go on, lad, you're not needed here," Murdoch says gently.

I stumble away. The square is littered with bodies, most of them Outsiders, but there are Metz officers too. Sightless eyes stare into the milky grey sky. I've never seen so much death. So much destruction.

Is fighting for equality really worth this? If everyone dies, who is there left to fight for?

I find Bryn and Abby trying to treat the wounded. I throw my arms around Abby but pull back when she sways. "Sorry. I just thought ..." My words get choked up.

She blinks and shakes her head slightly, then smiles. "I know. I was out for a good few minutes, I think?"

"Five," growls Bryn. He's trying to secure a bandage around another man's leg with one arm and his teeth. I drop down to take it from him. "Thanks, Trey." He spits the bandage from his mouth. "Five minutes. I counted them."

I look at him and then back to Abby, who's still swaying. "I know you want to help, but ..."

"You look about to fall on your faces and add to the problem," a friendly voice says. A woman of about thirty with curly auburn hair stands with her hands on her hips. She wears a long overcoat with bandages and dressings stuffed in every pocket. "I'll take over here. Go and get some rest."

Abby smiles weakly at her. "Thanks, Amber."

The woman purses her lips. "You alright?"

Abby nods and winces. "Just one hell of a headache. I've got more supplies at home."

"Great. Now *get* home." The woman smiles.

Bryn gets to his feet. His left hand is tucked up in his jacket and blood seeps through the bandage across his shoulder. His eyes flick behind my shoulder and his forehead creases in a frown. "Aleesha."

I turn around slowly. She stands five metres away, uncertainty clouding her face. Her hands twist in front of her and she seems to be debating whether to come closer or run away.

Abby pushes past me, walks unsteadily over and pulls her into a hug.

"I'm sorry, I thought you w—" Aleesha's voice breaks and she squeezes her eyes shut, but not before a tear falls to Abby's shoulder. For a moment they cling to each other, then Abby gently pulls back. "I didn't know if ..." Aleesha's voice trails off and she looks at me. "I'm sorry."

I nod. "I know."

The familiar lance of pain strikes me again. But I don't feel the same anger I did before. Perhaps it's exhaustion. Or just that there has already been too much violence and anger today.

"Come back home?" Abby asks.

"I need to go to the Snakes' headquarters. They're taking the Metz officers there for now. To keep them safe." She hesitates.

"Come over after that," Bryn says, limping forward. "There's something I need to talk to you about."

Aleesha nods and turns to go.

I scramble after her. "Wait! Can ... can you give me a hand with something on the way?"

She looks puzzled but nods.

I turn to Bryn. "I'll catch you guys up."

We walk in silence across the square and down the alleyway.

He's still there. Lying alongside the wall, hands crossed on his chest.

"He saved me," I say, kneeling down and pressing the back of my hand to his cheek. His skin is cold to the touch, his jaw already stiffening in death. *He looks so young. Just a boy.* "I didn't even know his name."

A tear leaks from the corner of my eye and runs down my cheek. It drips off my chin and onto the boy's forehead. I wipe it off with my thumb.

"Shall we carry him up?" Aleesha asks quietly.

I nod.

He's heavy, but between the two of us we manage to carry him up the street and into the square. There's already a row of bodies lined up for identification. We put the boy down at the end and step back.

Aleesha moves along the line. She pauses, kneels beside a man and gently brings his hands up to rest on his chest. Bending over, she presses her forehead briefly to his clasped hands.

I walk over to her. The man's body is dotted with bullet wounds, but I recognize the snake tattoo and the unique half-braided hairstyle. "Jonas?"

She nods. "He died protecting me. He held his shield in front of me. And I ... I wasn't quick enough to save him." She stands and looks down the row of bodies. "Wasn't quick enough to save them."

"No one could." I reach out and touch her arm. "And you did save us. You and whoever created that box."

She shrugs me off and turns, wiping her sleeve across her eyes. "I'd better be going. Don't want to leave Jay alone with that lot. I-I'll see you in a bit."

"See you in a bit," I echo, but she's already running off across the square.

* * *

A few hours later, the three of us sit at Abby's kitchen table. One of her neighbours had come over shortly after we'd got back with pails of hot water. There was enough for us all to have a decent wash and for Abby to clean and dress Bryn's gunshot wound. I had to leave the room at that point, but I could still hear his shouts of pain, muffled by the piece of wood she'd given him to bite down on.

Why does it have to be like that? He should be able to go to a medic, like anyone else.

Like any Insider, I correct myself.

I stare down at the green herbs floating in the mug in front of me. I still catch myself thinking that way sometimes, though I feel more Outsider than Insider now. Perhaps I am both. Or neither.

Another neighbour donated us some food. From the shifty look in his eyes, I suspect it was stolen, but Abby thanked him anyway. Her eyes lit up when she unwrapped the parcel. "Chicken!"

Not real chicken, obviously. But in a stew with some freeze-dried vegetables and homemade dumplings, even I had to admit that it was hard to tell the difference.

Good food, clean clothes and a hot drink. Things I used to take for granted have become a rare treat.

The last portion of stew waits in the pot on the hotplate.

Abby yawns and pushes her hair back from her face. Bryn gives her a worried glance and she smiles. "It's okay, I'm just tired."

He frowns. "You shouldn't sleep yet. Not with that bang to your head. Any memories come back?"

Abby shakes her head and freezes, wincing. "I must stop doing that. No, I just remember leaving the house to go and help ... everything after that's a blank until I woke up."

The wind's picking up outside. The back gate slams. I glance out the window and catch sight of a dark figure. A moment later, there's a tentative knock on the door.

"Come in!" Abby calls.

The door opens. Aleesha stands on the step. Her clothing is torn and filthy, but the box still bulges under her jacket. She sways and reaches for the door frame to steady herself.

"Well don't just stand there, you're letting the cold in," Bryn says gruffly.

She stumbles inside and pushes the door shut. Leaning back on it, she glances around uncertainly.

"I saved you some dinner," Abby says, pushing her chair back. She ladles the remainder of the stew into a bowl and places it on the table. "It's still warm."

Aleesha's nostrils flare but she doesn't move. I look more closely at her face. Under the dirt and blood, a dark bruise stands out on her jaw.

I did that.

My hands clench around my mug.

Abby walks over to Aleesha and gently manoeuvres her into the spare chair next to Bryn. She places a spoon in her hand. "Eat. Then we talk."

Aleesha gulps the food down, barely swallowing. She scrapes the bowl with her spoon. "What was that? It was ... amazing."

"Stew. "Abby smiles and takes the bowl from her, replacing it with a steaming mug. "Drink this. It has chamomile and lavender, and a little sweetener."

Aleesha gives it a suspicious look.

"It's good for you," Abby soothes.

She takes a tentative sip and gives Abby a weak smile. Then she glances over at me and the smile falls from her face. "I ... I wanted to explain. About your father."

I stare down into my mug. A spark of anger flashes in my belly but I'm too tired to fuel it. I don't *want* to be angry. But I do need to understand. "You wanted answers?"

She nods. "Yes. I wanted to know why he did it. And I wanted him to feel how she felt, facing her death." She shakes her head. "I know I shouldn't have done it, but I just felt that finally, after all these years, perhaps I could move on."

"By killing him?" I can't keep the bitterness out of my voice.

"Yes. Except then I realized that wouldn't help. That killing him would make me feel worse, not better. That it wouldn't bring her back ... It would just make me lose ..." She swallows and scrubs a sleeve across her eye. "A friend. And I ... I know what it's like to lose a parent. I didn't want you to go through that."

I stare down at the table.

Aleesha takes a sip from her mug. "When I let him go, I didn't realize Katya and the Chain were out there. They caught him. And Katya ... she said I needed to avenge my mother's death. But I couldn't do it. So, she did it for me."

Still, I can't bring myself to look at her.

Bryn breaks the silence with a deep sigh. "Aleesha, whatever Katya said ... She would have killed him anyway."

I jerk my head up and look at him. Of course, he'd mentioned something yesterday, when we were at the headquarters. It feels so long ago now.

"You said the Leader ordered it?" I say slowly, trying to remember. "He wanted to set an example or something stupid."

Bryn nods. "That's what I told you. But it wasn't the full truth."

"What do you mean?" Aleesha asks.

He takes a deep breath and turns to look at her. "Andrew Goldsmith's death wasn't your fault. As soon as you reported back his name as being the authorizing officer for Operation Nightshade, his fate was sealed." He glances back at me. "You're right. The Leader did feel that having a government figure brought in front of the crowd would help rile them up and make them more likely to join us. But it couldn't just be any government figure. It had to be your father."

"But why him?" Aleesha whispers.

Bryn turns back to her. "Because for the Leader, this was never just about the city. London is personal. This was personal." He takes a deep breath. "He wanted revenge for your mother's death as much as you did.

Aleesha stares at him, and the colour drains from her face. Her eyes speak the question she can't voice.

Bryn nods. "Yes, he's Ricus Meyer. He's your father."

31

Aleesha

Bryn's still talking but his words pass me by.
The Leader. My father.

His picture appears in my head as clear as the day I'd stared at it on the file in the Metz compound, determined to memorize every feature, in case one day I found him.

A hand shakes my arm, jolting me out of my stupor. I look up into Bryn's eyes. "You know him?"

"Yes." He pulls back and winces, his hand flying to his shoulder. "He doesn't go by that name now, but when you mentioned your mother's name, I suspected. When he briefed me on this job, he mentioned a woman called Maria Ramos. Said that if I ever heard the name mentioned, I was to find out everything I could and report back. When you described him, I was sure." He shakes his head. "That scar is pretty distinctive."

"Does he …"

"Know you exist? I don't think so. I didn't mention you in my report back to him and I'm pretty sure Katya didn't either."

"I think she was going to tell him about me that day. The day she died. Did he tell you what happened? Why he wasn't there?" My throat chokes shut, and I stare down at the grain on the wooden table.

"No. He's never mentioned it." Bryn sighs again, this time in frustration. "I thought something felt wrong about this from the beginning. The other cities we've operated in, we've concentrated on building a better system of governance. Here, he's been far more focused on taking the government down than thinking about what could replace it."

He pauses, and I feel his eyes on me. "Do you want me to tell him about you?"

"No." I shake my head vigorously. "But I want to meet him." *So he can look me in the eye and tell me the truth about that day.*

"Well, you might get that chance."

"He's coming to London?" Trey leans forward.

"Yes. Says he wants to oversee things personally."

My breath catches in my throat and my heart begins to race. I raise my head. "When?"

"Won't be for a few days at least. He moves to his own timescales. He'll be here when he's here." Bryn yawns. "The next few days are going to be busy. We need to figure out what to do with those Metz officers you've caught us for a start." He eyes the bulge under my jacket. "Who gave you that thing anyway?"

"A friend." I picture Giles in his cave and wonder what he's doing now. If he knows how many lives he saved today.

"Fine, be mysterious." Bryn yawns again. "But tell him – or her – I owe them a drink if we ever meet."

"Are you hurt, Aleesha?" Abby stands and moves over to the hotplate. "There's a bit of water left for you to wash with."

I crick my neck. My whole body feels like one big hurt. "Nothing serious, I don't think. Just scratches."

Abby puts a kettle of water on to boil and comes over to me. "That looks like it needs a good clean." She gently touches my shoulder and a stab of pain lances up my neck. She hands me a small pump bottle. "Clean it well with water, then spray some of this on it and any other open cuts. It's a natural antiseptic."

I pick up the bottle and take a sniff. A strange but distinctive floral scent.

Abby leaves the room and returns a few minutes later with a pile of clothes and a towel. "They may be a bit big on you but at least they're clean." She looks pointedly at Bryn. "I think it's time you went to bed before you can't stand."

Bryn grunts and staggers over to the door. Abby turns to Trey. "I'm sure you two have a lot to talk about, but maybe let Aleesha get washed and changed first?"

Trey blushes and stammers something unintelligible as he leaves the room. Abby smiles at me. "Sure you don't need a hand?"

I shake my head.

"Okay, well I'll be off to bed. Please stay here tonight? There's the mattress upstairs or the sofa's free." She hesitates as if about to say something else but decides against it and turns toward the door. "Goodnight, Aleesha."

"Goodnight," I echo.

The kettle whistles. I pour the water into a bowl, undo my jacket and carefully place the black box on the table. It doesn't look any the worse for wear for the abuse it's been through. I strip down to my underwear and wash, biting my lip as the hot water stings my wounds. The water soon turns a dirty grey, but I've saved enough for a second bowl. I even manage to get the worst of the dust out of my hair by dunking my head in the bowl.

The antiseptic spray stings a little. I stick a dressing over the bullet wound and get dressed. The clothes are a little on the large side, but they're soft and comfy. I pour some cold water into a bucket and rinse my clothes as best I can before hanging them up to dry.

When I open the door to the hallway, Trey's waiting outside.

"Can I come in?"

I nod.

"You look better." He smiles at me tentatively.

"Smell better too, I bet." I return the smile.

"I—"

"I—"

We laugh awkwardly. "You first," I say.

He walks over and sits down in a chair. I sink into the one opposite.

"I'm sorry I hit you. I-I was mad and upset. I don't know what came over me …" He shakes his head. "It was like this other person took over my body and—"

"It's okay," I cut in. "I'd have probably done the same. Except I'd have hit harder. Your punching could use some work." I manage a tentative half smile.

Trey looks down at his hands. His long fingers are interlocked, thumbs up. "I understand why you did it, I think. But I don't know if I can forgive you yet. Not completely. I'm sorry, it's just too soon …"

A crushing weight presses on my chest, gripping my heart in an iron claw. "I understand," I whisper.

My only friend. And I beat him away.

It gets hard to breathe. I close my eyes and focus on trying to relax the tension in my throat. Somehow the raw emptiness inside me feels so much more painful than any wound or aching muscle.

I look up and meet his eyes.

"I'm broken," I whisper. "A bad person."

"No, not a bad person." Trey reaches across the table to take my hand. My skin tingles under his touch. "Just a person who has sometimes done bad things."

I cling to his fingers as if they're a lifeline connecting me to a better place.

"Do you think I can ever change?" The words catch in my throat. The questions I dare not ask even myself. "Can I ever be good?"

"You have a lot of good in you." Trey squeezes my fingers. "You saved a lot of people today. And you've saved my life more times than I can count. Besides, Abby says that it's our faults as much as our strengths that makes us who we are."

I smile at him through the tears brimming in my eyes. "She always thinks the best of everybody."

"And Bryn always thinks the worst. They make a good pair."

Trey pulls back and, reluctantly, I let go of his fingers. Immediately, I crave his touch and the focus it brings, keeping me here, in the present, in this warm, homely kitchen. Without it, my mind turns to darker thoughts.

Trey searches my eyes. "My father used to say that everyone can be who they want to be if they want it enough." He hesitates. "Do you want to meet your father?"

I look down at my fingers twisting around themselves on the table. "I think so ... I don't know. I'm confused. It's like I had this idea of who my father would be. The kind of man my mother would have loved. I thought he'd be an Insider, maybe. Rich, successful, kind. But this person they call the Leader? I don't know who he is at all. Except that I don't think he's anything like what I thought."

I glance across at him. "My mother would never have wanted

revenge for her death. So perhaps ... perhaps he's not the man she thought he was either." My throat is thick again.

"Well, I guess you won't know unless you meet him."

"No."

We sit in silence for a minute. Then Trey clicks his tongue. "I knew there was something important I had to tell you! The officer who knocked Abby out, the one who nearly killed us. It was Rogue. But he didn't recognize me ... Or, if he did, he didn't hesitate to nearly blow my brains out." He frowns. "Were we wrong about him?"

I shake my head. "No. Samson saw me with him before we broke into the compound. He told the President there was a rogue officer and the President had all their chips reset. It must have happened after we left the compound but before the fight." A thought flashes through my mind. "So, he'll be one of the officers we captured?"

Trey shrugs. "I guess so. But if he's been reset, will he remember us? When he's out of the suit?"

"I don't think so. Giles said the reset wipes their memories." I reach for the black box and turn it over in my hands.

"Does it really only work for you?"

I nod.

Another silence.

"So, what are you going to do with them?"

"I don't know." I sigh. "They can't stay with the Snakes for long and we can't send them back to the compound. What do you think I should do?"

Trey looks uncomfortable. "Well, I'm not sure you should just hand them over to the Chain. Katya sounded like she either wanted to use them as killing machines or execute them. What about this Samson?"

"I'm not sure he's any better," I admit. "He helped me out today, but I'm still not sure whose side he's really on."

"You mean whether he wants to help the government or Outsiders?"

"Yes. He claims to be on *both* sides, but I'm not sure that's possible." I hesitate. If anyone will understand, Trey will. "But if we use them as weapons – as Katya and others want to do – doesn't that make us just as bad as them? As the Commander?"

I spin the box, weaving it through my fingers until it moves in a blur.

"You think we should let them go?" Trey asks after a pause.

The box slips from my fingers and falls to the table with a clatter. "I think we should give them the choice. A real choice."

"You mean remove their implants? But couldn't that kill them?"

I shake my head and gesture to the box. "It has a deactivation option. To turn the chips off. To make them human again. Then we show them what life is like out here and let them decide what they want to do."

Trey looks dubious. "And if they all want to go back to the compound?"

"Then we let them go," I say quietly. "It's their choice."

"Katya's not going to like it."

"I don't care if Katya likes it. It's the right thing to do."

I look up. Trey has this odd smile on his face. "What?"

He shakes his head. "Nothing."

I scowl at him. *What does he mean, nothing?*

"You're right. It is the right thing to do." He yawns and rocks back on his chair legs. "Let's test it out tomorrow, okay?" He crashes back down. "You know, you may want to stay away from the Chain. I wouldn't put it past them to force you to hand

369

over the box."

"I'd like to see them try."

Trey doesn't look convinced. "Well, let's go one step at a time." He stands and stretches. "You can have the bed, if you like. I don't mind sleeping on the sofa."

I push back my chair. "No, it's fine. I'm not sure I'll sleep much anyway."

"You and me both." He yawns again and walks over to me. Gently, almost hesitantly, he reaches up to my cheek. His fingers ripple down my skin like a feather that both tickles and soothes. "You may be broken, but so are we all, in one way or another."

Then he turns and walks toward the door, disappearing before I can find the words to reply.

* * *

It turns out I don't have any problem dropping off. As soon as I've wrapped the blanket around me, I'm sucked down into a dark, dreamless sleep.

But part way through the night, something jerks me awake. I'm not sure what it was but I'm suddenly wide awake and alert. I pad over to the shuttered window and peer out, but the street outside is quiet and empty. I lie back down and pull the blanket over my shoulders, but I know at once that it's useless. Sleep will not come a second time. Sitting up, I turn the black box over in my hands.

I need to prove they're human. People who think and feel. Damaged people perhaps, but people all the same.

Perhaps I can help fix them.

I stand and tiptoe through into the kitchen. A small clock face shows it to be two in the morning. Plenty of time to get out and back before anyone else wakes up.

The streets are empty, and it doesn't take me long to get to the Snakes' headquarters. A sleepy guard stops me, and I'm kept waiting until someone else checks with Jay that it's okay to let me in before I'm allowed through. I don't mind. I'm glad security is tight.

The huge main room of the old warehouse is dark; the only light is the faint haze of the moon through the skylight windows. Rows and rows of Metz officers fill the space. When you look at them like this, they look like machines just waiting to be switched on. An army of giant robots. I wonder if they're asleep or awake inside the helmets. If their suits hold them up or if their legs will tire at some point and they'll fall over like a set of dominoes.

I activate the black box and bring up the display. Row upon row of flashing lights, but no way of knowing which is the one I'm looking for.

I shut the display back down and begin to walk along the line. I reach the end of one row and turn up the next. Already the numbers are starting to blur in my head. *Where are you, Rogue?*

The eerie quietness is getting to me. Perhaps I should have waited until morning. Come here with Trey or Jay. I pass the third row and move onto the fourth.

Something stops me. I frown and look at the officer in front of me. MD345. Not Rogue. I backtrack a few paces to the previous officer.

ML486.

He looms above me, his masked face expressionless.

"Rogue?" I whisper.

There's no sign of acknowledgement. I bring up the display and select his chip. "Follow me."

I set off up the line. Rogue falls into step behind me, his

footsteps echoing in the silence. At the end of the room is a stack of chairs. I pull two off and place them opposite one another.

"Sit on the chair."

The officer obeys, his bulk dwarfing the small chair.

I sit down, clutching the box.

Giles said it would bring their memories back from before they were officers. But he wasn't sure about the time they were officers. Perhaps it would be better if they didn't remember those.

Will this even work? And should I take off his helmet before or after? I should have checked with Giles.

Before. Then you can see his face. And he can see what's really here. Not what the helmet shows him.

I place the box on the chair and walk around to the back of Rogue's chair. Using the stiletto blade, I release the catch on his helmet and, with an effort, lift it off his head.

He looks just the same. Except his blue eyes are vacant. I wave my hand in front of them. "Rogue?"

No response.

I place the helmet on the floor and am surprised to find my hands trembling slightly.

Come on, what's the worst that can happen?

I eye his belt. The gun has gone but there's a baton and a knife at least that I can see. Quickly, I strip him of anything that looks like a weapon and hide the kit in the pile of chairs. Then I return to sit on the chair opposite him.

"Okay." I blow out a breath. I wish I'd thought to bring some water.

I switch the setting from "control" to "deactivation" and bring up the display.

Once you've turned off the chip, there's no going back. They will be able to make their own decisions.

My finger hovers over the green dot. Is this the right thing to do?

"What if he doesn't want to remember?" I whisper into the silence. But no answer comes back.

I select the green flashing dot and give the command.

It stops flashing then fades to a dull grey.

I look up. He's still staring straight ahead. "Rogue?"

His face twitches. Then his whole body starts as if he's been given a huge electric shock. He springs to his feet, looking around wildly.

I jump up, the chair crashing to the ground behind me, ready to run.

"Who are you? Where am I? What ...?"

His voice trails off as his eyes finally come to rest on me.

"I ... my name is Aleesha. We've met before." My voice comes out as a croak.

"Have we? I don't remember." He looks around and frowns.

"You may have some gaps in your memory." I try to sound calm, but I can't stop the tremor in my voice. "That's normal. Do you remember your name?"

He comes to attention as if I've given him an order.

"My name is Kian Eamon Anderson. I am twenty-two years old. I ... I ..."

He turns to look at me and his eyes are filled with such horror that I look away, unable to meet his gaze.

"What have I done?" He looks down at his hands. Those hands that have caused so much bloodshed, without the knowledge or consent of their owner.

"What have I done?" he whispers again, turning to me as if I can provide the answer.

But I just shake my head, tears welling in my eyes.
What do I tell him?
The battle for Area Four is over.
But his own battle is only just beginning.

Coming soon... Defenders

Defenders (Book 3 of The Wall Series) will be coming out at the end of 2018. To be notified when it's available and receive fortnightly updates from me with free short stories, writing news, giveaways and book recommendations, join my Readers' Club.

As a welcome gift, I'll send you a FREE copy of *Outsider* (the prequel to *The Wall Series*) when you sign up.

Interested? Sign up here: bit.ly/alisoningleby-outsider.

I look forward to having you on board!

Alison

P.S. If you're a fan of dystopian fiction, come and join my private Facebook group, The Last Book Café on Earth (bit.ly/LastBookCafe). We share book recommendations, fun quizzes and futurist news.

If you enjoyed Infiltrators...

Please leave a review!

As an independent author, reviews are really important to me. They help make my books visible to people who are browsing Amazon or other sites and they help readers decide whether they'll enjoy reading my books.

I also take into account the reviews my books get when deciding which series to continue with and what stories to write next.

So, if you enjoyed reading *Infiltrators* and want to read more in this series, I'd really appreciate it if you could take five minutes to leave a review. You can jump straight to the pages using the links below.

Amazon: mybook.to/InfiltratorsReview
Goodreads: http://bit.ly/InfiltratorsGoodreads

Thank you!

Alison

Acknowledgements

I truly believe that creating and publishing a book is a team effort, and would like to say a huge thank you to everyone who helped me make *Infiltrators* the best it could be.

Thanks to my amazing team of beta readers: William McCullough, Isabel Hosier, Anni Willis, Candy Robosky and Kate Ingleby. Your comments were invaluable in helping me improve my manuscript.

A huge thanks to my fantastic editor, Sophie Playle of Liminal Pages, for picking up on my mistakes, polishing my prose and pushing me to become a better writer. I promise that one day I will learn how to use commas properly ...

My gorgeous cover was designed by Meg at Jolly Creative Cover Design (bookcovers.megcowley.com).

I thought that my first book would be the hardest to write. But in many ways, I found writing *Infiltrators* much harder. I have suffered the same crises of confidence and battles with my inner critic as I did with Expendables and have come to accept them as part and parcel of being an author.

But, as the person who bears the brunt of these crises, along with my long working hours, the final thank you has to go to my husband, Sam. Without you, I would spend even more hours in front of the computer and probably turn into a hunchbacked hermit.

About the Author

Alison Ingleby is an author of sci-fi and fantasy fiction for young adults and adults who are still young at heart.

Alison holds a Master's degree in Geography from the University of Cambridge and a Master's degree in Emergency Planning and Management from Coventry University. She's worked as an emergency planner and sustainability professional in cities across the UK and now happily spends her days as a freelance writer, specialising in helping businesses who love the outdoors as much as she does.

When not writing or curled up in her reading chair with a cup of Yorkshire Tea, Alison loves climbing up cliff faces, running across the Yorkshire moors and hiking up Scottish mountains. Her dream is to live in a Scottish castle by a loch. (Preferably one with central heating and hot water.)

You can find out more about Alison, sign up for her Readers' Club and get a free story by visiting her website: https://alisoningleby.com/

Alison's Books:

The Wall Series:
Outsider (prequel)
Expendables (Book One)
Infiltrators (Book Two)
Defenders (Book Three) - coming autumn 2018

Short stories & novellas:
Red Sun Rising: A Story from the Alteruvium Expanse
The Faerie Flag - coming summer 2018
The Climb (featured in *Future Visions Anthologies*) - coming summer 2018